Beneath the Surface

Beneath the Surface

Melynda Price

Montlake
Romance

This is a work of fiction. Names, characters, organizations, places, events, and incidents are either products of the author's imagination or are used fictitiously.

Published by Montlake Romance, Seattle

www.apub.com

Amazon, the Amazon logo, and Montlake Romance are trademarks of Amazon.com, Inc., or its affiliates.

ISBN-13: 9781503937222
ISBN-10: 1503937224

Cover design by Damonza

Printed in the United States of America

CHAPTER

I

Quinn's heart leapt into her throat and beat a wild staccato when the doorknob to her apartment came loose in her hand. Looking closer, she could see the jamb was fractured; small slivers of wood littered the ground around her feet. She pressed her ear against the door, listening for movement. Silence answered.

Oh, God . . . Emily!

Fear for her roommate gripped her as she dug through her purse and pulled out her cell. Her hands shook as she scrolled through her contacts and selected Emily's number. Time stopped, the air frozen in her lungs as she waited for the phone to ring, praying to God she wouldn't hear the resonating echo on the other side of that door.

This was all her fault. She never should have come back here. If anything had happened to her roommate . . . The cell rang on Quinn's end and hope rose with each millisecond that passed in responding silence. Then her heart broke as "All About That Bass" sounded in their apartment. Frozen by indecision, she was torn between going in and running for help as Emily's phone sang on about that boom, boom that all the boys chased, and how she had all the right junk in all the right places.

With a trembling hand, Quinn pressed on the door. The hinges protested loudly as it opened and she winced, hoping and praying that whoever had broken in wasn't still inside. *Please be all right, please be all right . . .* she prayed as music echoed through the apartment, claiming to be all about that bass, no treble. The song abruptly cut off, rolling her call over to voicemail.

"Hey, this is Emily. Leave me a message."

Quinn disconnected the call mid *beeeeep*.

"Em?" she called, stepping inside. Simon, Emily's Siamese, meowed a greeting from the living room, but there was no answer from her roommate. She forced one tentative step into the entryway and let out a startled yelp when the cat darted across her path.

Her gaze fell to the bloody tracks left behind on the tile and her hand flew up to cover the scream building in her throat. "Em!" she cried, racing forward and then stumbling to a halt. This time there was no stopping the terrified cry that tore from her lungs as her mind refused to reconcile the horror her eyes could not unsee. There wasn't one thing left in its rightful place. Blood splattered the walls and the overturned furniture. Emily's broken body lay in a crimson pool like a centerpiece in this sick macabre scene. Sightless eyes stared at the ceiling, frozen in an expression of terror. The awkward angle of her head caused by the deep gash across her throat was Quinn's final undoing.

The scent of death assaulted her, slamming into Quinn like an invisible wall. Sharp and pungent, the sickly sweet smell mixed with the apple cinnamon air freshener. Bile surged up her throat and her stomach rebelled. She took a step back and the heel of her boot slipped out from under her when it came down on her sister's wedding photos scattered over the floor. She stumbled back and knocked into Simon. He let out a shrill meow and hissed. Quinn's ankle rolled, pain searing through the joint as she lost her balance and fell, whacking her head against the overturned end table. Stars burst behind her eyes and a wave of dizziness washed over her, but she pushed it back, scrambling to her feet.

Quinn limped over to the phone, lifted the receiver, and was dialing 911 when her gaze landed on a vase of roses sitting in the middle of the dining room table. The beautiful bouquet amidst all the destruction was its own obscenity, but what stopped Quinn cold was the sight of her name written on the envelope. Her breath froze in her lungs.

Oh my God . . .

Somewhere in the back of her mind she was vaguely aware the phone was ringing on the other end of the line. She was shaking so badly, it took several attempts to pluck the envelope from the forked holder among the blood-red roses. She pulled out the small floral card, her stomach lurching at the blood smeared across the bottom of the envelope. Her pounding heart seized inside her chest.

Quinn Summers,

You can run but you can't hide.

I'll be seeing you soon . . .

"Hello, 911. Please state your emergency . . ." said the voice on the phone.

Quinn couldn't speak, she couldn't breathe.

"Hello, 911. Do you need assistance?"

The phone fell from Quinn's numb hand, hitting the floor as she took a step toward the door. She had to get out of here—now! The pain in her ankle grounded her to reality as this horrifying moment threatened to steal her sanity.

Nooo . . . She shook her head in denial, but she already knew the truth. This was no random act of violence, and she was holding the proof of it in her hand. She'd been back in the States only forty-eight hours and already someone was dead. Not just someone—Emily.

———

"Violet . . . ?" Quinn's knees buckled in relief at the sound of her sister's voice. Thank God they were all right.

"Quinn? Is that you? What's wrong? Are you okay?"

No, she wasn't. She wasn't okay at all. The adrenaline flooding her veins was the only thing keeping her standing. Her ankle had its own heartbeat, throbbing in time with the rapid pounding of her pulse. Unsure where to go, she'd made it as far as the library. She didn't know if she was being followed, but common sense told her the safest place to be was in public. Finding a remote corner where she could still see the entrance, she hid between two towering shelves of the paleontology section. Out of breath, her words came in a whispered pant. "I'm in trouble, Vi."

"What kind of trouble? Quinn, you're scaring me."

"I know. I'm sorry. I just . . . needed to hear your voice. I needed to know you were all right." Swallowing back the rise of tears, she took a deep breath, trying to steady her voice.

"All right? Why wouldn't we be? Are you still in Haiti? Quinn, if you're in trouble, you need to go to the embassy."

"I'm in New York, Vi. And I can't go to the police."

"Why not?"

"Because someone's trying to kill me, and I think the government could be involved. I don't know who I can trust right now." Even as she said the words, she could hardly believe them herself. This sounded insane. Over and over, her mind tried to reject that this was actually happening. But there was no other explanation. She'd gone straight from the airport to the US attorney general's office in Washington, DC. She hadn't contacted or seen anyone else since returning from Haiti, and forty-eight hours later, her apartment had been ransacked and her roommate was dead.

"Someone's trying to kill you?" Her sister's shout blasted into her ear. The fear in her voice mirrored the terror pumping through Quinn's veins. She shouldn't have called. The last thing she wanted to do was pull Violet into this, but she didn't know what else to do, where else to turn. Desperation clawed at her insides as her mind raced with dwindling options.

"Clover, who are you talking to?" Quinn could hear the deep voice of Nikko, Vi's husband, in the background and a pang of envy sliced her heart. Never in her life had she felt more alone and hopeless than she did at this moment. Her faith in humanity was destroyed—her trust in the government shattered. She had no one to turn to, no one she could trust with her secret. No one to help her . . .

"It's Quinn," Vi whispered. "She's in trouble."

"Let me talk to her."

She was about to protest when Nikko's voice came across the line with a decisive calmness she really needed right now. "Quinn? Quinn, talk to me. What's going on?"

"I'm in a lot of trouble, Nikko." It was hard to speak with the tears clogging her throat. Taking a deep breath, she swallowed past the lump and tried again. "I was doing this story in Haiti, and I found out some stuff I shouldn't have . . ."

"Where are you at right now?"

"The Mid-Manhattan Library."

"How are you calling?"

"My cell."

He growled a nasty curse. "Quinn, you need to get off that phone. Back up your contacts and then destroy it. If there's someone after you and he's worth a shit, he'll be using that cell to track you. Go to the ATM and pull out all the cash you can get—debit cards, credit cards, all of it. Go to the train station and buy an Amtrak ticket to San Diego. If you buy it at the counter and use cash, they won't require an ID to board. You'll be safest traveling in a large group that makes several stops. Get off in Salt Lake City and I'll pick you up there. If you exit midroute, it'll be harder to track you."

"You can't come get me." It didn't matter how much she wanted to take Nikko up on his offer, she couldn't put his family at risk. Not after what happened to Emily. "I can't bring you guys into this. It's really bad, Nikko. They killed my roommate." Her voice broke.

It was the first time she'd said those words out loud, and somehow hearing them made this all too real, forcing her mind to accept with finality what it was trying so hard to deny—the government was trying to kill her before she could go public with what she'd discovered in Haiti. What she didn't understand was what the US government had to gain by covering it up.

She was in too deep now to let this go, even if she wanted to. They would never let her live, not with what she knew, and Quinn refused to let Emily's death be in vain. Rallying her nerve, she let the seed of anger take root and watered it with injustice, clinging to those emotions like a lifeline. In that moment she made a decision—she could either become a victim—like Emily, like those children in Haiti—or she could become their voice for justice. Many people had martyred themselves for less. If she was going to die, at least it wouldn't be for nothing. She'd die telling her story to the world.

"If you won't let me come get you, Quinn, then you need to go to Asher. He'll keep you safe."

Asher? Asher Tate from her sister's wedding? Nikko's whoring best man? No freaking way. The guy was such an insufferable prick, she never wanted to lay eyes on him again.

She was about to tell Nikko she'd rather take her chances on her own when he pressed the issue. "Listen, I realize you two didn't exactly hit it off."

That was an understatement.

"But you need to be with someone who can protect you, Quinn. Someone who's trained in this kind of stuff and can help you get this shit straightened out."

A lot of words came to mind when she thought of Asher Tate, but "protect" and "safe" were not two of them.

"There's no one I trust more, Quinn."

There had to be some other way, some better alternative. But as her mind raced through options, she was coming up blank and running out of time. She couldn't very well stay holed up in a library.

Well, shit . . .

"Do you have a pen and paper?"

"Yeah, just a minute . . ." Her hands shook as she dug through her purse. She pulled out a pen and then fished around to find something to write on. Her fingers connected with the sharp edge of the floral card she'd shoved inside the pouch. She pulled it out and a shiver of dread coursed down her spine at the sight of her name penned by her roommate's killer. She flipped it over. "All right, I'm ready."

"Get off the Amtrak in Denver. Then take a cab to Grand Junction, Colorado. There's a little bar outside of town called The Rabbit Hole. When you get there, ask for a man by the name of Robert Tate. He's Asher's father. He'll be expecting you. I'll call him and arrange for him to take you to Asher's."

Colorado? Was he crazy? Nikko was sending her halfway across the United States to get protection from a guy who hated her just as much as she loathed him, and he didn't even know she was coming?

"Can I get his number? Why can't I go straight there?" If she was seriously considering doing this, then perhaps she should at least talk to the guy first.

"He isn't taking calls or answering any e-mails. I think his cell's turned off. Since this Nisour Square shit hit the press, he's gone off grid. I'll keep trying to contact him, though."

"He was part of Nisour Square? Seriously, Nikko, what are you getting me into?" She hadn't been back in the States more than two days and even *she* knew about the Nisour Square massacre. The news coverage she'd seen at the airport had focused on the Peterson trial. She hadn't been aware Asher was involved.

"You can't believe everything you hear on the news, Quinn. Asher didn't kill those people."

Maybe not, but guilt by association and all that crap. In her experience, all lies tended to have some fabric of truth woven into them. He might not have pulled the trigger, but she'd be surprised if he wasn't complicit to those murders in some way, shape, or form. For all she knew, she could be running from one killer straight into the hands of another.

"I'm not sure this is a good idea, Nikko. I don't trust him—"

"Do you trust me?"

"Of course I do."

"Then go to Asher."

"What if he refuses to help me?" Lord, she must be out of her mind for actually considering this. But what better option did she have? Stay here in the city and be hunted down like a rabid dog? She never thought she'd be saying this, but right now Asher Tate really was the lesser of the two evils. And make no mistake, that man was quite possibly the devil incarnate.

You can run but you can't hide. I'll be seeing you soon . . .

Well, at least he wasn't trying to kill her—yet. Considering their last encounter, once she got there, all bets would probably be off. Shit . . . was she really going to do this?

"He won't refuse. He'll help you if you tell him I sent you."

CHAPTER

2

As the train pulled away from the station in Chicago, Quinn released a breath she hadn't realized she'd been holding. They were moving again. She was safe—for now. The train began to pick up speed, and she settled back in her seat and tried to relax. Tension strung her muscles tight until her whole body ached. She still couldn't believe this was happening, that a simple publicity piece for the Children's Global Resource Network would have her running for her life.

Her mind vacillated between moments of shock, denial, and paralyzing fear as she tried to process the last twenty-four hours. She couldn't sleep, exhaustion fueling the panic inside her. Every time she closed her eyes, she saw Emily's lifeless eyes staring back at her and the guilt nearly crushed her. The god-awful images flashed through her mind like one horrific slideshow playing on an endless reel, joining those she'd collected in Haiti.

She looked out the window into the darkness, seeing nothing but her reflection in the glass. Quinn barely recognized the woman staring back at her. This wasn't her—afraid and helpless. She was used to being on her own. If fact, she preferred it. Quinn was a bold and independent spirit that stared the face of adversity in the eye without blinking.

But this . . . this was unconscionable. What had happened to poor Emily, what was going on over in Haiti, what was happening to her . . . it was a nightmare she couldn't wake from. She could barely do anything more than draw in one breath after another, praying the next one would be a little easier. But it wasn't. Fear and grief suffocated her. Never in her life had she felt so helpless and utterly alone.

But her solitude was about to change in a hurry. And with each passing hour that brought her closer to Asher Tate, an all-encompassing sense of dread took root deeper in her gut. There was a very real possibility she was making a huge mistake here. Perhaps Nikko didn't know his friend as well as he thought he did, because the man she'd met didn't seem capable of protecting anything more than his bottle of Jack Daniel's. She doubted much had changed in the months since she'd last seen him.

Thinking of Asher Tate shouldn't have conjured a mental image of the man as easily as it did. Four months had been plenty of time to forget the infuriating jackass who seemed to possess the unique ability to bring out the worst in her. But thinking about Asher was better than the horrifying images that had been haunting her for the last twenty-four hours, so she let herself go with it, desperate for the mental reprieve, even if it was found in dwelling on the thoughts of the last person she ever wanted to see again.

———

"You are the most arrogant, conceited, egotistical asshole I've ever met," Quinn hissed past her painted-on smile. Her arm was looped through the bended forearm of her counterpart as they started down the aisle. Even through his tux, she could feel the corded muscles beneath her touch and did her damndest to ignore the flutter of feminine awareness heating her blood, attributing the unwelcomed burn to anger.

Asher's top lip quirked in amusement. He leaned close and whispered, "You kiss your boyfriend with that mouth, Quinn?"

His question twisted the knife Spencer had plunged into her heart. The wound that two years and half a world apart still couldn't heal. Men . . .

they were nothing but a bunch of self-serving assholes, and she was on the arm of their king.

Asher's lips brushed the shell of her ear when he spoke, sending goose bumps erupting over her flesh. Her response to his nearness fueled the flame of her ire. "I don't have a boyfriend," she snapped between gritted teeth.

"Big surprise there," he grumbled under his breath.

The bastard knew full well she could hear him. Quinn discreetly jabbed her elbow into his ribs, but his chuckle wasn't the response she'd been hoping for. Nor was the shiver shuddering through her from the auditory caress of that throaty masculine rumble. She swore to the Lord Almighty that if they weren't standing in front of an altar with three hundred guests staring at them, she would introduce her knee to his groin.

"Stop it, you two," Nikko growled as they split apart, retreating to their respective corners. Quinn moved left, standing on the top step across from Asher. Nikko, her sister's husband-to-be/referee, was in the middle, waiting for his bride to come walking down the aisle any moment.

Raven, a bridesmaid and Nikko's fifteen-year-old daughter, snickered beside her. Holding up her bouquet, the girl tipped her face into the flowers. Her beautiful smile was infectious. Quinn winked, giving her future niece a conspiratorial grin, and whispered, "Your dad's kinda scary . . ."

And in truth he actually was. When Violet had called her six months ago to tell her she was getting married and asked Quinn if she'd be her maid of honor, this was not the mental image she'd painted of the man who'd stolen her sister's heart. Violet was the pragmatic one between them, a freaking psychologist, for chrissake—you didn't get any more straightlaced than that. She'd always gone for dull and boring men, but there was nothing dull or boring about Nikko Del Toro.

"Nah . . . he's not so bad," Raven whispered back, the interlude music filling the church and muffling their voices.

The girl was teasing her. Quinn knew Raven adored her father. In the few days she'd spent with them before the wedding, she'd watched them all together—Nikko, Raven, and Violet. Truth be told, she envied her sister.

Violet was finally getting the family she'd always wanted and Quinn was genuinely happy for her, she really was. But it also highlighted the painfully obvious fact that Quinn was nowhere near finding true love or settling down, and knowing her luck, she never would.

But this was good—Nikko and Violet. Quinn might not know the ex-marine turned MMA fighter very well, but she knew he loved her sister and his daughter—fiercely—and that was good enough for her. Despite her initial reservations, she genuinely liked the man, even if she didn't necessarily agree with his choice in friends.

Quinn was still smiling when she caught Asher's gaze across the aisle. Surprise briefly registered in his eyes, along with something else she didn't dare name. He looked at her like he couldn't believe she was actually smiling—at which point her grin promptly left her face.

She held zero affection for that man. Honestly, she held most men in rather low regard, but this one was a particularly sharp burr in her ass she could well do without. Perhaps it was his audacious arrogance, or maybe because he'd been in town only three days and had probably fucked as many women. Every time she saw him he had a new flavor of the day hanging off his arm. The last one of which she'd had the distinct displeasure of walking in on when she'd entered the coat-check room to retrieve her jacket at the rehearsal dinner last night. The girl who should have been working at the desk was up against the wall with her legs wrapped around Asher's bare ass, his slacks sagging around his knees.

She wouldn't think about the perfection of that ass or the flex of muscles on display as he thrust into the woman pinned between his huge body and the wall. He didn't even have the decency to look embarrassed at being caught. The least he could have done was stop fucking her long enough for Quinn to get her coat. Sure he was shit-faced, but that was no excuse, and now she was partnered with the pig throughout this wedding and the reception. Best man and maid of honor . . . Oh joy. Her plane for Haiti couldn't leave fast enough.

Quinn's thoughts fast-forwarded through the wedding, which was now mostly a blur. She wished the obscurity of her memories had done her the courtesy of blotting out the rest of that day. It was frustrating what the mind recalled with startling clarity and which other things it chose to forget. If only her memories were like e-mails, and she could scroll through her inbox and archive the things she wanted to remember and delete the others. Asher's inbox would be titled: Proceed with Caution.

———

"I pray the guy my sister just married isn't as big of an asshole as you."

Asher's grip on Quinn's hand tightened until she winced, his arm around her waist flexing as he sucked her up tightly against him. She stumbled forward, her breasts mashing into his chest. Damn, this guy was huge. The top of her head came just below his chin—typical male that he would try to use his size and strength to bully her. But what disconcerted Quinn the most was her reaction to him. Heat flooded her veins at the close contact, making her breasts tingle. A rush of electricity ran straight into her core. She prayed Asher wouldn't feel the pebbling of her nipples or the hammering of her heartbeat through his thin dress shirt.

He'd shed his jacket and tie during the dinner, unfastening enough buttons of his shirt to give her a glimpse of smooth tanned skin and a hard muscled chest. His sleeves were rolled up his forearms, revealing several gray-wash tattoos. The only one she could read was the Old English scripting "Semper Fi" underneath his right forearm as he held her hand up, waltzing her around the dance floor.

Curiosity beckoned her to look at his ink, but she refused to give him the satisfaction of staring at him long enough to decipher the imagery sleeving a good portion of his arms. However, she had to admit the dichotomy of a large, well-built, tattooed man in a tux was a sexy combination. Too bad it had to be this jerk sporting the look.

They'd just started the bridal party dance. Aiden, Nikko's other grooms-man, was dancing with his wife, Ryann. Quinn would have been happy to dance with her niece, Raven, but to her father's obvious displeasure, some other guy had stepped in and swept the girl onto the dance floor—which only left the maid of honor and the best man. Fantastic . . .

Asher was a surprisingly good dancer. It wasn't a skill she'd expect a man of his caliber to possess. Most men his size didn't have the control over their body or the fluid grace to move without looking like a bull in a china shop.

God help her, how long could this song last? Her breasts were still crushed up against his chest. He held her so close she could feel every muscu-lar detail of his body molded against hers. And he made no attempt to hide the very prominent erection that was digging into her belly, grinding against her as they stepped and turned, their waltz morphing into a modified salsa that was drawing the eyes of many guests.

In fact, if she had to guess, she'd say he was taking great pleasure in the ardent, wanton gazes of the single women watching them. A spark of jealousy flared to life inside her that she dismissed as nothing more than simple feminine rivalry. Her traitorous body took a secret thrill that she was the one who aroused him—the one he wanted. For the moment, anyway . . .

Quinn took pride in knowing she was probably the only single woman in the universe who wouldn't spread her legs for this man, and the thought of sending him back to wherever the hell he came from with a severe case of blue balls pleased her immensely. They both had flights scheduled to depart in a few hours and would need to be leaving for the airport soon.

When he dipped his head, she felt Asher's breath skate down her neck and resisted the involuntary shudder in the base of her spine. The man was sex-on-a-stick hot. That, she wouldn't even try to deny, but just because the woman in her could appreciate an impressive specimen of male flesh didn't mean she would ever indulge in it.

"Fair warning." His whisper was a low throaty growl in her ear. *"You keep sweet-talking me like this and grinding your hot little body against mine, I might lose all control and ravish you right here on the dance floor."*

An affronted gasp broke from her throat. Sweet-talking? She'd just called him an asshole, and he was the one doing all the grinding. *"If you so much as touch me, I swear I'll shank your foot with the heel of my shoe."*

"Sweetheart, I'm already touching you." Again that deep, masculine chuckle rumbled in his chest.

She refused to admit how much the sound of it affected her, or the way the vibration teased her nipples, sending little currents of pleasure tingling between her legs. Damn him . . .

"Do I amuse you?" she snapped, craning her head, which was a huge mistake. Looking into Asher Tate's eyes was like peering into a kaleidoscope. The variation of color staring back at her was absolutely mesmerizing.

"A little," he confessed. *"But when you've spent the last six months staring at sand, it doesn't take much. If you really want to amuse me, I'll bet my ass I can come up with something more entertaining than this."*

"I've already seen your ass. Trust me, it wasn't that impressive, and I certainly wouldn't bet on it."

She was a damn liar. It was and she would, but she'd eat dirt before she ever admitted as much to this arrogant jerk. The look of surprise on his face was almost laughable. He missed a step and sent them bumping into Aiden and his wife. After a mumbled apology, Asher moved them to a quieter area of the dance floor. The teasing light in his eyes was replaced by something more serious. She didn't think she liked the intensity of what she saw staring back at her.

"Is that why you've been so pissy with me today? Listen, sweetheart, I'm really sorry, but I've gotta confess, I don't remember jack shit about what happened last night. Did you and me . . . did we . . . hook up?"

What? Was he serious? *"No, we didn't 'hook up'!"* she hissed, stomping on his instep. *"But I'm sure the coat-check girl who you did screw would be glad to know that you don't even remember her!"*

His top lip curled in a crooked grin. Understanding lit his eyes as if it all made sense to him now. "I get it . . . You're not pissed that we fucked, you're pissed that we didn't."

Heat flooded her cheeks—and everywhere else as her mind inadvertently took the place of the coat-check girl. "I think I actually hate you right now."

"Don't hate the player, sweetheart. Hate the game."

"You make me sick!" She tried to step back and put a little distance between them, but he wouldn't let her go.

Instead, he pulled her closer—if that was even possible. Dipping his head to her neck, he let his lips brush against her thundering pulse as he growled, "That may be true, but I guarantee I could make you come harder than you've ever come in your uppity little life. Of course, you'd have to actually give up your precious control first, and I'm willing to bet you've never done that, have you? Given a man total freedom with your body?"

Quinn gasped, and this time when she took a step back, he let her go. Using her momentum, she slapped him across the face. He didn't even flinch, the bastard.

"Took you long enough . . ."

What the hell was that supposed to mean? Had he wanted her to hit him? What purpose could that possibly serve? No . . . it didn't matter. She was done. Quinn took another step back, then turned and stormed away. Asher's words were a low blow dealt with lethal precision. If she never saw this man again as long as she lived, it would be too soon.

CHAPTER

3

"This AR-15's got really smooth action. Stays right on point."

"I told you it would."

"You did a great job modifying it to fully auto. How soon can you get one ready for me?"

"A week?"

Jayce flipped the safety, dropped the magazine, and double-checked the chamber with speed and fluidity that came from years of practice. He handed Asher the weapon and then pulled his pistol from a holster behind his back. Pointing it at the target seventy-five yards out, he emptied the Glock .45 semi-auto, forming a tight cluster of holes around the center ring. Impressive fucking shooting, especially from this distance. Then again, Asher wouldn't expect anything less from his old Recon Six sniper and fellow team member.

"Missed one . . ." Asher nodded downrange.

Jayce chuckled. "Blow me, Tate. Let's see you do better." He reloaded the .45, slammed the clip home, and handed Asher the gun.

He took aim and fired the weapon with the same rapid succession as his friend, blowing out the abused center of the target.

"Ha! Missed one!" Jayce threw a sharp elbow into his ribs. "Where'd you fucking learn to shoot?"

"From the same asshole that taught you, obviously."

"Remmy . . ." they answered in unison, and shared a nostalgic chuckle. Asher made the sign of the cross over his chest and lifted his eyes toward heaven.

"Fucking miss that guy," Jayce murmured. "Best goddamn sniper I ever knew."

Asher couldn't disagree. "So, you gonna tell me what you need the gun for?"

Jayce cut him a glance and holstered his weapon. "Not unless you want in. This one's off the books."

"All your jobs are off the books."

"They are since Nisour."

He didn't miss the disgruntled tone in Jayce's voice. "No thanks, man. I'm actually thinking about retiring." He was prepared for his friend's surprised look, but not the disappointment that ground the salt deeper into Asher's festering wound.

"Come on. You can't let that shit get to you. Some missions just go to hell and there's nothing you can do about it. Insurgents look like civilians. You can't tell them apart. That's what I told them at Peterson's trial and that's what I'm telling you right now. It's what makes those ragheads so goddamn dangerous. She was warned to stop and kept driving at us, what the fuck were we supposed to do?"

"She had a fucking kid in the car."

"Then she should have stopped the goddamn car when she was warned. It wouldn't be the first time one of those radical bastards blew up a kid."

Asher shook his head. "I wish I had your conscience." He grabbed the AR off the rest and carried it back up to the house. "I sure as hell would be sleeping a lot better."

"You just got to turn it off, man. Quit fucking caring about shit."

That sounded tempting, but Asher knew it wasn't that easy. Every action caused a reaction and every decision came with a consequence. Asher suspected Jayce's had cost him his soul a long time ago. The man had changed since they'd served together in Recon Six. Then again, hadn't they all? Who was he to cast judgment? They were all just trying to make it through, one day at a time.

Asher mounted the steps of the back porch and entered the kitchen.

"Nice place you got here," Jayce commented, following him inside.

"Thanks." He wasn't one for company, but Jayce had dropped by today to see him about getting his AR-15 modified to fully automatic. He'd turned his cell off a couple of weeks ago when Peterson's trial began and the press started swarming him like fucking piranha. Asher walked over to the pantry cupboard he'd modified into a weapons safe and opened the door.

"You build it yourself?" Jayce glanced around the kitchen, craning his head to peer around the corner into the living room.

"Most of it." He entered the key code and turned the lever. "The logs are from the property. I had it shelled when we were on our last ops. Been working on it since we got back."

The one-bedroom log house tucked in the foothills of the Rocky Mountains wasn't anything you'd find on *Lifestyles of the Rich and Famous*, but he wasn't about luxury. Sniper's blood ran through Asher's veins. He was reclusive by nature and there was no undoing the years of training and conditioning that had turned him into a hardened soldier—a killer. The A-frame was a basic design with a master bedroom loft that led to a balcony off the front. The vantage point and height elevation gave him the perfect view to monitor the inner perimeter of the property.

Jayce chuckled. "Who would have thought, carpenter by day, Black Ops soldier by night. Impressive . . ."

"The labor's cathartic. It's nice to build something rather than destroying it for a change."

"How many acres you got here?"

"A hundred and fifty. They head up into the mountains."

Asher opened the safe door and set the AR back in its place. He was closing it when Jayce said, "Holy shit, man. You preparing for a war?"

The safe was stocked with guns and a multitude of armaments— military issue shit he could probably get in a hell of a lot of trouble for having, but over the years he had collected quite a diverse stockpile. Asher shrugged. "You never know, right?" He closed the door, then the pantry cupboard. "Want a beer?"

"Sure."

Asher crossed the kitchen and opened the fridge, pulling out two Landsharks. Sliding one down the table toward Jayce, he took a seat across from him and stretched out into a lazy sprawl.

"You heard from the boys?" Jayce twisted off the cap and took a pull from his beer.

He posed the question as casually as if inquiring about the weather, but Asher wasn't fooled. "Not since the depositions."

"It wasn't your fault, you know. Nobody blames you."

"You can keep sayin' that, but it doesn't change a thing. It was my team, my mission—I'm responsible for those men, it was my fuckup to hire Peterson."

"I don't blame Peterson."

Of course he didn't. These were two very opposite sides of the coin they stood on, a sensitive subject they'd both be better off not broaching.

"His trial will be wrapping up this week. I think it'll go a long way with the jury if you spoke on his behalf."

And here was the rub. Was that why Jayce was really here? To try to convince him to intervene in Peterson's trial? He should have known the guy wanted more than a souped-up AR. Asher tipped back his beer and downed a good portion of it. He was considering the possibility of getting piss-ass drunk when the red light above the fridge began to flash and a high-pitched beep sounded in the living room.

"What the fuck is that?"

"Someone's coming up the driveway." Asher rose from the chair, opened the sliding lid on the breadbox, and pulled out his Sig Sauer P226 from its spot beside a loaf of Country Hearth 12 Grain.

"Holy shit, Tate, is there anywhere you don't have a weapon stashed around here?"

Probably not . . . Asher tucked the gun into the waistband of his jeans and headed for the living room to silence the alarm. "I live thirty miles from the closest town and have a half-mile-long driveway. No one comes here by mistake."

He glanced out the picture window and saw the plume of driveway dust heading toward them. Instinct told him whoever was on their way wasn't a threat. Anyone who'd come here with ill intentions wouldn't be dumb enough to announce their arrival, but one could never be too careful. Asher had made plenty of enemies during his career in the Special Forces—foreign and domestic.

His dad's truck came into view and pulled to a stop in the turn-around. What was he doing here? This time of day, he'd be at The Rabbit Hole. It had always been his dad's dream to own a little dive bar, and last year he'd checked it off his bucket list. Funny, the things people coveted. Asher's mind began to spin with reasons for this impromptu visit and a knot of dread fisted in his gut. Was something wrong with Mom, or Fisher? His little brother was in PBR nationals this week— had a bull finally kicked his ass?

Asher rushed to the door. As he broke out onto the porch, his feet skidded to a halt at the sight of the most gorgeous woman's ass bent toward him—long legs, dark-wash skinny jeans, calf-high black boots . . . That was all he could see of her leaning over the driver's window, talking to his dad. *What the fuck?* Jayce rushed out behind him, no doubt alarmed by Asher's hasty dash, but was a little late on the *Whoa*, because he ran into him, nudging Asher farther onto the porch.

"Holy shit . . ." The appreciative curse was whispered behind him.

Asher shot his friend a scowl over his shoulder, not that the guy would notice. His eyes were fixed on the woman's rear end. Without breaking gaze, Jayce lifted his beer and took a long swig. As she straightened, Asher got his first glimpse of pale blonde hair and was hit with a disconcerting memory blasting him back to Nikko's wedding.

———

Quinn Summers was a piece of work. Gorgeous beyond words, but not even close to being worth the effort it would take to tame that shrew. It was odd, her disdain toward him. Women usually liked him. Fuck, who was he kidding? They loved him, especially when he was in uniform. Maybe they thought it was their patriotic duty, or maybe it was a big coup to bang a Marine Special Forces officer. Well, ex-officer now, not that it really mattered.

But Asher had never come across a female as prickly as Quinn before, and he'd be lying if he said she didn't amuse the hell out of him. She hadn't been a fan of his since the day they met, but today the woman had become downright nasty. Too bad he couldn't remember what the hell happened last night to piss her off so much. And it wasn't for lack of trying, but he'd been lit as shit and whiskey had an amnesic effect on him. It was a blessing and a curse, because most times he drank to forget, but there were those rare moments, like now, when he was pretty sure something significant had happened and he had no fucking clue what it was.

Quinn walked down the aisle beside him with the regal elegance of a queen—an ice queen. And she looked like one too, with her pale blonde hair piled on top of her head in a fancy twist. Quinn's bone structure was defined and delicate, her lips full and lush with that Angelina Jolie look that automatically made a man imagine what they'd feel like wrapped around his . . . Yeah, not going there . . .

Quinn was hot. No doubt about it. But her resting bitch face was enough to make a man's dick want to crawl up his own ass. Were Asher a lesser man, he might have let the holier-than-thou midge get to him. But he wasn't any ordinary man. He'd stared death in the eye more times than he cared to count, and the last thing he was going to let intimidate him was an ornery female, half his size, who walked around with some skewed perception that he actually gave a shit what she thought of him.

He wasn't here to impress some chick. He was here to stand up for his friend, see him married, and then be on his way. Unfortunately, the maid of honor was a royal pain in the ass. He'd decided early on that if he was going to be forced to spend the day with her, he was going to at least enjoy himself, which meant pissing her off at every opportunity. Was it childish? Perhaps, but he didn't really give a fuck. So then why did it please him so much to discover she didn't have a boyfriend?

When it was time to separate, he didn't let her go until he absolutely had to, enjoying her discreet attempts to get free as she pulled, once—twice—third time was a charm, and she stumbled a little when he abruptly released her.

"Stop it, you two," Nikko growled.

Asher gave his friend a teasing wink and a supportive shoulder squeeze as he walked past him, taking his place at Nikko's right. As happy as he was for Nikko, and honored as he felt to be standing here as his best man, the thought he couldn't seem to get out of his head, the thought that had been plaguing him since he'd stepped off that plane three days ago, was that he didn't belong here. This should be Remmy's job—Remmy's honor . . . and as hard as he'd tried to distract himself with pussy and booze, the gut-wrenching knowledge never left him.

Shoving aside the memories that were always too close to the surface, his gaze strayed to the woman across from him while the piano played on and they waited for Violet to make her appearance. Quinn was whispering something to Raven. The smile gracing her beautiful face was genuine and unguarded, giving him the first glimpse of the woman beneath the mask. He'd never seen her look so free, and the sight of her hit him like a palm strike to the chest. His heart actually stuttered. Holy hell . . .

The ceremony flew by with a lot of promises and "I do's." Before he knew it, he was watching his friend kiss his bride and the room erupted into cheers. The traditional parting music began to play, and the bride and groom headed down the aisle together. When it was Asher's turn to follow, he stepped toward Quinn. Her eyes were moist with unshed tears, and for the briefest moment something deep inside him, something he didn't even know existed, stirred.

He wasn't sure if it was a response to her tears or something else, but he quickly quelled the shit by courting her temper. Giving her a mocking bow, he held his arm out for her to take. "Shall we get this over with?"

There was that flash of temper. "My thoughts exactly," she replied with saccharine sweetness as she looped her arm through his and they descended the steps.

This was safer ground—her anger he could deal with, her snark he understood, but God help them both the day he decided he wanted Quinn Summers . . .

———

"I've gotta get back to the bar. See ya Sunday for the barbecue." His dad's voice pulled Asher back from his thoughts. A hand extended from the window, giving him a quick wave as he pulled away.

Asher leapt off the porch and hit the ground at a determined clip. He was halfway to the woman and about to yell for his dad to stop, when she turned around and all the air left his lungs. *Holy shit . . .*

"Quinn? What the hell are you doing here?"

She looked up at him, meeting his glare with an impressive amount of bravado he suspected was just for show and notching her chin in that stubborn defiance that grated on his nerves like hellfire.

"I need your help."

And fuck him if just for a moment that woman's bottom lip didn't quiver.

———

Okay . . . so she'd been hoping for a slightly warmer reception. It seemed their last meeting had stuck with him just about as fondly as it had her. For the millionth time, Quinn found herself asking what in the hell was she doing. If she'd thought this was a bad idea before, she only needed to look at the man glowering at her with a mix of *You're fucking kidding me* and *Get your ass back in that truck and go back to wherever you came from.*

Only problem was, she had nowhere to go. Bottom line, Asher was her only option. She'd had two days of traveling to come up with a better idea. None had surfaced, and believe her, it wasn't for lack of trying. She had no contingency plan, and if he refused to help her, there was a good chance that whoever was trying to kill her would succeed.

So Quinn found herself doing the one thing she vowed never to do in front of Asher Tate—she cried. And it was humiliating. Not because she was using the age-old ploy of female manipulation to get to him, because truthfully, she was desperate enough right now to do it. No, she was humiliated because her tears were real. After seeing her roommate murdered, running for her life, and nearly forty-eight hours of traveling across the country with little to no sleep, she was just plain exhausted. And now, seeing Asher standing there looking so strong, so safe, that steely resolve she prided herself on just crumbled.

She held his stare until her vision swam. He said nothing to her confession as he stood there watching her with that unreadable expression on his too-handsome face. When a tear slipped down her cheek, she quickly swiped it away and notched her chin a little higher. Maybe he was a sucker for a crying woman, because after another moment of hesitation, Asher muttered a curse that sounded a lot like *fuck me* and closed the distance between them.

"Come here . . ." He pulled her into his arms, and for the first time in longer than she could remember, Quinn finally felt safe. It made no sense because this was the last man she ever imagined taking comfort from. Yet here she was, pressed against a wall of hard muscle as he held her close.

It wasn't the first time he'd had his arms around her. They'd danced together at her sister's wedding, walked together arm in arm down the aisle . . . Perhaps that was why she was allowing the close contact now from a man who was, by all rights, a stranger, and one she professed to despise, at that. Each shuddering breath pulled his scent deeper into her lungs. He smelled of the outdoors, clean and fresh, with just a hint of masculine spice. His touch was comforting—more than she wanted to admit. And for just a moment, she allowed herself to melt against him.

"What have you gotten yourself into, Quinn?"

His low, husky voice resonated in his chest, rumbling against her ear. But it was his words she took offense to. Was he implying she was somehow to blame for this? She stiffened in his arms and he must have felt the tension ripple through her because he let her go and took a very wise step back. That was when she noticed the other man standing on the porch, drinking a beer and watching them with interest. His legs were crossed at the ankle, one shoulder leaning casually against a log support beam.

Asher must have seen her attention diverting to the man behind him. Stepping to the side, he made a hasty introduction as he escorted her up to the house. "Quinn, this is Jayce Rivers, a friend of mine. We served in the Special Forces together. Jayce, this is Quinn Summers—"

"The shrew from the wedding," Jayce finished for him, shooting her a wolfish grin.

"*Not* what I was going to say," Asher growled, his pointed glare warning his friend to behave. "But thanks, asshole."

His friend smirked and raised his half-empty beer as if to say *No problem*, then resumed downing the drink.

"Quinn is Nikko Del Toro's sister-in-law."

Now that got his attention. The man stopped chugging and gave a cough, clearing his throat. "Oh, shit . . ." He stood with a little more attention and held out his hand as she approached the steps. "My apologies, Quinn. It's nice to meet you."

So this guy knew she was from the wedding, but Asher had failed to mention her other than to call her names. Nice. She wanted to tell Jayce where he could shove his apology—insincere jackass—but considering why she was here, she thought better of making enemies of Asher's friends. Painting on a smile, not unlike the one she'd worn with Asher at the wedding, she climbed the steps and begrudgingly placed her hand in his.

"It's a pleasure to meet you too." His hand folded around hers, his grip firmer than she was expecting.

"All right, Casanova. It's time for you to hit the road," Asher interjected, climbing the steps behind her.

Jayce released her hand, and Quinn didn't miss how Asher put himself between her and his friend. The sense of relief she felt at his protectiveness drove home the revelation that although she may not like this man, she could trust him to protect her. And right now, that was exactly what she needed . . . someone to keep her safe.

CHAPTER

4

She watched Asher from the kitchen table as he poured her a glass of iced tea. He set it down in front of her, and she politely thanked him as he took the opposite seat. Before sitting down, he reached behind his back and pulled a gun from his waistband, depositing it in the center of the table.

She startled at the weapon, not used to seeing firearms lying out in the open or handled so casually.

"Relax, I'm not going to shoot you, Quinn."

Well, that was reassuring. Fixing her with his stare, he waited, probably expecting her to say something, but the words were stuck in her throat. She was surprised to see this side of him—serious and all business. Where was the carefree, flirtatious rogue she'd met at Vi's wedding? If she didn't know better, she'd swear they weren't the same man at all and Asher Tate had an evil twin.

"Why are you here?" he pressed at her silence.

Okay, so there wasn't going to be any easing into this. No "Hey, how have you been?"

"Oh, you know, just trying not to get killed. How about you?"

She ran her palms down the thighs of her jeans, drying her sweaty hands. It would have been nice if Asher's father would have at least given the guy a heads-up that she was coming. Why wouldn't he have said anything? He'd seemed quick to dump her and run.

God help her, where should she start?

"Are you going to make me repeat myself? Given how we parted the last time I saw you, I hardly think you're here to take me up on that fucking I offered you."

Yep, same asshole . . . And for a fleeting moment, she was embarrassed to admit the thought actually crossed her mind to let him believe she'd done just that. It would sure as hell be easier than telling him the truth. She may have had no other choice than to trust him with her life, but that didn't mean she trusted him with her secrets. Could she swallow her hatred for the man long enough to hide out here as his whore? Probably not . . .

She just needed enough time to discover the connection between the US and the Children's Global Resource Network. Once she connected all the dots and got the proof she was waiting for, she'd tell the world about the atrocities she'd discovered while doing her human-interest story in Haiti.

No one would find her here, tucked away in the foothills of the Rocky Mountains. She'd been careful and was sure she hadn't been followed. There was no one to connect her to Asher, so she should be safe . . . right? At least that's what she kept telling herself.

"Five minutes, Quinn. That's how long you have to explain to me what you're doing here or I'm loading your ass into my truck and dropping you off at the closest bus station."

The tension radiating from him and the look on his face told her he wasn't messing around. All right, if he wanted to cut to the chase, then so be it. "Someone's trying to kill me."

Asher studied her a moment. Why didn't he look nearly as surprised as she thought he should?

"Aside from the obvious reasons, why do you think someone is trying to kill you, Quinn?"

Asshole! Did he think this was some kind of joke? She didn't appreciate his tone or his condescending attitude. "Because whoever is trying to kill me just murdered my roommate," she snapped.

Now that got his attention. Where were the smartass jokes now, funny guy? His brows drew tight, and damn, was that a flicker of concern she saw in his eyes? Couldn't be . . .

"How do you know it was you they were after? Perhaps your roommate had a tiff with a jealous boyfriend that ended badly. It happens . . ."

"I know because I'm not supposed to be back in the country for two more weeks. And when I found her, there were a dozen red roses sitting on my kitchen table with my name on them." She grabbed the note card from her purse and slapped it down on the table, sliding it toward him. "I think he got into the building by posing as a florist."

When Asher read the note his face lost all softness, and he didn't have a lot there to begin with.

"You still haven't answered my question. Why would someone want to kill you?"

She wasn't sure she wanted to tell him, especially not without him agreeing to help her first. The last person she'd gone to with the truth had tried to have her killed. Putting on her best poker face, she looked him square in the eye. "I can't tell you."

He met her stare and raised his brow. "Can't or won't?"

She upped the ante. "Both."

All chips in. "Who's trying to kill you, Quinn?"

"I don't know . . ." Truthfully, she really didn't.

He called her bluff. "Bullshit." Asher crossed his arms over his chest, putting those impressive muscles on display. "You expect me to believe that you have no clue who's trying to kill you, and you don't know why. I'm not a fucking idiot, Quinn, and I gotta be honest, you're not making a very compelling case for yourself."

She exhaled a defeated sigh, unsure how much she should say right now. "I know, but I'm asking for your help anyway, Asher. All I can tell you is that it has to do with a story I was working on in Haiti for the CGRN."

His brow rose in question and she clarified, "Children's Global Resource Network. Something happened when I was over there and I did a little digging and discovered something I shouldn't have. Just keep me safe until I can finish this story and get the evidence I need to go public. If I'm going to die, then I at least want it to be for something I believe in."

"Spoken like a true soldier . . ."

Was that grudging respect she heard in his voice? It couldn't possibly be, yet there was a note of curiosity in his eyes she hadn't seen earlier. But she didn't want him thinking she was someone she wasn't. She was no soldier, no hero. In the face of danger, she'd run—halfway across the country even, leaving her poor roommate behind. Common sense told her there was nothing else she could have done for Emily after calling 911. But the thought that Emily's death was her fault broke her heart and riddled her with so much guilt it felt like she could hardly breathe.

"I'm not brave, Asher. I'm scared out of my freaking mind."

He studied her until she felt her cheeks begin to heat. She wished she knew what he was thinking. She hated this vulnerability, the feeling that everything around her was spinning out of control and she was helpless to stop it. This wasn't her—at someone else's mercy, constantly afraid and looking over her shoulder, wondering if every stranger's eyes were those of her assassin.

"You said you weren't due back in the States for a couple more weeks. Who knows you're home?"

He was going to keep pressing until he got the answers he was looking for. Was it fair to pull him into the middle of this without full disclosure? Would the truth make him more or less likely to help her? She couldn't know, but she got the feeling that unless she took a step of good faith, he wasn't going to budge. "Besides Nikko and Violet, just the attorney general's office in Washington, DC."

Asher muttered a ripe curse and scrubbed his hand over the back of his neck. Yeah, he was thinking the same thing she was.

"No one else?"

She shook her head.

"You're sure?"

She nodded. "Forty-eight hours after I went to them with my story, I came home to Manhattan and found Emily dead. I don't know how long she'd been there—a while. That note card was waiting for me. I don't know who I can trust and I have no idea how deep this goes."

"Why did it take you so long to get home from DC?"

"My flight was delayed because of weather. Otherwise I would have been there."

"Holy hell, Quinn, you're in a lot of shit. And I'm no bodyguard. I'm a fucking mercenary, for chrissake."

"Is there a difference?"

He stared at her, bold and unapologetic, when he said, "Yeah, I get paid to kill people."

Was he serious? Quinn studied the man, trying to decide what the hell she was supposed to say to that. It wasn't like she had a lot of options here. Asher was her plans A, B, and C. She'd heard it said that the eyes were the windows to the soul, and if that was true, then this man was in trouble.

"Isn't that . . . illegal?"

He chuffed a masculine grunt. "I suppose that depends on who you're doing the killing for."

Setting her shoulders and notching her chin stubbornly, because there was no way she was taking no for an answer, she said with a hell of a lot more confidence than she felt, "Well . . . now I'll be paying you to keep me alive."

"I don't want your money, Quinn."

That surprised her. Was it possible she'd misjudged him? Could it be that there was more to Asher Tate than a sexy smile and a hard-on? Before she could think on it long enough to give the idea any serious consideration, he gave her a roguish grin and said, "Of course, gratuity is always welcome."

Pig. Was she really this desperate? Was she really going to put her life in the hands of this egomaniacal jerk? Sadly, yes, yes she was . . .

———

What the fuck was he thinking? Was he actually considering helping this woman? Letting her stay here? He'd never lived with a woman before. Hell, he'd never spent any length of time with one before. Well, time that wasn't horizontal, anyway. Spending the last fourteen years with a team of men in the Middle East had not made him a very good candidate for Bachelor of the Year, that's for sure. Of all the women he knew, and there were a lot of them, this was the last one he'd ever wanted to see again. The idea of sharing four walls with her was a less-than-appealing proposition.

He didn't give a shit about Quinn Summers. So then why did the thought of someone trying to kill her sit so ill with him? Maybe it was the desperation and fear in her eyes, but something about her stirred his protective instincts to life. Something churned deep inside him, unsettling his soul. What could this woman possibly have discovered that would put her on the government's hit list? Something serious enough that they'd send someone to hunt her down. But who wanted her dead, and why?

Problem was, if he started making queries, he would more than likely get the answers he wanted, but it would also paint a big target on both their backs. The longer she could hide out here undiscovered, the better. No question, whoever was hunting her would eventually find her. No sense in bringing that to fruition any sooner.

"Who sent you here, Quinn? How did you find my dad?" He was sure he already knew the answer to that and it would undoubtedly seal his fate to this cantankerous woman.

"Nikko."

Fuck . . .

"He wanted to help me himself, but after what happened to Emily, my roommate, I couldn't risk putting my sister's family in danger."

No, no she couldn't. Nor could he turn this woman away, no matter how much he might be tempted to do just that. The moment he'd met Quinn, he knew she was going to be nothing but trouble. Only he hadn't expected that trouble to come knocking on his door four months later.

"I've already put her at risk as it is. Before I left Haiti I gave my SD card to someone I trusted and had them mail it to Violet, just in case something happened to me and I didn't make it home. It's a good thing I did, because my luggage disappeared. I had to check my bag at the Haitian airport. It was either lost or stolen, and my camera and laptop were in there. All my photos and CGRN interviews are on the SD card. I regret getting Vi involved at all. I just . . . I just never thought this would happen. I thought once I got back to the States that I'd be safe."

"Why didn't you upload the card before you left?"

"I couldn't. There wasn't any Internet access. I was afraid someone would discover what I knew and I didn't want to risk getting caught with the SD card."

"What's your plan, Quinn?"

"Besides not getting killed?" Her laugh held no humor. "I'm going to find out what the US government has to do with all this and why they would want to keep me from telling this story. Then I'm going to the press. I can only hope that once the truth comes out, it will be my protection. No good would come from killing me after the fact."

"I hate to be the bearer of bad news here, but if you're right and the government did hire someone to kill you, going public with this story isn't going to stop him."

"How do you know?"

"Because it wouldn't stop me."

She visibly paled and looked like she was about to be sick. Shit . . . Maybe he shouldn't have said that, but goddammit, pussyfooting around wasn't his style. He was used to dealing with men—Marines—and they were direct, blunt, and to the point. They didn't waste words dancing around the truth. Besides, he didn't want her going into this with any false expectations. If the government indeed hired someone to kill her, she was in serious danger. And nothing short of taking out that assassin and exposing the truth before they could hire someone else to take his place would stop them.

Ah, hell . . . was he really going to do this? The woman had obviously been through a great trauma. She looked exhausted, but more than fatigue marred her beautiful eyes—eyes that were such an odd shade of blue they looked violet—it was the desperation he saw there that got to him. She obviously had no one else to turn to, otherwise she wouldn't be sitting in his kitchen right now. This woman liked him about as much as he cared for her. He could only imagine the pride she must have had to swallow to come here and ask him for help.

Even so, as foul tempered and prickly as he knew she could be, he couldn't send her away. She had no place to go and doing so would undoubtedly be sending her to her death. He'd made enough mistakes in his life. He didn't need to add this woman's death to the toll.

Exhaling an exhausted sigh, he dragged his fingers through his hair and fixed her with a hard stare. Neither of them said anything for the longest time, and then finally, he broke. "If I'm going to do this, I want full disclosure, Quinn. I need to know what the hell you've gotten yourself into."

She nodded her agreement, not seeming surprised by his request, but looked relieved when he didn't push for any more details, though that conversation would be coming soon enough.

"I only have one bedroom. It's the loft." He canted his head to the left, indicating the stairs. "You can stay there and I'll take the couch."

"I don't want to inconvenience you. I'll stay on the couch."

It was too late for that, and was she really going to start this off by bucking him already? "You'll stay upstairs. I prefer you out from underfoot."

Something flashed in her eyes—hurt maybe?—but he couldn't tell for sure because her gaze broke away and shifted to the floor before he could interpret the emotion. She nodded, saying nothing. He continued on, refusing to worry about offending her. It wasn't the first time and it certainly wouldn't be the last.

"The living room is behind you and the bathroom is down the hall. There's another one upstairs. This place doesn't have a lot of room, but it's safe—for now." That got her eyes back on him. "The house is wired with a military-grade security system. I'll teach you how to use it and give you a passcode. Always keep it armed. The property covers one hundred and fifty acres. The main perimeter around the house is secure. I'll take you through it tomorrow, show you where to go, where not to go."

"Do you think they're going to find me?"

"Yes. How long it takes will depend on how good he is and how well you've covered your tracks."

"I bought a train ticket to San Diego and I exited when we stopped in Denver."

"Any idea how long it's going to take you to get your story together and go public with this?"

She shook her head. "I won't know until I start digging and hopefully find what I'm looking for. And I need my SD card. That's where all my photos are. I don't suppose you have a secure phone and Internet access with an impenetrable firewall I could use?"

"I do."

Her top lip twitched, but didn't quite make it to a smile. "Thank you for helping me."

He wasn't sure what to say. "Thank you" were just about the last words he expected to ever hear coming out of Quinn's mouth, and it

made him uncomfortable as hell to hear them. He didn't want her gratitude. In truth, he didn't want anything to do with her. His initial assessment of the woman had been spot-fucking-on. Quinn Summers was
a spitfire and he couldn't shake the feeling he was going to get burned.

"You can thank me if you make it through this alive," he grumbled,
rising from the chair and walking out of the kitchen.

CHAPTER

5

Quinn followed Asher up the stairs after getting a tour of the main level and stopped behind him when they reached the loft. The log home was rustic, quaint, and, surprisingly, a lot cleaner than she'd expected a bachelor pad to be—especially his bedroom. Braided rugs covered areas of the hardwood floor, giving the place a homey feel. A king-size bed sat in the center of the room with a plain navy blue comforter adorning a wrinkle-free mattress with tight, mitered corners. Was that the military in him coming out? She was tempted to walk over and see if she could bounce a quarter on the bed.

This glimpse into Asher's private life didn't reconcile with the flagrant playboy she knew him to be. By his home, it would appear that Asher was a man who liked order and structure—not at all like the guy she'd met at her sister's wedding, who got shit-faced and whored it up with a different woman every night.

She wasn't entirely sure what she was expecting, maybe some clothes strewn on the floor, left wherever they'd fallen the night before as he'd hastily ripped them off to get naked with whoever struck his fancy for the evening. She took a step forward, looking around the large room.

"What's the matter, Quinn? Not what you were expecting?"

"I have to be honest, I was preparing myself for condom wrappers scattered all over the floor and panties hanging from the ceiling fan."

Asher chuckled. "Sorry to disappoint you." He looked toward the open beam rafters, up to the ceiling fan set on a lazy spin. "You'd have to be one hell of a shot to snag a pair all the way up there." Dropping his gaze back on her, he added, "I ain't sayin' I'm not up to the challenge, but uh . . ."

"Don't even think about it," she snapped, brushing past him. "Tell me, are you always such a pig? I'm just asking so I don't get my hopes up that you actually have a chivalrous bone in your body."

His brow arched and he crossed his arms over his chest in that stubborn pose he seemed to like so much. "I think it's pretty chivalrous of me to be saving your ass."

Okay, that took the wind out of her sails a little bit. Quinn's rebuke abruptly died on her lips. He was right. It was. And she needed to remember that. She winced at the guilty pinch in her chest. What was it about this man that sparked her temper so fiercely? Admittedly, she was attracted to him—who wouldn't be?—but it annoyed the hell of out her because the last thing she wanted was to find herself drawn to this incorrigible ass.

Besides, just because she felt physical desire for Asher Tate didn't mean she liked him, and even though she may be indebted to him, it didn't mean she'd whore herself out to the man—even if the thought had very briefly crossed her mind.

Quinn's biggest problem was that she lacked a filter between her brain and her mouth. Whatever she was thinking just seemed to come spilling out, consequences be damned. She'd been like that ever since she was a little kid. One would think that over the years, she'd grow out of it. Guess not . . .

"You're right, I'm sorry. I shouldn't have said that," she conceded. "I don't want you to think I'm ungrateful—"

"For chrissake, Quinn, that's not what I meant. I don't expect you to fuck me for letting you stay here. What kind of a douche bag do you think I am?"

She wasn't sure she should answer that. Her mouth had gotten her into enough trouble for one night. "It's getting late and I'm really tired. Would it be all right if I took a bath?"

When he didn't answer her right away, she glanced back to find him staring at her—scowling actually—those colorful eyes boring into her with an intensity that made her shift uncomfortably. She ignored the fluttering in her stomach and the quickening of her pulse. She was just hungry, and it was hot in here. And she was a dirty liar because that man was too damn gorgeous for his own good—or maybe her own good.

That he could incite this response in her after everything she'd been through these last few days warned Quinn she needed to be careful around this man because Asher Tate was far more dangerous than she'd thought, but for a whole other set of reasons.

After taking a deep breath, his exhale was long and drawn out. *He* was the one who sounded exhausted. "The bathroom's behind you." He indicated the door with a nod.

"Umm . . . I don't have any clothes, other than what I'm wearing." God help her, she hated to ask, but what other option did she have? She'd been in these clothes for the last two days and the thought of putting them back on was not appealing.

"T-shirts are in my top dresser drawer, far left. Help yourself." He turned and walked out before she could thank him. The fading sound of footsteps drew her to the balcony in the hall. Her hand rested on the railing as she watched him leave.

He stopped at the bottom of the stairs and looked up. "Something else you needed, Quinn?" It wasn't what he said, it was how he said it that warned her she'd exhausted his patience.

Taking a step back from the rail, she shook her head. She wasn't sure what she wanted to say, but thought better of pushing her luck. He was the first to break eye contact and turn away, muttering something to himself that she couldn't hear and was fairly certain she didn't want to either.

She headed back toward the bedroom, closed the door behind her, and crossed the room to sit on the side of his bed. It was softer than it looked. For a moment, she considered lying back and just going to sleep. But she was also wearing two days of travel on her and the lure of a long, hot bath was more enticing than rest.

Commanding her reluctant muscles to move, she rose and dragged her ass over to the dresser. She opened the top drawer and grabbed a T-shirt. When she entered the bathroom and saw the whirlpool tub in the corner, she almost cried tears of joy. It was a luxury she hadn't expected to find.

Closing the door behind her, she quickly shed her clothes and headed for the tub. The tile floor was cool against her feet, sending a chill of goose bumps prickling over her flesh. Stopping at the shower, she grabbed the shampoo and body wash and set them on the tile rim before turning on the bathwater.

She retrieved a towel and then paused as she passed the sink, catching a glimpse of herself in the mirror. Oh heavens, was she a mess. Her hair was wild and unruly, and the pieces coming loose from the braid she'd put it in had given her a hair halo. Dark circles rimmed her eyes from lack of sleep. She was pale, her face drawn and washed out. Good grief. Had she really been concerned about Asher hitting on her? She doubted he was into necrophilia, so no worries there.

What she wouldn't give to brush her teeth, or to shave her legs . . . . Quinn hesitated only a moment before opening the medicine cabinet, the temptation to feel clean and refreshed more alluring than her concern for Asher's privacy. Who knows, maybe she'd get lucky and find a spare toothbrush still in the package. Disappointingly, no such luck. But there was a razor, spare blades, and a bottle of shaving cream.

Oh, and a box of Magnum condoms—Ultra Thin—XL. Quinn picked it up and gave it a shake, the foil wrappers scratching against the inside of the box. It felt light . . . She was tempted to peek inside for a quick count but told herself it didn't matter. It was none of her business who or how many women Asher Tate slept with. The image of catching him in that compromising position with the coat-check girl returned, and so did her ire.

With a caustic snort, she set the box back on the shelf and grabbed his razor, a fresh blade, and the shaving cream. She set the supplies on the side of the tub, turned off the water, and pressed the button to start up the jets. The water surged to life, bubbling and swirling as she climbed into the hot, steamy bath. Quinn's breath left her lungs in a soft, throaty moan as she leaned back against the tub and closed her eyes.

This was the first time in four months she'd had a real bath. It was funny the things one took for granted living in a first-world country—things like running water, flushing toilets, or toilets at all . . . Her travels as a freelance journalist had taken her to some remote areas in the world, but the conditions in Haiti had been some of the worst. Water was a scarce, precious commodity there and she almost felt guilty surrounding herself in what many people would labor tirelessly for. How many homes would have drinking water for days in what she was bathing in right now?

Her thoughts began to drift to Meille and the family that had been so gracious as to take her in and share their home with her. Sweet, precious Aileen . . . Her chest tightened with grief every time she thought of the girl. Quinn's heart broke for her, her family, and the countless other girls—missing. She may not be able to bring them back, but she could sure as hell tell the world what was happening over there.

Tears pricked her eyelids and she forced the memory from her mind, only to have it replaced with images of Emily. She couldn't even contact her roommate's family to tell them how sorry she was. How had a simple publicity piece for the CGRN turned into such a nightmare? She was so sure she would have found an ally in the US government. Instead, she was running for her life. But why? What part of this story was she missing?

Was the killer, even now, watching her? Waiting for his chance to strike? No, he couldn't have found her. Not yet, anyway. She'd been careful to do exactly as Nikko had instructed. But Asher had no qualms about making sure she knew it was only a matter of time. He was coming, and when he found her she could only pray that Asher would be able to keep her safe.

Taking a breath, she slipped below the water's surface to cleanse the gruesome scene from her eyes, but nothing could wash away the horrific images. Holding her breath until her lungs burned, she let the jets blast against her face, swirling her long hair into a mercurial tangle around her. Her need for oxygen forced her from her oasis and she pushed up, breaking through the surface.

Quinn took her time bathing, trying to relax and allow the turbulent water to beat against her tired, aching muscles. Once she began to prune and the water turned tepid, she shut off the jets, drained the tub, and reached for the towel she'd draped over the tile ledge. After she dried off, she twisted her hair up into the towel and pulled on Asher's T-shirt. It smelled like him—fresh and outdoorsy.

The shirt dwarfed her. She'd known he was large, but this was ridiculous. The V-neck settled deep between her cleavage, and the hemline hung midthigh. "USMC" was emblazoned over her abdomen. The white cotton shirt was soft and thin from wear—like one of those boyfriend tees girls would buy and wear as a nightshirt. She glanced at her reflection in the mirror as she passed by. Yeah, she probably should have picked a color other than white. Something her nipples wouldn't show through would be nice. Oh well, she was just going to bed, anyway. She'd figure out her clothing situation in the morning.

As Quinn headed for the bedroom, she pulled the towel from her hair and began drying the ends as she walked out of the bathroom.

"Holy fuck!"

———

Quinn stumbled to an abrupt halt and shoved her fall of wet hair out of her face. He hadn't meant to startle her with his outburst, but Asher hadn't expected her to come walking out yet, and definitely not looking like that. He knew it was rude to stare, but short of poking his eyes out with a stick, there was no help for it. He'd always known Quinn Summers was a beautiful woman, there had never been any question about that, but he wasn't prepared to see her standing half-naked in his bedroom, wearing nothing but his T-shirt. There was just something about seeing a gorgeous woman wearing your clothes that was . . . totally fucking sexy. His blood rushed south so fast his head felt light.

The T-shirt she'd picked was one of his favorites. An old white, threadbare, red-lettered USMC shirt he'd gotten back in boot camp. The V exposed a generous amount of her cleavage, and damn, that girl had an amazing rack. Her rosy, pebbled nipples shone through the thin cotton and areas she hadn't dried very well made the material transparent in various teasing patches.

"Asher? What are you doing up here?"

The accusation in her voice was sharp, sparking his temper, which was exactly what he needed to rein in his desire. "What does it look like I'm doing?" he shot back, fluffing the top sheet with a sharp flick of his wrist. The linen cracked in the air like a whip, drawing her eyes to his bed. "I'm putting fresh sheets on the bed, or did you want to sleep in mine?"

A blush bloomed on her cheeks and quickly stole down her neck. Yeah, she should be embarrassed. Her assuming the worst of him was gonna get old pretty damn fast. He settled the sheet over the bed, lifted the foot of the mattress, and folded in the corners before turning to her. "Listen, Quinn, as much as you may want this to happen," he glanced up and waved his finger back and forth between the two of them, "I'm sorry to disappoint you, but I'm not interested. I don't do shrew."

She gasped—an eyes-rounded, jaw-dropping gasp, and it was a test of self-control not to laugh at the look on her face. But this woman needed to be knocked off her high horse and he was just the guy to do it. He'd be damned if he was going to let some chick come in here and make him feel like a lecher in his own home. She may be pretty on the outside, but that beauty was only skin deep. He refused to tiptoe around her for the next God knew how long.

"You're such an ass!"

She sounded surprised—like she was just figuring that out or something.

"And you have an overinflated opinion of yourself," he shot back as he settled the comforter back over the bed then grabbed the dirty sheets off the floor. "Give me your clothes. I'll throw them in the washer."

She wadded up her towel and chucked it at him. He caught the thing before it could smack him in the face, but not before he was nailed with a blast of her scent. Tucking the damp cloth beneath his arm, he cursed the throbbing in his cock, telling that shit to heel because this was not going to happen. Quinn Summers was hands off. It was bad enough he had to live with her. The last thing he wanted to do was make a bad situation worse by getting romantically involved with the woman. If he didn't owe Nikko his life, he likely would have sent her uppity ass on down the road. He was serious when he told her he wasn't a bodyguard. He killed for a living, and Quinn would do well to remember that. If she kept pushing his buttons, he'd do her assassin's job for him.

No longer seeming self-conscious about her state of undress, Quinn spun around and marched back into the bathroom. She was standing in the doorway when she bent over and collected her clothes. The hemline of his shirt rode up, flashing him the bottom of her bare ass. No panties? Seriously?

Perhaps she wasn't aware of the show she was giving him. Maybe she was pissed off and didn't care. Or just maybe this was her way of saying "fuck you." Either way, the lust firing through his veins was starting to make him sweat because, yeah, as much as he pretended not to, he wanted to fuck Quinn Summers in the worst way.

Guess he did shrew after all . . .

CHAPTER

6

"You'd better be calling to tell me she's dead."

His grip on the cell tightened as he ground his teeth to keep from telling this bureaucratic son of a bitch to go fuck himself. If he thought this job was so easy, he could get off his fat ass and do it himself. But it was always seventy and florescent in their world. Just like a typical office bitch—sit behind a desk and wield a pen like a sword, expecting the same result. Real life just didn't work that way.

Shit happens . . . What should have been a quick, easy job had just turned a fuckload more complicated. He was starting to feel like Lemony fucking Snicket in A Series of Unfortunate Events. If only that bitch would have been home instead of her roommate, this all would have been over by now. But no, that would be too goddamn easy, and nothing about this mission had gone as planned. He knew once she came home to her welcome present, she would run.

It wasn't Quinn's running that had been the problem, it was the where to that was the challenge, leading them both into a dangerous game of cat and mouse. If it hadn't been for those wedding pictures he'd found, he might not have located her as quickly as he had. It'd been a fifty-fifty guess where she'd run—to her sister's or into the arms of the man she'd been standing with in that photo, a man who'd been the focus of nearly twenty-four-hour media coverage of the Nisour Square trial. After a few days of reconnaissance at Violet Del Toro's and no hint of her sister, he figured she'd avoided involving the woman in this and he'd moved on to option B. As of seven thirty tonight, it looked like that gamble had paid off.

"I'm going to need some more time."

"We don't have more time. If she goes public with that story and releases those photos, the media will crucify us."

Yeah, well, if this fucker kept ordering him around like some degenerate piece of shit, he was going to find himself on the sharp end of his blade. He wasn't going to fuck this up by acting hastily. He'd already underestimated the woman once. He wouldn't do it again. This kill had to be clean, and that bitch had just seriously muddied the waters.

"She's with Asher Tate."

Silence.

Yeah, not so simple now, is it? Asshole . . . Anyone who owned a TV and watched CNN knew who that bastard was.

"Kill him."

What? Was this guy fucking serious?

"Take them both out. Make it look like an accident."

When this was over, he was going to make this cocksucker look like an accident. That was the problem with these goddamn people—bunch of self-serving assholes who had no loyalty to God or country. Then again, he was hardly one to judge. He'd sold his soul to the devil a long time ago. But still, killing a decorated war hero didn't exactly sit well with him.

Well, he wouldn't be by the time this was all over.

———

Quinn stood outside the apartment door and commanded herself to run. She knew what she'd find the moment she pushed it open, the horror that awaited her on the other side. The nightmare was a rerun set on a continuous loop. Despite her warning, her body moved as if commanded by another force beyond her will, beyond her control. *Run!*

she commanded, but still her feet refused to listen. Her hand rose to the door and she walked into the apartment . . .

A shrill cry tore through the air. "Emily!" Quinn's scream echoed through the room as she bolted upright, her heart slamming inside her chest. Disorientation clouded her mind, panic choking her. "It's just a dream, it's just a dream," she chanted between gasping breaths, trapped in that mental haze between sleep and reality, unable to fully wrestle her consciousness from the grip of her nightmare. But it wasn't just a dream at all . . . dreams were fictitious imaginations. This was real—a horrible memory. And perhaps that was why she could never fully escape it. Every time she closed her eyes, she relived Emily's death—over and over.

Quinn squinted against the bright light flooding the room and rubbed her eyes, discovering excess moisture on her cheeks. As things slowly came into focus, she gradually began to reorient. She was no longer on the train. Asher . . . She was at Asher's house. *You're safe* . . . Taking slow, deep breaths, she tried to calm her rioting heart. *But for how long?* The responding question haunted her.

I'll be seeing you soon . . . The promise of Emily's killer played through her mind, ratcheting her fear and kicking her fight-or-flight response into action. But where else could she go? She had no one else to turn to. How pathetic was that?

Quinn closed her eyes and took another breath. If she'd learned nothing else in her yoga classes, it was how to breathe. Slowly, the panic began to release its grip on her throat. Although it begrudged her to admit it, she really did feel safe here with Asher. She wasn't sure if it was the isolation and solitude of the mountains, or if it was him, but for the first time in days, she finally felt a small measure of reprieve from the constant fear that had been riding her since that horrible night in Haiti.

She supposed that suffering the infuriating man's presence was a small price to pay for security. He wasn't pleasant to be around. Then again, she was no picnic herself these days. They'd started off on the wrong foot months ago, and it appeared they'd continue down that path until someone made the effort to build a bridge and take the high road. Considering she was on his turf, asking him for help, she supposed that person should probably be her.

While she was here, she'd do her best to be cordial. With any luck, the SD card would arrive at Violet's soon. She regretted getting her sister involved even this much, and never would have done it if she'd had any idea this would happen. Never once had the possibility of a US connection entered her mind.

She had originally planned to visit Violet after coming home, and pick up the package there. But now, she couldn't take the risk of traveling and leading anyone to her sister—not after what happened to Emily. The apartment had been ransacked. To do that kind of damage would have taken time—time one wouldn't want to spend around a crime scene unless they were looking for something. The attorney general she'd spoken with knew about the SD card, but he didn't know it wasn't with her. Quinn cursed herself now for being so trusting. What a fool . . .

The shrill cry rang out again, briefly startling her. Only this time she recognized the sound. Horses . . . Asher had horses? She hadn't noticed them when she'd arrived yesterday. Funny, he hadn't exactly struck her as an animal lover. The whinny sounded like it was coming from the backyard. Curiosity had her tossing aside the covers and crawling across the bed to investigate. She padded toward the window and stopped at the sight of Asher standing in the yard below her.

Sweat glistened on his bare, muscular shoulders as the sun beat upon his tanned flesh. He wore a pair of jeans that hugged his hips, the handle of a gun poking out of the waistband. A large black horse was attached to a lunge line held loosely in his hand. Asher's muscles rolled and flexed as he transferred the rope from one hand to the other, with the horse trotting in a circle around him.

Once it passed in front of him again, he shifted his weight and bent his knees. The horse abruptly stopped, pivoted on its back hooves, and reversed direction. Amazing . . . It was like watching the two of them acting out a choreographed dance. They were completely in sync with each other.

Unbidden, the memory of dancing with Asher came to mind— being in his arms, guided and controlled by the lead of his powerful body. He'd moved with such fluid grace, just like now . . . only this time he had a much different partner.

She wasn't sure how long she stood there watching him lunge that horse. He must have sensed her watching him after a while, because his head lifted and he looked up at her. Asher's brow arched, a shit-eating grin tipping the corner of his mouth. What was he smiling at? It took her a moment to figure it out. When he pointed up at her, she realized just exactly what it was that he found so damn amusing.

Oh good Lord, he could see up her shirt!

Quinn gasped and stumbled a few steps back from the window. Grabbing the hem of the T-shirt, she pulled it between her legs. She could see him laughing as he turned around, shaking his head, and resumed working the horse. Her cheeks burned with embarrassment, though she wasn't sure why. What did she have to worry about? He'd made it abundantly clear last night that he wasn't interested in her.

"He doesn't do shrew, remember?" she snarked to herself as she turned away from the window and left to go find the laundry room and retrieve her clothes. She didn't have far to look. When she opened the bedroom door there they were, folded in a neat little pile on the floor with her white lace bra and panties sitting right there on top. Perhaps she should have found the gesture thoughtful, but the idea of Asher taking the liberty of touching her unmentionables annoyed her.

She snatched her clothes up off the floor and carried them over to the bed. After checking first to make sure she was out of sight, she pulled off his T-shirt, tossed it onto the bed, and began to get dressed. Yeah, it was definitely the laundry that made him smell so good, because now her clothes smelled like the guy. It felt good to be dressed again, though. It'd feel even better when she could brush her teeth and comb her hair. A cup of coffee probably wouldn't hurt either.

Quinn headed into the bathroom and struck out on the comb, so she ended up braiding her hair until she could get to a store and buy some much-needed toiletries. She hadn't brushed her teeth with her finger since she was a kid and it worked no better this time. Heading downstairs, she was greeted by the aroma of coffee. Score—one out of three was better than nothing.

As she walked through the living room, she spotted a folded sheet and blanket draped over the couch and felt a brief twinge of guilt for displacing Asher. It didn't last long when she reminded herself she was still mad at him. Well, in all honesty, she should be angry at herself. It wasn't his fault she'd flashed him. His amusement had just been the salt in the wound.

Quinn entered the kitchen and headed straight for the coffeepot. She poured herself a cup and settled into a chair. Looking around the room, she was struck by how surreal this was. She was sitting here in Asher Tate's home . . . Four months ago, if someone had told her the man she was walking down the aisle with would be saving her life, she never would have believed it. Not that he seemed any more thrilled by the prospect than she was. Best-case scenario, they could manage not to kill each other long enough for her to get the evidence she needed to go public with her story. In the meantime, she would do her best to stay out of his way.

She'd no sooner had the thought than the door behind her opened and closed. She couldn't help the ripple of tension shuddering through her as the energy in the air instantly charged with Asher's presence. The scents of leather, horse, and clean male sweat greeted her and she forced the swallow of coffee down her suddenly tight throat.

She'd never been around a man who affected her so strongly before. It seemed where he was concerned, every emotion was heightened—albeit, that feeling was predominantly anger—but either way, he'd managed to hijack her emotions and she didn't like it one bit.

"You're up," he said in way of greeting.

"Uh-huh . . ." She kept her gaze fixed straight ahead and took another sip of her coffee.

"And dressed . . ."

She didn't miss the teasing lilt in his voice. "Glad I could provide some entertainment for you," she snapped. "I hope you got a good look, cuz that's the only one you'll ever get." Hadn't she just told herself she was going to try to be nice? It wasn't her fault, though. He was baiting her.

Asher laughed, a deep, masculine rumble she felt in places she'd just promised this man he'd never go. The cupboard door opened and closed behind her. He walked over to the coffeepot and poured himself a cup. Taking a sip, he watched her with smirking amusement. "Whatever you say . . ."

His unimpressed tone told her he didn't count her declaration a loss.

"It's coming on noon. You hungry?" he asked, jumping subjects as he headed for the fridge.

It was? She glanced at the clock on the wall for confirmation. Damn, she hadn't realized it was so late. She never slept in so long. "I guess."

Opening the door, he pulled out some sliced cheese and a butter container and set them on the counter before squatting down to pull a pan from the cupboard near the stove.

"Do you always wear a gun?"

"Yes. After fourteen years of carrying one, it's kinda like putting on underwear, you know?" He stood with the pan in hand and shot her a wicked grin over his shoulder as he set the pan on the stove. "Or maybe not . . ."

"Okaaay . . . enough of the underwear jokes, huh?"

He chuckled. "Fair enough. I'll take you into town this afternoon so you can get some more clothes and whatever else it is that women need." He stepped over to the sink and washed his hands. "Hand me that bread over there, will ya?"

Quinn got up and lifted the slider door. "Jeez, you've got a gun in here too?" Grabbing the loaf, she carried it over to him as he finished drying his hands.

"You never know when a man's going to have to protect his twelve grain."

Okay, that was funny. Quinn laughed. She couldn't help herself. If she wasn't careful, she might start to find this man charming. "Or . . . when some crazy woman will show up on your doorstep begging you to help her."

He fixed her with that multihued stare. This man really was too handsome for his own good. It didn't help matters that he was standing here half-naked. Though admittedly, her experience with men was limited—she'd never seen one in the flesh before with this hard of a body. The thought crossed her mind for the briefest moment—what would it feel like to be taken by a man like Asher Tate?—possessed by him?—dominated by him?

All right, she must be suffering from PTSD or something, because she should definitely not be thinking about him like that.

"You're not crazy, Quinn. A little odd, maybe . . ." His lips curled in a teasing grin, giving her a flash of straight white teeth. "But definitely not crazy."

She gasped in mock outrage and playfully punched him in the shoulder. It was like hitting a brick.

"My culinary skills leave something to be desired," he warned, taking the twist tie off the bag and pulling out a stack of bread. "I've lived on MREs for years and I hate cooking, so if you want anything fancier than a grilled cheese, you're going to have to make it yourself."

He gave her his back and began buttering the slices, then slapped them down on the pan.

"Grilled cheese is fine. Thank you. Do you have any fruit I can cut up?"

"It's in the fridge. Help yourself."

She pulled the door open and was surprised to find the refrigerator reasonably well stocked, and with healthy options. Then again, he probably wouldn't have a body like that living on junk food—no Twinkies and Ho Hos for this guy. She pulled a few peaches out of the produce drawer and set them on the counter. He handed her a plate from the cupboard above him as she retrieved a knife from the block. "Thanks. I didn't know you had horses."

"Yeah, two. I grew up on a horse farm. My parents live about a half hour into the mountains. Horses come in handy around here. You ride?"

"Me?" She looked up from the peach she was peeling. "No. There's not much of an opportunity to go horseback riding in Manhattan."

"You like it there? In Manhattan?"

"Not especially. But then I haven't really thought of it as home since—" She caught herself before Spencer's name left her lips. "Well, in a long time, anyway. I've been traveling for the last two years so I haven't been there a lot. That's why I got a roommate."

Her chest tightened at the thought of Emily, a sharp ache reminding her that although she may be far from the city, the memories were just a moment away. She didn't finish what she was saying. It didn't matter and she wasn't in the mood to talk anymore. If Asher noticed her discomfort, he ignored it. She returned to her task, focusing intently on cutting the peaches.

They settled into companionable silence after that and she helped him finish making lunch. It was nice—surprisingly amiable. She should have known it wouldn't last.

CHAPTER

7

Asher studied the woman sitting across from him, eating her grilled cheese and peaches in contemplative silence. He suspected she was thinking about her roommate and wanted to give her the silence she needed to process. Grief was a tricky thing . . . You think you're fine one minute and the next you're not. It was a traumatic shock, seeing someone you cared about dead like that—especially when you weren't used to it. He knew what she must have been going through—been there, done that, too many times to count. He was no stranger to grief. The doubts, the guilt, and the what-ifs that plagued your mind during the day and haunted your dreams at night. They'd eat you alive if you didn't find a way to shut them off. After all these years, he still remembered his first. S'pose you never forget your first anything.

The problem wasn't always shutting the emotions off—sometimes that was the only way you could survive the next five minutes. No, the problem came when you refused to turn them back on, which had become the problem for many men like Jayce, and the temptation Asher lived with every fucking day. Once you become numb to everything—eventually your conscience just withers up and dies. He'd seen it happen time and time again to good soldiers—great men—destroyed by the atrocities of war.

Everyone had their breaking point, and Asher had reached his two years ago when he'd watched one of his best friends gun down a kid on the streets of Kandahar. He couldn't have been any older than thirteen.

Then again, many of them were killers long before that. The kid was reaching into his jacket. Slater thought he was carrying a bomb and reaching for the detonator.

That was the day Asher decided he couldn't fucking do it anymore and resigned from the Special Forces, taking an early out. He knew if he didn't, there wouldn't be anything left of him and he'd be blowing his brains out just like Slater did after he'd realized his mistake. He was one bad call from a pine box.

He should have just retired. If he'd known then what he did now, he sure as shit would have. But no, he'd gone and started up his own private security consulting agency. He should have fucking named it Mercenaries "R" Us, because that's exactly what they turned out to be, but it didn't quite have the same ring to it as Tate Security.

Their last mission was doomed to fail from the start. Then again, how in the hell would he know the job they'd been hired to do was a setup to undermine the emergence of the Iraqi military? Asher couldn't help but wonder if Del Toro had taken that job when he'd offered it, instead of Peterson, would things have ended differently? There was a good possibility seventeen people would still be alive.

Shoving his own mental shit aside, he cleared his throat and focused his attention on his houseguest. He almost didn't want to disrupt the unspoken truce that seemed to have settled between them, but he knew she wouldn't volunteer the information on her own and he needed to know what the hell was going on. "I discovered something I shouldn't have in Haiti" just wasn't going to cut it. If he was going to risk his life for her, he damn well wanted to know why.

"You're staring . . ." She spoke into her bowl of peaches without looking up.

Yes, he supposed he was. But he was still having a hard time believing Quinn was actually here. He hated to admit how many times in the past four months he'd thought of her, none of those times fondly, however. But nonetheless, she'd gotten under his skin at that wedding—bad.

Mumbling an apology, Asher dragged his hand through his sweat-dried hair. He needed a shower and to wash off this dirt clinging to him like a second skin. The heat index was pushing ninety already, and he'd shed his sweaty shirt to work out Jack, the horse he'd left behind when he'd gone to scout the property earlier this morning. So far, there wasn't any sign she'd been followed.

"I need to know what happened in Haiti, Quinn."

She tensed but refused to look at him. It was just as well. He was a sucker for those violet eyes and he didn't need her making him soft—or hard, which seemed to be the case more often than not. As much as he tried to fight it, Quinn's effect on him was far more visceral than he cared to admit. He'd known it back at the wedding and foolishly thought it would pass. But seeing her again had brought all that desire, and more, rushing back. He needed to figure out a way to get a handle on that shit and fast, because he could not do his job, could not keep her safe, if all he could think about was being with her. Chrissake, at this rate he was going to get them both killed.

He hadn't slept at all last night. The only thing that was harder than that god-awful couch was his cock. And that crotch shot she'd given him this morning had been the last damn thing he needed. So far, he'd done a pretty decent job of pretending he didn't want her—now if he could only convince his dick of that lie, he'd be doing pretty fucking swell.

She sat her fork down and reluctantly lifted her gaze to his. "What do you want to know?"

"Everything. The more you can tell me, the better chance I'm going to have at keeping you alive."

She looked hesitant, like she was trying to decide whether she could trust him or not—a little late to be having second thoughts now. "Listen, Quinn, you're in some serious shit. I know it and you know it, or else you wouldn't be sitting in my kitchen right now. It's pretty apparent that you're not here for my company. You don't have to like me, but you're going to have to trust me."

He must have made a convincing enough argument because after a minute she nodded. "I was hired to do a publicity story on the Children's Global Resource Network to raise awareness and support for the organization. They are the main and sometimes only source of food for many villages in Haiti."

"I've heard of them. They're known for their humanitarian aid to third-world countries."

"Right. I was staying in Meille. It's one of the smallest, poorest villages in central Haiti. Most of the huts are one-room dwellings. There was a family there that was kind enough to let me stay with them. They have five children, their oldest is a girl named Aileen—she's sixteen." She glanced up and the pain in her eyes made something in his chest cramp. "A few weeks ago, she was out with two of her friends and they disappeared. Her parents were devastated. We searched everywhere, but no one saw anything, or if they had, no one was talking. I began doing more digging and discovered that Meille wasn't the only village where teenage girls were going missing. It was happening all over the area. One here, two there . . . Once I began documenting the location and details of their disappearances, I discovered a commonality—the CGRN."

"Fuck . . ." It didn't take a rocket scientist to figure out where this story was headed or what happened to those kids.

"I wasn't the only one who suspected they were taking these girls and selling them, but no one would say anything because if the CGRN gets pulled out of their region, many more people will starve to death."

"So they turn a blind eye to the atrocities of a few to save the lives of many—it's utilitarianism."

"It's barbarianism."

"I don't disagree. But many underdeveloped countries operate with this mentality."

"Well, it has to stop. And I'm going to do everything in my power to see that it does."

The conviction in her voice, the determination in her eyes, was admirable—inspiring even. It'd been a long time since he fought for something he believed in, or believed in something enough to fight for it.

"Since I was already doing a story for the CGRN, I was able to get access to different areas, take a lot of pictures, and interview people without raising suspicion. I don't believe the majority of the people in the CGRN even know this is going on. I think there's a small group within the organization that's using them as a front for human trafficking. A lot of what I learned was circumstantial and I knew I needed proof before coming forward with a story that was so damaging. So I waited. Night after night, I waited and watched until I finally found the proof I needed. I witnessed some of the men with the CGRN military team selling these girls to another group of men."

Her voice broke, vacancy filling her eyes. She was looking at him, but it wasn't Asher she was seeing anymore. A knot fisted in his gut at hearing her story, at seeing the agony she struggled with. He had to fight against the impulse to go to her, to take her in his arms and tell her it was all going to be okay. But he didn't, because it wasn't. It wasn't going to be okay for those girls and it sure as hell wasn't all right for her roommate. And if he fucked this up, it wouldn't be all right for Quinn.

"I had nothing but my camera. There wasn't anything I could do to stop them from taking those girls. Standing right there, they stripped them naked and treated them like cattle—grabbing at their breasts and inspecting their teeth . . . It was so horrible. The girls were crying, begging the men to let them go. They clung to each other as they were loaded into a canvas-covered truck. And I just let it happen . . ." Tears filled her eyes, and when one spilled down her cheek, she angrily swiped it away.

"You said it yourself, Quinn, there was nothing you could do to stop it. If you would have tried, you would have gotten yourself killed—or worse." Because, yeah, there were some things a lot worse than death.

The thought of how close Quinn could have come to disappearing rocked him harder than it should have. He didn't care about this woman, he reminded himself. And he was a fucking liar too. Quinn had sunk her quills into him four months ago and it appeared those barbs were still imbedded pretty deep.

"They raped one of them—right there in the dirt, each of them taking their turn with the girl. It was all I could do not to throw up. Every time the bile would surge up my throat, I'd swallow it back down and keep taking pictures."

Fuck . . . "You were lucky they didn't catch you."

She nodded. "I left the next day, claimed I had a family emergency I needed to return home for. I transferred all my notes and interviews onto the SD card from my camera and gave it to Aileen's father. He mailed it to Violet for me. I'm hoping it will be here by the end of the week. Instead of going home, I flew into DC, and like I told you last night, I went straight to the attorney general's office and reported what I'd seen, what was happening over there."

"Who did you speak with?"

"The attorney general, Mark Madison."

"And what did he tell you?"

"He asked for my proof, which I don't have right now. I checked my bag before boarding the plane and never saw it again. He said he would look into my report and wanted me to contact him when I had my evidence. Then he thanked me for coming in. I went home from there, back to New York, but my flight was delayed because of bad weather. I arrived to find my roommate dead and—" Her voice broke and she buried her face in her hands.

"Shit . . ." He came around the table and pulled Quinn into his arms. He was filthy and probably smelled like a sweaty horse, but she didn't seem to care. She felt so small, caged against him. So fragile . . . Her shoulders shook with grief and he held her tighter. He rested his chin on the top of her head and tried not to let his mind wander down the tragic road this could have taken. He knew how easily she could have been killed—had been on too many missions fucked up by one mistake or another not to know how this could have played out.

Inhaling a deep breath, he drew her scent into his lungs and closed his eyes. She was here now—safe. He just needed to keep her that way.

———

Once the tears started falling, she couldn't get them to stop. Putting voice to those memories had been harder than she'd expected, making her relive them with startling clarity. The emotions were too raw, the horror too close to the surface for her to hold them back anymore.

When Asher's arms wrapped around her, the feeling of safety enveloping her was her final undoing. She just . . . cracked, breaking down and sobbing against him. He held her close, tucking her head beneath his chin as he stood there letting her cry. It shouldn't feel this good, being in his arms, but when his large hand slowly moved up and down her back, she melted into him, molding against every hard, muscled peak and plane of his body. He was dirty and he smelled like leather, sweat, and horse. And God help her, she never wanted him to let her go. She told herself it was his strength she needed, but as the flicker of feminine awareness slowly awakened inside her, she knew it was more than that.

She wanted Asher Tate, and if she was being completely honest with herself, she'd wanted him from the moment she'd laid eyes on him. It was his arrogant, cocky attitude she'd hated, the flagrant whoring that had given her the self-control to stay the hell away from him. But this was a side of Asher she hadn't seen before, and she wasn't sure she wanted to, because the last thing she needed right now was to fall for this man.

She'd had her heart broken once and vowed she'd never give another man the chance to do it again. She had no doubt if she lowered her guard and let Asher in, he would devastate her. Maybe not on purpose, but she knew guys like him, and they had no interest in long-term anything.

When she felt him harden against her, she knew it was time to step back. She wasn't sure exactly when this sweet gesture of comfort had turned to something more, but the energy shifted in the room, charging with sexual tension, and she knew without a doubt she wasn't the only one feeling it.

Slamming her walls into place, she pulled back, feeling his reluctance to let her go. Grasping for control of not only her rioting emotions, but of the situation, she played her bitch card. It was her old standby and one well used. "I think we should finish talking about this some other time. You need a shower, and you should probably make it a cold one."

The tenderness on his handsome face turned expressionless. But what stung was his lack of surprise at her remark. He'd expected as much from her, she realized. He really thought she was a bitch . . . and why wouldn't he? She could play the part so well.

CHAPTER

8

This was the second time in as many days Asher had found himself comforting this woman, and that shit needed to stop. What was it about her that tugged at the frayed ends of his heartstrings so damn badly? He was a hardened killer, dammit, not some cuddly babysitter, and he'd do well to remember that.

Moving out from under the shower's spray, he turned the water to cold and let it beat the arousal out of his cock. It took a hell of a lot longer than it should have, and by the time he stepped out of the shower, goose bumps pricked every inch of his flesh. It felt like ice crystals were forming in his veins. This was fucking ridiculous. She was just a woman, and it wasn't like he was in short supply of them.

But then that wasn't exactly true, because Quinn Summers was like no other woman he'd ever met, and perhaps that was the rub. She was sharp tongued, quick witted, and off-the-charts intelligent. He knew all this because, yeah, he'd done some digging into his little houseguest last night when he hadn't been able to sleep. She'd started attending college at the age of seventeen and had a master's in cultural anthropology with a minor in English, literature, and writing—impressive. But more than having a fancy resume, and most importantly, she was the first woman he'd come across in a long time that didn't want him. It wasn't just that gorgeous face and killer body that made her so damn irresistible. That was the icing on the cake. It was what was underneath—her standoffish, abrasive attitude that drove him nuts. It also courted his inherent nature to conquer and possess.

Muttering a foul oath, he shut off the shower and snagged the towel he'd draped over the door. After a quick rubdown, he fastened it around his waist and headed for his bedroom. She'd been here only a day and already it felt like he was invading her private space.

Before exiting the bathroom, he rapped his knuckles against the door to warn Quinn he was coming out. He'd learned from her mistake last night not to assume the room was empty. Silence answered him and he slowly opened the door. The bed was still rumpled, the pillow indented from where she'd laid her head. Annoyingly, something in his chest tightened at the sight of seeing his bed in her disarray.

Grinding his molars, he marched over and jerked the covers back into place. By the time he was finished, all evidence of Quinn was gone, and not even a wrinkle in the bed remained. He quickly dressed and headed downstairs. When his foot hit the landing he abruptly stopped, his grip on the railing tightening as a rush of anger flooded him, erasing any chill lingering in his veins.

Quinn was sitting on the corner of the couch watching TV. She hadn't changed the channel from the CNN station it'd been left at the last time he'd turned that fucking thing on, before promptly hurling the remote into the fireplace. This time, there were news anchors chattering on about something irrelevant, but it was the headlines flashing across the bottom of the screen that caught his attention. *Nisour Square Massacre . . . Peterson's trial expected to conclude by the end of the week. Iraqi officials are demanding justice for the death of seventeen civilians and officers. Asher Tate, owner of Tate Security, acquitted of criminal charges against . . .*

At the sight of his name, Asher quit reading and marched over to the TV. He jerked the cord out of the wall and the anchors' voices cut out, leaving the room in silence. He ignored the look of surprise on Quinn's face, his own expression locked down to contain the rush of

guilt and anger that assaulted him every time he heard Peterson's fucking name. He should have shot that bastard when he'd had the chance.

It didn't matter that Asher hadn't been the one to pull that trigger;
he was still to blame. Those were *his* men—*his* responsibility. The White
House didn't see it that way, though, and after an exhaustive investigation, he'd been cleared of any misconduct. But it still didn't stop the
press from breathing down his neck.

"I prefer the TV stay off," he told Quinn gruffly, giving her no more
explanation before heading for the kitchen.

———

Did he just rip that television cord out of the wall and tell her she
couldn't watch the news? Quinn stared at him, too shocked for words
as she watched him walk away like he hadn't just revoked her First
Amendment rights. Was this guy for real? She shoved herself to her feet
and followed him out with a mind to give him an earful, then thought
better of it when he pulled his gun from the breadbox and chambered
a round before sliding the weapon into the holster behind his back.

"You ready to go?" he asked, barely shooting her a glance as she
hovered in the doorway.

"Aren't you worried you're going to shoot yourself in the ass?" Her
annoyance over his stunt in the living room sharpened the edge in her
voice.

He looked at her now, his raised brow posing the unspoken question, *Are you serious?* "If I shoot myself in the ass, then I have no business
protecting you. Might be worth the bullet . . ." He grumbled the last
part under his breath, but she heard him.

So this was how it was going to be? Lovely. "Look, I'm sorry I
snapped at you earlier. Okay? You were just trying to be nice—"

"I don't want your apology, Quinn. It's not necessary."

Apparently it was, because he was clearly pissed off at her. "How long are you going to keep this up?" she asked, frustration edging her toward her boiling point. She stepped into the kitchen and snatched her purse off the counter, shouldering the strap.

"Keep what up?"

As if he didn't know. "Acting like a dick."

He closed the lid on the breadbox with more force than necessary. The sharp rap against the granite countertop startled her. He turned to face her, his expression locked down except for the lines of tension bracketing his mouth and that little muscle flexing near his jaw. Okaaay, so she wasn't the only one close to losing their shit right now.

"What do you want from me, Quinn?" he barked impatiently.

Did he really not know, or did he just want to hear her swallow her pride and say it? One thing she knew about this man, which admittedly wasn't a lot—especially now that he was censoring her media exposure—was that he wasn't stupid. "This tension between us . . . It has to stop. We have to figure out a way to get along."

"How about you stay out of my way and I'll stay out of yours."

"That's it? That's your big plan?"

"You got a better one?" he asked, pulling his charcoal-colored Henley down over the back of his jeans and heading for the door.

His dismissive attitude made it obvious he didn't want to talk, but too damn bad. She was determined to resolve this tension between them and find some common ground. Quinn wasn't too prideful to admit her part in this strife. The least he could do was meet her halfway. "Maybe we should, you know, try to be friends."

That got her a surprised look and a dark chuckle that was anything but friendly. "Friends? Like 'Kumbaya' and campfires? I don't think so, Quinn. Thanks anyway, though."

He turned to walk out on her when she shouted after him, hot on his heels. "No, you jackass. Friends like 'I'm going to go grab a beer—you want one too?' 'Sure. Thanks for asking.' Or 'How was your day?' 'Great. How about yours?'"

He stopped abruptly and spun back around. She almost ran smack into his chest. "The beer is in the fridge. Help yourself. And I think you know exactly how my day has been, seeing as how you're practically on top of me. Listen, Quinn, I don't mean to sound like a jerk, but I don't *want* to be your friend."

His words hit her like a stinging slap across the face and she took an involuntary step back, trying like hell not to let the shock and hurt reflect on her face. "I can't be your friend and do my job, because the moment I start caring about you is when I'm going to make a mistake. I can't afford the distraction, Quinn. I can't get emotionally involved with you. Perhaps I gave you the wrong impression this morning, and you think I wanted there to be something here." He waved his hand between them. "If I've done that, I apologize. But I want to be very clear, my job is to keep you safe and nothing more. I'm not here to be your friend or meet any other needs you may have. That's how it has to be because that's the only way I'm going to be able to keep you alive."

He didn't wait for her to respond before turning away and heading to the truck. It was just as well. For the first time in her life, she was actually speechless.

CHAPTER

9

"Are you about finished in there?"

The sharp rap of knuckles against the dressing-room door startled Quinn as she unzipped the back of a sundress she'd tried on. The zipper caught between her shoulder blades, snagging on the daisy-printed fabric. Great. Now she was stuck.

"Just a minute," she snapped, struggling to reach behind her back as she spun around, trying to get a look in the three-sided mirror to see where she was hung up.

"It's been thirty. I'm standing in a women's dressing room, Quinn. I feel like a perv."

"I never asked you to come in here." She tugged harder but the zipper wouldn't budge, and cursed herself for giving in to the temptation to try the damn thing on. Not exactly an "essential" item, true, but she'd left Manhattan with nothing but the clothes on her back and wanted to buy something other than granny panties and jeans from the limited selection of the local department store. Big mistake by the way.

"I'm sure as hell not leaving you in here alone."

"It's a dressing room, Asher. I think I'll survive." She huffed a stray piece of hair out of her eyes as she craned her neck to see over her shoulder.

"Yeah, and there's a back exit twenty feet down the hall. I could have abducted and killed you five different ways by now."

Nice. She certainly didn't need the reminder, but leave it to Mr. Congeniality to plant that swell little visual in her mind.

"You've been in there a half hour . . ."

"I didn't realize you were timing me." It wasn't like she was going on a shopping spree here. In fact, she enjoyed shopping just about as much as Asher enjoyed loitering in the women's dressing room. But she needed a few things to wear and he could just deal.

"I didn't realize it took you so long to take off your clothes. Perhaps you need some more practice."

"Not with you, I don't," she grumbled, wrestling with the zipper.

"I'm not offering."

"Shit . . ." she cursed, tugging to get the stubborn fabric free. Her hand slipped off the zipper and she banged her elbow against the wall. "Ouch! Dammit!" Pins and needles shot down her arm and her hand went numb. Fantastic . . .

"You sound like a bull in a china shop in there. What the hell are you doing?"

"Nothing . . . I'm stuck," she whispered, praying no one else was in there to hear them.

There was a pause of silence before a snort of masculine laughter erupted on the other side of the door. "You're what?"

He heard her. He just wanted to make her say it again. Asshole . . .

"I'm stuck, all right? S-T-U-C-K. Stuck. You startled me when you began beating my door down and the zipper snagged."

"I was not beating your door down."

"Whatever. This is all your fault—stop laughing at me!"

"You really can't undress yourself, can you?"

"It's not funny, Asher . . ."

"I think it's fucking hilarious. Looks like you need my assistance after all."

She'd rather wear the damn dress home than ask him to help her get out of it.

"Open the door. I'm coming in."

"What?" she squeaked. "No way . . ."

The knob rattled. "Open the door, Quinn." Impatience was starting to replace his humor.

"Are you crazy? I'm half-naked. I'm not letting you in here."

"I've seen naked women before. Lots of times."

"I'm sure you have," she snapped, letting out a sarcastic snort.

"Just open the goddamn door."

It was no use. She wasn't going to get this thing off by herself. Exhaling a dramatic sigh, Quinn turned the lock and he stepped inside. "Hurry up and close it," she hissed when he got stuck between the open door and the wall.

"Could this room be any smaller?" he complained, forcing the door closed behind him.

"I don't think it's meant for two. Or someone your size," she grumbled. There wasn't a lot of room for them to move around, and things were getting too close for comfort really fast.

"Let me see the problem."

Quinn twisted her hair up and held it piled on top of her head. Asher grabbed her hips and turned her back toward him. "I can't get it to go down."

"Are you planning on buying this thing?"

She lifted her gaze and met his in the mirror, but he wasn't looking at her eyes. "Maybe . . ." She shrugged defiantly. "Why?" She had no intention of buying this dress but wasn't going to give him the satisfaction of telling him that. Besides, what the hell did he care what she wore?

His brow arched but he didn't respond. Quinn followed the direction of his gaze and then gasped, slapping her splayed hand over her exposed cleavage. "Quit staring at my boobs and just unzip the damn dress."

Her cheeks flushed hotly with embarrassment. Yeah, it was definitely embarrassment, and those were not butterflies coming to life in her stomach when she felt his hands at her back. His fingers brushed against her spine as he worked to free the fabric.

"You get it out yet?" she asked impatiently, feeling warmer by the minute.

"Does it feel like I got it out?" he snapped back with growing impatience.

"Well, try jerking it a little harder . . ."

"Shit, Quinn. Will you just stop talking?"

Finally, she heard the *ziiip* . . . and felt the dress let loose. If her hand hadn't been on her chest, the thing would have been around her ankles.

"There. Anything else, or do you think you can manage from here? Those bra clasps can be tricky."

"Get out."

He actually laughed, taking sadistic pleasure in her discomfort and embarrassment. Jackass . . . Asher opened the door and maneuvered past her. It was another tight squeeze but he was finally able to make it out. Once the door closed behind him, she quickly dressed and gathered the clothes she wanted to buy into her arms. He didn't offer any more smartass remarks as they left the dressing room—miracles never ceased. Instead, he dutifully followed her out.

Quinn dropped the armful into the shopping cart parked outside the dressing room, already filled with other essentials. Shampoo, conditioner, body wash . . . It was surprising how quickly this stuff added up to a cartload—shaving cream, razors, because she couldn't keep using Asher's. Loofah, toothbrush, toothpaste . . .

As she steered her cart toward the checkout lane, Asher's presence loomed behind her. Was this what it felt like to be famous? Having your every step shadowed by a gun-toting bodyguard? Because she'd only been in here an hour and it was already getting old. At least she didn't have to buy tampons or Monistat, because that would have been totally embarrassing and Asher was not letting her out of his sight. That fiasco in the dressing room was bad enough, and it certainly didn't help that her feelings were still bruised by his little speech. Perhaps if he didn't try so hard to piss her off, she wouldn't have been as annoyed by his looming presence.

The cashier made small talk with Quinn as she rang up her items and piled the bags on the other side of the conveyer belt. It surprised her to see Asher reaching for his wallet. Did he think she expected him to pay for all this stuff? "I have money," she told him briskly, refusing to be softened by the gesture. He wasn't doing this to be nice. He probably thought she didn't have a dime to her name, and she wouldn't have if Nikko hadn't told her to take out all that cash. Her train ticket and cab fare hadn't been cheap, but she still had about a thousand left.

Quinn pulled some cash out of her purse and paid the woman. When she turned to collect her sacks, Asher was reaching for them. "I've got them," Quinn snapped, grabbing her shopping bags. "You're my bodyguard, not my friend. Remember?"

Asher raised both hands and took a *Suit yourself* step back. Between her bare essentials, clothing, and toiletries, her arms were loaded down as she struggled to get her burden to the truck without collapsing under the weight of it all. But she'd be damned if she'd accept any more help from him than she absolutely had to.

He reached the truck before she did and opened the rear passenger door before heading to the driver's side. Quinn hefted her bags inside and slammed it shut. She was about to climb into the front passenger seat when a niggling of uneasiness swept through her like a hot flash. She froze midstep and turned to look behind her.

"What's the matter, Quinn?"

She took another second to search the lot. No one was there. But before she could tell Asher it was probably nothing more than her over-active imagination, he was out of the truck and rounding to her side with gun in hand, blocking her with his body as he none too gently ushered her into the vehicle.

"Stay down and lock the doors," he demanded, heading toward a cluster of cars to the south of them. Her heart rioted inside her chest. She wasn't sure what shook her up more—the fear that someone might really be out there, or the sudden change in Asher.

She could hardly believe this was the same guy who'd laughed at her not even twenty minutes ago for getting stuck in her dress. It was like hanging out with freaking Jekyll and Hyde. It took him a while to return. Long enough that she was starting to get really worried. She hated this feeling of helplessness . . . How long would she have to live with this constant fear that, at any moment, her life could be over?

The truck door swung open and she let out a startled yelp. Asher tossed a bag into her lap and climbed into the driver's seat. "Found your stalker. You forgot a bag at the checkout. I think I scared the shit out of the poor guy chasing after you." He fired up the truck and pulled out of the parking lot. "Almost killed a guy over your underwear. That's just awesome, Quinn."

What? Oh, please no . . . Quinn opened the sack on her lap and peeked inside. Her cheeks flushed and she closed her eyes, dropping her head back against the seat.

Yep, it was official. God hated her . . .

CHAPTER

10

Asher left after supper for an evening ride to scout the property, giving Quinn the place to herself for a little while. She was taking advantage of the solitude and sitting on the back porch, sipping a vodka lemon iced tea and admiring the view of the Colorado Rocky Mountains.

The darkening sky was lit by pink- and orange-hued clouds, the mountain peaks silhouetted against the setting sun. It really was beautiful here. And so peaceful . . . She could almost forget the rest of the world existed—almost. It was easy to see why Asher loved this place. *She* could love this place. It was everything the city wasn't—quiet, spacious. The earth felt alive here in a way she couldn't describe. It was like the air was a living element that infused the soul with each drawn breath.

If she survived this nightmare, someday she would find a place like this to call home. New York had stopped being that for her when Spencer left her. And now, after what happened to Emily, she didn't think she could ever go back. Too many painful memories . . .

For the first time since she could remember, she finally felt safe. Perhaps it was the vodka warming her stomach and lulling her into a false sense of security. She didn't know, didn't really care. She just needed to shut it off for a while—the thoughts, the fears, the images that would flash through her mind without warning, sending a surge of adrenaline flooding her veins and panic clawing up her throat at random points throughout the day.

A soft nicker drew Quinn's attention to the barn. She tipped back her glass and drained the contents. The ice cubes clinked together as she set it down on the table and rose. She'd never been up close and personal with a horse before, but she had just enough liquid courage in her to head down to the barn and go check it out. Halfway across the yard the call came out again.

She slid the large barn door open and felt for the light switch, clicking it on before stepping inside. Quinn walked past the first stall and found it empty. She stepped in a bit farther and almost collided with a large black head inches from her face. "Oh!" she gasped, reaching up to press her hand over her pounding heart. "You scared me." Holy crap, this horse was huge. "Is that you making all the racket in here?"

The horse snorted, blowing a fine mist all over her cheek. He threw his head up and down like he understood what she was saying. Cute. Quinn laughed and took a step back, wiping her palm down her cheek and onto her pants. This was the horse Asher had been working earlier that morning.

"Did you get left behind again?" she cooed, raising her hand and letting the horse sniff her palm like one might do to a stray dog. Funny, he hadn't looked that large from the window or standing beside Asher, but up close, this animal towered over her. He was the most beautiful, magnificent thing she'd ever seen. His dark eyes watched her with curious intelligence. His ears tipped forward, nostrils flaring slightly as he smelled her.

He must have decided she was okay, because a moment later he dropped his nose into her hand and wiggled his lips. The heat of his breath and the soft rub of his leathery nose made her smile. "Are you looking for a treat?"

Quinn glanced around the barn, looking for something she could give the horse. She spotted a sack in the corner and a grabbed a handful of grain. She carried it over and opened her hand, taking care to keep her fingers out of the way. He cleaned off her offering in one nibble.

"You want some more?"

The horse threw its head up and down.

She made another trip over to the sack and came back with more grain. This time as he munched the oats, she reached up with her free hand and gently ran it down the length of his nose. He stood there, letting her pet him a moment, and then his head bobbed again, as if prompting her to go get him another snack.

Quinn smiled, a glimmer of joy entering her heart that she hadn't felt in longer than she could remember. Who would have thought one could get such joy just being around an animal? She read studies about the therapeutic effects of owning a pet, especially for people suffering from PTSD, but she'd never had any pets herself. Not that she hadn't desperately wanted one when she was growing up. But in the building where she'd lived in New York, they hadn't been allowed.

Quinn made another grain trip and raised her hand to give the sweet animal another treat.

"You're going to spoil him."

She startled and jumped back, dropping her hand. The grain spilled on the ground, scattering at her feet as Asher entered the barn and led the other horse in behind him. They stopped at the first stall and he unclipped the reins before gently sliding the bit from the animal's mouth.

"I'm not spoiling him. I felt bad for him," she explained, running her hand down the horse's neck. "He was left in here all alone. Why did you lock him up?"

"He's limping on his front right leg. If I left him in the pasture he'd race the fence and I don't want him making the strain worse."

"Is he going to be all right?" She stood on her tiptoes, reaching up to pet the tuft of his mane between his ears.

"He'll be fine in a few days." Asher made a hand gesture to the horse before turning his attention back to the one he'd just brought in. The one she was petting immediately dropped his head so she could reach him easier.

"Did you just do that?"

Asher flipped the stirrup over the seat and began unfastening the saddle. "Do what?"

"Tell him to lower his head?"

"Yeah . . . He's tall. It makes bridling him easier."

The horse lowered his head even more, resting his forehead against her chest when she began to scratch his ears. Asher glanced her way, then did a double take before shaking his head and lifting the saddle and blankets off the chocolate-colored one. He stepped out of sight and returned a moment later with a brush.

"What?" she asked him, scratching her nails down the horse's neck.

"Nothing . . ." He began brushing his horse with long brisk strokes, working his way around the animal with swift efficiency. "Jack doesn't like many people, is all. He likes you."

"Well, at least someone around here does." The caustic remark was out of her mouth before she could call it back.

Asher stopped midbrush. His head snapped up and his eyes collided with hers. Seconds ticked by, each one growing more interminably uncomfortable than the last. Finally he spoke, his voice edged with frustration.

"I never said I didn't like you, Quinn."

And then the brushing resumed—this time with a lot more vigor than before. What was that supposed to mean? *I never said I didn't like you.* He sure as shit did. Whatever . . . she wasn't about to stand here and argue with him about it. With a final pat, she stepped back and placed a kiss on Jack's nose before turning and heading out of the barn. She didn't even spare Asher a parting glance as she walked out, but she sure as hell felt his eyes on her.

———

That woman just kissed his horse.

Asher stared at her in shock as she walked past him in typical Quinn fashion—chin notched in that stubborn lift that set his teeth on edge, violet eyes fixed straight ahead. The glimpse of her tenderness toward Jack hit him in the gut like a sucker punch. His chest tightened uncomfortably, leaving him a little breathless. Just when he thought he'd figured Quinn out, she went and did something completely unexpected.

But then again, did he really know her well enough to make that kind of assumption? The more time he spent with her, the more he was beginning to suspect there was a lot more to Quinn Summers than what met the eye. If she only knew the significance of what she'd just done, would she still have done it? First of all, you kiss a man's horse, you might as well be planting those lips on him. And secondly, Jack didn't let anyone touch him but Asher—ever. And here the beast was, practically drooling all over that woman.

"What the hell was that?" he grouched to the stallion as he opened Marley's stall and ushered the gelding inside.

Jack nickered a response.

"Yeah, I know she's pretty. Those are the ones you've gotta watch out for. She'll wrap you around her little finger, I'm tellin' ya." He closed the stall door and set the lock, not sure who that warning was meant for—him or the horse. Both would do well to heed the advice.

He headed to the back of the barn and grabbed a square bale. He dropped it between the stalls, then cut the twine with his pocketknife and stuffed a few flakes in each feeder. "She's gonna break your heart, boy. Don't say I didn't warn you."

Jack nodded his head, his common response to whatever Asher said. With those parting words, Asher slid the barn door closed and latched it. As he walked up to the house, his gaze was drawn to the loft that was lit up like a fucking Christmas tree. Quinn was standing there by the dresser, her back to him. She was wearing nothing but a pair of white lace panties, the cheeky cut only covering half her ass.

Lord, have mercy . . .

First thing tomorrow morning, he needed to get some curtains on those damn windows.

CHAPTER

11

*B*ang, bang, bang!

Quinn looked up from the article she'd been reading on Asher's laptop to the ceiling above her. What in the hell was he doing up there? She'd set up camp at the kitchen table, needing some room to spread out. Notes were scattered around her as she searched for the CGRN/US government connection. So far nothing was flagging. She'd been racking her brain, but she couldn't remember the name of the military team that had escorted them into Meille. It was in her notes somewhere, but they were all on the SD card with the photos. It was frustrating, but she had to believe if she kept looking, something was bound to show up. Right now, she was chasing a bunch of dead ends and it was making her irritable.

Bang, bang, bang!

Exhaling an annoyed sigh, she shoved her chair back and headed up the stairs to investigate the racket. Quinn rounded the corner and stepped into the bedroom to find Asher nailing a bracket above the window. His arms were stretched above his head as he pounded nail after nail with impressive precision.

"What are you doing?"

"Hanging up curtains," he answered past the nails held between his lips.

"Why?"

He shot her a Really? arched brow glance and then resumed hammering.

What was that supposed to mean? And then the answer sent an icy chill invading her veins. Her pulse quickened with the rush of dread that was never very far away from the surface. She stepped closer to the glass and looked out to the woods surrounding them. For the first time, she saw all this rustic beauty from a killer's perspective. No longer were the woods a place of peace and serenity. He could be anywhere and they'd never even know it. "You think he's out there, don't you? He's watching me . . . That's why you're hanging up curtains."

"I don't know if he's out there, Quinn. I haven't seen any sign of anyone in the woods yet, but you gave *me* a hell of a show last night."

What? Embarrassment usurped her anxiety. "You were spying on me?" she accused, her tone sharp with indignation.

That earned her an annoyed scowl. He grabbed the end of a sheet and hooked it over the bracket, then stretched it across the first window before moving to the next one. "I wasn't 'spying' on you. If I was, do you think I'd be hanging up curtains?"

Good point . . . In truth, she was surprised he was doing this. The Asher she knew didn't seem like the kind of guy not to take advantage of a prime opportunity for a peep show. Then again, how well did she really know him? Obviously not very, because she would have thought her privacy would have been Asher's last priority. Yet here he was, pounding away.

"Well, thank you," she conceded, turning to head back downstairs. "I should be getting back to work."

"How's it coming along?" he asked over the banging.

She could understand him better now that his mouth wasn't full of nails. The roped muscle of his arms flexed as he swung the hammer. Her gaze dropped to the flash of tan skin exposed at his waist. Her glimpse of hard abs sent a flicker of heat budding in her core. His dark-washed distressed jeans hung low on his hips, giving her a teasing flash of an Abercrombie & Fitch waistband. Hmm . . . He seemed more like a Hanes guy to her. Not that she'd spent a lot of time imagining what kind of underwear Asher wore, because that was just creepy and . . . yes, pathetic. Oh for chrissake, she shouldn't be thinking about his underwear at all. She had a story to focus on. She did not need this distraction. But a distraction he was—and a big one.

"Not very well . . ." she confessed when she realized she hadn't answered him yet. "I've got pages of conspiracy theories and nothing to support them. I have no idea why Mark Madison would want to cover up a human-trafficking operation halfway around the world."

"Maybe you're looking at it wrong. Hand me that sheet over there, will you?"

She walked over to the bed and grabbed it. "Did you make the bed?" This was the second day in a row she'd come upstairs to find it wrinkle-free. Sadly, this bed was becoming a metaphor for their lives— he liked his orderly and neat, and she was messing it up.

"Sorry, it's a habit." He held out his hand for the sheet and she gave it to him.

"What did you mean by maybe I'm looking at it wrong?"

He shook out the sheet and turned back to the window. "Maybe you're internalizing this too much because of how personal it has become for you. It could be affecting your objectivity. You're looking at this on a micro rather than a macro level. One thing I've learned, being in the military, is that the buck rarely stops where you think it does and everyone is a pawn."

She looked at him, studying the man hanging her makeshift curtains while giving his comment careful consideration. Was he always this insightful? She'd known he was intelligent. That had never been a question. You didn't get put in charge of your own Special Forces recon unit or own a private security agency by being an idiot. Maybe he was right. She *was* looking at this personally. She'd been doing all this research on the attorney general, trying to find his connection to the CGRN. She needed to broaden the cast of her net and see what it dragged in.

He must have felt her staring at him because after he got the sheet hung, he glanced over his shoulder and shrugged. "Or not . . . It's just a thought."

He walked out, leaving her standing there, no doubt looking as dumbfounded as she felt.

———

"Do you really think this is a good idea?"

Anything that involved Asher not sitting in a nine-hundred-square-foot house with this woman was a good idea. Keeping his distance from Quinn was proving harder than he'd ever expected. After hanging her makeshift curtains, he'd gone outside to work on the modifications for Jayce's AR, but his mind just wasn't into it.

All fucking day it was meditating on a slender, bare back and white lace panties. Some shit you just couldn't unsee . . . His mind wouldn't stop imagining that tiny waist he'd bet money he could fit his hands around and the flare of those feminine hips. Quinn had the kind of ass a man's fingers itched to curl into as he lifted her up and pinned her against the wall. She was right under his roof and he couldn't fucking touch her.

He'd talked a big talk with his *I can't be your friend* speech, and he'd meant every damn word. Problem was, friend or not, he wanted her, and there weren't enough curtains he could hang or cold showers he could take to change that. And worse yet, he was discovering he actually liked her. He liked her sharp tongue, her quick wit, and her courageous spirit. She fought for what she believed in—no matter the cost. And fuck him if he didn't admire the hell out of her for it.

She stoked his temper as much as his lust. But after what he'd been through these past few months, it was just nice to feel something other than guilt and self-loathing for a change. Quinn stirred something inside him that went soul deep. He didn't want to give it consideration or let it get a foothold, because as much as he tried to tell himself that this was just lust, that she was just a job, he knew if he gave himself even an inch of leeway, he'd consume her with the ravenous hunger of a forest fire that would burn them both to the ground.

He was under no delusion that she wanted anything from him other than the security his presence provided. She had walls that would rival his own, making him wonder if any man had ever scaled them. Would the reward be worth the effort? Something told him it would be. Was there a bastard in her past responsible for putting them there? If yes, he wanted to meet that fucker so he could throat punch him.

Her knack for running cold was impressive, and he had zero doubt his rebuke of her olive branch yesterday would come with some hefty consequences. But he'd known it would. In fact, he'd been banking on her ire because he wasn't so sure he trusted himself not to say "fuck it" and take them down a road where neither one of them should be headed.

He pulled up to The Rabbit Hole and parked around back to save space up front for the paying patrons. The place wasn't big and parking was limited, but it was always busy. His father ran a good business, and the locals were a loyal lot.

"It shouldn't take me too long to look at this cooler. It's not holding temp and probably just needs a charge. I'm not comfortable leaving you alone at the house when I'm this far away. Besides, you've been glued to that computer all day. It'll do you some good to get away from it for a little while—clear your head."

"It's easier said than done."

He cast her a quick glance and could tell she wasn't happy he'd dragged her away from her research. "I know . . ." And he did. "Nothing about this is easy." He knew exactly what it felt like to blame yourself for someone's death. He knew what it was like to be haunted by the what-ifs. But if Quinn didn't find a way to balance this out, to take her mind off it, even just for a little while, it was going to destroy her from the inside out.

"We can get supper while we're here. I promise it'll be better than anything I can cook at home. The Rabbit Hole's got the best broasted chicken around. We'll order some to go."

That seemed to sway her and she nodded her acquiescence. He cut the engine and climbed out, heading to the rear to grab his tool bag from the bed of the truck. She still hadn't gotten out by the time he closed the tailgate. Heading around to her side, he opened the door. "Come on . . ."

She climbed out and followed him up to the building. He opened the door for her then followed her in. The contrast of brightness outside to the dark hall rendered him momentarily blind. He didn't realize she'd turned around to wait for him until he ran into her.

She connected solidly with his chest and let out a surprised yelp. Her breasts crushed against his ribs, sending a jolt of heat arrowing straight into his cock. She stumbled back and he slipped his arms around her waist to steady her, pulling her closer. Her hands flew up and she planted her palms against his chest, for balance or to push him away, he wasn't sure. But if she was smart, she'd do the latter, because he was having a hard time forcing his arms to let her go.

"Are you all right?" he asked, his eyes finally adjusting to the darkness.

"I'm fine. You know, for a Black Ops specialist, you're not very stealthy."

He chuckled. "Black Ops, huh? You make me sound like an Xbox One character. I'm not even going to ask you what my name would be."

She laughed now. That beautiful cadence bubbled up and nailed him with a kill shot right through the heart. Quinn Summers didn't laugh often, but when she did, he swore to God it was the most beautiful sound he'd ever heard. And he found himself wanting to hear it again.

"How about Private Jackass?"

"Really? You're demoting me to a private? You can at least call me Gunnery Sergeant Jackass."

Her laughter rang out again, and it was then that he realized he was still holding her. How long before she realized it too? Damn, she felt good . . .

"All right, I'll give you rank, but you know that just means you're an even bigger jackass, right?"

His own throaty laugh resonated in the hall. "I suppose it does."

"I thought I heard voices back here."

A light clicked on overhead, and just like that the moment was gone—wiped away with the flick of a switch. Quinn tensed against him and dropped her gaze, a blush quickly staining her cheeks. Was she embarrassed she'd let her guard down and allowed her sense of humor to show? Or was she afraid he might discover she wasn't such a shrew after all? Maybe she was embarrassed to be caught standing here in his arms? He glanced over the top of her head to his dad, who was giving Asher a knowing grin. It was obvious what the old man was thinking—or hoping he saw, anyway.

Sorry to disappoint him, but despite how things looked, or how much he may wish things could be different, Quinn was off-limits. Before he could let her go, she pushed against his chest and stepped out of his arms.

"Hey, Pop. I got your message about the cooler not holding temp. Thought I'd take a look while we got some supper ordered up."

"Absolutely. You want the usual?"

"That'd be great."

"I'll just add it to your tab."

His dad waved them forward and gave Quinn a teasing wink. She returned his smile and Asher refused to let himself wonder what it would be like to be the recipient of that unguarded brilliance. Had she smiled at him like that in the dark?

"It's nice to see you again, Mr. Tate."

"Please, call me Robert." Then to Asher he said, "Well, you know where the cooler is, so I'll leave you to it and go put in for two specials. Should be ready in about a half hour or so."

"Thanks, Pops." Asher led Quinn down the hall and dropped off his tool bag in the supply room where they kept the cooler. "You want to sit at the bar? You can have a drink while you wait. I'm sure Pops would love to keep you company."

She shrugged. "That's all right. I think I'll stay here with you."

Definitely not the answer he was expecting to hear. Why would she want to be in here with him? Was she afraid to sit at the bar? She'd be safe with his dad. Rather than make a big deal of it, he got to work checking the charge on the unit while Quinn found a spot to sit on one of the boxes. He could feel her eyes on him. The sensation was almost as tactile as her touch in the hall had been, and his body's response was just as swift.

It was distracting as hell and she was fucking with his concentration. "You sure you don't want to wait at the bar? Have a glass of wine or something?" he offered again, hooking the meter up to the refrigerator line.

"I'm fine. Unless you want me to get you something. Do you do this a lot?" she asked, changing the direction of their conversation. "Fix things around here for your dad?"

He shrugged. "Sometimes. This cooler and I have a love-hate relationship. It loves to break down and I hate to fix it."

She laughed again and that sound rolled right through him . . .

"I have a grenade at home with this damn thing's name on it. I swear, someday I'm going to take her out back and blow this bitch up." More of that light melodic music caressed over him. "Pops always dreamed of owning a small bar like this. Maintenance issues are par for the course, I guess. I was on leave a few years ago when it came up for sale. So, I bought the place for him. I knew he'd never do it himself."

"Wait, *you* own this bar?"

"More like a silent partner." Yep, the charge was low. He disconnected the gauge and then readjusted his erection before standing. How pathetic was it that just the sound of her voice, her laughter, could make him this hot? Before turning to face her, he tugged the hem of his Henley over the bulge in his pants and tried to focus on their conversation rather than the path his mind was trying to lead him down. "My dad does most of the work. I've been taking care of the building, doing repairs and maintenance since I got back, but this is really his gig."

"So that crack about your tab was really a joke."

He chuckled. "Shit, I hope so, or else I'd probably be payin' for the place twice."

"You're pretty much a jack of all trades then, huh? Special Forces soldier, mercenary, bar owner, handyman . . ."

She had no idea how handy he could be . . .

"That about cover it?"

She was giving him shit and he couldn't resist giving it right back to her. Despite what he'd told her yesterday, he suspected, under different circumstances, they might have been friends—maybe more. He rather enjoyed her sharp, sarcastic sense of humor.

Taking a step toward her, he nudged her shoe with his boot. It was the closest he dared come to touching her. He was breaking the rules. He knew it and yet he was having a hard time caring at the moment.

"You forgot about babysitter." He flashed her a teasing grin and her feminine snort should not have been as sexy as it was. Fuck, he had to get out of here, put some space between him and Quinn Summers, because she was about two seconds from going up against that cooler.

"I gotta go get some refrigerant. Would you mind grabbing me a beer from the bar?" He was out the door and down the hall before she could respond.

CHAPTER

12

He was squatted down, bent over the unit, filling it with refrigerant when a pair of breasts pressed against his back and a beer dangled in front of his face. He had a momentary flash of *Holy shit . . .* then a reactionary *Oh fuck* when he realized it wasn't Quinn. His first clue was the heady perfume searing his nostrils. And if he still had any doubt, Quinn didn't wear hot-pink nail polish.

Asher rose to his feet and spun around to find his dad's waitress standing way too close to him, pinning him between her large, surgically enhanced rack and the cooler. Tina might have been going for sexy, but it wasn't working for her. The woman's smile reminded him more of a cat that ate the canary, and he was missing a few pinfeathers. Goddamn, this woman was tenacious . . .

She planted one hand over his shoulder, bracing it against the cooler, while holding his beer in the other. "I heard you were back here. Thought you might like a beer."

Tina was pretty enough, but not even close to Quinn's league. Then again, not many women were. This wouldn't be the first time he'd turned Tina down. He'd told her the last time she'd cornered him in the back storeroom that he didn't fuck his father's employees—no exception.

"I'm good, thanks," he replied, trying to put some space between them.

She stepped closer, rubbing her breasts against his chest. It did nothing for him.

"Oh, come on . . . We both know you want it," she purred, and she wasn't talking about the beer.

Asher wanted something all right, but Tina wasn't it. Problem was, the woman he wanted he couldn't have. She slipped her beer hand up around his neck, pressing in for full frontal contact. He grabbed her hips and was about to forcibly move her back when Quinn's voice echoed in the doorway—way too close.

"You never said what kind of beer you wanted, so I got you an Arrogant Bastard—"

Her sentence died on her lips and so did that rare smile. "Guess it was a good choice," she added, slamming it down on the shelf. A mountain of foam bubbled up over the rim, spilling onto the boxes below as she spun around and walked out.

"Quinn, wait . . ."

He tried to go after her, but Tina blocked his path.

"Tina, stop. I've told you before, this isn't going to happen. If you touch me again, you're fired."

He rushed past her to go find Quinn, cursing his damn luck all the way. Tina's timing couldn't have been worse. And he knew what Quinn was thinking. No way in hell would the thought ever enter her mind to give him the benefit of the doubt. Not after the shit he'd pulled around Nikko's wedding. Guilt churned inside his gut, which was ridiculous. He hadn't done anything wrong. Yet here he was, feet in motion, chasing after the woman he had no business wanting.

He stepped into the bar, stopping in the doorway when he saw Quinn talking to another man, and jealousy burned through his veins. He recognized the guy—Luke fucking Thompson. He had a reputation of being a player, and rumor had it, he liked to play rough.

The guy said something to Quinn as Asher approached, but the music playing in the background and the occasional crack of pool balls drowned out any hope of catching their conversation.

Quinn glanced his way and dismissed him just as quickly, nodding in agreement to something Luke had said. Just before Asher reached her, she slid off the stool and turned to leave.

Asher caught hold of her arm before she could walk away. "Where the hell do you think you're going?"

Luke paused, giving Asher a surprised look. "Are you two together?"

"Yes," he answered at the same time she responded with a resounding "No."

"I'll meet you over there," she told Luke, who seemed a little uncertain now as he headed back toward the pool tables.

When Quinn turned her violet eyes on him, they were sharp with anger. Any of the softening that had been there earlier was long gone, and the sudden ache of disappointment blooming in his chest pissed him off.

"Let go of me, Asher."

His grip tightened, fingertips biting into her biceps. "What do you think you're doing?" he demanded.

"I'm going to play a game of pool over there with Luke, while you play whatever back there with your little barmaid."

Dammit, he didn't owe her any explanations, and that's exactly what he found himself wanting to give her. "Quinn, Tina and I—"

"Save it, Asher," she snapped icily, holding up her hand. "You don't have to answer to me."

Then why in the hell did it feel like he did?

"You're free to fuck whomever you want. It's not like I haven't walked in on you doing it before."

Her response hit him like a sucker punch in the gut. It was a low blow and completely uncalled for. You know what, she was exactly right. He didn't owe her a damn thing.

"I don't want you around that guy, Quinn."

Her brows popped up, her expression a challenging *Oh really?* "Do you think he's the man who's after me? The guy who killed Emily?"

"No, but—"

"Then your babysitting services aren't needed, Gunnery Sergeant Jackass." She tugged her arm from his grip. "Take the night off. It looks like your 'services' are wanted elsewhere."

———

Quinn told herself she didn't care whom Asher messed around with, that it didn't matter. It was a dirty lie. She cared. She cared a hell of a lot more than she ought to, and walking in on him with that waitress stung. She didn't need an instant replay with him and the coat-check girl. Had she really thought he'd changed? That she'd misjudged him?

Was that why he'd sent her to go get him a beer, so he could have his little hookup? He'd tried twice before to get her to leave and wait for him at the bar. Like a fool, she'd refused, enjoying the few rare moments when they weren't at each other's throats. It made perfect sense now. How else was he going to get laid? He couldn't get any privacy at his house. She felt like a complete idiot.

Well, now was his chance. She'd taken his advice and forced her mind to rest. Right now she was just a stranger in a small town, drinking a beer and shooting a game of pool. Asher could go fuck off—literally.

Only he didn't. He'd taken a seat at the bar and just sat there watching her. She was acutely aware of his eyes on her, felt everywhere they touched, like the bold caress of a possessive lover—which was absolutely ridiculous because she wasn't that to him, and she never would be.

"That's a great shot." Luke smiled at her from across the table.

"Thanks." She sunk the eight ball in the left corner pocket, winning her first of the three games they'd played. Quinn suspected this last one was a pity win.

"You want to rack up another game?" he offered. "I'll grab some more beers."

That probably wasn't such a good idea. She was testing Asher's patience as it was, and she had the feeling he was about two seconds from tossing her over his shoulder, caveman-style, and hauling her ass out of there.

"Thanks, but I can't. It's been a lot of fun, but I really need to get going." She went to walk around the table and misjudged the distance, whacking her hip on the corner. "Ouch . . ." She cursed, steadying herself on the rail.

"Are you all right?" Luke was at her side before she could blink, slipping his arm around her waist.

Quinn shouldn't have let him. She really didn't need the help. She'd only had two beers, but apparently that was enough to mess with her better judgment. The spiteful, reckless side of her wanted Asher to know what it felt like to be the one on the sideline for once.

"I need to use the bathroom."

"Sure. It's this way," he said, guiding her toward the hall. Once they passed Asher's line of sight, she pulled away from him. "Really, I'm fine, Luke. I've got it from here."

She dismissed him with a polite wave and didn't wait for him to respond before entering the bathroom. As she closed the door, she caught the briefest flash of something darkening his eyes that sent a prickle of apprehension needling up her spine. What had Asher been about to say when she cut him off as he'd tried to warn her about Luke? Quinn locked the bathroom door behind her and took her time in there, hoping Luke would be gone by the time she came out.

When she swung the door open, she was startled to find Asher standing in the hallway waiting for her. He was leaning against the wall, arms folded over his broad, muscular chest. "What are you doing here?" she asked, surprised, and admittedly a little relieved, to see him.

"Saving your ass . . . Come on, let's go."

Saving her ass? What was that supposed to mean? He didn't give her a chance to ask. Taking Quinn's hand, he led her back to the bar. His grip was firm, his stride a determined clip that, no lie, was a challenge to keep up with. He made no attempt to disguise his anger, and she didn't want to risk making an even bigger scene by asking him to slow down. Already, they were attracting more than a few curious looks. Asher's dad was waiting for them up at the bar with a clear plastic bag in hand.

"Sorry about the wait. It's been busy tonight."

"Don't worry about it, Pop."

As they stepped into the hall, Robert said, "I'll see to it he's not allowed back here, Asher."

"He comes back again, he won't be walking out."

Asher took the bag from his dad, and she noticed his knuckles were bruised and bleeding. They briefly paused near the exit and she heard him quietly tell his father, "You can't report him to the cops, Pop. Quinn would have to make a statement, and no one can know she's here."

What the hell had happened while she was in that bathroom?

Robert's voice was low, but not so quiet that Quinn couldn't hear him say, "I understand. I'll take care of it."

———

"Are you going to tell me what that was all about?"

Asher looked up from his broasted chicken and stared at her, saying nothing. It wasn't the first time she'd posed this question in the last hour, and this one was met with the same response as the last—silence. Quinn had never seen him this angry before. She'd always imagined Asher was the kind of guy that exploded when mad, but nope. He was a simmer-and-boil type, and those were the worst kind—dangerous and unpredictable.

Clearing his throat, he wiped his face with his napkin and closed the clamshell. "Do you have any idea how close you came to becoming a statistic tonight?"

His voice was deep, lacking any inflection of emotion whatsoever. She wasn't sure if it was what he said or how he said it that made the fine hairs on the back of her neck rise.

"I'm wondering how it's possible for a woman as smart as you to do something so stupid."

"What?" She couldn't believe the words that were coming out of his mouth. "I'm stupid because I played pool with a guy? Seriously? Maybe the problem, Asher, is that you're jealous. Have you ever thought of that? Maybe you're just pissed that your 'I can't be your friend or anything else' plan is backfiring!"

"You're stupid because you accepted drinks from a man you didn't know!" he snarled, slamming his fist down on the table. The bang made her jump in her chair. His bruised knuckles split open and began to bleed again, though she doubted he noticed the crimson drops splattering on the table. "You hung out with a guy I warned you to stay away from, just to spite me. When you were in the bathroom, that bastard *mickeyed* your goddamn drink!"

That stopped her cold. But it didn't take more than a heartbeat for her shock to dissolve back into anger. So this was *her* fault? Typical dickhead male, blame the woman because she was almost raped. "Well, maybe if you could manage to keep the women you're fucking off of you for two seconds, I could stand to be around you without wanting to puke!"

"I already tried to tell you, I'm not messing around with Tina. Maybe you shouldn't make assumptions because it makes an ass out of you and m—no, it just makes an ass out of you."

"Wow, you sure have a silver tongue, Tate. I don't know how I'm controlling the urge to leap across this table and jump you right now."

"Easy. I'm not trying to fuck you, Quinn. If I were, you'd sure as hell know it."

Another verbal slap. And then the realization hit her . . . He was telling her the God's honest truth. He really didn't want her. For some embarrassingly dense reason, she hadn't truly believed him before now. Maybe he was right and she really did have an overinflated opinion of herself. Humiliation burned through her anger, leaving her feeling just plain exhausted. It spooked her to realize how close she'd come to being assaulted when she'd believed she was safe. And if Asher could have been just a little bit nicer and a lot less insulting, she would have told him thank you for protecting her tonight and offered to patch up his hand, because it sure wasn't looking very good.

But now, she just wanted to go upstairs, throw herself a pity party, and pretend this whole day never happened. In fact, she wanted to pretend the past few weeks never happened. Maybe then she could close her eyes at night without Emily's sightless ones staring back at her. Maybe then she could stop remembering the brutal rape and molestation of those poor girls in Meille. Maybe then she could stop looking over her shoulder wondering when that assassin was going to find her.

Rising from the chair, her appetite ruined, she closed the lid on her Styrofoam box and set her dinner in the fridge. All out of fight, she found herself unable to meet Asher's pissed-off glare.

"I'm sorry I've caused you so much trouble, and I'm sorry about your hand." She left the kitchen and headed up the stairs to the loft. As her feet landed softly on the wooden stairs, she heard Asher's curse echo from the kitchen and the scrape of his chair against the tile floor. "Quinn, wait . . ."

But she didn't stop. They'd said just about enough to each other for one day.

CHAPTER

13

The sun was just coming up over the mountains as Asher cinched the saddle strap tight. It was a little early to be heading out for his morning scout, but he couldn't sleep and hoped a ride would help clear his head. It had been three days and Quinn was still refusing to speak to him, and although he knew it was probably for the best, he felt bad for lashing out at her like he had. He'd been rude and insulting. His fear for her safety had caused him to react badly—and if he was being honest, his jealousy hadn't helped the situation.

Now she was just flat-out avoiding him, which was what he'd been hoping for, right? So then why was her avoidance driving him so insane? Even now, just the thought of her had his cock swelling as quickly as his anger. And if that shit didn't stop, he was going to have a damn uncomfortable ride.

Sure, he talked a big game, and he might have been able to convince Quinn he didn't want her, but just like Pinocchio, every time he told himself the lie, his cock would grow like that damn wooden puppet's nose.

Despite his repeated efforts, he hadn't been able to work her out of his system—and it hadn't been for lack of trying. But his hand was a poor substitute for the gorgeous blonde that set his blood on fire. He'd worried that getting involved with her would be a dangerous distraction, but at the rate he was going, that woman had him so tied up in knots he'd be better off fucking her and getting it over with. It's what he would have done four months ago. But it was getting complicated now because, dammit, he liked her. He liked her a lot.

Asher grabbed the hoof pick and ran his hand down the front of Jack's leg. When he reached his pastern, the horse obediently lifted his leg for Asher to clean out the packed dirt and stray gravel from his hoof. After finishing all four hooves, he bridled the horse, then retightened the cinch one final time before climbing into the saddle. Gathering the reins, he guided Jack around with the press of his knee and headed out of the barn. They weren't more than a few steps into the yard when a prickle of unease settled over him. He shifted his weight, directing Jack to stop.

Perhaps he was feeding off Asher's tension, but the animal's head snapped up, his ears turning forward and at attention—listening. Maybe he sensed it too. Something or someone was out there.

Asher's gaze scoured the wood line, straining to see into the shadows. Jack pawed the ground and gave a restless toss of his head, requesting permission to advance. Horses were notoriously creatures of flight, but not Jack. They'd hunted enough predators together that if Asher didn't know better, he'd swear this horse was part bloodhound.

As Asher searched the woods bordering the perimeter of the yard, his eyes kept returning to the east corner. The prickling sensation put his nerves on edge. As he nudged Jack forward, Asher slipped his hand behind his back and pulled the Sig from his waistband. He was about to cut into the woods and flank around the back when a deer bolted out of the trees.

Jack stopped abruptly and let out a snort, watching the doe bound across the yard. It looked like Asher wasn't the only one feeling punchy today. Hopefully the ride would do them both good. On the way back, he'd flank around and check the woods for any sign, but he suspected he'd discovered the source of their unease. The doe picked at the acorns in his front yard as she meandered west, and Asher urged Jack onto the trail.

———

He lowered his rifle and took his finger off the trigger. That was close—too close. How in the fuck had he known he was here? It was as if Tate had sensed him up in this tree. If it hadn't been for that deer coming out when it had and the cover of the predawn darkness, this could have ended very badly for the both of them. No doubt Tate would prove to be a formidable adversary, and he'd do well not to underestimate the man.

He waited a little while before slipping his arm through the rifle's sling and descending the oak that had become his post for the last several mornings. Though, now that her back bedroom window was covered, he was certainly enjoying the view a hell of a lot less. Quinn was an early riser and a creature of habit. To his luck, she showered in the mornings and had given him more than one teasing glimpse of that incredible ass. Her tits were a man's wet dream, and he'd bet his left nut her cunt was just as glorious.

It hadn't been his intention for the mission to take this unexpected turn. He was a professional, and emotions were an assassin's worst enemy. But from the moment he'd laid eyes on this woman, he couldn't deny it had turned very personal indeed. It would be a boon, a credit to his skill and talent, to take this woman out from under The Great Asher Tate's nose. He would have Quinn before he killed her—he'd decided that days ago. And by the looks of it, this just might be his lucky day.

The horse Tate left behind called for its pasture mate. The answering whinny put him a good quarter mile north of here. Far enough he could make a play for the house without Tate being able to reach her in time. It was a calculated risk he was willing to take. He wasn't thrilled about the prospect of killing the man—not that he wouldn't do it if he had to, but Tate's death, under any circumstances other than an accident, would raise a lot of brows, and a thorough investigation.

The man was well connected. His ability to walk through the Nisour Square scandal and come out smelling like a rose was proof enough of that. That man had a lot of friends—dangerous friends—who would not take his death lightly. The last thing he needed was for the hunter to become the hunted.

He stayed to the cover of the woods as he made his way toward the house, coming out on the trail Tate had entered, being mindful not to leave any sign in his wake. Traveling the path Asher took from the house, he stepped onto the deck. The boards creaked beneath his weight as he approached the back door. Energy thrummed through his veins, his pulse accelerating with anticipation.

There were so many ways he'd played this scenario out in his head. A thrill raced through him as he imagined the look on Quinn's face—the flash of terror in her eyes, just like her roommate's. That beautiful moment when all hope was lost, right before his victims realized they were going to die. There was just something about that kind of intimacy, the connection that tied their souls together forever—hunter and prey. It was the most euphoric, powerful feeling in the world. Nothing could be better, except maybe being buried inside this woman when the realization struck her. Just the thought of it made his balls ache and his cock twitched impatiently, anxious to get this party started.

He pulled the thin leather gloves from his back pocket and slipped them on before placing his hand on the doorknob. The handle didn't move. Then again, he would have been disappointed if it had. Tate wouldn't be that careless with his treasure. He wasn't sure how much longer he'd enjoy the advantage. Once Tate discovered who he was dealing with, all bets would be off. How long before he figured it out? A day or two? A week? With any luck this would be over and he'd be long gone by then.

He removed the slim pouch from his pocket and pulled out two metal tools, slipping the small torque wrench into the bottom of the lock, and then turning it left. Feeling no give, he turned it right and the cylinder shifted ever so slightly. Keeping tension on the wrench, he slid the pick in and pushed the pins up, turning the lock until he felt it click.

It was too easy. He replaced his tools and pocketed the kit before turning the knob on the door. It rotated with silent ease. He was about to push the kitchen door open when the light in the hall clicked on. Not wanting to lose the element of surprise, he spun around, pressing his back against the rough-hewn logs, and waited. The kitchen faucet turned on. As it ran, cupboard doors opened and closed. The water shut off and several seconds later, the high-pitched whir of a coffee grinder fired up. The noise would drown out her scream. This was his chance . . .

He turned the knob and was about to open the door and slip inside when he heard the rumble of an engine coming up the driveway and the crunch of gravel beneath approaching tires.

Fuck. Someone was coming.

———

Quinn startled when the alarm sounded in the living room. Her heart leapt into her throat as she spun around, the little red light above the fridge flashing the warning of an approaching vehicle. She glanced at the clock on the stove—6:30 a.m. Who would possibly be coming here this early? She rushed into the living room and peered out the window as Asher's dad's truck, pulling a trailer full of hay, came into view then disappeared around the side of the barn.

Quinn exhaled a breath she didn't realize she'd been holding. She silenced the alarm and opened the front door, waiting to greet him.

"Morning, Quinn." He smiled as he approached the house. "Asher around?"

"You just missed him. He's out riding."

"That's all right, I'm a little early. Brought him a load of hay."

"Well, I don't know how long he'll be, but I just put on a pot of coffee. Would you like a cup while you wait?"

"I would. Thank you."

Asher's father followed her inside and took a seat at the kitchen table as she grabbed two mugs from the cupboard. "Black or cream?"

"Just a dash of cream, please. How are you doing?"

"I'm fine." She handed him the cup. "Thank you for asking."

"I feel bad about what happened the other day at the bar. I hate the idea of women coming into my bar and not being safe. That Luke Thompson has been trouble since he and Asher were kids. I would have called the police, but—"

"I'm glad you didn't," she cut in. "Besides, by the look of Asher's hand, I'm guessing he took care of it."

Robert grunted in agreement. "Listen, I'm not going to pretend to know what brought a city girl like yourself running to my son's door, and I won't ask, but I'm glad you're here."

Her eyes snapped to his, finding him watching her intently over the rim of his cup as he took a sip. "You are?"

"I am. I suspect Asher needs you just about as much as you need him, though for entirely different reasons."

"Is that why you didn't tell him I was coming?"

At least his dad had the decency to look chagrined. "I knew it'd be harder for him to refuse you in person."

Well, she could certainly see where Asher got his candidness, though to his credit, his father seemed to have a bit more tact with his words. Settling into the chair, she took a sip of her coffee and then asked, "Why do you think he needs me?" She had a hard time imagining Asher Tate needing anyone for anything.

"The war was tough on him. It changes a person . . ." Robert sounded like he was speaking from experience. "You live around death and violence long enough, you start to forget who you are, and think that's all you're capable of. But Asher is so much more than that. He just needs someone who can help him see that."

"And you think that person's me?" She hated to disappoint him, but she could hardly help herself, let alone someone else.

Before his father could respond, the pound of horse hooves sounded outside. Quinn was about to rise and look out the window when the kitchen door flew open.

"Quinn!"

Asher flooded the doorway. Her heart kicked inside her chest at the wild look in his eyes. If she didn't know better, she'd swear she saw fear, and something else that gave her pause, but she quickly dismissed it. It was his responsibility to keep her safe. She wouldn't fool herself into thinking his reaction was anything more than that.

Exhaling a ripe curse that sounded a lot like relief, he scrubbed his hand over the back of his neck and sagged against the doorframe.

Robert turned his head to look from his son back to her and said, "Yep, I do."

She hated to tell him he was wrong. Asher didn't care about her. At least not like his father might be hoping. He was just doing his job, and she'd do well to remember that.

"The security alarm went off," he said in way of explanation for barreling in like a hurricane.

"Sorry, son. That was me." His father raised his hand. "I didn't mean to worry you. I came by with the hay a little early. The truck's parked down behind the barn."

"How did you know the alarm went off?" Quinn asked.

"I have an alert on my phone that lets me know whenever the alarms are tripped inside the house. Shit. I thought . . ."

He didn't finish his thought. Then again, she didn't need him to. She'd been thinking the same thing—that she'd been found. Just the thought sent a shudder of fear racing through her heart. "I should go upstairs," she said after a moment, rising from her seat. "I've got a lot of work to do. There's fresh coffee in the pot."

Asher's scowl deepened at her dismissal. He looked like he was about to say something, then his gaze cut to his dad and he must have thought better of it. "I gotta get Jack put away," he told Robert, turning to head back out. "Come on, Pops. We'll get that hay unloaded."

Was it just her, or was that a definite note of frustration in his voice? Ever since their fight the other day, she'd been working in the bedroom, avoiding him at all costs. It wasn't nearly as comfortable, doing her research upstairs, but she'd put up with a backache over the unbearable tension that seemed to be a constant presence between them now.

CHAPTER

14

Quinn? Oh my gosh, I've been so worried! The FBI has been calling here. They're looking for you."

A chill ran through Quinn at her sister's news. She shouldn't be surprised to find out the FBI was looking for her. "I'm sure they are. What have you told them?"

"Nothing. That I haven't seen you. They wanted to talk to Mom and Dad. I gave them their number and told them they were out of the country. I don't know if they called or not, but I contacted them and told them you were safe and not to believe anything they said. My God, Quinn, I still can't believe this is happening."

"Me neither. It's like I'm living a nightmare."

"Is it safe to talk?"

"It's safe. I'm on Asher's phone." It was good to hear Violet's voice—so good, she was having trouble fighting the emotion swelling in her throat.

"Nikko said you were at Asher's. How's that going? Better than the wedding, I hope."

"It's going . . ." Three more days had passed with barely a word spoken between them.

"That good, huh?"

They seemed to have reached a stalemate. Despite their lack of conversation, it did nothing to ease the tension brewing between them. The air verily crackled with it whenever they were in the same room together. How long could she keep going on like this? Pretending like he didn't exist when he was all she could think about?

"You might not know this, Vi, but I'm not always the easiest person to be around."

Her sister busted out laughing. "You don't say . . ."

"Hey, whose side are you on, anyway?" she grouched, annoyed by the pang of guilt pricking her chest. Perhaps she should have stayed and talked with Asher, rather than walking away the night they'd come home from the bar. He'd tried to stop her, his tone full of regret, but old habits die hard. She'd been pissed, and Quinn had never been one to sit down and peaceably talk things out once her temper flared. She was more the shoot first and apologize later type. Vi was the levelheaded one in the family. Not her. Unfortunately, sometimes Asher reminded her a little too much of herself.

Would they still be at this impasse if she's handled things differently? Probably not, but honestly, her feelings had been so raw and bruised. She'd been afraid she'd break down into a puddle of tears and the last thing she'd wanted was to cry in front of him again—twice was more than enough.

Since her conversation with Robert, she hadn't been able to stop replaying his words in her mind. Did Asher really need her? More than likely, those were the hopeful ramblings from an old man who didn't want to see his son become a hermit.

"I'm on your side, Quinn. Always. You know that."

She did, and she loved her sister to death for it. "Listen, I called to see if a package has arrived there yet. I had it sent to your office before I left Haiti."

"I haven't received any package, but I can call you as soon as it arrives. Quinn, I'm worried about you. All this cloak-and-dagger stuff is really freaking me out."

"Me too. But I'm safe here." She left the "for now" part off her sentence. No reason to cause her sister any more stress.

"I know you didn't hit it off with Asher at the wedding, but he's a really good guy. You'll see if you'd just give him a chance."

Where the hell did that come from? What was with all the raving endorsements for Asher Tate? "A chance for what, Vi? Are you and Asher's dad the new Chuck Woolery or something? I'm not here to make a love connection. I'm here to stay alive."

"Asher's dad?"

"Don't ask . . ."

"All I'm saying is that not every guy is like Spencer. That's all . . ."

Just the mention of her ex made her gut churn. "Yeah, sometimes they're worse."

"I know Spencer hurt you. Bailing on you like that was a douche bag move, but you can't judge all guys by the actions of a few. Some of them are really great."

"Look, Vi, I'm happy for you that you found Nikko, really I am. But not all of us get our happily ever after, you know? Sometimes Prince Charming is really just a frog."

"And you think Asher is a frog?"

"No, I think he's a toad that hides his warts really, really well."

"Don't we all?"

Ouch. "You know I hate it when you're always right," she grumbled, exhaling a frustrated sigh.

"Well, I am a psychologist. I'd be a pretty shitty one if I were always wrong."

Quinn laughed.

"He's a war hero, you know . . ."

No, she didn't. Actually, now that she thought about it, there wasn't a lot she did know about Asher. The conversations they had never seemed to end well.

"Nikko said he was given the Medal of Honor for throwing himself on a bomb to save his recon team. It's a miracle it didn't go off. That's the only reason he's alive today."

Great, now she really felt like shit . . .

"I'm only telling you this because I know you don't trust easily, Quinn, and I want you to know you can depend on Asher. If he says he'll keep you safe, he'll do everything in his power to keep that promise."

"Thanks, Vi. I love you, you know that?"

"I love you too, Quinn. I pray this is over soon."

"Me too."

"I'll get that package to you right away."

"Thanks, Vi. I owe you . . ." They ended the call just as the door downstairs slammed shut. Taking a deep breath, Quinn steeled her resolve. This was crazy. Six days was enough dancing around each other. She just needed to go talk to Asher, at least apologize for her part in making a bad situation worse. Then the ball would be in his court and she could stop tiptoeing around here, feeling like the tension festering between them was her fault. She was grateful to him for everything he was doing for her. She could at least extend the olive branch and tell him that.

Quinn closed Asher's laptop and swung her legs over the edge of the bed. After days of searching for the connection between the US and the CGRN, she'd yet to yield any results that would link them together. She'd found figures and statistics in articles documenting the United States' financial and food contributions to the CGRN, but nothing on the US providing any military aid. It didn't make sense. She should have been able to find something. It wasn't like she didn't know how to do her research. She was a journalist and a damn good one. Bottom line, without her notes and interviews to look back on, she was just grasping at straws.

Quinn's feet had just hit the top step when she heard voices downstairs and the snick of two beer bottles opening.

"Thanks for modifying that AR for me. I can't wait to try it out."

"No problem."

She stopped on the stairs, not wanting to interrupt Asher if he had company, and would have headed back to her room if they hadn't started talking about her.

"Your little houseguest still hanging around?"

She recognized the voice as Asher's friend, the guy she'd met when she'd arrived. "Yeah, she's here."

Asher couldn't have sounded any less enthused if he'd tried. And why did that hurt? She didn't care what he thought of her. But even as she told herself the lie, it sat ill with her. The sad reality was she did care—too much, actually.

"How's that working for you?"

His deep chuckle rang out, followed by Asher's scoffing masculine snort.

"Shit, don't even ask."

"That good, huh? I don't get it. If you're not fucking her, then why is she here?"

Her stomach knotted at Jayce's question. Wasn't that what everyone would wonder? Why was she here? She strained to hear his response over the drumming of her pulse, praying all the while he wouldn't say something to expose her secrets. She may trust Asher with her life, but his friend was another matter entirely.

"It's a favor for Nikko. I'm helping her out with something. It's no big deal."

She exhaled a sigh of relief when Jayce didn't press for more details.

"Maybe you just need a break for a little while. Don't you have that barbecue thing at your parents' house this afternoon? If you want, I'd be happy to hang out here and keep an eye on things."

"Thanks, man, I appreciate the offer. But I value our friendship way too much to do that to you."

Jayce chuckled.

It wasn't funny.

"It's not a problem, man—honestly. How much trouble could she possibly be? If I can handle an army of Taliban insurgents trying to blow my head off, I think I can handle your little midge."

Asher laughed—a throaty rumble that lit up her nerve endings. How could just the sound of his voice spark such a visceral response, it made her core ache? She had hoped her attraction to him would pass. If anything, it was getting worse, growing stronger by the day. Not even their avoidance of each other was working to temper the flame of desire Asher sparked inside her.

"You think so, huh? Well, you don't know Quinn."

"Can't say I'd mind getting to know her a little better. She's smokin' hot."

"Stay the fuck away from her."

His response surprised her. It was sharp and immediate, all friendly warmth gone from his voice. Quinn could feel the chill frosting the air all the way up here. Gone was the camaraderie of two friends having a beer and shooting the shit. Asher's ability to go from friendly to foreboding could give a person whiplash. Goose bumps prickled up her arms. If she didn't know better, she'd swear she heard possessiveness in that low warning growl, but it couldn't be. He didn't like her. He'd all but admitted as much to his friend thirty seconds ago.

"Take it easy, Tate," Jayce shot back, a warning with equal menace. "You're getting kinda testy for a guy who has no claim on that woman. Which means you're either lying to me and you're fucking her, or you're lying to yourself and you want to be."

Her breath stalled in her lungs as she waited to hear Asher's response.

"Or there's the third option. She's too damn good for you."

Silence.

Jayce busted out laughing—a deep, throaty sound that echoed from the kitchen. Quinn wasn't sure what he found so funny, because she didn't think Asher was joking.

"Yeah, you definitely want to fuck her," his friend ribbed.

"About as much as I want to fuck a porcupine."

His friend broke into laughter again. Quinn turned and headed back to her room. She'd heard enough. Tears stung her eyes and she blinked them away, embarrassment and humiliation burning in her chest. He thought he knew her so well. Thought he was so funny making his little jokes. Did he think she wanted to be like this? Afraid to trust, afraid to let a guy get close to her again? She didn't *want* to be alone. But after Spencer's betrayal, she wasn't sure she could open up her heart and trust another guy not to shatter it, especially one as flagrantly noncommittal as Asher. Sex to him was nothing but a sport, and she had no doubt he was the MVP. Quinn had zero interest in playing, not that she'd been invited.

But still, his snarky dismissal bruised her feelings. She hadn't always been like this, guarded and closed off. There had once been a time she was sweet and trusting—and naïve. She'd believed in the power of true love, thought that life was all rainbows and butterflies. What a crock . . .

Reaching her room, she slammed the door behind her, cutting off their mocking laughter.

———

A soft rap of knuckles sounded on her door a little while later. Not looking up from the article she was reading, Quinn ignored the knock the first time, but could tell by its increasing persistence that Asher wasn't going to leave.

"Come in." She was careful to school her expression as the door opened. She grabbed the wadded-up tissue by her knee and stuffed it beneath her leg. She didn't want him to know how much his words had hurt her.

Asher stood in the doorway, studying her for a moment.

She returned his stare with one of bored impassivity. "Something you want?" she inquired coolly. On his own admission, it sure as hell wasn't her.

The sigh he exhaled seemed to be one searching for patience. "My family is having a barbecue this afternoon. I want you to come."

"Me? No thanks. I think I'd rather stay here and comb my quills."

Something flashed in his eyes. Embarrassment? Regret? Yeah, right . . . Asher Tate wasn't a man who went around apologizing for anything.

"Heard that, did ya?"

"Yep . . ." she answered coolly, turning her attention back to the computer screen. Perhaps if she pretended he wasn't there, he'd get the hint and go away.

"What did you expect me to tell him, Quinn?" The frustration in his voice got her attention. "You want me to tell him that you're the most amazing woman I've ever met? That I'm falling for you?"

"Of course not. Don't be a dick," she scoffed, angry that he'd even joke about something so serious.

He chuffed a harsh bark of laughter. "Only you would call me a dick for giving you a compliment."

"That's because I know you don't mean it."

His brow arched in question but he didn't dispute it.

"Look, I'm not asking you to lie. I'm just saying you don't have to be so brutally honest all the time."

"He's not a good guy, Quinn. You don't want Jayce interested in you, believe me."

No, she didn't, but that wasn't the point. Was Asher so dense he couldn't see that? "And yet he's your friend?"

"I'm not a good guy either."

His admission surprised her. He met her stare unwaveringly. Did he really believe that? The lack of hesitation in his response told her he did. There might have been a time not too long ago that she would have agreed with him. She'd been a proud card-carrying member of the *I Hate Asher Tate* fan club, and she wasn't exactly sure when that membership had expired, but at some point over the last week something between them had changed. Maybe it started when he'd agreed to take her in and protect her when she knew he didn't want to. It might have begun with the kindness he'd shown her when she'd told him of the tragedy she'd witnessed in Haiti. Or, it could have been the fearless way he'd protected her when he'd thought she was in danger in that parking lot, only to return with a bag full of her underwear. Perhaps it was those few stolen moments at The Rabbit Hole—right before everything had gone so horribly wrong between them—when he'd started to open up to her just enough to glimpse the man behind the mask.

And then there was Violet's raving endorsement that carried more weight with her than she wanted to admit. "That's not what my sister said. She claims you're a hero."

His brows drew tight in a frown. Not the response she'd been expecting. Instead of being flattered by the compliment, he seemed . . . annoyed. "I'm not a hero, Quinn. I'm a killer. I told you that the day you got here. Nothing's changed."

Yes, he had. And she had no doubt it was true. But he was wrong about one thing—everything had changed.

"The barbecue isn't optional. I don't feel comfortable leaving you here alone."

She wanted to ask him why not. Was he worried she'd been found? Surely he wasn't forcing her to come along for her sunny disposition.

"We're leaving in an hour. Pops told everyone you were my girl-friend so they're all excited and expecting to meet you."

All . . . ? How many people were they talking about here?

"He's trying to protect you, and it's easier than explaining the truth. So try not to act like you hate me for the next couple of hours, huh?"

Was that what he thought? "Asher, I don't hate you . . ."

He glanced back and continued to talk without acknowledging her confession. He either didn't believe her or he didn't care. Quinn wasn't sure which thought hurt more. His walls were so high the builders of Jericho could have taken architecture lessons from this guy.

"My brother Jaxson is a human lie detector. So try not to say any-thing that isn't true if you can help it."

Great. Well, this oughta be fun . . .

CHAPTER

15

The calm, always confident, and in-control Quinn Summers looked . . . nervous. Tension radiated from her in the seat beside him. He recognized the silent, restless agitation. Had seen it in a lot of soldiers he'd served with over the years. Those were the ones you had to be worried about. On the surface everything appeared just fine—until they cracked.

"Relax. It's a barbecue, Quinn, not the Spanish Inquisition." Asher reached across the center console and gave her hand a reassuring squeeze. He immediately realized his mistake when heat raced up his arm like an electrical current. His cock stirred with awareness of the woman he'd been fighting like hell to resist for the last week. Obviously, it was a battle he was losing. Hell, if he was honest with himself, he'd been losing it since the day he walked her down the aisle.

Maybe she felt it too, or maybe she just didn't want him touching her. Either way, she tensed. Shit . . . no one was going to believe they were dating. It wasn't that he didn't trust his family with the truth, and under normal circumstances he would never have lied to them, but Quinn's secret wasn't his to share. His father must have been of the same opinion or he wouldn't have fronted the story in the first place. Or perhaps the old man had an ulterior motive in throwing them together like this . . .

He removed his hand from hers and she cast him an anxious glance. "How many people are going to be there?"

"My parents, Sandra and you know Robert. My three brothers, Rory, Jaxson, and Fisher. Rory's wife, Kim, and their twin girls, Megan and Maddie."

"That's a lot of people."

He pulled into the driveway and parked behind Rory's burnt-orange Ram. Cutting the engine, he turned to face her. He wasn't used to seeing her without that tough, prickly exterior. Her appearance of vulnerability and the apprehension in her eyes hit him in the chest, stirring something deep inside him—a need to comfort her, to protect her. It wasn't the first time she'd courted the emotions in him, but it was the first time he'd felt the pull this strongly.

"Hey. You'll be fine. Just stick to the facts without getting into the details. You're a journalist, we met at your sister's wedding, and you became instantly infatuated with me."

She let out a light feminine bark of laughter that heated the blood in his veins. "I thought you said this should be believable."

She was teasing him. It was a good sign. She was rallying some of her moxie. He should have known Quinn wouldn't leave her guard down for long. A lopsided grin tugged his top lip. She really was a beautiful woman, and as much as she ignited his temper, she also ignited another fire inside him he wasn't sure he was going to be able to deny much longer. He'd discovered that realization after talking with Jayce this afternoon. Asher had never been one for jealousy. There were more than enough fish in the sea for everyone . . . but not like Quinn. She was different. And she was off-limits. He'd made sure Jayce had no misunderstanding about that.

"That's the way it happened in my head."

"Well, I think you should have your head examined. You're obviously delusional."

He chuckled at her teasing tone. Was it possible the Ice Queen was thawing? After climbing out, he rounded the truck and opened the door for her. He held out his hand to help her down, because that's what any doting boyfriend would do, right? And he just wanted the chance to touch her again.

She hesitated a moment, shooting him a nervous, uncertain look before taking it. Her hand was so incredibly soft, nothing like his rough, calloused ones—and delicate. The fine bones were so fragile and tiny, such a stark contrast to her personality. Sometimes he forgot how small and breakable she really was.

"I think we should tell them that *you* fell for *me*."

"We probably should," he conceded, closing the door behind her. "It's more believable . . ."

She took a step then stopped, glancing up at him with surprise. "It is . . . ?"

Was that a note of vulnerability he heard in her voice? It was so atypical of her to have any crack in her armor, and damn him if he didn't want to exploit it, if it didn't lay siege to his guard, lowering his own defenses. He studied her a moment, searching those stunning violet eyes. What he found in there made his pulse quicken and his chest ache with an unwelcomed fullness.

The thought briefly crossed his mind—what would it be like to have this woman's love, her devotion? He imagined it would be akin to possessing a rare piece of art—something irreplaceable and priceless.

His fingers tightened around hers, not wanting to let her go. "Of course it is. You're a beautiful woman, Quinn. What man wouldn't want you?"

She let out a sarcastic snort of mocking laughter. "You'd be surprised . . ."

Wait a minute . . . She didn't actually believe his ruse, did she? Did Quinn honestly think he didn't want her? He was fighting like hell to do the honorable thing here—to keep his distance and maintain his focus on the task at hand, which was Quinn's safety. Or was this about someone else? Fuck, *was* there someone else? He hadn't considered the possibility until this moment. The idea of her pining away over another man filled his veins with jealousy's bitter poison. He wanted to find out more, but before he could ask her, the front door opened and his mother stepped onto the porch.

"Asher, thank God you're here. Your brother's grilling."

"Oh, come on, Mom. It's not rocket science," Jax hollered from the kitchen. "I'm not going to burn the burgers."

"Then why is there smoke billowing out of the grill?" she called over her shoulder.

"Oh, shit . . ."

A streak of his brother flashed across the doorway as Jax ran out the back. His mother shook her head and laughed. "Your father said you were bringing a guest. Come over here and introduce me to her."

"You ready for this?" he asked Quinn under his breath, giving her hand a gentle squeeze.

Her grip on him tightened and she cast him a nervous smile. "As I'll ever be . . ."

———

The press of Asher's hand at the small of her back was a terrible distraction as he took her around and introduced her to his family. The heat coming off his palm radiated through her soft rayon top, warming her in places that had long been denied a man's touch. She tried to concentrate on what he was saying, to smile and shake hands and remember everyone's name, but she was pretty sure that wasn't going to happen. Her attention span was limited to Asher and the occasional gentle brush of his thumb up and down her spine.

Everyone was kind and welcoming—especially Asher's mother. Sandra had pulled her in for a hug the moment she'd gotten within arm's reach of the woman, telling Quinn how wonderful it was to meet her. It was a completely different experience than meeting Spencer's parents for the first time, and perhaps that unpleasant memory had added to her anxiety today.

Quinn came from just enough money that she and Spencer had rubbed shoulders at a few parties, but not so much that she would ever be accepted by Manhattan's elite. If she'd only known that back then, she could have saved herself a lot of heartache later on. She'd caught Spencer's eye at a fundraiser event, and it had been a whirlwind, fairytale romance—without the happily ever after. It had seemed too good to be true . . . and it was. As far as his parents were concerned, he was slumming it with Quinn, and they made no attempt to hide their feelings about her.

Ultimately, he'd chosen his parents over her. Well, his parents' money, more specifically. Once they'd threatened to cut him off after discovering he'd proposed to her, it had been a short engagement— forty-eight hours to be exact. That was precisely how long it took for Spencer's balls to shrivel up and drop off, and for him to go crawling back to his mommy and daddy, begging their forgiveness. And to think she'd wasted her virginity on him . . .

What a crock. She wanted a refund, dammit—a do-over. Instead, she'd hocked his ring worth enough green to help support her while she'd traveled the world for the next two years doing freelance journalism.

Not a bad deal if it hadn't been for the broken heart. She'd loved Spencer like crazy and stupidly believed he'd loved her more than his wealth. She hadn't cared about or wanted his money. He knew that, but in the end it hadn't mattered. Just as time healed all wounds, it also had left one hell of a scar behind. In the two years since Spencer left her, she hadn't dated or been with another man. Quinn didn't do casual sex, and she had no interest in opening her heart up to getting broken again.

But this experience of meeting Asher's family was nothing like she'd expected. Sandra was so sweet and excited to see her with Asher, she wondered if his mother had been told the truth and was just playing along, or if she really did think they were together. It made Quinn uncomfortable, lying to these people, even if it was for a good reason. But what surprised her the most was how convincing Asher was. If she didn't know better, *she'd* swear they were a couple. Was he just that good of a liar, or did the ruse settle better with him than it did her?

To watch him with his family, he seemed so at ease, so . . . normal—which was not a word she would have used to describe Asher Tate. The man was many things, but "normal" implied ordinary, average . . . mediocre. These adjectives were the antithesis of the man standing beside her right now. Not even the way he made her feel was "normal."

As they visited with his brother Rory in the living room, the casual caress of Asher's thumb made her skin tingle with raw energy that hummed beneath her flesh, sending shivers of desire racing through her veins. She had no idea if he even realized he was doing it, but she'd be damned if she let him figure out how deeply his touch was affecting her. Let him think her a porcupine, because honestly, that illusion was the only thing saving her from making a serious mistake in judgment where he was concerned. She'd talked a big game, but when it came right down to it, she was just as weak as the next girl when it came to resisting Asher's charm.

She'd given it the old college try, though. But spending a week with this man under the same roof was enough to erode the resolve of a nun. And now that he wasn't giving her the cold shoulder, allowing her a glimpse of what it would be like to have Asher Tate's affection, it was a heady experience she hadn't been prepared for.

"Jax and Fish out back?" he asked, glancing around, looking for his missing siblings.

"Yeah," Rory said. "I was just going to grab the girls and a beer before heading out. I think Kim could use a break."

She shot her husband a grateful smile and mouthed *Thank you . . .*

"You can thank me tonight," he told her under his breath, but not quietly enough because it brought a scandalous gasp from her and a chorus of whooping laughter from everyone else in the room.

Quinn smiled as she watched Rory scoop a child into each arm. They squealed with delight at going airborne as he twirled them around. The girls were adorable three-year-old identical twins with deep red hair and bright blue eyes. In that moment, Quinn's womb ached. She could practically hear the countdown of her biological clock mocking her. Sure, twenty-eight wasn't that old, but with no prospects in sight, the odds certainly weren't in her favor.

"I'll get the beers and meet you out there," Asher offered.

He left her long enough to grab a few bottles from the fridge. After twisting off the cap, he handed one to her, which she gladly accepted, following him out after excusing herself. She exited the patio door and came to an abrupt stop when her eyes locked on the man at the grill. Her gaze darted to Asher standing beside her, and then back to his brother. The first words that came to her mind tumbled out in typical filterless fashion.

"Holy shit . . ." There were two of them.

His brother chuckled, seeming to enjoy her shock as he tipped back the beer Asher had given him. "I take it my little brother didn't warn you he was a twin."

Little brother?

"By like two minutes," Asher grumbled, giving her the feeling this was an ongoing rub between these two. But from the looks of it, Asher wasn't his little anything. He had maybe half an inch on the guy, and about twenty more pounds. However, the differences ended there—same dark brown hair, strong angular jaw, proud aquiline nose, and sinfully sexy mouth that made a woman dream of what it would feel like crushed up against hers. Undeniably, the man at the grill was an impressive piece of fine male flesh—an exact replica of Asher, right down to those gorgeous multicolored eyes.

His brother stepped around the grill and walked up to her, offering his hand. God help her, even that confident, arrogant swagger was the same. She took his hand, expecting the same fluttering response in the pit of her stomach that she felt whenever Asher touched her, and was surprised to discover it wasn't there.

What the hell? Oh, this didn't bode well—not at all.

She'd told herself her attraction to Asher was purely physical, so then why in the hell weren't these butterflies fluttering? She gripped his hand tighter, holding on a little longer than she probably should have, waiting for those things to wake up. Nothing . . .

His grip tightened in response, his expression curious as he studied her. He was taking her measure and making no attempt to hide it. Wasn't this the brother Asher had called the human lie detector? She released her grip, but he didn't reciprocate.

A nervous glance Asher's way brought him up beside her. His arm slipped around her waist and he pulled her into his side, breaking Jaxson's contact. Yep . . . there they were, traitorous little bastards, battering around inside her stomach like it were a field of wildflowers.

"Jaxson, this is my girlfriend, Quinn. Quinn, my twin brother, Jaxson."

"It's nice to meet you," she offered, torn between stepping away and leaning into Asher's side. The current of awareness thrumming through her veins set her pulse on a chaotic course. He felt so good and yet she didn't think it was a wise idea to stand in his arms for very long. Her only saving grace was that he had no idea how strongly his touch was affecting her.

"Dad mentioned you were seeing someone. I didn't believe it." Turning his gaze back to her, Jaxson said, "It's nice to meet you, Quinn . . ."

"Summers," she supplied honestly, because Asher had warned her not to lie if she could help it. She was safe with his family, and wasn't worried about giving her full name, but that didn't mean she wanted to get into the dirty details of what brought her to Asher's doorstep.

"Jax is a homicide detective in Denver," Asher finished their introduction. "Don't mind him. He can be a little . . . intense. And then there's this yahoo over here . . ." He guided her around, pointing Quinn in the direction of a guy lounging in a lawn chair wearing nothing but a pair of tight, low-riding jeans, cowboy boots, and a shiny silver belt buckle. A Stetson was tipped low over his brow, shielding his eyes from the sun. "My youngest brother, Fisher."

The man climbed out of his chair, moving with a slow, easy grace that defied his size. Wow, these boys had some good genetics. He ambled toward her, the neck of his half-empty beer bottle trapped between his fingers, dangling at his side. He tipped his hat with his knuckle and gave her a nod. "Ma'am . . ." Was that a hint of a southern drawl? If the size of his belt buckle matched his ego, then women beware.

He shook her hand and she smiled politely.

"PBR nationals ended a few days ago. When Fish isn't traveling, he trains the horses here on the ranch."

"PBR?"

"Fish is a professional bull rider."

"Ahh . . . that explains the belt buckle," she teased.

He winked and shot her a sexy grin, pointing at the silver metal. But he was off by a few inches. "Eight seconds, baby . . ."

"You know, there are some women that might not be so impressed by that record." She winked back.

Asher caught her meaning right away and busted out laughing, a deep throaty sound that resonated right through her. She'd never heard him laugh so hard before or seen him look so at ease and relaxed. There was a difference between this man and the presumably carefree one she'd met at Violet's wedding. Had she been privy to this side of him, perhaps they wouldn't have gotten off to such a rocky start, because this Asher was charming, attentive, and downright sweet. Until now, she'd only seen the arrogant, cocky version or the withdrawn, broody one. Neither had struck such a chord with her as the one holding on to her right now, and she felt a flicker of fear skitter through her. She did *not* want to fall for this man—but if she was being totally honest with herself, it might be too late.

Jaxson let out a deep, masculine bark of laughter. She probably shouldn't have said what she did. She hardly knew this guy well enough to be giving him shit, but then again, when had that ever stopped her? She was relieved when Fisher joined in. Apparently, his ego could take the ribbing.

"That's a good one," he conceded, giving her a nod of approval. "Asher, your girl's got sass. I like it."

"Oh, you don't even know . . ." he told his brother, wrapping his other arm around her and pulling her in for a hug. His scent surrounded her and she found herself taking a deep breath, drawing him in as he planted a quick kiss on her temple before letting her go. She tensed, startled by the unexpected show of affection. The whole thing happened so fast and seamlessly, it was over before she knew it. But holy hell, the effects would be lasting for a while. Heat rocketed through her, flushing from the top of her head to the bottom of her toes and hitting a few key areas in between.

Like a scratching record, time momentarily stood still while her mind scrambled to catch up with what had just happened. He was being kind and affectionate—and it was all a lie. She'd do well to remember that before she got the delusional notion that Asher actually cared about her, before she lowered her defenses and got hurt again. Not even three hours ago he'd likened her to fucking a porcupine, so there was no way in hell this wasn't for show. She just wished she hadn't felt such a sharp sting of disappointment at that revelation.

She scowled in annoyance with herself, turning away before anyone could see it, but Asher's answering frown told her she was too late. He was perceptive to a fault. She could feel his eyes on her as she excused herself to go get another beer, hating that he saw the weakness inside her. Even if underneath all that bravado he truly was this attentive, affectionate guy, she didn't know if she could ever open her heart again and trust him enough to find out.

"'Bout time you met a woman who made you work for it," Jaxson joked, slapping Asher on the shoulder.

But he wasn't laughing anymore.

CHAPTER

16

He probably shouldn't have done that. Correction—he definitely shouldn't have done that. Pulling Quinn into his arms and kissing her, even for an impulsive, chaste peck, was a mistake. Raw need roared through him like testosterone-fueled octane. Her light, floral shampoo reminded him of a field of wildflowers. He craved to bury his nose in those silky blonde strands and draw her scent deep into his lungs. The moment his lips had brushed her temple, he'd felt her flinch and quickly let her go.

She hid her unease well, excusing herself to head back to the house for another beer. He doubted the others noticed, but her rejection was another stinging slap. He wondered if Quinn was like this with all men or just him—cool, reserved, and wary. Even knowing she needed to act the part, she seemed unable to tolerate his affection longer than a few minutes before coming up with an excuse to skitter away like a frightened doe.

Admittedly, it unsettled him how easily he could pretend with her and how much he enjoyed the freedom the guise provided to touch her. This last week had been torture, and he wouldn't think about how good, how right, it felt to have had her at his side since they'd gotten here. So good, he needed to stop this train of thought before he grew a cockstand. That was the last thing he needed someone noticing. He took enough ribbing from his brothers as it was.

Flames shot up on the grill, the whoosh and hiss of frying burgers demanding his brother's attention and thankfully taking the focus off of him. "Shit!" Jax cursed, turning back to the burning meat. He grabbed the water bottle and shook it. Swearing again, he handed it to Asher. "Go get me some water, will ya?"

"Sure."

"Thanks." He poured his beer on the flames, temporarily averting ruin.

"You're wasting good beer . . ." Fish complained.

"Better than burning Mom's burgers."

"Good point. Here." Fish handed Jax his beer too, and returned to the lawn chair.

Asher noticed him wince as he lowered himself down. "You all right?"

"Yeah, just landed bad on my last ride is all. I'm fine."

Fish wouldn't say so if he wasn't. Before Asher could ask him about it, flames roared from the grill again. "For chrissake, how high is that thing turned up?"

"Don't you worry about it," his brother shot back. "Just get me some water. I'm running out of beer."

Asher shook his head at the sorry burgers and walked toward the house. It was no use arguing with him. Jax was the most stubborn, bullheaded man he knew. If he wanted to be in charge of the grilling, then all the power to him.

"Grab some more beers while you're in there," his brother called over his shoulder as Asher opened the patio door.

He crossed the living room and was about to round the corner of the kitchen when the sound of his mother's voice ground him to a halt.

"So, tell us, how did you and Asher meet?"

"Yes, tell us," Kim added with conspiratorial excitement. "We're dying to know how you managed to capture that man's heart. He's like the elusive white buffalo," she laughed.

For a moment, Asher considered taking pity on Quinn and saving her from the nosy twosome, but he wanted to hear what she said. They had her cornered in the kitchen. He could only imagine her deer-in-the-headlights look as her violet gaze darted around nervously, looking for the easiest escape route.

"Umm . . ." He could hear the hesitation in her voice. "We met at my sister's wedding. Asher was the best man and I was the maid of honor."

"And you took one look at each other and fell madly in love." His mother, a hopeless romantic, hijacked Quinn's story with her wishful thinking.

Asher held back a sarcastic snort of laughter, the memory of that day an all-too-familiar reminder that Quinn's bark was just as bad as her bite.

"Something like that," Quinn said evasively. "If you'll excuse me, I think Asher is waiting for me."

"Let him wait," his mother said dismissively. "I've been waiting his whole life for him to finally settle down and bring a woman home for us to meet."

"I'm the first?"

He couldn't decide if she sounded flattered or concerned about that little revelation. And why was the subject now suddenly turning to him, he'd like to know? If they didn't tread lightly here, he was going to have to do some serious damage control where Quinn was concerned. She already thought he was a commitment-phobic man-whore. Then again, she wasn't that far off in her assumption.

His father obviously hadn't let his mother in on the ruse, and he wished he would have. Asher knew how important it was to her that he meet someone and settle down. The last thing he wanted was to fill her with false hope, because he was fairly certain Quinn Summers was not his one true love—if such a thing even existed. His one true lust, perhaps . . .

"Asher's a very special man," his mother continued.

Oh, God help him, his mother made it sound like he belonged on the short bus. He couldn't believe she was sales-pitching him to this woman.

"He's been through a lot, especially since what happened in Nisour Square."

Shit, she was *not* going there. Yes, yes she was . . .

"He doesn't let people in easily. You must be a special woman if he's opening up to you."

Please stop talking . . . Asher closed his eyes and pinched the bridge of his nose. He couldn't believe this was happening. Note to self: *Do not let Quinn out of your sight again.*

All right, it was time to intervene. He was about to enter the kitchen and break up their little chatfest when Quinn spoke, and her confession stunned him like the concussive blast of an RPG.

"Sometimes you meet someone and without even realizing it, they become the difference between life and death. Asher is that for me, and I'm incredibly thankful I met him."

Was that honesty in her voice? It sure as hell sounded like it, or perhaps it was wishful thinking. Either way, it made his chest tighten at this rare glimpse of her. Before he could think any harder about the significance of her words, the patio door slid open and Jax shouted, "Hey, jackass . . . What in the hell is taking so long with that water? I'm all out of beer."

Shit. Busted . . . "Just wait a goddamn minute," he growled back, stepping around the corner and entering the kitchen. "And turn down the temperature on that grill!" All eyes focused on him, and was that a blush staining Quinn's cheeks? Holy hell, she was beautiful . . .

Pretending he hadn't just walked in on the middle of their conversation, he twisted the cap off the water bottle as he headed over to the sink. "Hey, Quinn, could you grab some more beers and bring them when you come out? Jax poured everyone's on the grill."

"Sure." Amusement lightened her voice as she headed for the fridge. "I'll be there in a minute. I was just helping your mom and Kim throw together this fruit salad."

That wasn't all they were doing in here. He turned off the water and recapped the bottle as he left the kitchen. The moment he rounded the corner, the room erupted into a fit of feminine laughter.

"Do you think he heard us?" Kim whispered.

"Lord, I hope not," Quinn answered.

———

"Hey, Quinn, you want to play corn hole?"

She swallowed wrong and began choking on her beer as she busted out laughing. For some reason she found Fisher's question ridiculously hilarious and completely inappropriate. She drained her fourth beer and decided to switch to soda because she was starting to get a little buzzed. She'd consumed her first and second fairly quickly to curb her anxiety over meeting Asher's family. It was an unfounded fear, because they'd all been incredibly friendly—except for Jaxson. He was polite and kind, but more reserved than the others. She'd occasionally catch him watching her. Not in a lewd or creepy way, but pensive and thoughtful, as if he was trying to do the math and she and Asher didn't quite add up. He watched her interacting with Asher and the rest of the family, spending a lot more time listening than talking as the group gathered around the picnic table for lunch.

She drank her third and fourth beer during lunch, in hopes of numbing her body's traitorous response to Asher's frequent touches, which, by the way, did not work. If anything, it heightened her craving and she found herself sitting closer to him at the picnic table than necessary, her thigh resting against his, her arm occasionally grazing his while they ate.

Despite his attempt to stifle his reaction, she knew she was affecting him too, and she was just tipsy enough to find it amusing. It pleased her to know she wasn't the only one who wasn't immune to this "innocent" contact, and she was taking a great amount of pleasure in getting a little payback of her own.

"It's a flattering offer, Fish, and I can honestly say no one's ever asked me that before, but I'm not so sure your brother would appreciate us 'corn-holing.'"

The others at the table laughed. She even got a chuckle out of Jaxson, and Quinn couldn't be sure, but she thought she might have made that tough bull rider blush.

Asher slipped his arm around her and pulled her a little closer. Dipping his head, he told her with a throaty chuckle of amusement, "Corn hole is like a beanbag toss game—but with corn."

"Oh," she laughed, joining the others. "Well then, in that case, I'd love to. I don't know how to play, though," she warned. "We don't have 'corn hole' in Manhattan."

"No worries, sweetheart. I'll teach you," Fisher offered.

"What about you?" she turned to Asher, making the mistake of glancing up into his eyes. How many different shades of blue, green, and brown were in there, she wondered, too buzzed to care that she was staring. "Don't you want to play with me?"

Hunger flared in his eyes. It was so raw and unguarded, her core clenched in response to his need.

He bent a little closer, his lips brushing the shell of her ear as he whispered, "I think I'm going to have to sit this one out."

The rumble of his voice set her nerve endings on fire. Her gaze dropped to his lap and she saw the reason he wouldn't be moving from this spot anytime soon. Maybe she shouldn't have enjoyed the flare of feminine satisfaction that gave her. If she didn't put some space between herself and this man soon, she was likely to do or say something her sober self would regret. They were in dangerous territory here. This ruse would only give them so much leeway before they got themselves in trouble.

"Your loss," she told him with a flirty grin. "Well, Fish, it looks like I'm all yours. Teach me to corn hole."

A low groan meant for her ears only rumbled in Asher's throat. Fisher chuckled as he slipped out of the bench across from them and gave her a gentlemanly bow. "Darlin', I'd be honored."

Quinn braced her hand on Asher's muscular shoulder as she rose, using him for balance as she carefully stepped one leg over the bench and then the other. She took her time, not only because the world was spinning a little, but also because she knew her breasts were in his face and she couldn't resist giving him a generous shot of cleavage.

She listed forward and Asher reached up, catching her hips to steady her. His grip was firm, his fingertips pressing into the flesh of her backside. The image of him gripping her like this as she rode him flashed through her mind. Her sex moistened, welcoming the fantasy. God help her, she needed to get away from him for a little while.

"You going to be all right?" Asher asked, concern replacing the burn of lust she saw blazing in his eyes only a moment ago.

"I'm fine. I just stood up a bit too fast, that's all. I don't usually drink," she confessed quietly.

"You sure you want to play?"

His hands were still on her hips. Her heart rioted inside her chest. This wasn't helping her stability any, that's for sure. "I'm good." She pulled out of his reluctant grasp and followed Fisher toward the two rectangular boxes with a hole cut out of each one. She could feel the heat of Asher's stare burning into her ass every step of the way. Jaxson and Rory were already there, marking off the distance between the two boxes.

"He's got it bad for you," Fisher told her as they walked across the yard.

He wasn't the first person to tell her this since they'd arrived, and she cursed the little leap of joy her heart took every time she heard it. This was crazy, reminding herself for the hundredth time that this wasn't real. Asher was just a really good actor. But then, she couldn't very well tell his brother that.

"How do you know?" she found herself asking him instead.

"Are you kidding me? He hasn't been able to keep his eyes off you all day." He glanced over his shoulder. "He's still staring at you."

She resisted the urge to look, but couldn't contain her grin.

"You've got him in knots, sweetheart."

They were almost to the boxes, about to join the others, when he slowed his steps and turned unexpectedly serious. "Don't hurt him, Quinn. That guy's been to hell and back, and he deserves a little happiness."

Before she could respond to his warning, that carefree grin flashed across his face again and he threw his arm around her shoulder, pulling her in for a brotherly hug. "Now let's play some corn hole."

CHAPTER

17

"Your family is really great," she told Asher after they said their last goodbyes eight hours later and walked down the sidewalk toward his truck. It was almost midnight. Once the sun went down, Robert had started up a bonfire and the boys passed around a bottle of Crown Royal, telling stories of their youth. She'd switched to iced tea long before then, and it was a good thing she had, because someone needed to be sober enough to drive home, and that someone was not Asher.

She'd learned quite a bit about him and his brothers tonight, more than he probably wanted her to know. Quinn couldn't remember the last time she'd laughed so hard. Rory was the trickster of the family, Jaxson was the cautious skeptic, Asher was the badass brawler, and Fisher was the daredevil. His mother and father certainly had their hands full raising that brood, but they'd done well.

Quinn felt honored to be a part of that family, even if it was only for one night—even if it was a lie. It felt good to belong for once, and she would miss them when this was over and she returned to her old life, wherever that may be. Neither she nor Violet were very close with their parents, and her relationship with her sister, although better now, had been strained over the years. She'd been traveling for the last two, and knew she hadn't been there for her sister when she'd needed her. The guilt ate at her for that, but she was hoping she would be able to make up for lost time. She knew Vi thought she was selfish, opinionated, and overbearing. Who knows, maybe she was right . . .

As they walked together, Quinn tipped her head back to admire the cloudless night lit by the sparkling stars as crickets harmonized with the bullfrog serenade. It was beautiful out here—so freeing . . . so different from the city or the other parts of the world she'd traveled. This land, these mountains, held a peaceful serenity that could have only come from God Himself. She could see why Asher loved it here. Away from it all, she could almost believe she was safe.

Her steps slowed and so did Asher's. She wasn't ready for this night to end. Was there a chance he felt the hesitancy too? She knew the moment they climbed into his truck and shut those doors, the charade would be over and her carriage would turn into a big fat pumpkin once again.

"Everyone liked you, especially Fish. Who would have thought you'd be such a great corn holer?"

She laughed. "That's a terrible name for a game, you know that, right?"

He chuckled. "Yeah, it is . . ."

"I'm not sure Jaxson was a big fan. You could have warned me you had a twin." She elbowed him in the ribs.

"It was funny to see the look on your face, I'm not gonna lie."

"I'm so glad I could amuse you."

"Jax liked you. Don't worry. He's a cop. It's his job to mistrust everyone. It was hell growing up together. People always think twins are supposed to be so close, but we fought constantly growing up—sibling rivalry bullshit. And it didn't get any easier when we got older. We've always had the same taste in women. They seemed to prefer him, though . . ."

His confession surprised her. "Why would you think that?"

Asher shrugged. "He's always been the better version of me. He saves lives and I take them."

Quinn grabbed his hand and tugged him to a stop just outside the truck. "That's not true, you know. You're saving my life."

He chuffed a masculine grunt. "That remains to be seen."

Quinn knew what it was like growing up in someone else's shadow. How much harder must it have been having that person be your twin? She wasn't sure what prompted her action; maybe it was their ruse and pretending to be a couple all day, or perhaps it was her genuine concern for his feelings of inferiority where his brother was concerned. She could give a hundred different reasons without touching on the truth—she just wanted to kiss him. After spending the day together, seeing him with his family, hearing the stories of a life beyond the negligent playboy, she knew there was so much more to Asher Tate than she ever imagined.

Taking a step closer, she slipped her arms up around his neck, stood on her tiptoes, and whispered, "I'd choose you, Asher." She brushed her lips against his and he tensed as if surprised, whether by her confession or by her kiss, she couldn't know.

It took a few seconds for him to respond, and then holy hell, did he ever . . . A low growl rumbled in his throat as his arm slipped around her waist, sucking her up tight against him, molding her to his hard, muscular body. His other hand slipped into her hair, angling her head so he could take over. His tongue plundered her mouth, stroking, teasing—demanding. It was all she could do to keep up. In all her life, she'd never been kissed with so much hunger and raw, primal need . . .

She was losing her breath, swept away by a maelstrom of emotion she was too afraid to name. Instead of letting him go and stepping back, which was what she probably should have done, she hung on tighter, giving herself over to the moment. Holy shit, he could kiss . . .

His mouth was pure sin, the way it moved over hers, firm and consuming. He woke places inside her she hadn't even known existed. She was on fire and the only thing that could quench this inferno was Asher's touch. A soft moan escaped her lips and he devoured it with an answering growl that made her aching sex clench with need. It had been so long since she'd been with a man, too long . . .

His lips were softer than she'd expected them to be when he was so hard everywhere else. And boy, was he hard. It wasn't the first time she'd felt his arousal pressing insistently against her stomach, but it was the first time she wasn't sure she was going to have the willpower to stop. So it surprised the hell out of her when Asher did—albeit, it was with a tortured groan.

He lifted his hands and cupped her face, resting his forehead against hers. His breaths came in ragged pants that held the vapor of whiskey but smelled like the mint he'd eaten from his mother's candy dish on the way out.

"I can't believe I'm fucking saying this . . ." She didn't know if his voice was raw from drink or desire. "But we gotta stop."

Nooo . . . Her mind screamed in protest and her body seconded it. "Just a little longer . . ." she whispered, knowing the moment he let her go the fantasy would be over.

"Fuck, Quinn, I'm so lit right now . . . I don't want to do this with you when I'm drunk. You're better than that. You're better than me."

Of all the times for him to step up and show a little chivalry, it had to be now? Seriously? It wasn't like she was asking him to fuck her. For crying out loud, they were in his parents' driveway. She hadn't forgotten that, but a little more kissing sure would be nice, because hands down, Asher's was the most talented mouth she'd ever had against hers. But Quinn refused to beg, and the sting of his rejection helped cool her jets.

Perhaps he'd forgotten, but she hadn't. She'd seen Asher out of control before, wild with lust, and this was not it. Maybe she just didn't do it for him like those other women did, because the Asher four months ago wouldn't have cared if he was drunk or not. Hell, he probably wouldn't have even cared if he was in his parents' driveway. For chrissake, he'd fucked another woman in front of her, which was a much-needed dose of reality. What the hell was she thinking?

Quinn, you're an idiot!

Gathering her last semblance of self-respect, she nodded, refusing to meet his stare, because his rejection hurt more than she wanted to admit, and there was no way in hell she'd give him the satisfaction of seeing it in her eyes. She pulled away from him, and he must have sensed the shift in her mood—guess he wasn't too drunk to realize that—because he followed her forward and reached for her.

"Quinn . . ."

She sidestepped him and moved back. "Give me the keys, Asher," she cut him off, holding out her hand. "I want to go home and you're too drunk to drive."

Exhaling a frustrated sigh, he shoved his hand into his pocket and gave her the keys. He knew she was upset, but what he didn't know was that she was equally embarrassed for being just like every other woman who fell at his feet, only that wasn't exactly true. Those girls he hadn't said no to.

"Quinn, listen to me . . ." He tried again, but she was in no mood to hear it.

"Just get in the truck, Asher. This was a mistake."

Maybe she would have chosen him, but he didn't choose her . . .

———

Well, this was a first—a woman getting pissed at him for doing the right thing. Goddammit, he couldn't win for losing. What in the hell did she want him to do, fuck her in the bed of his truck? There had been a time, not long ago, when he would have done exactly that. But there was something about Quinn that was different. She wasn't like all the others, and she sure as hell deserved to be treated better than that.

Problem was, his control was slipping, and so was hers, whether she realized it or not. He'd felt it in the way she'd responded to him, softened against him. It had been so fucking hot—so perfect. He could still feel where her hard little nipples had pressed into his chest. She tasted better than he'd ever imagined. Quinn Summers was a spirited ball of fire, to be sure, but she'd tamed so beautifully in his arms . . . Had he really called her a shrew?

What she needed, what he suspected she secretly craved, was a strong man to take control, to show her the woman she was, the woman she could be. She didn't always have to be in charge; there was freedom in letting go. And damn if he didn't want to be that guy for her, but this was not the time or the place.

She didn't realize that her innocent request for "just a little longer" would have ended with him buried balls deep inside her. And he didn't want to be the crass bastard who pointed that out to her, not that she would have believed him, because she still clung to the illusion that she was the one in control here. Which roused another burning question in his mind; how experienced—or inexperienced—was Quinn Summers in passion? Because she'd been playing with fire and he doubted very much that she knew how close she'd come to getting burned.

"Quinn, slow down. These corners coming up are sharp."

Maybe he should have driven after all. Except for the years he'd been pounding sand, he'd lived in these mountains as long as he could remember, knew them like the back of his hand, and knew with absolute certainty that if Quinn didn't slow the fuck down, they were going over the side of this cliff.

"Quinn!" he snapped, his voice sharp as the adrenaline spiked in his veins, burning through the alcohol and ushering in a blast of sobriety. Then he realized that the tension in her as they headed toward this turn wasn't anger, it was fear.

"Asher, I'm trying to slow down. Something's wrong with the brakes." She shot him a panicked glance and the bone-deep fear he saw staring back at him arrowed right through his fucking heart. "I don't know what to do!" she cried, stomping hard on the brakes with no response. "I can't stop!"

The night all but swallowed up the little patch of light the halogens cut through the blackness. They couldn't see the curve yet, but he knew it was there. If he didn't slow this truck down there was no way they were going to make this turn. In the reflection of light from the dashboard, he could see her foot still pressed hard into the brakes. A quick glance at the speedometer confirmed they were picking up speed—55 . . . 60 . . . Asher snarled a fowl curse and grabbed the emergency brake between them and wrenched it up.

Nothing happened.

"Fuck!"

"Asher . . ." Terror strained her voice as the high beams landed on the sign warning them of the 30-mile-an-hour curve coming up.

65 . . .

Panic filled her violet eyes as she turned them on him in desperation. Her tight, white-knuckled grip on the wheel kept the truck heading down the mountain road, but not for long. They were running out of options, and a jump from the truck at this speed would surely kill them both. If he could just make this corner, the next one had a cable guard he could take them into. Asher reached over and cut the engine; the loss of power slowed the truck down, but the steering became a lot tougher.

"What are you doing?" she cried. "I can't steer!"

Asher glanced at the speedometer—50—still too fast. "Hang on!" he shouted, unfastening his seat belt so he could reach the wheel. She wouldn't be strong enough to control it without power steering.

"What are you doing?" she cried. "Put your seat belt back on!"

He didn't have the heart to tell her, but these seat belts weren't going to save either one of them. Grabbing the wheel from her hands, he jerked it hard to the left. The momentum sent her shoulder slamming into his chest. Air whooshed from his lungs and he grunted at the impact. The tires squealed in protest against the pavement, the back end skidding, kicking out as it hit the gravel shoulder, sending up a spray of rock and debris pinging off the metal undercarriage.

Quinn screamed a shrill cry of terror that shredded right through him, and he swore to God if he lived through this, that sound would haunt him the rest of his days.

———

Quinn closed her eyes and braced for impact, unable to stop the scream that tore from her lungs as they barreled toward the cliff. At the last second, the wheel was wrenched from her hands and the truck careened left. She was propelled right, her shoulder slamming hard into Asher. Gravel pelted the truck and she waited for that weightless feeling of falling to overtake her.

We're going to die . . .

The knowledge was such a bone-deep truth, the fear a suffocating reality, and in that moment where time seemed to stop, regret overwhelmed her. Asher was going to die and it was her fault—just like Emily. How many lives would she have to stand before God and account for? It was selfish of her to come here, to put him at risk like this. A stupid, selfish mistake . . .

The truck veered hard to the left, tires screeching . . . She felt like a bobblehead, slamming from side to side. Her temple connected with the window as the truck slammed into rock before ricocheting right. Glass exploded, pain blasted behind her eyes, and a wave of dizziness washed over her, pulling her under. The truck lurched forward and the screeching metal was the last thing she heard before everything went black.

CHAPTER

18

"Quinn! Quinn! Baby, open your eyes."

She could barely hear the muffled demand over the ringing in her ears. Her world was tilting to the right and her ribs hurt where the center console pressed into them. Warm hands cradled her face and lifted her head. Pain spiked into her brain with the tempo of her beating heart. Her lids were heavy, refusing to obey her command to open.

The brush of a calloused thumb swept over her cheek, followed by a nasty curse. Then the demands started in again. This time his voice was sharper, his worry an audible bark. "Goddammit, Quinn, open your eyes!"

Struggling to climb out of the haze, she was tempted to slip back into unconsciousness. There it didn't hurt, there her stomach didn't roll with nausea, and there it didn't feel like her head was going to explode. She tried to force her lids apart, and moaned with the failed effort. She'd try again later, after she rested some more and took a break from the pain.

The twanging sound of a snapping cable and the groan of scraping metal accompanied the hard jerk that ripped her back into consciousness. She startled awake, her eyes coming open but still not focused.

"Quinn! Look at me!"

She blinked a couple of times before her vision began to clear. Slowly, her senses came back online, orienting her to time, place, and situation. Oh God, they'd crashed! Asher was in her face, his brows drawn tight with worry as his gaze roved over her.

"Fuck . . ." His thumb swept over the knot at her temple, and she winced at the spike of pain. "Quinn, listen to me. You need to climb out of the truck."

He reached over and she felt her seat belt let loose. Gravity dumped her into Asher's arms and he caught her before she could fall into his seat. The truck was nearly tipped onto the passenger side. The only way out was through the shattered driver's window. The groan of metal sounded outside and the truck slipped again, the tires skidding against gravel.

Her breath caught in her throat, a startled gasp as the precariousness of their situation settled on her. They weren't at the bottom of this mountain, she realized. They were at the top, and the truck was about to go over the edge. She had no idea how they were still up here, but she had a feeling it had something to do with the snapping twang of those wires outside.

"Quinn, we need to go." Asher's tone was firm and commanding—determined—and, God bless him, calm, because only one of them was allowed to lose their shit and that person was going to be her.

"We're going to fall off this mountain . . ." She muttered the thought out loud with absolute certainty.

"No, we're not. You're going to very carefully climb out of that window and slide down to the ground."

"What about you?"

"I'm going to help you get out."

"What if the truck slips and falls?"

"If we don't get out, it's going to. Now let's go."

His tone told her conversation time was over. He grabbed her waist and helped support her as she lifted her legs, being careful not to hit her knee on the steering wheel. She fought against the dizziness making the cab swim as she slowly climbed up. Asher changed his grip, bracing his hands on her bottom and boosting her up. He held her suspended in the air as she slid one leg out of the broken window and then the other. She dipped her head to clear the top of the opening and then hesitated before sliding out, glancing back at him. Tears filled her eyes and panic threatened to choke her. She had no idea what was keeping this truck from going over the edge, but she was terrified that when she dropped out, she was going to make it fall and Asher was going to be stuck inside.

"I don't want to do it," she cried, her voice breaking. "It's going to fall . . ."

Her gaze locked with his and she saw the horrible truth reflecting in his eyes. He knew it would. He'd known all along that her climbing out was going to push it over the edge. And still he'd made her get out. He was sacrificing his life for hers and she didn't want him to do it.

"Jump down, Quinn." His voice was calm—too calm.

Please, God, no! This man was going to die for her! The acceptance of his fate broke her heart. She saw no fear, no regret . . .

"I choose you, Quinn."

A sob tore from her throat as he spoke her words back to her. The same confession that left her lips only a short while ago would be the last she'd hear from his. She wouldn't do it. She wouldn't save herself at his expense.

"Give me your hand." She braced one hand on the doorframe and reached back inside for him with the other.

"Dammit, Quinn, get the hell out of this truck!"

"Not without you. We're going out together or not at all."

He hesitated a moment, seeming shocked that she'd refuse to leave him. Something softened in his eyes—respect, admiration, affection?

"You can't even do this one thing without a fight, can you? Goddammit, I think I could have fallen in love with you . . ."

His confession made her freeze. Her heart stuttered as her mind registered his words. He reached for her, but instead of grabbing her hand, he shoved her out the window. Quinn screamed as she fell out, her teeth jarring as she hit the ground—hard. Sharp pain shot through her knees and back at the impact, gravel grinding into her palms as her hands shot out to catch her. The shifting weight inside the truck made the cable snap, and the twang of whipping metal cord snapped through the air. The pained groan of metal scraping against metal gave way to the cascade of falling rock as the truck began to slide over the edge.

"Asher!"

———

The cable gave way and the truck began to slide over the edge. Asher's precarious world tilted and a jarring boom filled the cab as the metal cable whipped against the door. Adrenaline flooded his veins, and his heart hammered inside his chest as his body fought to admit what his mind already knew—he wasn't making it out of this alive. But still he wasn't going down without a fight. Acting on pure instinct, he dove for the window. The truck dropped down, then caught on the edge of something as it went over, precariously balancing for a few precious seconds, giving him just enough time to clear the opening and leap out before the truck tumbled down the side of the mountain. Quinn's gut-wrenching scream was followed by the crunch of metal and shattering glass that exploded into the night.

"Asher!"

Her plea gutted him, her grief a palpable force that thrust into his chest and took hold of his heart, squeezing until he swore it'd stop beating. She thought he was dead. And if it wasn't for this ledge of rock, he would be. Fuck, this was the second time in his life he'd faced certain death, and the second time he'd survived it. How many more times would he escape its clutches?

"Nooo!"

Her sobs echoed above him, a heartbreaking wail. He would have called for her but he couldn't breathe. The pain in his chest was so crushing, the hammering of his heart so violent, he felt like he was having a fucking heart attack.

Asher drew a slow, deep breath, pulling the crisp night air into his lungs, trying to calm his rioting pulse. "Quinn . . ." He called her name, his voice hoarse from the swell of emotion clogging his throat. God help him, he'd almost lost her. She must not have heard him over her own sobbing. He called for her again—louder. The crying stopped. Gravel crunched beneath running footsteps that skidded to a stop, sending little pieces of gravel raining down on him.

"Asher?" she cried, her voice shrill with hope.

"I'm down here, Quinn—on the ledge." Remembering his cell, he grabbed it from his pocket and turned on the flashlight. He held it up and the invisible band around his chest tightened. Sweet Jesus, there wasn't a more beautiful sight in the world than this woman.

"Asher! I thought—" her voice broke.

"I'm all right," he reassured her. Thankfully, he was only a few feet down. The rock wall was jagged enough he should be able to crawl back up it. He tipped the light down to get a better view of his surroundings and his stomach dropped. Less than two inches separated him from death. He'd come that close to missing the ledge when he'd leapt out that window. He held the light farther over the edge, looking for his truck, but the beam couldn't cast that far down. Damn, that would've been one hell of a rough way to go.

"I'm going to toss my phone up to you. I need you to hold the light against the rock so I can see where to climb."

She nodded and he sent the cell into the air, praying to God she was a good catch.

"Got it."

She angled the light against the rock face, and he scoured the stone for the best route. Finding his path, he climbed back up and hoisted himself over the ledge. The moment he was back on his feet, Quinn crashed into him. Throwing her arms around his neck, she squeezed him tight. But her welcoming embrace was short-lived because she pulled back and promptly smacked him in the chest.

"I can't believe you did that!" She was still holding his phone, lighting the area between them. He could see the fresh tears streaming down her face. "You knew that truck was going to fall when you shoved me out!" She raised her hand to hit him again and he caught her wrist, yanking her back into his arms. This time he hugged her tight, and he had no intention of letting her go.

"Shhh . . ." he whispered against the top of her head when she broke down again.

"You almost died . . ." she sobbed against his chest.

"I'm right here, it's all right. We're going to be fine . . ." he soothed, squeezing tighter still and pressing a kiss into her silky hair. He thought he'd never smell the scent of wildflowers again, or hold her in his arms—feel her soft little body pressed against his.

Adrenaline coursed through his veins at how narrowly he'd escaped death, and his emotions were riding high. That had to be the fullness in his chest right now, making his heart ache, because God help him if he'd fallen for this woman.

CHAPTER

19

Quinn couldn't stop shaking. Even as the hot water beat down on her flushed skin, the steam billowing into a cumulous cloud around her, she couldn't stop the tremors from racking her body. She reached for the soap and the bottle slipped from her hands, crashing onto the floor. Tears blurred her vision anew as she bent to retrieve it. Shit, she was a wreck. No matter how many times she told herself that Asher was all right, she couldn't get the terror out of her heart at seeing that truck sliding off the cliff.

Guilt consumed her, a suffocating weight that threatened to buckle her knees. Asher had almost died tonight saving her. The resounding reality of his sacrifice shook her to her core, forcing her to face feelings she'd been denying. In one selfless act, Asher had managed to lay siege to her walls and obliterate her defenses.

The urge to go to him now, the need to see him alive and safe, tugged at her heart. But she didn't think he was alone and didn't want to interrupt. He'd called his dad to come pick them up, and instead of dropping them off, he'd stayed to talk to Asher. She'd wanted to give them some privacy and had hoped a shower would help calm her nerves, but it wasn't working.

She thought she heard pounding on the door but couldn't be sure if it was that or the hammering of her heartbeat in her ears. Quinn turned off the water to listen. The knock came again.

"Quinn? Are you all right? I heard something bang up here. Are you hurt?"

Was she hurt? If he only knew . . . Just the sound of his voice made her chest ache. She'd tried so hard to protect her heart, but looking a man in the eyes right before he gave his life for yours . . . there was no coming back from that. In that moment, her heart had become irrevocably lost to Asher Tate and there wasn't a damn thing she could do about it.

"I . . . I'm fine," she called, glad when her voice didn't betray her turbulent emotions. "I just dropped a bottle. I'll be out in a minute."

There was a long pause. For a moment, she wondered if he was going to come in and see for himself that she was all right. Her pulse quickened at the thought. A twinge of disappointment cramped in her chest when he said through the door, "Just be careful. You hit your head pretty hard tonight. I want to take a look at it before you go to bed."

Had his father left? Were they alone? Before she could tell him he could stay, his steps echoed on the wooden floor and the hollow cadence descended the stairs. She opened the shower door and grabbed her towel from the rack. After drying off, she wrapped up her hair, taking care not to hit the bump on her temple. A low-level headache thrummed to the beat of her pulse.

When she opened the bathroom door, a blast of cool air rushed in. Goose bumps prickled her flesh and she hurried to the dresser they now shared. As she stepped into a pair of black lace panties, her gaze strayed to his drawer of T-shirts. Would he mind if she wore one tonight? Her sleepwear was limited and she wanted something warmer. If she was really being honest with herself, she just wanted to feel closer to Asher.

He'd told her the first night she'd come here that she could help herself. Going on the assumption that was a standing offer, Quinn opened the drawer and saw the T-shirt she'd worn the night she'd arrived folded neatly on the pile. Had it really only been just a week ago that she'd come here with nothing more than a desperate plea for help and the clothes on her back? How could so much change this fast? She grabbed a navy blue T-shirt and pulled it on as she headed for the door.

As Quinn passed by, she caught her reflection in the full-length mirror on the wall and stopped to make a quick self-assessment. The hemline hung halfway down her thighs. She supposed she looked presentable enough to head downstairs for some ibuprofen and a glass of water. Stepping closer, she inspected the knot on the side of her head. It was bruised and swollen. Tender to the touch, but she'd live.

Quinn made her way downstairs and had just stepped into the living room when she heard Robert's voice in the kitchen. He was still here. Crap. She might be all right with Asher seeing her half-dressed, but his dad was another story. Quinn turned around to go back upstairs but his father's question stopped her cold.

"How much trouble is this girl in, Asher?"

There was a long pause, as if he was trying to decide how much he wanted to say. "Enough that my brakes went out and the emergency brake failed."

Quinn's heart stuttered at the confirmation of what she feared— that this accident had been no accident at all . . .

"You think someone did this?"

"I wouldn't know for sure unless I got a look at the brake line. Seeing as how my truck is lying at the bottom of a mountain, I don't see how that's going to happen anytime soon."

Guilt came over her like a crashing wave—crippling, consuming . . . Her hand shot out to steady herself on the railing. Her knees felt weak as her heart hammered inside her chest. If Asher was right, then this really was her fault and Quinn's killer had found her. It was only a matter of time before he succeeded. They were up against a nameless, faceless enemy. How could they ever hope to survive? The fear she'd felt for herself a week ago had now transferred to Asher. The soul-deep regret she felt for pulling him into this was beyond words. She never should have done it. Maybe it wasn't too late to undo her mistake. If she left, Asher would be safe . . .

His dad swore a ripe curse. It was the first time she'd heard Robert use foul language. It didn't suit him. "How serious are you about this girl, Asher?"

"What do you mean?"

"Are you in love with her or are you putting your life on the line for a piece of ass?"

"Jesus, dad. Really?"

"Answer my question." His father's demand held the authoritative tone of a man who'd raised four willful boys.

"Neither. I'm not sleeping with Quinn."

"That's not what I asked you, and that's not what it looked like in the driveway tonight. Your mother's practically picking out color patterns and flower arrangements."

Asher cursed. "You should have told her the truth right away, Dad. Quinn and I—it's . . . complicated."

His father chuckled. "Yeah, I hate to break it to you, son, but you're in love with her."

"I'm not in love with Quinn," he denied. "The woman drives me nuts."

Disappointment pierced her heart. It hurt a lot more than she wanted to admit, especially because she couldn't say the same about him. Oh shit, this was Spencer all over again. Only with Asher, she feared the fallout would be so much worse. She knew she hadn't been easy to get along with, and they'd had a rocky start together. But she'd thought after what happened tonight, that just maybe . . .

His father's humor stung. She failed to see what was so funny. Her heart was breaking and his father was laughing.

"Sounds like love to me. Do you think about her all the time? Do you want to strangle her one minute, and hug her the next? Does she make you want to be a better man?"

Quinn waited in breathless silence for Asher to answer.

"Oh, God . . ."

Asher couldn't sound more disgusted at the thought. It only made his dad laugh harder.

"I don't love Quinn," he said, this time with a lot more adamancy. "I can't, Pop."

"Well, that's a shame, because that girl's the best thing that's happened to you in a long time."

The scraping sound of a chair sent Quinn scrambling back into the shadows. She took another step toward the loft and silently retreated. Asher said something else to his dad but she couldn't hear what. It didn't really matter. She'd heard enough and her course was set. Tomorrow morning she was leaving.

She entered the room and grabbed her brush off the dresser before taking a seat at the foot of his bed. Despite the profound ache of disappointment in her chest, she told herself this was for the best. Especially with the likelihood she'd been found. If she thought there was a chance they could be together, it would only make leaving him all the harder. She'd survived a broken heart before, and she'd do it again—maybe . . . if her assassin didn't find her first.

Quinn would call Violet in the morning and see if Nikko could meet her somewhere with the package rather than mailing it. She had no plan beyond that and would just have to take it moment by moment, day by day. All she knew was that she couldn't stay here—not anymore, knowing the danger she was putting Asher in. Maybe she'd just board the Amtrak and see where it took her. It'd gotten her this far in one piece, right? If she kept moving, hopefully she'd stay safe long enough to find the connection she was searching for and finish her story.

She'd just gotten done working through the knots in her hair when Quinn heard a soft knock on the door. Despite herself, her pulse quickened and butterflies began a nervous dance inside her stomach. This was crazy. She wasn't some hormonal teen with a schoolgirl crush. She was an adult, for chrissake.

"Come in."

The door slowly opened and Quinn's breath caught in her lungs at the sight of Asher filling her doorway. He still wore his clothes from earlier. Dirt streaked his T-shirt, and she could see the muscular outline of his pecs through the thin cotton. His jeans hung low on his hips, bearing more evidence of his treacherous climb. A tear in the knee and one on his thigh pulled her gaze below his waist.

"I thought you were going to come down."

"I was, but I saw your dad was still here and I didn't want to interrupt."

He studied her, eyes raking over her head to toe—taking everything in and giving nothing away.

"Nice pajamas . . ."

The lift of his mouth was so subtle she almost missed it.

"I hope it's all right. I should have asked—"

"I don't mind, Quinn."

If she didn't know better, she'd think he looked pleased to see her in his clothes. Nervous energy flooded through her, and she could feel her cheeks heating beneath the scrutiny of his stare.

He stood there a moment watching her. As the silence stretched between them, so did the tension. But there was a new element to the vibe charging the air. She wished he weren't so damn difficult to read.

"You all right?" His husky voice skated over her like a caress.

Her response to him was immediate and uncontrollable, just like when he'd kissed her tonight. It made her feel exposed and vulnerable—and defensive. "Of course I am," she answered briskly. "Why wouldn't I be? I'm not the one who fell off the side of a mountain." Her voice was gruff and curt, a last-ditch effort to pull herself together because she did not like the loss of control she was feeling around him. But instead of being put off by her front and leaving, he seemed to see right through her act and took it as an invitation to stay.

They hadn't spoken much since the accident. Asher had called his dad right away to come pick them up, and this was the first they'd been alone since. But something was different about him—there was intensity in the way he watched her, unguarded concern in his eyes. Dare she hope something more? No, it would only make things harder. Besides, she'd heard the denial from his lips less than twenty minutes ago.

The storm of emotion raging inside his eyes was just the aftereffect of a terrifying experience, and she'd be a fool to read any more into it than that. He'd been so adamant they couldn't be friends, that he didn't care about her. But as he stood here in her doorway now, there was an undeniable spark of desire crackling between them that made her nerve endings tingle with anticipation. No, he may not love her, but she wasn't an idiot either—Asher Tate wanted her.

Exhaling a sigh, he stepped into the bedroom and walked toward her. No man had a right to be this handsome. Her pulse quickened when he knelt between her legs and met her eyes. Emotion clogged in her throat, tears pricking her lids anew at the thought of how close she came to losing him tonight, and how hard it was going to be to let him go tomorrow.

"I'm all right, Quinn . . ."

He took her hand, his grip strong and sure. Heat traveled up her arm as he brushed his thumb over her palm, uncurling her fingers, and placed it against his chest. The strong, steady beat of his heart sent her own hammering in a chaotic tempo.

"See . . ." he said, seeming oblivious that she was melting inside. Her core was like molten lava ready to erupt. "I'm just fine. Everything's going to be okay."

Lord, she needed to hear that, even if it wasn't true. Quinn was losing the battle with her tears. She couldn't keep looking into those soulful eyes without losing it. In this moment, she was sure she'd never wanted a man more than this one staring up at her right now, and never would again. How had everything gotten so out of control so fast? She was a heartbeat from throwing herself into his arms and taking the pleasure she knew only he could give her.

After what happened tonight, she needed to feel alive, to feel *him* alive—his heart beating against her breasts instead of her palm. But she was scared. She hadn't been with a man since Spencer, and if Asher's kiss tonight was any indication of the passion he was capable of, Asher Tate was totally out of her league. And not only that, but what if he turned her down? She wasn't sure she could handle that kind of rejection—not again.

"How's your head?" he asked, letting go of her hand and threading his fingers into her hair. He angled her head just enough to get a better look at the bump on her temple.

She winced as his fingers gently probed the area.

"Sorry . . . you have a cut here. I want to make sure you don't need any stitches."

His mouth was close to hers. She could feel his breath skate across her lips as he studied her contusion. What would he do if she closed the distance?

Had she once honestly thought Asher was a man ruled by his emotions . . . or his hormones? What a joke. In the week she'd spent with him, he'd exhibited nothing but discipline and strict self-control. *She'd* been the one to kiss him earlier tonight. *She'd* been the one urging him not to stop when he'd tried to cool things down, and *she* was the one tempted to do it again.

The irony wasn't lost on her that she was proving to be just like the other women she'd seen him with. Perhaps she had misjudged him all along and Asher wasn't the flagrant, whoring womanizer she'd accused him of being. Maybe he was guilty of nothing more than being a gorgeous man that women, including herself, couldn't seem to resist.

After a thorough inspection, he got off his knees and stood. "I think it'll be fine. Let me know if you get dizzy or start having headaches." Before he let her go, he pressed a chaste kiss to her forehead near the knot. Her eyes drifted closed, soaking in the heat of his touch, but it was over all too quick.

"It's late. I'm sure you're exhausted."

When he turned to leave, she bit her bottom lip to keep from calling him back. He stopped at the dresser to grab some clothes before heading for the door.

"Asher . . ." His name broke from her lips before she could stop it.

He paused. Tension radiated from him as he stood there with his hand on the door. He seemed hesitant to turn around. Would he stay if she asked him to? At the last minute, her nerves failed her. She cleared her throat and said, "I want to thank you again for saving my life tonight."

"Don't mention it." He kept his back to her, his voice a bit rougher than normal.

Maybe he wasn't as immune to what happened as he pretended. Her resistance broke. She was about to climb off the bed and go to him when he said, "Good night, Quinn," and walked out, pulling the door closed behind him.

CHAPTER

20

Just keep walking, Tate. One foot in front of the other . . . He gave his feet their marching orders and despite their dragging protest, they were good little soldiers, taking him down the steps and away from Quinn before he did something he would undoubtedly regret. He'd seen that look in women's eyes enough times to know what it was. He just never thought he'd see it in Quinn's. And, like a coward, it had sent him running. He hadn't trusted himself enough to turn around and face her when she'd called his name for fear he'd tell his honor to go fuck itself. As it was, that shit was hanging on by a thread.

Quinn was vulnerable and understandably shaken up over what happened tonight. She was just confusing gratitude with desire—that's all. The emotional high of escaping death could fuck with one's mind. He knew that. Hell, he was fighting the effects of it himself right now. He would not take advantage of her like this. It was the worst asshole move he could make. Especially when he knew Quinn Summers didn't do casual sex.

But is that what it would really be? Was it possible to do anything with Quinn and call it casual? Asher wasn't so sure anymore. Fuck, he wasn't sure about a lot of things and he hadn't appreciated his dad's two cents muddying the waters even more. Could he really be in love with Quinn? His mind flashed back to his confession a moment before he'd gone over that mountain. *I think I could have fallen in love with you . .*

. Had it been the meaningless rambling of a man about to die? Or did his heart know something his mind wasn't ready to admit?

Hell if he knew . . . It was late and he was exhausted. He was in no frame of mind to be making decisions about anything. The smartest move he could make was to hit the shower and then the couch. He let the bathroom door slam shut with a little too much gusto—the low level of sexual frustration setting his blood on a slow boil. Add in his concern that Quinn's killer had likely found her and yeah, sleep was going to be a forgone wish. What he'd really like to know was how in the hell had that bastard found her so quickly?

He contemplated the answer to that question as he pulled off his clothes and stepped beneath the shower's hot spray, making quick work of washing away most of the evidence of his near-death experience. Aside from a few cuts and bruises, he wasn't any worse for wear. He'd been through a hell of a lot worse.

As if summoned, those memories threatened to resurface—the screams, the sharp report of gunfire as he yelled for his men to stand down. Peterson's refusal . . . the explosion . . . Fuck, he swore he could still smell the sharp, sulfuric scent of gunpowder, the phantom pains of smoke-filled air burning his lungs, consuming his oxygen. With a snarled curse, he pushed the images back, refusing to go there. But the echo of guilt was never very far away. It did wonders to kill his cock, though, so he guessed he could at least be thankful for that.

Asher stepped out of the shower, then dried off and slipped into a pair of lounge pants, not bothering with a shirt. He headed into the living room after a trip past the front door to make sure the lock was secure. After checking the security system, he paused in the kitchen to swallow a few ibuprofen tablets because he was sure he'd be feeling the effects of that Evel Knievel stunt in the morning. Asher tipped his head beneath the faucet and turned it on, chugging down some water. Drying his mouth with the back of his hand, he clicked off the lights and headed to the couch.

He sprawled out, one hand tucked beneath his head as the other slipped beneath the couch cushion to check for his Sig. After sleeping with a sidearm for so many years, it was just a force of habit. As his fingertips brushed over the cool metal grip, the thought occurred to him to find out if Quinn knew how to shoot. If she didn't, she was going to learn. An image filled his mind of her wearing those sexy calf-high boots and skinny jeans, legs parted in a shooting stance with her arms outstretched, elbows locked, as she aimed his gun and pulled the trigger. Just like one of Charlie's Angels . . .

So fucking hot. With a groaned curse, he reached down to adjust the bent angle of his hard-on, straightening himself out. The ache in his balls warned him they weren't happy about being denied their release—again. He'd spent so much time at the barbecue hard for her, it wasn't funny. And then she'd kissed him outside his truck and holy shit . . .

His cock leapt at the memory, jerking with impatience. Yeah, well, Cujo was just going to have to heel, because this dog was not getting anywhere near Quinn. No sooner did that thought cross his mind than the bed above him squeaked beneath her weight, a painful reminder of just how close she was. He closed his eyes and tried to block out the visual of her wearing nothing but his navy blue T-shirt.

"Are you asleep?"

His eyes flew open at the sound of her voice. She was standing at the top of the stairs. The light from the lamp on the end table didn't quite reach her face, but from the way she fidgeted with the hem of his T-shirt, she looked nervous. It took him a moment to find his voice. When he did, it sounded like he'd been eating gravel. "No . . . I'm not sleeping. What do you want, Quinn?"

She took a hesitant step down and his gut clenched, each subsequent one knotting that fist tighter and tighter.

"I can't sleep . . ." she confessed, her bare feet taking that final step down.

Well, that made two of them then.

"Every time I close my eyes . . ."

Her voice broke and so did his heart. Fuck, this woman was going to be the death of him. Without consulting his brain, he was speaking before he even realized words were coming out of his mouth. "Come here, Quinn." He sat up on the sofa and held out his hand.

She didn't hesitate to race toward him, and the moment her hand connected with his, he pulled her into his lap. Her arms circled around his neck and she hugged him tight as she buried her face into the side of his neck. God help him, she felt incredible in his arms. Her scent enveloped him and his body responded with a visceral awareness like nothing he'd ever experienced before.

Her shoulders began to shake and moisture trickled down his neck. Her tears gutted him, and the invisible band around his chest tightened until he could hardly breathe. "Shhh . . ." he soothed, holding her a bit tighter, letting her get it out of her system. Over the years he'd seen so much bloodshed and tears, he thought himself immune to the maelstrom of emotion. Yet somehow Quinn's tears seemed to resonate deep inside his soul. If he could, he would bear this pain, this grief for her. He'd do it in a heartbeat, because it was easier to deal with the emotion himself than the feeling of helplessness that came over him at watching her crumble.

"You're going to be all right," he said as her sobs phased into stuttering breaths.

"It's not . . . me . . . I'm scared . . . about," she hiccupped. "It's . . . you . . ."

He tensed. Him? She was crying for him? Asher reached up and took Quinn's face in his hands, her cheeks damp against his palms. He leaned back and he tipped her chin to get a better look at her. His breath caught in his throat. She was beautiful. Her violet eyes glistened with unshed tears. Seeing her like this, with no walls, no defenses . . . his heart fucking melted.

Never in his life had a woman looked at him with such genuine concern and caring—and she was the last person he'd ever expected to see it from. It was humbling and gut-wrenching at the same time, heartwarming and terrifying, because he wasn't the man worthy of this woman's devotion. She just didn't know it yet. Once she learned the truth about him—what he'd done—that would change.

Two giant drops broke free of her lashes and rolled down her cheeks. He wiped them away with his thumbs. "Stop it . . ." he crooned softly, pressing his lips to one briny cheek and then the other. "I don't want you crying over me, Quinn." His mouth brushed over hers lightly. He meant it only as a comforting gesture, but her lips parted so sweetly beneath his, yielding so deliciously, he couldn't resist taking another taste.

He pressed his mouth more firmly against hers. Her lips were so full and soft, with just the faintest hint of her tears. He could feel his resolve slipping as she snuggled closer. His thin T-shirt did nothing to hide the pebbled hardness of her nipples pressing against his chest as her bottom ground against his erection. This was a bad idea . . . getting involved with Quinn like this. He was crossing the line. Who the fuck was he kidding? He'd crossed the line so long ago the damn thing was a speck in his rearview mirror. But still, she was upset, emotional, and vulnerable. She didn't know what she was doing . . .

Her tongue teased over his top lip and retreated. She slipped her fingers into his hair and they curled into tight little fists as she shifted in his lap. Okay, maybe she did know what she was doing a little bit. But that didn't make him any less of a bastard for taking advantage of her. "Quinn . . ." he whispered against her mouth. His throat was dry as ash, making her name a broken, husky plea. "I don't think—"

"Don't, Asher," she interrupted him. "Don't say it. I just . . . I need this," she pleaded softly. "I need you. I need you to make me forget. I need to feel alive and that everything is going to be okay, even if it isn't."

Her request was more than he had the strength to deny. She knew what she wanted, even if it was just his body. He could give that to her. Hell, if he could give it to scores of women he didn't care about, he could give it to Quinn. But this was different—*she* was different, his heart tried to warn him before it was too late. He didn't listen.

He could take away her fear, her hurt, and replace it with pleasure. He could make the world go away—even if it was just for the night . . .

———

No regrets . . . It was Quinn's vow when she'd climbed out of bed and into this man's arms, and it was her vow right now as she made her plea for him not to stop. She could feel the tension inside him, his hard body veritably humming with it—a living, breathing force of restraint. His will was impressive. What would it take to break him?

In all her wildest dreams, she'd never imagined she would be the one to proposition him. Then again, she'd never believed it was possible to fall so hard or fast for a man like this. She was a humanitarian in love with a mercenary . . . The irony of it was laughable if the hopelessness of a future together wasn't so heartbreaking.

She wasn't going into this with blinders on. She knew Asher didn't love her, but sadly that didn't stop her from wanting him. And if she couldn't have his heart then she at least wanted this—one night with him before she left. This wasn't just about her safety anymore. She cared too much about Asher to let him keep risking his life for hers. She would never forgive herself if something happened to him.

She'd almost experienced that loss tonight—and she vowed she'd never do it again. Tomorrow morning she would leave—it was the only way to keep him safe. But before she left, she wanted one night to experience what it was like to be in this man's arms. She was going to walk away from him brokenhearted either way, so she might as well do it with no regrets.

"You don't want to do this. This isn't you, Quinn . . ."

How would he know? *She* hardly knew herself anymore. She'd been hiding behind her walls for so long, afraid to love, afraid to trust, that she'd lost sight of who the real Quinn Summers truly was.

She knew he wanted her, could feel the evidence of his impressive arousal against her hip, making her ache with long-denied need. "Please, Asher . . ."

And that was all it took to snap his restraint. With a growl that sounded more animal than man, he rolled her beneath him, his hard, muscular body pinning her against the couch. His mouth took hers in a hot joining that left her breathless. His hips rocked against her sex, the friction making her gasp as little jolts of pleasure arrowed into her core. The thin barrier of his lounge pants and the damp scrap of cotton between her legs were the only things preventing him from entering her.

She exhaled a throaty moan that he devoured. His breath infused her lungs as his tongue tangled with hers. One hand fisted into her hair while the other slipped beneath her shirt, capturing one of her breasts. The calluses of his palm abraded her nipple, sending a direct current of energy between her legs. She squirmed beneath him, seeking the friction of his erection to relieve the mounting tension coiling deep inside her.

"Fuck, Quinn, hold still . . ." he growled, tearing his mouth from hers.

His hand left her breast to grab her hip and pin it down. The feeling of his fingertips biting into her flesh was an erotic mix of pain and pleasure. "You're going to make me come before I even get inside you."

The rough gravel of his voice and the vulgar honesty of his confession thrilled and excited her. Every nerve ending was lit up, alive in a way she'd never felt before. She wasn't sure she *could* hold still. The need was nearing unbearable. Her breaths were coming in a ragged pant. Perhaps Asher recognized the desperation in her eyes, because his lips curled in a grin of pure masculine approval as his hungry gaze swept over her.

"As hot as it is to see you in my clothes, I think I'd prefer you out of them. Take my shirt off."

A moment of uncertainty skittered through her at his command. It'd been a long time since a man had seen her naked . . .

"What's the matter, Quinn? Having second thoughts?"

"No . . ." she quickly answered, afraid he'd get the wrong idea and change his mind.

A few seconds ticked by and he chuckled. Lord, she felt that throaty rumble roll right through her.

"You're shy . . ." He sounded surprised, like the thought had never occurred to him before. "How long has it been since you've done this— been with a man?"

His brow arched, waiting for her to answer. She was embarrassed to tell him. This wasn't something she would normally talk about. How incredibly unromantic was it to have this conversation right now? She took his hand to tug him closer. He didn't budge. He wasn't going to do this unless he was absolutely sure it was what she wanted. She should feel relieved by that, but instead his hesitancy frustrated her. Again, he was shattering her preconceptions about him and she didn't like it. The more she discovered about him, the more she realized she didn't really know Asher Tate, and the deeper in love she fell with him.

Heat flooded her cheeks. "Over two years," she confessed softly.

Understanding softened his eyes and he reached up, gently brushing the back of his knuckles against her cheek. "I won't hurt you, Quinn. I promise I'll be careful. And baby, believe me, you've got nothing to be shy about. Come on, lift your arms up."

His compliment gave her enough courage to do as he instructed, but it didn't stop her heart from nervously hammering inside her chest. This was really happening . . .

He gathered the hem and pulled it over her head. The cool air kissed her nipples, drawing them tighter. Her breath stalled in her lungs, awaiting his response as his eyes devoured her.

The air left his lips with a reverent curse as he lifted his hand and gently cupped her breast, his thumb brushing over her turgid nipple. "So beautiful . . ."

He rose from the couch and scooped her up into his arms. "What are you doing?"

"Taking you upstairs. This couch is not the place for what I'm going to do to you."

CHAPTER
21

Asher's husky promise sent a thrill racing through her. She felt weightless in his arms as he climbed the stairs with surprising speed. His steps were quick and determined as he crossed the room, heading straight for the bed. She was glad she'd left the bathroom light on, casting the bedroom in a soft, ambient glow.

He laid her down and hooked his fingers into the lace of her panties, slowly dragging them down her legs. She didn't have time wrestle with the insecurity of being totally bare before him. He wasted no time loosening the string on his pajama pants, and freeing his erection. The gasp that caught in her throat was both awe and fear. The man standing before was undoubtedly the most magnificent male specimen she'd ever seen. Everything about him was huge, and every impressive inch was flesh-covered steel. She was torn between the impulse to indulge in this beautiful masculine gift or run for the hills, because Asher Tate was so out of her league, it wasn't even funny.

Her awestruck hesitation must have shone on her face because that low masculine chuckle brought her gaze up to his. "Now you look like you're having second thoughts."

She swallowed past the dry click in her throat and shook her head—words failed her.

"You don't have to do this, Quinn."

"No, it's not that . . ." She rose to her knees, fascination winning over fear. Raising a tentative hand she traced the line of his collarbone and followed the muscular mapping on his chest.

He inhaled a sharp hiss through clenched teeth, but other than the tension that seemed to hum beneath his skin, he didn't move, giving her a chance to touch, to explore . . .

"You're just so . . . beautiful." It was a feminine word, but there wasn't anything feminine about this man, and yet no other word could describe him more perfectly. Back up and over his shoulders, she ran her hands down the ropes of muscles flexing and straining over his biceps as he fought to allow Quinn her exploration.

With each touch her timidity began to ebb, emboldened by the effort it was costing him to give her this time to get familiar with his body. His hands curled into fists, the pattern of his breathing becoming chaotic as she traced her fingertips over to his ribs and the carved muscles of his abs—the V of flesh near his hips, guiding her to the erection straining just as large and proud as the man standing before her.

"And big . . ."

Her own breaths quickened at the glorious sight of him; the fire building in her core was making her melt. The ache he created in her was a soul-deep need only he could satisfy.

Her fingers drifted toward his length, but before she could touch him, his hand caught her wrist. Her eyes darted up to his in surprise, those simmering embers of uncertainty flaring back to life at the reminder of who was really in control here.

"I won't hurt you, Quinn."

His deep voice, normally smooth as aged whiskey, now sounded coarse as sandpaper. Goose bumps rose to her flesh in response and anticipation as she nodded her acquiescence. She believed him—trusted him with her body. It was her heart she wasn't so sure about, because his tenderness, his concern for her, contradicted his denial that he cared for her, and she'd be a fool to let herself hope there was something here that wasn't. This was just sex. That's all it ever could be. And that was okay, because tomorrow was going to come soon enough.

He slid her hand up instead of down, past planes of his abs, over his chest, and around his neck as he climbed onto the bed. He lowered himself on top of her as they both went down to the mattress. Bracing his weight on his forearms, his hand slipped into her hair as his mouth took hers. His kiss was tempered now, more gentle than downstairs, but just as intoxicating.

His touch was teasing instead of demanding—lighter, exploring, like hers had been. It was sweet torture . . . He brushed the back of his knuckles against the outer swell of her breast, his thumb tracing the bottom curve, making her nipples ache for the attention he denied her.

She knew what he was doing and it was working—fanning her flame until the fire inside her took hold and became a raging inferno. With each passing second, her inhibitions were dissolving, her worry burning away until there was nothing left but raw, aching need. His fingertips brushed up her inner thigh, each sweep back and forth bringing him closer to her silken folds, only to draw back at the last moment.

She was burning up. Frustration made her bolder. He was showing her she wasn't the insecure, unpracticed woman she thought. Giving her the time she needed to get more comfortable with herself, with him . . .

Quinn returned his kiss with more demand, her tongue doing the invading as she tugged him closer. Her hand dipped to the roadmap of his abs, and then lower. When she wrapped her fingers around his erection, it jerked in her hand and the throaty growl rumbling in his throat sounded like erotic torture. She was pushing him, edging him past the limits of his self-control, and the thrill it gave her to have this kind of effect on a man like Asher was a heady, intoxicating experience.

He'd masterfully worked her past her insecurities and doubts. The desire to be filled by him, to have him consuming her, quickly became her only thought, her only need. She stroked his length, and his hips rocked in rhythm with her hand. Moisture escaped him and slicked her palm. His whole body tensed above her, flagging restraint stringing his muscles tight, and he growled a curse that tasted absolutely delicious on her tongue.

"You have to stop touching me, Quinn. You're not ready yet and I don't want to hurt you."

She thought she was ready, and she told him so. He proved her wrong by parting her slick folds and slipping two fingers deep inside her. She gasped at the invasion. As sweet as it felt, the stretch was almost more than she could handle. "You're not ready. Just trust me . . ." he whispered beside her ear before kissing that sensitive spot on her neck.

She forced herself to relax into his touch, but the tension deep inside her grew impossibly tighter. When his mouth covered her breast, she couldn't hold back her moan as his thumb found the bead of her sex and her walls tightened around his fingers. She was going to come. Never in her life had she been brought so high so fast. Her heart rioted in her chest, thundered in her ears. Her breaths were a ragged pant as she tried to warn him, "Asher, I'm . . ."

But she didn't get any farther than that. Her confession died in her throat as his teeth grazed her nipple and then sucked the bud—hard. His fingertips stroked that perfect spot deep inside her and she shattered. A broken cry tore from her as she rode the euphoric wave of her release. At some point, his mouth found hers again, kissing her as if his very breath depended on it.

Her head was still spinning as he moved above her and she was vaguely aware of him reaching for the nightstand. She heard the tearing of a foil wrapper and a moment later he was settled between her legs, his erection hovering at her entrance. She felt liquid in his arms, her muscles relaxed and pliable. This was what he must have meant by ready, and she was glad he'd taken the time to prepare her, because she failed to fully appreciate his size until he entered her.

His mouth was on her neck, nipping and sucking as he eased himself inside. The invading fullness of him made her breath catch. She tensed.

He stopped moving. The quiver of his strained muscles and the fine sheen of sweat across his shoulder blades were proof of what his temperance was costing him. Asher didn't strike her as a slow or particularly gentle lover. This was all about her right now—her comfort—her pleasure.

"Relax . . ." he whispered, his breath hot against the shell of her ear. His mouth returned to hers. That coaxing, courting kiss was back, and so was the spark of heat igniting her core. He didn't advance, he just held his ground. When his hand slipped between them and found the bundle of nerves at the hood of her sex, a soft moan escaped her lips and the ache slowly began to build.

She returned his kiss with increasing demand, and soon she was writhing beneath him. She dragged her nails down his back and grabbed the tight muscles of his ass, urging him forward. Why wasn't he moving?

"Just give me a minute," he panted against her mouth. "Fuck, Quinn, you feel so amazing. So tight . . . I'm going to lose it if you don't hold still."

But he was driving her to the edge. His hand teasing the tight bundle of nerves, his mouth utterly pilfering hers . . . She wanted him home. Buried so deep she wouldn't know where he ended and she began.

"Please . . ." she begged, kissing his neck. She was too close to her own release now. His pulse hammered against her tongue, a testament to his flagging control. She playfully nipped his skin and sucked away the sting as she bit her nails into his ass and nudged him farther. With a tortured groan, he relented and thrust forward, burying himself deep inside her. He felt incredible . . . The head of his cock hit that sensitive spot inside her and she gasped at the explosion of pleasure.

Asher's restraint was shredded. He withdrew and drove home again, and again, and again. Her orgasm ripped through her at the same time a sharp bark of rapture tore from his throat. He pulsed against her core, her glove milking his release as wave after euphoric wave crashed into her.

Several minutes passed in silence as they worked to catch their breath. His forehead rested against her shoulder. She wasn't sure what to say—what to expect from him now that it was over. God's honest truth, she was speechless. Quinn never doubted sex with him would be anything other than incredible. She just wasn't prepared for the melee of emotions to come barreling through her in the aftermath of her postorgasmic bliss. Perhaps she'd been naïve to believe she could handle it, to think that sex with him would change nothing, but when he braced his weight on his elbow and slowly lifted his head to meet her eyes, there was no denying the soul-shattering truth.

It changed everything . . .

———

Asher had been with more than his share of women in his day, but hands down, none had ever rocked his world like Quinn Summers. And by the look on her face, he'd venture a guess that he wasn't the only one feeling the effects. Had he honestly thought this woman cold?—a shrew?—compared her to a porcupine? Nothing could be further from the truth. She was the hottest, sweetest thing he'd ever had the pleasure of taking to his bed, and now that he had her there, he had no intention of letting her go.

Did this complicate things? Hell yes. Was it worth it? Fuck yeah. Would she agree? Shit, he hoped so. If she wasn't sold yet, he had the whole night to convince her otherwise.

"You all right?" he asked, reaching up to tuck a strand of pale blonde hair behind her ear. He told her he'd be careful, gentle with her, but what had started as such certainly hadn't ended that way. Shit, he hoped he didn't hurt her. She was so damn tight, so tiny . . .

Quinn nodded but didn't speak. He studied her a little bit longer while attempting to sort out the riot of emotions battering around inside his chest. The fullness in his heart was an uncomfortable pressure. This couldn't be love—could it? He'd never had the experience before to know for sure, but his father seemed to think it was. The only thing he knew for sure was that he'd almost lost this woman tonight, and the thought of it terrified him. It made him want to wrap her up in his arms and never let go.

She broke his stare, looking a little uncertain—nervous? Maybe what she saw in him was scaring her as much as it did him. Fuck, he needed to get a handle on himself before he went and really freaked her out by telling her he was in love with her or some crazy shit like that. He might not know Quinn as well as he wanted to, but she wore those walls like a coat of armor. And he'd be willing to guess that there was a good reason for it.

That he was getting a glimpse of her now, unguarded, was a rare gift he wasn't taking for granted. He could already sense her rallying the troops to re-erect those damn barriers. But before the hedging doubts could take root in her mind, he waged his own assault on her defenses and kissed her. The last thing he wanted was her regretting this, regretting him, but then wasn't that just delaying the inevitable? If she truly knew him, would she really want him? Likely not . . . The only reason she was here at all was that she needed him.

When he tried to break their kiss, Quinn pulled him back to her. "Don't leave . . ." she whispered between kisses. "Not yet."

She thought he was leaving her? What kind of an asshole did she take him for? Someone who'd pull a bang and bail? Really? He was still inside her and getting hard again. His refractory period with this woman was nonexistent. But this condom wasn't going to hold up for round two, and as much as he didn't want to leave her, even for a quick dash to the bathroom, it was a necessary trip because he was not done with Quinn Summers. Not by a long shot.

CHAPTER

22

Quinn hadn't slept the entire night, though she feigned it now as she felt Asher stir beside her. After several rounds of mind-blowing sex, he'd finally pulled her against him somewhere around 4:00 a.m. and drifted off to sleep. She hadn't expected him to stay—never thought for a moment that he'd be capable of this kind of intimacy or affection. Oh, she'd known he could fuck like a rock star, and he'd definitely lived up to the expectation, but what was she supposed to do with this? What did it mean?

It didn't matter, she told herself, shutting down the sprig of hope blooming in her heart. It changed nothing. The man hunting her was still out there and she needed to run. Every minute she delayed was another minute she put Asher at risk. She just couldn't do it anymore. Besides, for all she knew, he'd just felt sorry for her last night. She'd gone to him in tears and practically begged him to sleep with her. She had probably been a pity fuck—nothing more. Her emotions were messing with her judgment, making her read something into things that weren't there. He'd no doubt be relieved to have her gone. Lord knows, she hadn't been easy to live with. And she'd nearly gotten him killed. What guy in his right mind would actually want her to stay after that? No, it was better this way—for everyone.

Asher's arm slipped away from her chest, their legs untangling as he rolled onto his back and stretched. Despite her hammering heart, she kept her breaths slow and even. Would he try to wake her for one more bout of amazing sex, or just slip away like it never happened? She got her answer a moment later when the mattress dipped and the covers shifted. Cool air kissed her backside as he rose. A moment later she heard the soft click of the bathroom door and a few seconds after that, the shower turned on.

Shoving aside the sharp pang of regret, Quinn rallied her walls around her breaking heart and focused on the task at hand—survival. Tossing back the covers, she crawled to the edge of the bed and froze. Condom wrappers littered the floor like confetti. The irony of the wisecrack she'd made to him the day she arrived wasn't lost on her.

Oh, no . . . I've become that *woman.*

Ignoring the embarrassment flushing her face, she quickly dressed and headed for the closet to retrieve the duffle bag she'd purchased the day she'd gone shopping. She grabbed her stack of articles and notes off the laptop and put them in the bag before turning to the dresser to pack her clothes. She moved fast, carelessly stuffing the items inside. She wanted to be packed, downstairs, and ready to go before Asher came out of the bathroom. This was going to be hard enough as it was. She didn't want to make it any more difficult or awkward by being in here when he came out.

Quinn pulled open the last drawer and grabbed a fistful of panties. She was about to stuff them into the bag when she heard the sharp report of Asher's deep voice fire off behind her.

"What the hell are you doing?"

Her gaze shot to his, then went back to her task. He looked pissed. Steeling her determination, she notched her chin and answered with more bravado than she felt. "I'm leaving. I decided last night it isn't fair what I've done to you. I should never have pulled you into this."

"You had no problem dragging me into this a week ago," he challenged. "So what's changed?"

"A week ago I didn't care about you." She grabbed her bras and shoved them into the bag. "A week ago you were just some jackass I met at my sister's wedding."

He let out a harsh bark of laughter that held no amusement. "Quinn, I hate to break it to you, but I'm still some jackass you met at your sister's wedding."

It wasn't true. He was so much more than that, and if nothing else, he was *her* jackass now, and she couldn't live with herself if something happened to him.

"And last night was what? A sayonara fuck, payment for services rendered?"

She winced. Ouch, that hurt . . . his words were just as sharp as his tone.

"A little late for second thoughts, don't you think, Quinn? If you honestly believe I'm just going to let you walk out of here, you're out of your goddamn mind. Despite what happened last night with that accident, you're still safer here than anywhere else. We're going to see this through together. And when it's over, you'll be free to go. But until then, you're stuck with me, sweetheart."

"When it's over, you could be dead! And this isn't your decision. I hired you, I can fire you."

"You're not paying me!"

"I almost got you killed!" She blinked back the sting of impending tears, knowing the minute she lost the battle, they weren't going to stop. There would be plenty of time for them later. "He's found me, Asher. Last night was no accident!"

"You don't know that, Quinn."

"Yes, I do! And so do you. I heard you talking to your dad so don't you dare stand there and lie to me."

"What are you going to do, Quinn? Where do you think you're going to go?"

She didn't know. She hadn't gotten that far. All she knew was that she couldn't live with Asher's death on her hands. Emily's was bad enough.

"You know what I think? I think you're scared."

"Of course I'm scared. I'm freaking terrified."

"Not about that, about us."

"About us?"

"You've been pushing me away every chance you could since the day you got here."

"Well, if that isn't the pot calling the kettle black, Mr. I-Don't-Care-About-You."

"I never said I *didn't* care. I said I *couldn't* care."

"Semantics."

"I think you're scared to let someone in, and after what happened between us last night, you're afraid that if you stay, you might actually have to admit you have feelings for me. Well, let me tell you, Quinn, you can't keep running forever. Eventually you're going to have to trust someone."

Oh, that was low. Now he was playing dirty—giving her false hope that last night was something more to him than a convenient fuck. Who the hell was he kidding? Asher Tate didn't do serious relationships. She knew it. Hell, even his family knew it. That was why they'd been so shocked to see her at the barbecue.

"I thought you didn't do casual sex, Quinn."

"And I thought you didn't do relationships."

"You're just going to walk away from this, pretend it didn't happen? That *this* isn't happening?"

"You've been more than clear from the first day I got here that you didn't want—" she waved her hand in between them "—*this*. Don't try to manipulate me into thinking that this was more to you than it really was so that I'll stay."

His brows popped up with surprise and he walked toward her—stalked was more like it. Her pulse quickened, adrenaline lit her veins. She felt like a cornered rabbit. He was completely naked except for the towel wrapped low around his hips, the split stretching farther up the inside of his thigh with each determined step.

"You think you know me so well, do you? Then tell me, what was this?"

His voice was a low, husky growl that sent goose bumps erupting over her flesh. Her nerve endings began to tingle in response to his nearness, the delicious soreness between her legs an all too fresh reminder of what this was—explosive, consuming, mind-blowing . . .

Despite his anger—and make no mistake, he was furious—he was also aroused. She could see the evidence of it tenting the terry cloth between his long, muscular legs—a dangerous combination that both frightened and excited her.

Tamping down the feminine awareness lighting her up, she ignored the ache blooming in her core and the temptation to experience heaven in his arms one more time. Because without a doubt, she'd never come close to having this kind of passion with another man as long as she lived, and that thought alone nearly crumbled her resolve.

"It was . . ." She scrambled to find the right words. She wouldn't tell him what it had meant to her. Those emotions belonged to Quinn and Quinn alone. She wouldn't further expose herself by telling him she'd fallen in love with him and that if she didn't leave now, she wasn't sure she'd have the strength to do it later. "It was a mistake."

His brows tightened, the little muscle in his jaw ticked. He was seriously pissed off.

"It was a moment of weakness, on both our parts," she continued to explain, but the more she talked the angrier he looked, and the closer he came. She took another step back and connected with the wall. Trapped . . .

Oh, shit . . .

He planted his palms against the logs on each side of her head, caging her with his arms. She stared up into his eyes, unable to look away from that mesmerizing kaleidoscope of color glaring down at her. Ropes of flesh-covered muscle surrounded her. The heat radiating off his bare skin set her on a slow boil. Her pulse was hammering inside her chest, everything feminine inside her humming with desire. She wanted to run and to throw herself into the safety of his arms at the same time. Why was he doing this to her? Why wouldn't he just let her go?

"It was more than that and you know it." He was so close she could smell the clean, masculine scent of his soap. "You're not going anywhere and don't you dare try to run from me, Quinn. There's a goddamn killer out there and until I find him, you're stuck with me. You got it?"

All she could do was numbly nod like some freaking bobblehead, too shocked by his words to manage anything more than that. Lowering his head, he stopped just before their lips touched. Hers parted in invitation; she could almost taste the mint of his toothpaste on her tongue.

"What happened between us wasn't a mistake," he growled. "And until you're willing to admit it, it isn't going to happen again."

He dropped his hands and spun away, leaving her standing there in jaw-dropping shock. Was he serious? Was he really going to just walk away from her like that? Guess so . . .

He didn't cast another glance her way as he shamelessly dropped his towel and made a bare-assed trek across the bedroom to the dresser. She couldn't tear her eyes off the visual feast—wide, muscular shoulders tapering to a trim, narrow waist. Not a spare ounce of flesh was on that man's body. His ass was perfection, with muscled dimples in each cheek that flexed with each step.

Did he really believe what he'd just said? That last night wasn't a mistake? If so, then what did he think it was? If she swallowed her pride and caved to his demand, would he take her back to his bed and prove it to her? Just the thought of being in his arms again had moisture gathering between her legs.

But Quinn wasn't a fool. She'd learned a long time ago not to take a man at his word. Guys said whatever they had to say to serve their own purpose at the moment, and she'd be a naïve idiot to believe Asher was any different. Especially when he'd told her to her face he couldn't care about her, and confirmed just as much last night to his father.

Bottom line, she may trust Asher with her life, but she didn't trust him not to break her heart. And the sad truth was, as much as she wanted the pleasure only he could give her, she desired the connection to his heart more. She wanted him to hold her in his arms, to tell her she was the only one—that he loved her . . . And those were dangerous desires, because she wasn't sure that Asher Tate was capable of that kind of emotion.

He wanted her to admit this wasn't a mistake, but she couldn't do that, because it very well may have been the biggest mistake of her life. She feared that in giving him her body, she might have just lost her soul.

CHAPTER
23

He was fucking this up . . .

Asher sat on the couch, head in his hands, as he replayed his argument upstairs with Quinn. He couldn't decide who he was more pissed at, Quinn for trying to leave him, or himself for making her believe he didn't care about her. He'd so thoroughly convinced her that he didn't give a shit, that he could make love to her for an entire night—because make no mistake, that's exactly what it was—and in the morning, she could still look him in the eyes and believe it hadn't meant anything to him.

She'd told him it was a mistake. And he just might have believed her if it wasn't for the moisture gathering in her eyes, making those beauties shine like amethysts. Maybe he hadn't been ready to admit he'd fallen in love with her last night, but after being with her, being inside her, over and over . . . After walking out that bathroom door and finding her getting ready to leave him . . . Something profound had shifted into place inside his chest, and he'd been faced with the hard slap of reality—he was undeniably in love with Quinn Summers. And he might have told her that too, if he'd thought there was a snowball's chance in hell that she'd believe him.

Sometime between pulling her into his arms and drifting off to sleep, and then waking this morning, he'd lost her again. Her walls were back up, higher than ever, as she wore that stubborn chin-tilt of determination that dared him to challenge her.

Well, challenge accepted, sweetheart. He didn't know what the hell had happened to her to make her such an untrusting skeptic, but he was determined to find out. Maybe he hadn't done this right. Hell, if he was being honest with himself, he'd been fucking things up with her since the day he'd met her. But last night was the first time he'd gotten it right, and as a reward, he'd been given a glimpse of the real Quinn Summers—and he wanted more. Dammit, he wanted *her*. The problem was going to be convincing her of that, because the one thing he knew about this woman, she believed actions over words. If he hoped to have any bit of a future with her when this was over, then he had his work cut out for him.

And not only that—the fuck of it was, here he sat thinking of ways he could get Quinn to fall in love with him when what he really needed to be focusing on was keeping her alive, because he was pretty damn sure that the killer had found her.

See, this was exactly what he'd meant by a distraction. Goddammit . . .

———

It was with mixed emotions that he stood at the cliff's edge and stared at the wreckage lying at the bottom of the mountain. No one could have survived that. He'd made sure the cables were loose enough that they wouldn't hold if the truck had made it this far and crashed into the barrier. His only regret was the bastard had taken Quinn with him. He hadn't been done with her yet—far from it. And the loss of a good kill left him oddly bereft. He'd had so many plans for her—for them . . .

He knew going into it he was taking a calculated risk, but he hadn't been able to pass up the opportunity to take Tate out of the game. There were only so many ways to make a hit look like an accident. When he'd overheard Tate's father telling one of his staff that his son was heading up to his place for a barbecue, it had been the chance he was waiting for. It wasn't uncommon for a truck's brakes to go out coming down a mountain.

He'd gambled that Tate would leave the woman behind, not wanting to get her involved with his family. He'd lost that bet—lost his chance to take out the competition and claim that sweet piece of ass for himself. Fuck . . .

He'd realized his misfortune after going to Tate's house shortly after dark and finding the place empty. It would have been perfect. Quinn there all alone . . . Imagining the fun he would have had with her made his dick hard, the ache in his balls demanding satisfaction.

With a foul curse, he turned away from the wreckage, climbed into his car, and headed for Tate's house. He hoped recovering the evidence wouldn't be like searching for a needle in a haystack. It had to be there. He'd wrecked Quinn's apartment searching for it. Her roommate hadn't been any help, too busy sobbing and begging him not to kill her to be of any use. He'd finally cut her throat just to shut her the fuck up. Of course, she would have died either way. She'd seen his face. Then again, so had Quinn. She just hadn't realized it, which told him she hadn't spent a lot of time going through the photos she took. Sometimes the best places to hide were in plain sight. Not that any of it mattered now. She was dead. Tate was dead. He'd retrieve the final piece of damning evidence and then he could put this all behind him.

His security team was heading out for another CGRN escort at the end of the month. It'd be nice to get a little R & R before heading back to that shithole of a country. Maybe he'd go to Grand Cayman and lie low for a few weeks, or maybe Turks and Caicos. Both places would be beautiful this time of year, and he fucking deserved a vacation—especially after dealing with this shit.

———

Quinn opened the bathroom door and entered the bedroom, her gaze falling on the foil wrappers still littering the floor. As meticulously clean as Asher kept his place, she'd thought he would've cleaned them up while she was in the shower, but nope. There they were . . . and once again, the evidence of their passionate night together hit her with a resounding smack of reality.

As much as she knew she should, Quinn couldn't bring herself to regret what had happened between them—mistake or not. Hands down, it had been the most incredible night of her life. She'd never felt that kind of pleasure in a man's arms before. Asher had consumed her, taking all she had and giving so much more in return. Even now, just thinking about his mouth on hers, tongues tangling to the rhythm of his hard thrusts, had her belly turning liquid. Had he really meant what he'd said about it not happening again until she admitted to him that this wasn't a mistake? Did she want it to happen again? The answer to that question was most resoundingly yes—yes she did.

She hadn't expected him to fight so hard for her to stay, and wondered if he was so adamant because of his sense of obligation to Nikko, or if he truly wanted her here. She was wrestling with her decision, and if it wasn't for the knowledge that Asher would undoubtedly come after her, putting himself at even greater risk, she would leave—not because she didn't love him enough to stay, but because she loved him enough not to.

"Well, it looks like the only thing we're missing are the panties hanging from the ceiling fan."

Quinn startled at his voice behind her, her hand tightening around the foil wrappers. How could he be so calm when she had a knot of emotions bouncing around inside her like a Ping-Pong tournament? Didn't he care he'd almost died last night? For someone who'd fallen off a mountain, he was acting terribly cavalier about the whole thing.

She shot him a look over her shoulder and grumbled, "I can't believe you're joking at a time like this." Didn't he see how much danger he was putting himself in by keeping her here? That the best thing for him was to let her go and forget he ever met her? Quinn grabbed the last wrapper and felt Asher's gaze on her ass. She carried them over to the trash can and dropped the handful inside.

"What do you want me to do, Quinn? You want me to say that I'm scared? Will that make you feel any better, any safer? All right . . ." He walked toward her until she was within arm's reach and then took hold of her shoulders, gripping her firmly as if preparing to shake some sense into her. The look in his eyes, the unguarded emotion and raw honesty she saw reflecting back at her, made her heart stutter in her chest. "I'm fucking terrified . . . but not of that bastard. I'm scared you're going to get it into your head again that you're better off on your own, and you're going to get yourself killed. Promise me, you will not leave. I don't need you to protect me, Quinn. That's *my* job. Let me do it."

Quinn nodded, unable to speak past the lump in her throat. She would never have thought it possible, but she loved this man more and more with each passing second. His grip on her softened, his thumbs brushing back and forth over her arms in a gentle caress. How could such a simple touch make her knees go weak?

He studied her a moment, seeming to search her eyes for any hint of deception. He must have been satisfied with what he saw, because after a long pause he nodded. "All right, then." He pulled her into his arms and hugged her tight. "No more talk of you going anywhere except with me."

Quinn could feel the beat of his heart against her breasts—strong and reassuring. She slipped her arms around his waist and held on for dear life. How was it possible that in such a short time this man had literally become her lifeline?

"I think I need to get you out of here for a while. Let the dust settle and see what happens. I have a cabin up in the mountains we can go to. It's remote, and safe. The only way to get there is on horseback or foot."

She pulled back far enough to see his face. The grim set of his brows told her his decision was already made. "What about the SD card? I need those photos and my notes. I still haven't been able to find the US connection I'm looking for, and I'm afraid I'm not going to without them."

"There's a generator at the cabin, so you'll have electricity to finish working on your story, but no Internet access. When the SD card arrives Nikko can call the sat phone."

"I don't want him to upload those files. I won't risk anyone discovering Vi has them if someone is monitoring her e-mail."

"We'll figure something out. We're also going to need to make a plan for how we're going to handle the news release. It's not going to be as easy as pressing the send button—believe me."

Quinn hadn't gotten that far. She'd originally planned to hand her story over to the attorney general's office and let them right this ghastly wrong, but that hope had died along with Emily. Journalism had never been her intended career. All her work had been overseas and she hadn't been interested in networking and making social connections. She didn't know anyone within the media circles who could help her. So along with finishing her research, she needed to start doing some homework and decide which media outlets she trusted with this story.

"How long do you think we'll be at your cabin?"

"How long do you think it'll take you to finish your work?"

"Once I have everything? A few days. Maybe a week at the most."

He nodded. "That should give me enough time to figure out a way to flush this fucker out. I want him dead before you release this story."

A cold chill snaked over her flesh, sending a shiver racking up her spine. Asher pulled her closer and pressed a kiss to the top of her head. "Don't worry, Quinn. You just focus on doing your job, and let me do mine. This is what I've been trained for."

She knew he intended his words to bring her comfort, but there was none. Quinn hated that she'd dragged him into this. And at the same time, there wasn't any other place she'd rather be—especially now, standing here in his arms—except maybe naked and beneath him. She had no idea how he planned to kill this man, but the idea of Asher putting himself at risk scared the ever-loving hell out of her.

CHAPTER

24

"A sher, I'm not comfortable doing this."

"I don't remember asking you," he said behind her, his voice a low, husky caress against her ear. "Spread your legs farther apart."

He wedged his foot between hers and knocked her left foot into position, then her right.

"I've never done this before . . ."

"Are you telling me I'm your first?" he chuckled. His chest was pressed against her back and the vibration rolled right through her. "Because that's fucking hot . . ."

His body was like warm steel pressed up behind her and she could feel exactly how turned on he was. How he could be hard at a time like this, she would never know—maybe it was a guy thing. His erection ground against her ass and Quinn's aim dropped. She couldn't concentrate with him standing this close to her—touching her—though aside from his very prominent erection, his touch was strictly platonic.

"Arms up," Asher told her, placing a hand beneath her elbow and inching it back into position. "Straighten out your shoulders, tense those elbows, and lock your wrists or you're not going to hit shit."

"I don't know . . ." she hedged, wondering how in God's name she'd ever let Asher convince her to do this.

"You'll be fine. I was taught how to shoot by one of the best snipers in the Marine Corps. Trust me, I know what I'm doing."

"You might, but I have no idea what I'm doing. What if I shoot you?"
He laughed. It was pure sex to her ears . . .

"That would be pretty hard, considering I'm standing right behind
you. I tell you what, how about we do the first one together?"

Asher pressed in closer, molding every inch of his body against her
back. His spicy, masculine scent enveloped her along with his arms,
his hands overlapping hers on the butt of the gun. He lowered his
head over her shoulder to see the target from her view and readjusted
her aim, a little higher and to the left. "Now, I'm not going to touch
the trigger. That's all you. When you're ready, squeeze it—slow and
easy. Don't pull it or jerk it, you'll throw off your aim. Remember, it's
going to recoil and it's going to be loud, but I want you to know what
it sounds like. Otherwise, if you don't know what to expect the noise
can be disorienting.

"All right . . ."

He turned his face into her neck and drew in a slow, deep inhale.

Her nerve endings began to tingle. "Asher?"

"Um-hmm . . ."

His low, throaty response sent a rush of desire flooding through her.
"You're distracting me," she scolded, tipping her head a little farther to
the side and inviting his kiss. She knew she shouldn't be encouraging
this, but he felt so incredible, it was hard to resist.

"You just smell so fucking good. What is that?"

"Lavender," she laughed. "But I think we're getting off topic here."

"Right." He cleared his throat and readjusted their aim, one last
time. "Sorry. As I was saying, everyone has an NRP, a natural respiratory
pause. That's when you want to take the shot."

"Okay."

"Now take a few deep breaths to relax, clear your thoughts, and
focus on aiming; then slowly exhale. When your lungs are almost
empty, pause your breathing and squeeze the trigger."

Easier said than done. Especially with the thoughts running through her head right now. "Okay." She tried to focus and squeezed her nondominant eye closed.

"When you're ready . . ."

She lined up the back two sights with the front one and pointed the barrel at the target twenty yards away. She felt more confident with Asher helping her, and did as he instructed. Breathe in, breathe out . . . breathe in, breathe out . . . breathe in, breathe out . . . pause. She squeezed the trigger.

Boom!

The gun went off, kicking back in her hands. The concussive blast of power that flowed through her was amazing. She'd never touched a gun before today and she certainly never expected to enjoy it. But after feeling so much fear these last few weeks, the helplessness and vulnerability that came with the inability to protect herself, this was . . . an unexpectedly empowering experience.

The recoil wasn't as bad as she'd been expecting. Asher had chosen his smallest-caliber gun with the slimmest grip. It was still a little large for her hand, but he'd said it would work all right. The blast was deafening, though. The only thing she could hear was a high-pitched ring that took a few moments to fade.

"I did it!"

Asher took the gun and was holstering it behind his back as she turned to face him. "I hit the target!" She beamed, throwing her arms around his neck for a celebratory hug. "It wasn't a bull's-eye, but at least I didn't completely miss it."

His arm slipped around her waist and he chuckled at her excitement. Perhaps he thought she was going a bit overboard, but he indulged her anyway. He couldn't possibly understand what doing this meant to her. Asher was giving Quinn her power back. He was teaching her to protect and defend herself. It was a gift she hadn't realized she needed, or wanted, until the moment she'd squeezed that trigger. But then again, maybe he understood her better than she gave him credit for, because the look of pride reflecting in his gorgeous eyes was enough to stop her heart.

"See, it wasn't as bad as you thought, was it?"

"It was scary, but it was also really fun."

"I knew you'd like it. With a little practice, I'll turn you into a sniper in no time."

She nudged him with her elbow and laughed. "Now you're teasing me."

He gave her a playful wink. "Stick with me and I'll have you doing all kinds of stuff you never thought you'd enjoy."

She busted out laughing at his assured and totally inappropriate remark. "Oh, you think so, do you?" In the days they'd spent together, Quinn hadn't been given much opportunity to glimpse Asher's wicked sense of humor. But today, something about him was different. He was more at ease with her, sweeter . . . attentive. Maybe deep down a part of him was still worried she'd try to leave and he was keeping a closer eye on her. Or could it be possible that he'd been telling her the truth and last night had meant something more to him than she'd wanted to believe? Dare she open her heart up enough to hope? She was having a hard enough time as it was sorting out her own emotions without second-guessing his. She needed to take it slow. Time would tell what this was budding between them.

"Yep," he said with the arrogant confidence she'd come to secretly adore. "After lunch we'll start your riding lessons."

Wait. "My what?"

"Horseback riding lessons."

That was *not* the kind of bareback she'd been imagining them doing. "It's the only way to get to my cabin."

"Can't I just ride with you?" She'd never been on a horse in her life and she wasn't sure she wanted to learn by climbing the side of a mountain on one.

"The hills are too steep in places and both our weight could throw the horse's balance off. Don't worry. I'll teach you the basics and Jack will do the rest. Let's take it one step at a time and focus on getting you proficient with a handgun first. We'll worry about keeping you in the saddle later. I've got some earplugs for you." He reached into his pocket and pulled out a small package.

"Thanks." She took them and opened the wrapper. "I'm glad we're doing it again. Practice makes perfect, right?" She balled up the soft foam and stuffed it into one ear.

He looked so incredibly gorgeous standing there smiling down at her, she nearly caved to the temptation to throw her arms around his neck and kiss him. "Sweetheart, we can keep doing it as long as you want to."

Her breath stalled in her lungs at the sexy rasp in his voice. Did he mean the shooting or was he giving her an open-ended invitation? Because there were a lot of things she wanted to do with Asher Tate.

———

Quinn was a natural markswoman. After two hours under his tutelage, she was shooting better than some of the guys who'd spent weeks in the corps. She was averaging a kill-shot accuracy of eight-five percent. Not bad, not bad at all . . .

She needed to learn how to protect herself. As much as he wanted to, it was unrealistic of him to think he could be with her every second of every day. With the likelihood that she'd been found, he wasn't taking any chances with her life. He hoped he was wrong and his brakes had just failed, but in his gut he knew the truth.

When he'd first suggested she learn to shoot, he'd been worried at her hesitancy. He knew a measure of comfort would come over time, but time was a luxury he didn't have right now. Quinn needed to know her way around a gun—like, yesterday. Thank God she was a remarkably apt pupil. He cursed himself for not putting one in her hands sooner, but looking back wasn't going to help them now. What he needed to focus on was teaching her to defend herself—that, and getting her the hell out of here.

Quinn fired the last round and the slide stayed open. She pulled out an earplug and turned to look at him. A big grin that almost brought him to his knees graced her beautiful face, and holy hell, the things he'd love to do to her from there. Her brow was raised, requesting his approval.

"Nice shooting . . ." He nodded toward the clustering near the center of the target. He'd had her practicing at a variety of distances, but it was more likely that if she needed this gun, she'd be firing it at close range.

Watching Quinn confidently handle his gun was hot as hell, and he'd spent the last couple of hours hard as fucking granite. If she hadn't called their night together a mistake, he'd be tossing her over his shoulder right now and treating her to an encore.

"Reload your clip," he told her, keeping his tone all business when his mind was on anything but. He grabbed a handful of bullets from his pocket and watched her as she double-checked the chamber like he'd taught her before releasing the clip. She took the bullets from his hand and quickly fed them into the clip like a pro. After returning it to the grip with a firm click, she grabbed the slide and chambered a round.

"Should we spend another clip?"

Listen to her, talking like a pro. How fucking sexy was that? "Why don't we take a break and get some lunch."

"That sounds good."

When she handed the gun back to him, he shook his head and dropped on bended knee before her.

"What are you doing?" Her eyes got big and she took a wary step back.

Her reaction caught him off guard until he realized what this must look like to her. "Stop it," he said, catching her pant leg and dragging her back toward him. "What do you think I'm going to do? Propose?"

She blushed. "No . . . It's just . . . not every day a guy drops to his knee in front of me." Then she mumbled, "Bad memory is all . . ."

His gaze shot to Quinn's, his grip on her pant leg tightening. He told himself it was to keep her from retreating, though it was a hell of a lot more than that. "What did you just say? Quinn, were you married?" Because that would actually explain a whole hell of a lot—her general mistrust of the male population as a whole, for one.

"I don't want to talk about it, Asher. Will you . . . just get up?"

"No. Not until you answer the question." He was starting to get pissed. He wasn't used to this pussyfooting around. He'd commanded his own team of Special Forces soldiers for eight goddamn years and when he asked a question, he expected a fucking answer.

She tried to tug her foot free but he wouldn't let go. She must have realized the only way either of them was moving was if she gave him the answers he wanted, because she exhaled a sigh and reluctantly dragged her violet gaze back to his.

"I was never married. I was engaged. Briefly."

Fuck. "How long ago?"

"Two years."

That's how long it'd been since she'd had a lover. Was her fiancé the last guy she'd been with before him?

"What happened?"

"I said I don't want to talk about it, and seeing you down there is bringing back a lot of really painful memories. Will you please just get up?"

Asher rolled up her pant leg and took the gun holster from his waistband. He focused on strapping it to her ankle, wishing he could get his hands on the guy who had hurt her. It was a struggle to calm the tide of jealousy crashing against the banks of his self-control. Someone had obviously hurt her—badly. He holstered the gun at her ankle and pulled her pant leg over the weapon before standing.

"This is yours now. Keep it on you or within reach at all times. Think of it as your new best friend. You don't go anywhere without it."

He stood and headed back to the house, frustration gnawing in his gut. It annoyed the hell out of him that after what they'd been through, done together, she still wouldn't open up and let him in. Her refusal to talk about something that was clearly a very raw and painful wound stung more than he cared to admit.

He thought he'd broken down her walls—thought they were moving past the I-don't-trust-you phase in their relationship. Then again, he was probably being a huge fucking hypocrite because he wasn't exactly anteing up the information on his past either. Though he seriously doubted she was responsible for killing scores of people, so it wasn't exactly tit for tat.

As he headed toward the house, the alarm on his cell began to beep. Someone was pulling up the driveway. "Get to the house," he told Quinn, shooting a glance at her over his shoulder. She was still several paces behind him. At the sound of a vehicle pulling up, he quickened his steps to intercept it but he was too late. As the KJTC News 8 van came to a stop, the side door slid open, and out poured a reporter and cameraman.

"Asher . . . ?"

He could hear the mixture of fear and apprehension in Quinn's voice as she came up behind him. "It's all right, Quinn. Go in the house."

She looked reluctant to leave him, and that moment of hesitation was all it took for her opportunity to escape to slip by.

Fuuuck . . .

CHAPTER

25

Asher stepped in front of Quinn and reached back, pressing his hand to the small of her back, pulling her in close behind him, and shielding her from the woman charging them like a bull seeing red. She recognized the woman from what little news she'd been able to watch. Danielle Rogers was a lead reporter for the local KJTC News 8 station. At first Quinn thought they were here for her. Had her story gotten out? How had they found her? Quinn's heart shot into her throat as a rush of panic squeezed tightly. She crowded closer to Asher, hiding behind him as he put himself between her and the news crew.

"Mr. Tate, Mr. Tate . . ." the woman called out. Two cameramen flanked her and Quinn was pretty sure she was going to have a panic attack right then and there.

It took her a moment to realize it was Asher the ravenous vultures were after—not her. But the relief she felt was a momentary blip because then the questions started flying at him.

"Mr. Tate, what's your reaction to the jury's decision to give Peterson life without parole?"

"No comment," he told her, continuing toward the house, but the woman and a cameraman followed him, walking backwards to block his way, the microphone vacillating between the reporter and being shoved in Asher's face.

"Did you know Peterson had been under psychological care since being discharged from the army?"

"No comment."

"What's your company's screening process for hiring ex-military officers?"

"No comment."

"Do you feel at all responsible for the Nisour Square massacre? Do you think your testimony at Peterson's trial could have affected the outcome?"

"No goddamn comment," he growled.

She kept firing the questions at him faster than he could answer them, not that he seemed to have any intention of doing so. All he kept saying was "no comment." But there was only so much he could do. Quinn knew he was pissed—could feel his anger reverberating off him as he kept moving them toward the house, keeping a tight hold on her.

She wished she could help him, but this reporter was tenacious. Not at all like the gentle, composed, mild-mannered woman that she appeared to be on TV. And then she saw Quinn, and the questions turned personal. This woman was hungry for a story and obviously had no intention of leaving until she got one.

"Who's the woman with you?" Giving up on getting any information from Asher, she turned her attention to Quinn. "What's your name?" she asked, shoving the mic at her. "Are you romantically involved with Mr. Tate? Does it bother you that he is debatably responsible for the murder of seventeen Iraqi civilians and officers?"

Asher snapped. He shoved past the news crew, giving Quinn an unimpeded shot up the stairs to the back door, and released her with a brisk command. "Go!"

She raced for the door as he turned on the reporter.

"That woman has nothing to do with this. Now get off my goddamn property!"

Quinn wasn't through the door thirty seconds before Asher charged in behind her, whipping it shut so hard she was surprised the glass didn't shatter. Outside, she could hear disgruntled murmurings, and the muffled slamming of the van doors. Neither of them spoke as the engine started and slowly began to fade into silence. If that was the kind of shit he'd had to deal with the past few months, no wonder he'd gone into seclusion. Was this a glimpse of what her life would be like when she released her story? Perhaps she had no idea what she was getting herself into. Asher was right. This wasn't going to be as simple as pressing the send button.

"Well, if your assassin didn't know where you were before, he's sure as hell going to know by six o'clock tonight. Fuck!" He jacked his hands through his hair and restlessly paced the kitchen.

"You think they'll show my picture?"

He stopped and looked at her. "Quinn, the cameras were rolling every second we were out there. It won't take them long to figure out who you are, not with the face recognition technology they have. Go start printing out whatever articles you haven't been able to get through yet, and gather all your notes. Pack whatever you want to bring with you because we probably won't be coming back."

Ever? She wanted to ask but refrained from voicing the question. This was just temporary, anyway, she reminded herself. As much as she loved it here, this wasn't her home. And she'd been prepared to leave it all behind this morning. But she hadn't wanted to go then either, and it was easier to make tough decisions when you were doing it to protect someone you cared about. The thought of leaving and never coming back intensified the dull ache in her chest.

She nodded and turned to head upstairs before he could see the tears already burning her eyes. She'd never been a crier, but these last twenty-four hours had put her on an emotional roller coaster and she was wishing like hell she could get off. This issue with the media was a complication neither of them needed right now.

Asher rounded the table and caught her wrist before she could leave. Just the feeling of his strong, sure grip was enough to push her over the edge. What would she do without him? What would happen to them when this was over? Both were questions she shouldn't be thinking about right now. They had more important things to be concerned with, like staying alive, yet she couldn't stop the questions from invading her mind.

"Hey." He stopped her, tugging her back around to face him.

She wiped away a tear before it could fall and met his stare with what she hoped were dry eyes.

"I know this hasn't been easy on you, but we're going to get through this. *You're* going to get through this. You're a strong woman, Quinn, and braver than you give yourself credit for."

Maybe she shouldn't be doing this—she was probably only making an impossible situation worse—but she slipped her arms around his neck and hugged him tight. When his arms came around her and squeezed, she soaked in his strength like a dry sponge tossed into the ocean. "You make me brave. I don't know what I'd do without you."

"You'd survive," he told her. "Because that's what you need to do. This is bigger than you or me. The world needs to know what's happening to those children over there. You have the power to stop it, and I have no doubt that you will."

———

He couldn't believe they were still alive. Tate's truck was lying at the bottom of a mountain for fuck's sake. He'd been so sure Tate and Summers were in it. How in the hell had they walked away from that unscathed? He'd planned so carefully, strategized and waited—biding his time for the perfect moment. They never should have survived. Right now he should be in Turks with a Mai Tai in his hand and his cock in some whore's mouth. Instead, he was holed up in a tree with a stick up his goddamn ass.

And now things had just gotten even more problematic because there was a fucking news van in Tate's driveway. This wasn't good, not at all. They didn't stay long but that didn't matter. It wouldn't take but a moment to undo all his hard work. He watched the media van pull out and head south. Training his scope on the license plate number, he committed it to memory.

That reporter had seen Quinn. No goddamn way they hadn't caught her on tape. If they discovered who she was, this could all blow up in his face by the evening news. Fuck, the last thing he needed was the police figuring out where she was and compromising his mission.

He'd hoped to have this over and done with before the conclusion of the Peterson trial, and he would have too, if last night had gone according to plan. But that was the thing about staging an accident—it wasn't as easy as pulling a trigger. There were some variables that were just out of his control.

Unfortunately, with as much press as Peterson's trial was getting, this was probably just the beginning of the barrage of media that would no doubt be knocking at Tate's door. His window of opportunity to kill Quinn was quickly closing, and this Channel 8 bitch was one more complication he didn't need right now.

After slipping the strap of his rifle over his shoulder, he descended the tree he'd been sitting in all afternoon. He made his way to his car and, after depositing his gun in the backseat, climbed inside and pulled out to follow the news van.

CHAPTER

26

"Quinn, come in here, you've gotta see this . . ."

Oh, no. The knot of dread tightened in her gut. Whatever Asher was calling her away for couldn't be good. She'd just finished hitting print on one of the last articles she wanted to read. It was about the CGRN's expansion into territories of Haiti that had higher civil unrest. Hopefully this article would make mention of the US or military support, because she knew the CGRN wasn't going in there alone. Once she got her notes and discovered the name of that security team, she could start cross-referencing them and hopefully begin connecting the dots. Perhaps the link to Attorney General Mark Madison was the military team instead of the CGRN. That would certainly explain why her research hadn't yielded any results so far.

The printer sucked a page into the feeder and began its monotonous left-to-right grind. One would think that as high-tech and sophisticated as Asher's computer, software, and security were, he would at least own a laser jet. For crying out loud, at this rate she was going to be at this half the night.

Sliding her chair back from the kitchen table, she stood and stretched, rubbing at the low ache in her back as she headed into the living room where Asher had on the six o'clock evening news. When she entered and saw the TV, she abruptly stopped, staring at the photos of the news crew who'd been there earlier. The pictures changed to a live scene of a news van lying at the base of a ravine, looking like a crushed milk carton. Quinn caught the last few lines of the news announcement: "The accident is still under investigation. The cause of the crash is unknown at this time."

"Asher . . . that's the news crew that was at the house earlier today."

"I know . . ." His attention was fixed on the screen.

"They're dead."

"Yep."

She came around the couch and stood beside Asher, sharing her time between watching him and the TV, though she wasn't sure what she was hoping to see from him. His expression, as usual, gave nothing away, but his eyes . . . That was where the truth could be found, and it chilled her to her core. "You don't think it was an accident, do you?"

"I think that I'm not the only one who didn't want your face plastered across the evening news, and this was one hell of a way to kill a story."

"Are you serious? You think the guy who's after me did this? But why?"

"I don't know. Maybe he doesn't want any attention being drawn to you. Maybe he figures it'll raise more questions if you turn up dead later. But I don't believe in coincidences. For whatever reason, that bastard didn't want Danielle Rogers running her story."

"What if it *was* just an accident?"

"You mean like ours was?"

Quinn's stomach lurched. If Asher was right, then that news crew died because of her. When would this stop? Guilt swamped her; her chest felt like there was a tight band around it preventing her from taking a full breath. She thought of Emily, her friend never far from her mind and always in her heart. Tears pricked her eyes. How many more lives would be stolen by this monster? And then the thought hit her, one she was sure hadn't been missed by Asher if the tight clench of his jaw was any indication. She might be a little slow on the uptake, but she was getting there.

"If you're right, then that means he was watching us today. That's the only way he could have known the news van was here."

The broadcast flipped to the national segment of the news and Asher shut the TV off, tossing the remote onto the couch. He shifted and gave her the full weight of his stare as she willed herself to breathe . . .

"Yep."

It was hard hearing him put voice to her fears. But one thing she knew about Asher was that he didn't sugarcoat anything. And honest to God, his next words were the proof that just about put her over the edge.

"Quinn, I think you need to prepare yourself for the possibility that this could get worse before it gets better. I'm going to do everything in my power to keep you safe. That's why I'm getting you out of here."

She nodded numbly, not sure what else to say as fear slowly unfurled inside her. It wasn't until she learned about the death of that news crew that Quinn realized somewhere deep down, she'd still been holding on to a scrap of hope that those brakes failing had really just been an accident. Asher was right; the accidents were no coincidence. It had only been a week . . . She thought she'd be safe longer than this. How had he found her so quickly? She'd been so careful . . . A blast of adrenaline hit her veins, her whole body humming with it as her mind raced for answers. How would he have known to look for her here? How?

She thought back to the night she came home and found Emily, replaying her steps through her mind. With vivid detail they came rushing back . . . Emily's ringtone playing on the other side of the door, the wood against Quinn's palm as she pushed it open . . .

Her heart hammering inside her chest, just like it was now, as dread became a living, breathing monster that wrapped its insidious claws around her throat and squeezed until she couldn't breathe. She wanted to run but her feet moved forward, propelling through the debris scattered all over the floor. Broken glass crunched under her feet, which ground to a halt when she entered the living room. Emily . . . Bile surged up her throat, the bitter burn an all too familiar feeling. She'd stumbled back, slipped on something beneath her boot, her ankle twisted, she fell . . .

Oh my God . . . that's it!

"Quinn . . . Quinn!"

She wasn't sure how long Asher had been calling her name. She hadn't seen him rise from the couch but here he was, standing in front of her, hands gripping her shoulders, concern etched in his otherwise stoically handsome face.

"Quinn, talk to me!"

"I know how he did it. I know how he found me. How could I have missed it? He's known I was here all along. I ran right into his hands. I have to call Violet!"

She tried to turn to go get his phone, but Asher wasn't letting her go. "Stop." His voice was firm but calm. "Tell me what you're thinking before you make any calls. How did he do it, Quinn? How do you think he found you?"

"The wedding pictures. They were all over the floor. He saw us together in those wedding pictures. And you're practically famous right now. He's going to know who you are. Of course I'd go running to you for help. I can't believe I didn't see it before now. I was so upset when I found Emily that it didn't even dawn on me. He knows who Violet is, Asher! If we leave and he can't get to me, he's going to go after her."

"Fuck . . ." He let her go and dragged his hand through his hair. "I'll call Nikko. Let me talk to him first. We need a plan before you tell Violet. I don't want you to scare her."

Quinn nodded numbly. Her hand was shaking as she raised it to cover her mouth.

"What about your parents? Where are they?"

"In Rome—they're in Rome until the end of the month."

"They should be safe there. It'd take too long for him to find them and then get back here to you. This guy went through a lot of trouble to make that hit yesterday look like an accident. He doesn't want your death raising any red flags. It'd be taking a big risk to go after anyone connected to you. But that doesn't mean Violet shouldn't be careful. He knows he's running out of time, and desperate people do desperate things."

———

"You all right? You've been staring at a blank screen for the last five minutes."

No, she wasn't all right. Nothing about this nightmare was all right. Quinn glanced up from the computer and met Asher's concerned stare. He was pocketing his cell after hanging up with Nikko. She didn't appreciate him retreating to the bedroom to make his call. He must have been talking about things he didn't want her overhearing. It bothered Quinn that he was keeping secrets from her. By the occasional sound of his raised voice, she'd venture a guess that the conversation could have gone better.

"I spoke with Nikko—I missed his call earlier. The SD card arrived today. He agrees we need to be careful. Violet's clearing her work schedule and he's taking her and Raven to Kauai for a few weeks until this is all over. Apparently, a friend of his owns a house there. We're meeting them in Salt Lake City to get the card, and they're flying out from there."

Asher came around the table and took a seat beside her, turning her chair to face him. She could tell he had more to say, but seemed to be hesitant or unsure how to proceed. His delay spiked her anxiety. It wasn't like Asher to be at a loss for words.

"What is it? What aren't you telling me?"

He studied her a little while longer, each second that passed ratcheting her panic higher and higher. "Asher, what is it?"

He scrubbed his hand over the back of his neck and exhaled a frustrated sigh. "He wants to take you with him."

Now the pieces fit into place. Asher wanted her to go and didn't know how to tell her. The thought of leaving him was like a lead weight settling in her gut. She didn't want to do it, but in her heart she knew it was the safest thing for him. Yet, now how much more risk would she be putting Nikko and her sister in by leaving with them? She was damned if she did and damned if she didn't. Well, she certainly wasn't going to make this any more awkward for him.

"And you want me to go . . ." she finished when he didn't speak.

His brows grew tight in a scowl that made her want to move back. "Fuck no, I don't want you to go. But I'm afraid you're going to leave anyway, especially after the way you nearly ran out on me this morning. And Nikko's being insistent. He thinks I'm being selfish to keep you with me. Hell, who knows, maybe I am. But goddammit, I don't want to let you go."

Her heart soared with his confession, and then plummeted just as fast. "Not yet . . ."

So he *was* planning to let her go. And then he kept talking and her heart just continued to spiral with disappointment. "I started this with you and I intend to see it through."

So it was his sense of duty that kept him honor-bound to her—not his heart. She should have known better than to expect any declaration of love from him. If she knew what was good for her she *would* go. It sure as hell wasn't going to be any easier to leave him when this was over. But nothing had changed; she couldn't put her family at risk by staying with them. Asher was going to be stuck with her. She just wished he wanted to be with her for the same reasons she wanted to be with him.

"I don't want to go, Asher."

The look of relief on his face helped convince her she was doing the right thing. He really did want her to stay, and not out of any obligation to Nikko or he wouldn't have been fighting so hard to keep her with him.

"When are they leaving?"

"In the morning. I have some things to finish buttoning up around here and I want to do some checking on security at the hotel. If it looks good, we might be able to lie low there for a few days. I was thinking if you have Internet access, you might be able to finish your story sooner. "

Lord, she hoped so, and knowing that Violet and Raven were safe was like a giant weight being lifted from her shoulders.

"All right. I'm already packed. I just have a few more articles to print out. I can read them in the car."

"That's good. I'll get supper started while you finish up."

He stood and Quinn grabbed his hand before he could walk away. Asher stopped and waited for her to speak. "Thank you . . . for everything. I can't tell you how much I appreciate what you're doing for me."

Something in his eyes softened. They wandered over her face as he reached up and gently brushed the back of his knuckles against her cheek. When his thumb slowly traced her plump bottom lip, her heart kicked inside her chest and that familiar spark deep inside lit, the flame fanned by the memories of being in his arms. He looked like he was going to kiss her.

"You're so beautiful . . ." he whispered, his naturally smooth voice rough with emotion. "It tears me up to think there's someone out there that wants to hurt you. I promise you, Quinn, someway, somehow, I'll find a way to end this."

Her lips parted as her eyes flittered closed, inviting his kiss. When his lips brushed against her cheek chastely, her eyes opened in surprise. Asher took a step back, but she wasn't sure if it was for his control or hers, because she was about to throw herself at this man—pride be damned.

"I'll get supper started." He turned away, heading to his respective corner of the kitchen.

Quinn watched in contemplative silence as she shared her time between printing articles and watching Asher cook for her. He'd refused her offer to help. Instead, he'd made her a lemon iced tea and spiked it with a shot of vodka. It tasted delicious.

Asher must have felt her eyes on him because he glanced at her over his shoulder. "You're awfully quiet. What are you thinking about?"

She wasn't sure she wanted to tell him. It was nothing deep or profound. After the stress of the day, her mind had chosen a safer topic to meditate on. It was strange she would think of Spencer as such, but all things considered . . . "I was thinking that you're the first man who has ever cooked for me. First grilled cheese and now this."

His brow arched in surprise and then another look came over his face that she couldn't interpret. It probably wasn't the answer he'd been expecting her to give, but it was the truth.

"What?" she asked, feeling a little self-conscious for her honesty.

"I'm really sorry I had to be your first."

An unexpected bubble of laughter burst from her throat and she slapped her hand over her mouth to cut it off. It felt so odd, maybe even inappropriate, considering their situation. But it also felt good, like a pressure valve inside her had released.

Asher's joining chuckle helped loosen some of the tension inside her. "There are a lot of firsts I could give you that would be a hell of a lot better than this experience is going to be."

"I bet there are . . ." Another chorus of laughter escaped her. "Spencer never did anything like this for me, so even if it's terrible, it's still going to be amazing."

Asher stopped cutting the potatoes and stood there watching her for a moment.

"What?" she asked, starting to feel self-conscious under the scrutiny of his stare.

"Do you do that often? Compare me to your ex?"

She shrugged, feeling her cheeks heat with embarrassment. It was something she'd found herself doing a lot lately. She didn't really know why, except maybe because Spencer was the first man she'd ever loved, so he subconsciously became the bar by which she measured all other men. And she was quickly discovering she'd wasted the last two years of her life heartbroken over a man that didn't even come close to measuring up against the one standing across the table from her right now.

"It's not much of a contest," she replied softly.

Asher's brows pulled tight. "I'm not sure how I should take that. You're either paying me a compliment, or insulting the hell out of me." Then under his breath he grumbled, "I never know where I stand with you."

How would he react if she told him the truth? That she was falling in love with him? Would he even believe her? She wasn't sure she had the courage to speak those words again, even if they might be true. Loving someone in secret was way safer than telling them how you felt and opening yourself up to rejection. Instead, she opted for the safe answer.

"Asher, I think you know there isn't a man in the world that could compare to you. Have you seen you? You're a gorgeous man. And not only that, but you're saving my life. For crying out loud, you're even cooking for me."

Asher set the knife down and exhaled a sigh that sounded a lot like frustration. Planting his palms on the table, he leaned closer. "It's not your gratitude I'm after, Quinn. Why can't you understand that?" His voice was a husky caress that woke the butterflies in her stomach.

"Then what do you want from me?" She sounded a little breathless, which wasn't surprising because her heart was hammering inside her chest so hard she couldn't breathe.

He studied her for a moment longer without answering. Everywhere his eyes touched, her flesh heated. Never in her life had she experienced this kind of visceral response to a man. It was exciting and terrifying at the same time, because whatever this was, it was beyond her control.

"I want you to admit that last night wasn't a mistake."

Was he serious? He didn't realize what he was asking of her. Why did it matter so much to him, anyway? Stubbornly, she dug her heels in. "I can't do that. But I can't promise you I wouldn't want to make the same mistake again."

"Careful, Quinn," he warned. "I'm not a man that you should be toying with. This isn't a game."

Then what was this to him? Did she want to know? Could she handle the truth? After a moment, she answered him with more unguarded honesty than she'd shared with anyone in a long time. "Asher, I'm scared."

He gave her an odd look that bordered on frustration. "Quinn, I'm doing everything I can to protect you."

"No, you don't get it, Asher. Who's going to protect me from you?"

He dropped into the chair across from her, looking . . . defeated. Snagging the vodka on the table, he forwent the glass and tipped the bottle back. She tried not to notice the strong, corded muscles of his neck working the liquor down his throat. Setting the bottle down with a loud *thunk*, he pinned her with a determined stare. "I would never hurt you, Quinn."

"Maybe not physically . . ."

"What the hell happened to you? What could that bastard possibly have done to take a woman any man would be lucky to have and so utterly break her?"

It wasn't easy for her to talk about, but there was something about Asher, about this moment, that made her want to open up to him. She wanted him to understand her, to see the woman behind the prickly image she projected, because that wasn't her . . . not anymore. And fortunately for her, she'd had just enough liquid courage to give her confidence a much-needed boost. "There's not that much to tell, really. I met a man and we fell in love. He promised me the world, and naïvely I believed he would deliver it. He was very rich, but that didn't matter to me—I didn't care about his money. His family didn't feel the same way. When they found out that he proposed to me, they threatened to cut him off if he went through with it. Bottom line, he cared more about his bank account than he did me. He made his choice. It wasn't me. End of story."

Quinn added another splash of vodka to her iced tea and took a healthy swallow. Asher watched her, his face void of all emotion except for that little muscle ticking in the corner of his jaw.

"He left you?" Asher asked when she didn't continue. "Just like that?"

"Just like that." Despite the years that had passed, it was still painful to talk about, but the memories were more like phantom pains now than true loss. Huh . . . was that because sitting here with Asher made it impossible to regret anyone else? When she thought she'd lost him over that cliff, the heartache she'd felt was far more devastating than anything she'd gone through in the last two years.

"You loved him a lot."

It was more a statement of fact than a question, and yet she still found herself nodding. "I did. He broke my heart and it devastated me to the point that I swore I'd never put myself in a position to let that happen again. The sad thing is, I honestly believe that he loved me too, just not enough to fight for me."

Asher reached across the table and took her hand in both of his, giving it a comforting squeeze. Without a flicker of hesitation he looked her in the eyes, and what she saw in his made her chest tighten uncomfortably.

"I will always fight for you, Quinn. No matter what . . ."

And she knew, without a doubt, that he would. Asher was a man who was fiercely loyal. But she wanted more than just his protection, she wanted his heart. Quinn cursed herself for being too big of a coward to tell him that.

CHAPTER

27

gotta say, for a guy that professes not to be able to cook, this is delicious."

Asher's brow rose in wry amusement as he watched Quinn across the table and chuffed a masculine grunt. "You must be drunk."

She laughed. "I am not. This is really good." Quinn forked some vegetables from her tinfoil pouch and chewed thoughtfully. "You know, you're nothing like you pretend to be. Why did you let me think you were such an asshole at Violet's wedding?"

He shrugged, tipping back his beer. "Why did you let me think you were such a shrew? Perhaps you and I aren't so different after all. I don't like letting people in any more than you do."

"Why not?"

A simple question with a very complicated answer. "Over the years, I've buried too many people I cared about. After a while, it's easier to just keep everyone at a distance."

Saying nothing, she studied him until he became uncomfortable beneath the scrutiny of her stare. He was afraid if she looked too close, she wouldn't like what she saw. Clearing his throat, he set his fork on his empty plate and went to rise. Quinn's hand shot out and grabbed his wrist, stopping him.

"No, let me. You cooked. It's only fair I clean up." She stood and took both their plates, carrying them to the sink. Her back was to him as she grabbed the dish soap and began filling one side with hot water.

Her hair was pulled up, giving him the opportunity to admire the long delicate column of her neck. As she worked, he'd occasionally get brief glimpses of the mark he'd left there last night as the ends of her pale hair flirted with her shoulders. His hands ached to twist into all that silk . . .

She was so beautiful it almost hurt to look at her, and with that thought, the uncomfortable fullness in his chest returned. It seemed to be a constant presence whenever he was around her. The desire to be close to her, the instinct to protect her, and the need to be buried deep inside her were a heady combination, making it difficult to remain seated.

"It makes me nervous when you stare," she commented into the sink, not bothering to turn and confirm he was checking her out. She just knew . . .

"Why is that?"

She shrugged.

"I have a dishwasher, you know," he told her, changing the subject. Quinn wasn't a woman who seemed to put a lot of emphasis on her looks. She was surprisingly shy, and he'd be lying if he said it wasn't totally fucking adorable.

"That's all right. It'll only take a few minutes to get these washed up. I don't mind."

Asher stood and went over to the drawer, pulling out a dish towel. He wasn't doing himself any favors sitting there gawking at her. His cock was so hard it strained the confines of his jeans. Busying his hands was about the only way he was going to be able to resist keeping them off Quinn. As she rinsed the first plate and set it in the drying rack, she shot him a glance over her shoulder and smiled. The unguarded radiance hit him in the solar plexus like a sucker punch. The effect this woman had on him was unbelievable.

It baffled him that any man could choose wealth over her. She was priceless—in every way—his little diamond in the rough, though admittedly she'd been caked in a lot of coal when he'd met her. But since he'd buffed her, good Lord, could she shine.

Asher grabbed a plate, dried it, and put it away in the cupboard. Stepping close behind her, he reached around her side to grab another. Every time he stepped near her and reached for a dish, her light floral scent teased his nostrils and he found himself drawing in deeper breaths. She tensed as if anticipating his touch, but he was careful to avoid contact. Handling Quinn was like courting a skittish colt—it took time and some finesse.

He'd imprinted enough foals at his dad's ranch to know the importance of getting them used to your touch, your scent. And he'd certainly imprinted the hell out of Quinn last night. Now, getting her comfortable with him and luring her in—that was going to be the challenge. Making her crave his touch and come to him for it, that's where the real work began.

And whether Quinn admitted it or not, she wanted him. The energy sparking off her was lighting up his own nerve endings like the Fourth of July. His blood heated in his veins until he was sure they would turn to ash. It was sweet torture, being this close without touching her. But he didn't dare, for fear that once he started he wouldn't be able to stop. Until Quinn came to him, until she was ready to admit her feelings, he wouldn't take her into his bed again.

But he'd be lying if he said he wasn't tempted to press in close and taste the graceful curve of her neck, to nip that reddened spot just below her ear. The sight of his mark on her filled him with possessive satisfaction that sent a wave of hardcore lust rolling through him. His mouth watered at the thought of all the other places he craved to taste her, to leave his mark. His cock twitched in eager agreement, straining against its denim prison.

Fuck, who was imprinting whom here?

Grabbing a handful of silverware, he stepped over to the drawer and dried them with meticulous precision before placing each piece back in its proper tray.

"Did you always want to be a journalist?" he asked, needing to get his thoughts anywhere other than where they'd taken him. Out of the corner of his eye, he saw her startle from her own thoughts. God help him, he'd never wanted to be clairvoyant more than he did at this moment.

"What? Oh . . . umm . . . no. Journalism is more of a hobby. I never intended it to be my career. I did it as a way to help cover the costs of traveling. I actually have a degree in cultural anthropology."

She "actually" had a hell of a lot more than that, but he wasn't going to tell her he knew that. And "degree" wasn't exactly accurate either. A master's in cultural anthropology with a minor in English, literature, and writing at twenty-eight was pretty fucking impressive.

"I went to Europe after Spencer and I broke up. Out of country, out of mind, right?" she laughed, but there was no humor in it. "Anyway, I began writing little pieces over there and selling my stories to newspapers and magazines. I discovered I enjoyed living abroad and experiencing different cultures. Violet's wedding was the first time I'd been back in the States for two years."

"That's a long time. You're not close with your parents? They didn't mind you traveling alone?"

"We're not particularly close. Growing up, they were always more concerned with their careers than Violet or me. We were an afterthought to them. I doubt they would have realized I was gone if I hadn't told them I was going."

So Quinn had been abandoned by more people than just her ex. No wonder she had trust and attachment issues. "What about your sister, Violet?"

"We were close growing up. She practically raised me. But after she married her first husband, we began to drift apart. He was a dick."

Asher chuckled. "That's what I hear."

"I feel bad about not being there for her through her divorce, though. She needed me and I let her down. That's a regret I've had to learn to live with. I'm glad she met Nikko. He seems like a really great guy."

"He is. How many years total have you been traveling?"

"A little over two. I studied several languages in college, which made getting around a lot easier. Freelance journalism has been, well, an adventure . . ."

"How many languages do you speak?"

"Five, fluently. It's kinda my hobby. I'm like a savant when it comes to that stuff. How about you? Do you know any other languages?"

"Some German."

"Really . . . ?" She rinsed a pan and handed it to him. "Haben Sie in Deutschland verbringen viel Zeit?"

"Yeah, not that well . . ."

She laughed and reached into the sink, pulling out the plug before stepping over to him to dry her hands on his towel. "I asked if you spent a lot of time in Germany."

"Some." He squatted down and opened the lower cupboard. "There's a large US medical base in Rheinland."

She braced her hip against the counter, watching him slide the pan onto the shelf. "Tell me something you know."

Tipping his head, he looked up at her and said, "Können Sie mir sagen, wo der nächste bar ist?"

Her laughter rang out, light and melodic. It was like an audible caress stroking his cock.

"So you learned the important stuff. I can see how knowing directions to the closest bar would be a necessity."

He chuckled and rose to his feet, finding her closer than she had been a few moments ago. "Hey, I know more than that. Du bist die schönste Frau, die ich je gesehen habe."

"Ah . . . so you can flirt in German as well. Why am I not surprised?"

He shrugged. "It's not flirting if it's true." Closing the last bit of distance between them, he reached up and tucked a fallen lock of hair behind her ear. "You *are* the most beautiful woman I've ever seen."

———

All trace of teasing left his eyes and what she saw in its place sent a rush of heat all the way to her toes. Quinn's pulse quickened as Asher's fingertips lightly grazed her cheek. It was all she could do not to close her eyes and tip her face into his hand. Like a moth to flame, she was drawn to this man, helpless to resist the unexplainable pull he had on her. Gone was his cavalier, flirtatious grin. The arrogant mask he so easily wore was replaced with raw, honest need.

"Ich fürchte, ich verliebe mich in dich." She whispered the confession with no fear he'd understand what she'd said.

He studied her a moment, and she could see his mind working to translate her words. "What did you say?"

Her nerves failed her. She shook her head and took a measured step back. "It doesn't matter. It's getting late and I have some work to finish before I go to bed." Quinn tried to brush past him but he blocked her path. He stepped closer; she moved back. Another step; she countered . . . and so they danced across the kitchen until she found herself connecting with the counter, the rounded granite edge digging into her lower back.

"What did you say?" he pressed, planting his palms on the countertop and caging her in, his eyes searching hers for answers. "What is it that you're so afraid of?"

So he'd understood that part. His German was better than he'd let on. Asher was close—so close she could feel the heat radiating off his powerful body, smell the spicy, masculine scent of his skin, and see the colorful pattern of his eyes that were so beautiful she could get lost in them if she wasn't careful.

Her heart ached, the pain in her chest competing with another ache deep in her core. She'd be a fool to let this man ease either one of them again, because when this was over and he walked away, it was going to break her.

He crowded closer. Her nipples tingled with anticipation as her heart rioted inside her chest. His gaze fell to her lips and she instinctively moistened them with the tip of her tongue. She could feel his breath brush over them—taste the faintest vapor of alcohol.

He was going to kiss her . . . and if he started, she'd never want him to stop. Her mind raced to give him the one answer that would free her from his cage. "I said I'm afraid you're going to break my heart . . ." It was the closet she would come to confessing the truth. Ducking under his arm, she raced for the stairs before she did or said anything else she would regret.

She was nearly to the top of the stairs when she heard Asher's growled curse echo through the main floor. A loud thud sent a tremor through the upper level that she felt beneath her feet as she raced into the bedroom and shut herself behind the door. Pressing her back against the cool, hard panel, she closed her eyes and tried to catch her breath.

She needed to go to bed—go to bed and forget what just almost happened. Quinn pushed away from the door, grabbed one of Asher's T-shirts from his top drawer, and began to undress. Her clothes were already packed and downstairs by the door. She left her shirt and pants on the floor in a pile and reached behind her back to unclasp her bra. Her breasts were still heavy from arousal, nipples tight, peaks sensitive. She was just pulling the soft cotton over her head when the bedroom door flew open, slamming against the wall.

Quinn let out a startled yelp and then took one apprehensive step back into the center of the room. Asher's brows were drawn tight, his jaw clenched, and those eyes were throwing off sparks she could feel burning her all the way across the room. His breaths were coming so fast, his wide, muscular shoulders heaved with the effort. He looked seriously pissed off and hotter than hell.

"That is *not* what you said, Quinn."

His voice was barely more than a growl—deep, throaty, and like sandpaper against skin that already felt too tight for her body.

"How do you know?"

"Google Translate . . ." He reached behind his head and yanked off his T-shirt, dropping it on the floor as he prowled toward her. Quinn's breath caught in her lungs at the display of all that smooth, sculpted muscle. Excitement warred with panic as he advanced with the determined grace of a predator cornering its prey. "You're afraid you're falling in love with me. Are you serious?"

He didn't sound pleased.

"*That's* how you decide to tell me something like that?"

Her heart felt like a jackhammer inside her chest. She stepped around the side of the bed to put more distance between them. "Asher, I . . . I'm sorry. You're right, I shouldn't have said that to you."

"You're damn right, you shouldn't have," he growled, stopping near the foot of the bed. "It's bad enough you lied about it. You tell someone you love them, at least have the fucking courtesy to say it in English."

Before she could respond, his gaze dropped to her chest and something flashed in his eyes—shock, terror, rage . . . ?

"Quinn, get down!"

Asher dove for her. His chest slammed into hers so hard, the air whooshed from her lungs as the ping of breaking glass sounded off to the left and a *thunk* echoed in the log wall behind her. Both sounded before she hit the ground, and pain exploded through her body. If Asher's hand weren't cradling the back of her head, she probably would have been knocked unconscious. The weight of his body knocked the wind out of her. She felt like she'd been hit with a ton of bricks. It took her longer to realize what was happening than it did him. With his body still covering hers, Asher reached above them, into the top drawer of his nightstand. And that's when she saw it, the red beam cutting through the bedroom.

Holy shit, someone just shot at me . . .

Even as the sound of gunfire rang out two more times, her mind still refused to believe it. Asher cursed. When he yanked his arm back, he had a gun in his hand. He raised it up over the mattress just far enough to fire off two shots, one at the ceiling light, and the other into the lamp across the bed. Glass shattered and the room suddenly went black. The red beam swept the room again, this time more slowly. She couldn't breathe. She wasn't sure if it was panic or Asher's weight crushing her, but air refused to enter her lungs.

Asher shifted above her. His hand slid to the side of her face and she had to choke back a frightened sob. "Are you all right?" he demanded. "Were you hit?"

She shook her head but then realized he wouldn't be able to see her respond. "No," she rasped, forcing what little air she had out of her lungs. "I'm okay. What about you?"

"I'm good."

She saw the red beam sweeping above them again and swallowed back a cry of terror. They were trapped in here behind the bed.

"Quinn, when I tell you to go, I want you to run for the bathroom and get into the shower. The bullets won't be able to penetrate both sets of logs. You'll be safe in there."

He shifted above her and she grabbed his arm, her nails digging into his biceps. "What about you?" she cried. God, this wasn't happening. Not again. She couldn't lose him again . . .

"I'm going to find this fucker and kill him."

His weight left her and Quinn pressed her hand over her mouth to hold back her broken sob. She could hear the closet door open and then close. The red beam was across the room, but getting closer to the closet by the second. He opened the French doors leading out onto the deck and the light swung left. A hail of bullets rang out, slamming into the wall above her. Quinn's scream was muffled by her hand.

"You all right?" Asher called across the room.

"Yes . . ." She could barely get the one word out past her trembling lips.

"Get ready to run, Quinn. On my go."

As soon as the red light swept over her again, Asher yelled, "Now!"

Quinn jumped to her feet and it sounded like she'd stepped into the middle of a war zone. Automatic gunfire erupted in the bedroom. It was deafening—disorienting. Quinn forced one foot in front of the other and ran for the bathroom, relying on memory to get her there because she couldn't see anything but blackness. The moment her foot hit the tile, she slammed the door shut behind her and ducked into the shower. And there she sat. On the floor, knees hugged tight to her chest, as she prayed to God He'd spare Asher's life one more time.

CHAPTER
28

When that red light centered on Quinn's chest, Asher's life literally flashed before his eyes, because if something happened to this woman, he wouldn't be able to live with himself. Time momentarily stopped, and so did his heart, before racing at a tempo that made his head spin. Acting on pure instinct, he'd dove for her as the bullet whizzed past them, slamming into the log wall. It'd come so close to hitting her, he'd felt the breeze against his back.

And this was exactly the reason why he kept guns stashed all over his house. You never knew when you were going to fall under attack. Needing to even the playing field, he'd retrieved his .45 from the night-stand and shot the lights. After making sure Quinn was all right, he timed the sweep of the red light scope and raced for the closet, grabbing his AR-15.

Rage burned through his veins like liquid fire as he beat feet to the glass doors and swung them open. The movement sent that red beam his way as an explosion of bullets tore through the bedroom. Quinn's muffled scream gutted him.

"You all right?" he called in the darkness, wishing to God he could see for himself.

"Yes."

She didn't sound all right. Not by a long shot. "Get ready to run, Quinn. On my go." He fixed his eyes on the beam shining out from the woods and flipped his modified AR to full auto. Aiming into the woods at the red light, he yelled, "Now!" and pulled the trigger, sending a hailstorm of bullets into the trees.

Once Asher was sure he'd given Quinn enough time to escape to the bathroom, he let his finger off the trigger and stepped back. Pressing his shoulder and hip against the wall, he waited for return fire, but there was only silence.

Could he have gotten lucky and hit that fucker? Or was this a trap to lure him into the woods? It didn't really matter. Either way, he was going out there. This was going to end—right fucking now. Tracking and vetting out Taliban insurgents was his specialty. He wouldn't have any trouble hunting this bastard down.

"Quinn, I'm going outside," he yelled through the door. "Stay right there until I come get you." He didn't wait for her to respond before sliding the strap of his assault rifle over his shoulder and charging down the stairs. He stopped in the kitchen and opened the safe. Slipping on a flak jacket, he pocketed another clip for his .45 and grabbed a pair of night vision optics before heading out the back door and into a world of bright green.

The night vision could be disorienting if one wasn't used to it. But his Recon Six team did most of their ops at night—this is what he was used to, what he trained for. Asher cut across the yard and into the woods. As he made his way south, he strained to hear over the high-pitched ringing in his ears. His eyes scanned the woods for movement—nothing. As he drew closer to the area he'd shot up a few minutes ago, Asher slowed his steps, doing a visual sweep of the trees. If that fucker was still out here, that's where he'd be. In the trees . . . waiting to ambush him. A twig snapped up ahead, maybe twenty yards, but the woods were too thick to see through. Shouldering his weapon, ready to fire, he advanced with cautious steps. A few paces later, Asher spotted a black blotch on the ground at the bottom of a large oak. Squatting down, he swiped his fingers through the moisture and rubbed them together. Blood. Perfect, now he had a trail to follow.

His pulse slowed and his breaths steadied as he drew the crisp night air deep into his lungs. He searched the woods for movement and spotted something just ahead. There . . . to the south. Someone was running toward the road. His unequal gait slowed his progress, giving Asher time to raise his AR, flip it to semi-auto, and fire off a few rounds. The trees were an unfortunate obstacle. The figure stumbled as he was hit, then returned fire. Asher ducked behind a tree as bullets whizzed past him, plunking into trees around him.

When the gunfire stopped, Asher took off after him. The bastard was on a hobbled run. Weaving in and out of trees, he raced through the woods. Up ahead, the man broke into the clearing and a moment later Asher heard the slam of a car door and the roar of an engine. Tires squealed on the asphalt as Asher ran toward the road. He cleared the trees just in time to see taillights flashing a taunting farewell as the car braked, fishtailing as it took the sharp corner, disappearing into the night.

"Fuck!"

—

Time stopped for Quinn as she sat on the cold tile floor, staring into darkness. Her ears still rang from the gunfire. Her heart hammered against her ribs so hard, her chest hurt. She could hardly breathe past the terror choking her. She'd almost been shot . . . And this very moment, Asher was out there with a killer.

Gunfire erupted again and she jumped. This time she didn't even try to hold back her startled cry. Minutes felt like hours as she waited for Asher to return. Where was he? Why was it taking so long? What if he was injured? He could be lying out there wounded, or dead in the woods for all she knew. She wasn't sure how much longer she could sit here, yet what other choice did she have? It was pitch black outside. She could hardly go running out into the night. Maybe if she could find a flashlight . . .

Quinn got to her feet, too panicked by what-ifs to heed Asher's warning to wait for him here. Her knees nearly buckled, she was shaking so badly. Stretching out her hand, she felt in the darkness for something to hold on to and took a hesitant step. Her fingers brushed against the edge of the sliding glass door and she braced herself against it. Her heart was pounding so fast, a wave of dizziness washed over her.

She made her way toward the door and once she orientated herself by locating the knob, Quinn ran her hand over the logs to find the light switch. She clicked it on and opened the bathroom door. The ambient glow shone into the bedroom, allowing just enough light to see the way to the stairs. Fear for Asher dwarfed her fear for her own safety. Her self-preservation instincts were running at an all-time low as she rushed down the stairs, images of Asher lying wounded in the woods flooding her mind. The weight attached to her left ankle was a comforting reminder that she wasn't defenseless.

Rounding the stairwell, she headed for the kitchen to find a flashlight. Quinn began opening and closing cupboards and drawers. Nothing. There had to be one somewhere—maybe under the sink? She opened the doors and squatted down to begin her search when the door beside her opened and slammed closed. She spun around, meeting Asher's glare.

"What are you doing down here? I told you to wait upstairs."

Relief flooded through her. She didn't care that he looked as pissed off as a grizzly bear. Quinn shot to her feet and rushed him, throwing her arms around his neck. "Thank God you're all right. I heard gunshots. And you were gone so long. I thought . . ." She couldn't say it. Her thoughts were too terrible to put voice to.

Asher set his rifle down and wrapped his arm around her, holding her tight. "You thought you were going to rescue me?" Emotion roughened his voice. "Fuck, Quinn. You can't keep doing stuff like this. You're going to get yourself killed."

"Me? Asher, you ran off into the woods, chasing a killer."

He exhaled a breath that sounded a lot like frustration and tried to release her, but she wasn't ready to let him go yet. She clung on tighter.

"Quinn, look at me."

Asher reached up and untangled her arms from around his neck, then tipped her head up to meet his stare.

"*I* am a killer. I am just like him." Asher pointed out the window toward the woods.

She shook her head in denial. How could he say that? "You're nothing like that monster."

"Yes, I am. The only difference is I'm *your* monster."

"Why are you saying this?"

"Because I don't want you believing I'm something that I'm not. I don't *ever* want you putting yourself at risk for me again. Do you understand me? I'm telling you this because I have done a lot of horrible things in my life, and I don't want you falling for an illusion. And I sure as hell don't want you dying for one."

Quinn was speechless. She watched in numb silence as he moved past her and headed for the pantry cupboard. Is that really what he thought? That he was no better than the man who'd almost shot her tonight? That he could even think something that was so far from the truth gave her a glimpse at the demons Asher must live with, and it made her heart ache.

She knew there wasn't anything she could say to convince him otherwise, and wondered if he would have even told her this much if it wasn't for her German confession. She hadn't intended to tell him she was falling for him, in English or any other language. It just sort of slipped out. His reaction hadn't been what she'd expected—at all. And then everything had gone to hell after that, so she had no clue where things stood with them now. She feared she'd changed the dynamics of their relationship, and not necessarily for the better.

Asher pulled the door open, and she realized it was no cupboard at all. He spun through the lock combination and opened the safe. She was surprised to see the cache of weapons, though she wasn't sure why. Asher had guns stowed all over the house; it only made sense he'd have a gun safe. But this wasn't just a gun safe. She didn't recognize half of the weapons she was looking at, but knew there was no way this stuff was legal.

He put the rifle away, returned the handgun, and pulled the clip from his pocket before removing his vest. It wasn't until he reached up to hang it on the hook that she noticed the crimson stain running down his side.

"You're bleeding!"

Asher lifted his arm a little higher and tipped his head to look down at his side. A three-inch gash cut through the flesh covering his ribs. He didn't seem nearly as alarmed as she was. Her observation was confirmed when he shrugged and said, "It's just a scratch. It'll be fine."

Dismissing the wound, he relocked the safe and closed the door. His negligence pinged Quinn's temper and her feet were in motion before she realized they were moving. "It's not 'fine,'" she snapped, taking hold of his arm and guiding him over to the chair. "And your 'scratch' looks like it needs about ten stitches." She tugged him to sit and he complied with an exasperated huff.

Her emotions were running high and she wasn't in any mood for his macho bullshit, though she suspected this was no show of masculine prowess. Asher really didn't care he'd been shot, and he seemed to think her doting attention was unwarranted. Well, too damn bad. If he insisted on running through the woods like Rambo, he was going to have to put up with her mother-henning him a little bit.

"Where's your first aid kit?"

"Under the sink in the bathroom."

She could hear the annoyance in his voice and wasn't sure if it was residual from finding her downstairs instead of where he'd told her to wait, or if he really didn't want her messing with his injury. Either way, she ignored the attitude and left to retrieve the kit. He was wrong. He was nothing like the man who'd tried to kill her, and she so badly wanted to make him see that. Though she knew words wouldn't convince him, Quinn was determined to prove it to him. Maybe Asher's dad was right and he needed her more than she realized.

———

As she disappeared down the hall, Asher exhaled a breath he didn't realize he'd been holding. With the immediate threat to Quinn temporarily neutralized—because with the size of that blood trail, there was no chance in hell that bastard was coming back tonight—it was as if the pause button had been lifted and the rocket of emotions that had sent him flying up those stairs after her were back with a vengeance. The last thing he'd expected her to say was that she was afraid she was falling in love with him, "afraid" being the key word here, because she *should* be afraid—very afraid. Despite his feelings for Quinn, her reciprocation of those emotions was not in his action plan, and that put this equation on a whole other mathematical level he wasn't sure he could solve.

Just because he had feelings for the woman, it didn't mean he was any good for her. She'd already had her heart broken once; he'd be damned if he was going to be the bastard that did it a second time. And yet, even as his mind told him all the reasons this was a terrible idea, his heart was doing a happy dance. He wanted her. He wanted her love, her affection, even if he didn't deserve it. She made him want to be a better man, and wasn't that the hallmark of a good woman? According to his dad, it was. As Asher sat there bleeding down his side and soaking the waistband of his jeans, he couldn't bring himself to give a shit because all he could think about was taking Quinn upstairs and making her his.

She didn't know how he felt about her and he wasn't sure what his next move here should be. This was all new, uncharted territory for him, and the circumstances that had brought them together only complicated it further. What if Quinn was confusing gratitude with love? What if, when all this was over and the threat element was gone, she decided she didn't really love him after all and went her separate way? Unlike her, he'd never had his heart broken before, and he wasn't keen on the idea of gaining the experience. Perhaps slowing this down and seeing where it went was the wiser move. Although, he wasn't sure he could slow it down enough to stay out of her bed. Even if that was exactly what he should be doing.

"I found it," she announced, carrying the box into the kitchen and setting it on the table. She also had a brown bottle and a few towels in her hand.

Quinn took the seat beside him and scooted it so her knees fit between his spread ones. She was all business, with that adorable frown of concentration on her face. Some women might be queasy at the sight of blood, and his was a good trickle running down his side, but not Quinn. She wasn't squeamish at all, and damn if that didn't earn her some more respect points.

The bullet wound could have been a lot worse than it was. He hadn't even realized he'd been grazed. Adrenaline was a wonderful anesthetic. He could have just taken a shower and let the water beat the laceration clean. It wasn't bad. He wasn't sure why he was indulging her now, other than he kinda liked the idea of her fussing over him, and he really liked the idea of her putting her hands on him. Just the anticipation of it dulled the burn in his side. The residual high of a firefight certainly didn't hurt either. He had a lot of testosterone pumping through his veins right now, and he wanted to work that shit out on Quinn.

"Lift your arm," she told him, all serious and no-nonsense. She was so damn cute it wasn't even funny.

Biting back a grin, he did as he was told, angling his side toward her.

Her scowl deepened. "Asher, this cut looks deep. Maybe you should go to the emergency room and get this stitched up."

"I'm not going to the ER. Gunshots are mandatorily reported, and I don't want the police involved. Besides, this isn't the first time I've been shot, and it's by far not the worst. Just bandage it up. It'll heal."

He could tell by the look of disapproval on her face that she didn't agree, but also knew arguing with him about it wasn't going to get her anywhere. "This is going to burn," she warned before popping the cap off the brown bottle. Holding a towel beneath the laceration, she doused the wound in peroxide.

Ho-ly shit! She wasn't kidding. Asher clenched his teeth to keep the profanity roaring through his mind from spewing out of his mouth, and sucked in a slow deep breath.

Quinn shot him a nervous glance. "Are you all right? I've got to get it cleaned out. I don't want this to get infected."

"It's fine," he gritted. "Do what you have to do."

And she did, dousing his side with another round of liquid fire. This time he was ready for it and the flash of pain wasn't as bad.

"Do you think he's still out there?" she asked quietly as she worked. Pink foam rolled down his side and onto the towel she held against his ribs.

"No. He's gone. I watched him drive away. He was limping pretty badly when he ran off. By the size of his blood trail, there's no way he'll be back tonight."

"You shot him?"

Asher nodded.

"You think he's coming back?" She carefully dried the wound and used the towel to clean the blood off his side. After opening a package of Steri-Strips, she pulled the skin together and began applying the tape.

Asher watched her work, wishing he could tell her that the threat was over. But he knew better. Unless the shot was fatal, the bastard would be back—and he was pissed. "Not right away . . .You're safe for now." But that was the only guarantee he could give her.

CHAPTER

29

"You probably shouldn't walk around barefoot in case I missed any glass."

The bedroom glowed with the filtered light coming from the bathroom. Quinn watched from her spot on the bed, appreciating the flex and roll of Asher's muscles as he swept the shards of glass into a pile.

The log walls behind her were chipped and gouged from the bullets. Wooden slivers littered the floor next to her. "I can do this, you know. I feel terrible about what happened to your house."

He stopped sweeping and turned to look at her. Quinn's stomach did that little flip and her pulse quickened. He hadn't put a shirt on yet, and the only thing covering his torso was the 4 x 4 gauze taped to his right side. His jeans sat so low on his waist she could see the V of muscles, drawing her gaze lower. Damn, he was impressive . . . and he'd saved her life—again. There just wasn't anything sexier than that.

Asher muttered a curse under his breath. "You gotta stop looking at me like that, Quinn."

"Why?" The question was out of her mouth before she could stop it. Yeah, she really needed to get herself one of those filters.

His grip on the broom handle tightened, making the muscles in his arm flex. "I already told you why."

She climbed off the bed and stood in front of him, her nerve endings tingling with anticipation. Despite her claim that what happened between them was a mistake, it was one she wanted to make with him again, and again, and again. Never in her life had anyone come close to making her feel the way Asher did. She had no idea what her body was capable of, but she had no doubt he would show her.

He hadn't brought up her German confession and she was glad for it, though she knew it was only a matter of time. He might have tabled the topic for now, but she knew Asher well enough to know he wouldn't let it go. Especially considering his reaction to his discovery—damn Google Translate.

She was so shaken by what had happened tonight that right now, all she wanted was the safety and security of being in Asher's arms again. And she was desperate enough that she'd do or say just about anything to get it. "Are you really not going to touch me again until I tell you it wasn't a mistake?"

He studied her for several seconds before exhaling a ripe curse and scrubbing his hand over his shadowed jaw. "Quinn, I'm not so sure that it wasn't."

His confession rocked her. This was not what she was expecting him to say. So he was having second thoughts about her? About them? Her confidence wavered and she took a step back, needing to put a little space between them, but he caught her wrist before she could get any farther.

"I don't like what this is doing to me, Quinn—what *you're* doing to me. And yet I don't think I can stop it. One night with you and I'm in fucking knots. I knew this was going to happen. That's why I told you I had to stay away. I need to be focusing on protecting you, keeping you safe, and all I can think about is getting inside you again. I can't stop wondering if the rest of you tastes as sweet as your kiss . . ."

His confession emboldened her, the raw honesty in his voice enflaming her until Quinn's need drowned out the last remnant of her inhibition. She slipped her arms up around his neck and whispered, "There's only one way to find out . . ."

He grumbled something that sounded like *fuck me* but she couldn't be sure. His hands settled on her hips, preventing her from arching up to her tiptoes so she could reach his mouth for a kiss.

"Quinn, we need to talk about what happened earlier."

And there it was. She should have known her reprieve would be short-lived.

"Did you mean what you said? Are you falling in love with me?"

She wanted to deny it. But she owed him the truth, and more than that, she owed it to herself to be true to her heart—even if he didn't feel the same way in return, even if she walked away from this with her heart shattered . . .

"Yes." It was a softly spoken confession, but one all the same.

Something flashed in his eyes, surprise maybe, but it was gone before she could be sure. Damn this darkness that shadowed his handsome face.

"You don't really know me, Quinn."

"You saved my life—twice. Your secret is out. You're not a dick after all."

He laughed, not a ha-ha-that-was-funny laugh, but more of a deep, throaty rumble. One she felt in all the places she wanted him touching her right now.

"It's okay." She gave his chest a patronizing pat. "Your secret is safe with me." Riding to her tiptoes, she whispered against his lips, "I won't tell anyone."

His hands on her hips forced her heels back to the floor and she exhaled a frustrated harrumph.

"Quinn, I'm serious."

"So am I."

"I think you're confusing gratitude with love."

"I'm not a child, Asher. Don't patronize me. And I know you better than you think. You keep your life neat and orderly right down to the mitered corners of your bed because you have a compulsive need for control. But it's only an illusion. What's inside here"—she pointed to her temple—"is beyond your control. And that torments you. You show the world a carefree, arrogant playboy, but that isn't who you are at all. You're a man with a strong moral compass who values his family above all else. You're selfless to a fault, and you'd give your life for someone else's without hesitation. You live by a code of loyalty and honor, but you also have walls and you try very hard to keep others out by pushing them away and by being a jackass."

She gave him a self-satisfied smile, confident in her assessment, but it was his turn to talk now, and she was not prepared for what he had to say.

"I've killed eighty-six people. Some of them were guilty of nothing more than being in the wrong place at the wrong time. I suffer from insomnia. I risk my life so easily because it means nothing to me. Don't try to make me into some hero, Quinn, because I'm not one."

Her smile fell as she listened to his confession. It shocked her speechless and was, no doubt, intended to do just that, yet every word struck a chord inside her and somehow made her fall more deeply in love with him.

"Recklessness is not heroic." He tapped his temple with his first and second fingers. "I'm fucked up. That's why I got out of the Special Forces. I couldn't take it anymore. Right before I left, I watched a kid get blown to shit by a guy in my unit who thought he was wearing a bomb. When Slater realized his mistake, I was wearing his brains until I could get back to base and shower that shit off. I drink—a lot—because it's the only thing that quiets the noise in my head. I'm probably an alcoholic and just don't fucking know it."

"Are you done? Because it isn't working."

"What isn't working?"

"Your list of all the reasons I shouldn't care about you. You're not scaring me away. If you don't want me then just say so, but your past is what has made you who you are, and I refuse to condemn you for it. It sounds like you're doing a bang-up job of that all by yourself, though. You're a good man, Asher, even if you refuse to see it. I wouldn't be alive right now if it wasn't for you.

"Asher, war is ugly, but sometimes it's a necessary evil. And because of it, people die. It's just the hard, painful truth. But because of it, people also live—because someone like you fought for their freedom. You count the lives lost, but you will never know the number of lives that were saved because of you, because of your sacrifice."

She slid her arms around his neck and stared into eyes that held a prism of pain, suffering, and regret. "I don't expect you to be perfect. God knows, I'm far from it myself."

Asher slipped his fingers into her hair, his palms cradling her face as he searched her own eyes. She wasn't sure what he was looking for, but hoped whatever it was he would find it. "Quinn, you're so fucking perfect it makes my heart ache to look at you."

Her heart swelled inside her chest a little more. Before she could tell him how wrong he was, he dipped his head. Her protest was replaced with a soft moan as his lips pressed against hers, his tongue taking the kiss deeper. He lifted her T-shirt and broke contact with her mouth only long enough to pull it over her head before he was back to kissing her with all the finesse of a freight train. In one fluid motion, he lifted her, carrying her those few steps to his bed. As he laid her out on the mattress, his gaze devoured her, sending a shiver of anticipation coursing through her veins.

His fingers curled into the lace of her panties and he slid them down her legs. Asher dropped to his knees at the side of the bed and her heart began to hammer with excitement and a little bit of fear when she realized what he intended to do. No one had ever touched her like this, kissed her . . . there. Spencer had been too "civilized," telling her that kind of intimacy was for the uncultured, the uncouth.

Asher slipped his hands beneath her legs and gripped her hips, dragging her closer. Her knees clamped together as another wave of anxiety washed over her.

"What's the matter, Quinn?"

He pressed a kiss to her knee, his strong, calloused hands slowly traveling up the sides of her thighs. Raw need warred with inexperience. "I've never done this before . . ." She felt her cheeks heat with her confession. What she wasn't expecting was the look of surprise that quickly morphed into total ravenous delight.

"Never?"

She shook her head.

"You have no idea how much it pleases me to know that whoever had this body before me had no idea what the fuck they were doing with it."

It did?

"It looks like this is going to be a day of firsts for you after all. I guarantee this is going to be a hell of a lot better than my cooking."

A nervous laugh escaped her and his deep, throaty chuckle joined in.

"Let me see you, sweetheart."

He coaxed her knees apart. Hesitantly, she let them fall to the sides, never feeling more vulnerable and turned on at the same time. Asher's response to the sight of her was what excited Quinn the most. Something dark and powerful, possessive and primal flared in his eyes. Maybe Spencer was right and this did bring out the animal in men, but civilization was overrated.

The way Asher looked at her had Quinn's heart pounding inside her chest . . . like she belonged to him and him alone—and he had no intention of ever letting her go.

"Fuck, you're the most beautiful thing I've ever seen." He gently brushed the back of his knuckles over her slick folds. She flinched at the contact, unaccustomed to being touched. A jolt of pleasure shot into her core, making her muscles involuntarily contract. "Absolutely perfect . . ." he whispered.

He took each of her ankles and placed her heels on the edge of the bed as he coaxed her thighs farther apart. Being open to him like this was unlike anything she'd ever experienced before. It almost felt more intimate than sex, because the way he was watching her stripped her completely bare of all pretenses, all walls, all remnants of self-preservation. And she knew, beyond a shadow of a doubt, that the moment he put his mouth on her, he'd capture not only her heart, but her very soul. And perhaps that was what scared her most of all. There would be no going back after this. From this moment on, she would irrevocably belong to this man.

But all her thoughts, all hesitancy, fled from her mind with the first touch of Asher's tongue against her flesh. The sensation was so powerful, so startling, her hips jerked up off the mattress. He chuckled at her startled gasp, the throaty rumble vibrating against the bundle of nerves at the top of her sex. His hands slid beneath her bottom and he dragged her back to him. Against her heated, sensitive flesh he whispered, "Ich fürchte, ich bin in der Liebe mit Ihnen fallen auch."

Wait, what? But then his mouth was on her again and Quinn's thoughts detonated. Her mind was so lust drunk it took her a moment to translate what he'd said into English and she couldn't string two words together to form a coherent response to his confession.

I'm afraid I'm falling in love with you too . . .

CHAPTER
30

The automatic doors slid open, granting him access to Rocky Mountain Regional. The congealed blood in his boot squished with each step, making a loud sucking sound as he limped across the lobby. It wasn't the fire in his thigh that bothered him. Hell, he'd been shot before, and a lot more vitally wounded than this. The problem that had him seeking professional medical assistance tonight was the lack of an exit wound. The fucking bullet was imbedded in his thigh, and that damn thing needed to come out. If it wasn't for his little lead problem, he would have cleaned it out and bandaged it himself.

He'd erred tonight, and he was furious with himself. After his fuckup he deserved a hell of a lot worse than a bullet in the leg. He was damn lucky that was the only damage he'd taken. Using the red light scope had been a serious error in judgment and one that Tate had taken advantage of. Quinn had been alone upstairs, and he'd made the split-moment decision to use the red light on his scope. It made it easier to hit a moving target. He hadn't expected Tate to go barreling in there, or to reach her before he could get his shot off. But the light had given away his position, and he'd paid dearly for that mistake, hence the 30-caliber bullet in his leg.

"Can I help you?" the nurse behind the desk asked, her eyes dropping to his blood-soaked thigh.

He sure fucking hoped so, and a little more give-a-shit might be nice.

"I got a bullet in my leg. I need someone to take it out."

"You were shot?"

"Nah . . . it was put there by angel kisses. Of course I was shot. For fuck's sake, lady, quit asking me stupid questions and get me a goddamn doctor."

He'd spent the last four hours with his belt tied around his thigh while he drove to Denver for treatment. He needed to go to a Level 1 trauma center, someplace that saw this kind of shit all the time, someplace he'd blend in with all the other bullet wounds of the night. You show up in a small-town ER with a gunshot wound, people remember that shit.

Needless to say, he was short on patience, low on blood supply, and Nancy Drew over here was pissing him the fuck off.

"Step into my triage room." She indicated the area to her right and he limped over to the room. She slid the curtain closed behind them and sat across from him. "Tell me what happened." The nurse placed a blood pressure cuff on his arm and pulse oximeter on his finger. After she pressed the start button, the cuff began to inflate and she turned to type his information into her computer. "What's your name?"

"Collin Anderson." He rattled off the info on the fake ID he carried in his wallet—name, address, date of birth.

"How were you shot?"

"In the Hunger Games. That Peeta's a real dick."

Nurse Ratched gave him an *I'm not amused* scowl and went back to clicking away on the keyboard.

The cuff released on his arm and the machine began to beep— 89/60, heart rate 120. Great, he was going into shock. The nurse looked at the machine and a flicker of concern flashed in her eyes. That was more like it. About fucking time . . .

"Are you dizzy? Light-headed?"

"A little bit."

"How long ago were you shot?"

"Couple of hours."

"How much blood have you lost?"

"Enough that I'm here instead of at home watching *Dancing with the Stars.*"

She pulled on a pair of gloves before grabbing her trauma shears and slitting the side of his pant leg to get a look at the wound. A slow trickle of blood oozed from the entrance wound, but he'd be willing to bet once that belt was taken off his leg, things were going to change in a big hurry.

"Wait here." She returned with a wheelchair a moment later and motioned for him to get into it. He didn't particularly want to, but decided it was probably his best shot at getting back there and in front of a doctor anytime soon. He should probably play nice, sit his ass down, and keep his fucking mouth shut so he could get fixed and get the hell out of there.

CHAPTER
31

Quinn rolled over, searching for Asher in her sleep. She startled awake when her hand glided over the cool sheets instead of his warm, muscled chest. Where was he? How long had he been gone? Long enough for his spot to grow cold. Concerned, she lifted her head and glanced at the clock on the nightstand—3:00 a.m.

He'd told her last night that he suffered from insomnia. Were the ghosts of his past haunting him? Or maybe he was keeping vigil in case the killer decided to return. He'd seemed confident that wouldn't happen, but Asher wasn't a man to take chances. Either way, she needed to find him. He didn't speak of it, but she knew the Peterson trial was wearing on him. She hoped now that it was over, the media interest would die down and he could finally let the guilt go.

Unfortunately, as was the case with most things, they always seemed to get worse before they got better. Maybe with her help, he could put this behind him and focus on moving forward. But would that forward include her? She hoped it would—especially after Asher's confession tonight. He was falling in love with her . . . Just remembering his words sent a burst of warmth spreading through her chest, and then remembering what he did to her in the hours after that made the heat pool lower.

Quinn tossed the covers aside to go find him. She didn't want him sitting up all alone with nothing but his demons to keep him company. She found his T-shirt balled up on the floor and slipped it on. The air was cool and goose bumps prickled her flesh as her bare foot touched the hardwood floor. She rubbed her hands up and down her arms for heat as she headed for the hallway. From the top of the stairs, she could see the glow of the TV lighting Asher's profile. He sat on the couch, feet planted on the floor. His elbows were resting on his knees and his face was buried in his hands, fingers threaded into his hair.

She watched him a moment, unsure if she should go to him or back to bed. He didn't look like he'd appreciate the interruption. But then his dad's words returned to her mind and were all the encouragement she needed to take that first step. It creaked beneath her weight. He tensed, but didn't move beyond that subtle shift.

As her foot landed on the bottom step, Quinn's attention was drawn to the TV and her heart took a nosedive into her stomach. The red word "mute" lit up the top right corner of the screen as the closed caption played across the bottom. CNN was playing footage of a car heading toward a Jeep filled with what appeared to be American soldiers. The camera panned to a woman driving the car. A child not more than eight was sitting in the passenger seat beside her. They were in the middle of a city, a town square maybe. It was difficult to see because whoever was filming didn't have a very steady hand.

Someone got out of the Jeep and faced off with the car. The camera zoomed in on the man and Quinn's heart stopped. *Holy shit, that's Asher* . . . He was yelling something at the car, then turned back at his men and shouted something. Another man got out of the vehicle and stood beside him. Wait . . . was that . . . Jayce? He drew his gun and aimed it at the car. Asher said something to him, and if she had to guess, he was telling him to stand down, because the man lowered his gun, refusing to take his eyes off his target. The car was getting closer. Asher yelled something again, and in the background she could see Iraqi soldiers running toward them from a distance.

Movement in the corner of the screen caught her eye. The camera panned left just as another solider stood up from the Jeep and fired on the car. It exploded. The concussive blast knocked Asher and Jayce to the ground. Smoke and dust filled the screen, and by the time it cleared, they were in a full-blown firefight. The Iraqi soldiers were firing at Asher and his team, and the Americans were returning fire. The bodies of Iraqi soldiers and civilians, caught in the crossfire, were lying in the streets. Blood flowed like a river. Death was everywhere. A pyre of black smoke billowed from the car, skewing the view of the camera as breezy gusts blew smoke past the lens.

Then the camera fell to the ground and Quinn's hand flew up to cover her mouth, holding back her startled gasp. The camera's angle now turned to the side, half of the screen filled with the vacant stare of the cameraman, the other half filming the running of feet, stampeding past the dead man until finally the screen turned to static. She'd never seen the footage of the Nisour Square massacre before and wished to God she never would have.

Running across the bottom of the television screen was the headline *Rolland Peterson found guilty in Nisour Square massacre. Sentenced to life without parole . . .* The news footage cut to a man being led down the steps of a courthouse. His legs were shackled and his wrists cuffed. Cameras flashed as reporters swarmed him. His lawyer tried to shield him, waving the media back, but they were stuck to him like a swarm of bees.

Asher was still as a stone statue. Quinn wanted to comfort him, but she didn't know what to say. Even without volume, that footage said enough—enough to convict a man to life in prison. It made her heart ache to think about what Asher had gone through that day—being caught in the middle of that firefight and bearing witness to all that horror . . .

Quinn sat on the couch beside him and laid her hand on his back. He flinched at the contact—in surprise or rejection of the comfort she offered him, Quinn didn't know. She couldn't begin to imagine what he was feeling right now. What he'd been going through these past few months.

"Asher . . ."

"Don't, Quinn . . ." he cut her off, pressing the heels of his hands against his eyes. "Whatever you have to say, I don't want to hear it. There's nothing you can say that will ever make this all right."

"But it wasn't your fault . . ." She didn't have to know all the details to be convinced of that.

He hit the power button on the remote and pinned her with a hard stare. "Of course it was my fault. Those were my men, my responsibility. It was a setup. I fucking knew Peterson was a hotheaded son of a bitch who couldn't follow orders."

"What do you mean it was a setup?"

He stared at her in silence, as if he wasn't sure how much he wanted to say. She hoped he'd open up and let her in. She'd trusted him with her secrets. Would he trust her with his? "Please, Asher . . . talk to me," she encouraged. "I want to be here for you."

He took her hand in his and studied it, brushing his thumb over the fine bones. His touch wasn't intended to be sexual, but even this simple contact sent a ripple of warmth spreading through her veins.

He turned her hand over, palm up, and traced the lines as he finally spoke, seeming to need the distraction of something else to focus on rather than the memories that had played out in vivid detail across the TV screen just a few minutes ago. "The Iraqi government started hiring ex-military officers to train their soldiers. Tate Security was given a six-month contract to go over there and work with their new recruits. There were a lot of people who didn't want us over there. The government wasn't happy about us taking their contracts, and the insurgents didn't want the Iraqi military to get stronger. Personally, I believe a terrorist faction staged the assault by putting a woman and her son in that car. What were the chances that a cameraman just happened to be there to catch the whole thing on tape, or that he had ties to al-Qaeda?

"They knew we'd think there was a bomb in that vehicle. I told everyone to stand down, but Peterson fired on it anyway. The car blew up and killed that woman and child. Some Iraqi officers in the square saw what happened and before we knew it we were in the middle of a firefight. By the time it was over, seventeen people were dead. We were deported back to the US and faced criminal charges. Al-Qaeda got what they wanted—us out of there and no one training the soldiers."

"Did you tell anyone you think it was a setup?"

"I mentioned it during my deposition. But it's only speculation and nothing that can be proven. And it doesn't justify what Peterson did. He disobeyed a direct order and a lot of people died." Asher took a deep breath and cleared his throat before continuing. "Anyway, what does it matter now? What's done is done."

He shrugged and stood. Apparently, discussion time was over. Quinn didn't move. Tipping her head back, she looked at him. "Clearly, it still matters to you."

He shook his head. Fatigue etched the fine lines of his handsome face.

"When was the last time you slept?" She stood and cupped the hard angle of his jaw, searching his eyes that seemed more predominately blue than she remembered. The day's growth of stubble abraded her palm.

"I told you, I don't sleep—two, three hours a night. That's it."

"And what do you do with the rest of those hours? Torment yourself with regret?"

"I've got a lot to be sorry for . . ."

"And you've got a lot to be proud of," she countered. Rising to her tiptoes, she kissed him softly, letting her lips gently brush over his. "Come on, let's go back to bed. It'll be light soon." He didn't resist her when she took his hand and led him back up the stairs. She may not be able to stop the demons that tormented him, but she could become the lifeline for him that he now was for her. His dad was right. Asher needed saving just as much as she did, only the enemy he faced was himself.

CHAPTER

32

"When you said you were booking us a room, I wasn't expecting it to be an apartment." Asher opened the door for Quinn to step inside. She looked around the suite as she slowly made the tour. The kitchen and living room were separated by a long countertop with a row of bar stools tucked beneath the overhang. He followed her into the bedroom and set their bags on the king-size bed.

"I wasn't sure how long we'd be here and figured a little room to breathe might be nice." Asher had booked the room on a private floor and had a meeting scheduled with the hotel manager in a half hour to discuss security protocols and operations. The only way to access the top floor was with a passcode entered into the elevator. The room was locked via keycard that changed access codes every twelve hours, which would provide added security if, by some chance in hell, Quinn was found here.

Depending on how savvy her assassin was, his government access, and the technology readily available to him, Asher wouldn't put anything past him. Hopefully by the time Quinn discovered the connection she was looking for, Asher would have a plan to take the bastard out. The problem was finding him and protecting Quinn at the same time.

It sure would make things a hell of a lot easier if he knew whom he was dealing with. He'd been reluctant to involve anyone in the search before now, because he didn't want to lead the assassin to them by sending out queries. But now that the killer had found Quinn, that wasn't an issue anymore, and Asher had lot of DNA in his woods that could give him the answers he was looking for.

Aside from Quinn's safety, catching this killer was his top priority, and he needed to exhaust his resources because he could be damn sure the bastard was doing the same.

"I need to make a call before my meeting with security. You going to be all right here by yourself for a while?" He couldn't resist pulling Quinn against him and stealing a kiss. She yielded to the pressure of his lips so sweetly it was tempting to take it further. She felt so perfect, tasted so sweet . . .

Despite all the chaos and stress surrounding them, he never experienced such peace as when Quinn was in his arms. For the first time in his life, all the pieces of his puzzle were in place. She had a way of making the noise inside his head quiet, the guilt that lived inside his heart abate—even if only for a little while. It was a welcomed reprieve.

"I'll be fine. I'm just going to take a shower and then rest until Nikko and Violet get here."

But along with the surge of lust flaring inside him, there was also a niggling of guilt. Although beautiful as ever, Quinn looked tired. She wasn't sleeping well and he certainly hadn't done anything to help rectify that. She was proving a temptation too strong to resist and he couldn't seem to get his fill of her. "I'm sorry I kept you up last night. You need your rest." He pressed a parting kiss on her forehead and took a step back, putting some much-needed space between them so he didn't miss his meeting.

"I'm not complaining."

Her teasing grin held a lot of wicked promises, all of which he wanted her to make good on. A deep chuckle rumbled in his chest at the playful light in her eyes. He took another step back, making his way toward the living room. "You're going to make me late. I'll be back as soon as I can. My number is on the notepad by the phone. Call me if you need me for anything."

"I'll be fine. Don't worry about me."

Easier said than done. She gave him a quick kiss before heading for the bathroom and he left before his feet aborted their mission and decided to follow her instead. He pulled his cell from his pocket and scrolled through his contacts as he stepped into the living room and dropped into an overstuffed chair. As the line rang, he contemplated hanging up, but the call connected before he could change his mind.

"Asher . . ."

"Hey, Jax."

"What's up?"

Caution laced his brother's voice. He felt like an asshole for calling, or maybe more aptly, for not calling. He should make a greater effort to close the distance between himself and his brother. It wasn't Jax's fault that every time Asher saw his twin, it was like looking in the mirror at a better version of himself. His issues were his own and it was about time he got over them.

"I need a favor. I'm wondering if you can help me."

"That depends. Knowing you, you're about to ask me to do something illegal."

"Only mildly. Can you find out if any of the ERs in the area treated someone for a gunshot wound last night?"

"Oh shit, who did you shoot?"

"I don't know. That's what I'm calling you for. I need a name. Someone unloaded about a dozen rounds into my house and I'm not too happy about it."

"What the fuck? Why in the hell would someone do that?"

"Don't ask me questions I can't answer."

"Then don't ask me to put my fucking job on the line. Tell me what's going on, man."

Asher exhaled a frustrated sigh and closed his eyes, pinching the bridge of his nose, trying to stave off the headache he felt coming on.

He should have known this wasn't going to be easy. "I can't. Not yet. Look, Jax, this is important. I just need a name—"

Asher heard the resigned sigh on the other end of the line. "Hold a minute and I'll see if anything pops up in the department's database."

Asher sat in silence waiting for his brother to get back on the line.

"There was only one in the system—slow night, I guess. The report says a Collin Anderson was treated at Rocky Mountain for a gunshot wound to his leg. Police were called by the hospital staff for a mandatory report. By the time the officer arrived the guy was gone. Security footage shows the guy slipping out behind a couple leaving the ER fifteen minutes before the officer arrived."

The name settled in Asher's gut like a lead weight. The blast from his past unearthed memories he'd worked long and hard to keep buried. It had to be a coincidence . . . yet he knew it wasn't.

"Rocky Mountain is four hours from my place. He drove all the way to Denver? What are the chances?"

"Pretty damn good, if this is your man. It's the closest Level 1 trauma center to you. You walk into a small-town hospital shot up and people are going to talk. Maybe he lives in the area. Who knows . . ."

"You running the name?"

"Of course I am. It's coming up a fake. Belongs to a dead soldier— died in a firefight in Afghanistan."

"I know. I was there. Collin Anderson is the first Special Forces officer I lost in my recon unit."

"You're fucking kidding me . . ."

"I wish I were."

"You got a pissed-off soldier coming home from the war who's got a grudge against you? Blames you for his buddy's death?"

"There are a lot of people who've got grudges against me."

"Yeah, well, anytime you decide to fill me in, that'd be real fucking swell. I'm not keen on the idea of some bastard running around taking potshots at you."

It wasn't him this fucker wanted. But who in the hell was this guy because he sure as shit wasn't Collin Anderson. Why in the hell was he using the ID of one of Asher's men? "If you want to help me catch this bastard, his DNA is all over at the bottom of a large oak tree on the east side of my property, two-thirds of the way up my driveway and about twenty paces into the woods."

"Where are you at right now?"

"I'd rather not say. This cell line is supposed to be secure but I don't want to take any chances."

"Was Quinn with you? She all right?"

"Yeah . . . she's fine."

"She must be pretty shaken up if someone's trying to kill you."

He felt like an ass for misleading his brother, but he wasn't ready to tell him what was going on yet—not when he wasn't entirely certain himself. "We've both had better days."

"I'll try to cut out a little early and head to your place after work. I'm going to have to open a case file to get the blood sample processed. Who knows, maybe your shooter's got a record and we'll get lucky with a hit."

Wouldn't that be nice? But something told Asher it wasn't going to be that easy.

"Watch your six," Asher warned. "If he comes back there and finds you digging around, he'll be gunning for you. This guy's no fucking joke."

———

Quinn's heart leapt with excitement when shortly after her shower, she heard a soft, persistent knock on the door. She knew before looking through the peephole that her sister was outside. But just to be safe, she put her eye to the glass and saw Violet's face grinning back at her as she waved to the hole.

She quickly unlatched the door and pulled it open, then stumbled back when her sister plowed into her, throwing her arms around Quinn and squeezing until she couldn't breathe. "Quinn! I've been a wreck worrying about you! Are you all right?"

"I'm okay . . ." she assured her, returning Vi's hug with equal vigor. She didn't realize how much she missed her sister until Violet was standing in front of her and all that emotion inside her came bubbling to the surface. She'd been gone too long, let too much time and distance separate them. When this was over, Quinn vowed things would be different—she'd be a better sister to Violet.

Vi let her go and took a step back, giving her a once-over.

"Really, I'm good," Quinn promised her. But then Vi's studious gaze paused on her neck and Quinn's cheeks flushed with heat as her sister's eyes grew wide with *Holy crap, is that a hickey on your neck?* Her surprised expression was all excitement and zero judgment—which was a graciousness Quinn was pretty certain her brother-in-law wouldn't be extending. But the mischievous glint in Vi's eyes promised they would be having a private talk later on.

Quinn cleared her throat a bit awkwardly and turned her attention to her niece. "Raven!" She grabbed the girl and pulled her into a hug. "You're even more beautiful than when I saw you last." Her straight black hair was so dark it almost looked blue in the light. And with her dad's silver-gray eyes, she was an absolute knockout. "You driving yet?"

She smiled and nodded excitedly. "Got my permit last month."

"That's awesome! The next time I come for a visit, we're going to steal your dad's car and hit the Vegas strip."

Raven laughed and the look Nikko gave Quinn promised *Not on your life.* "Oh, quit your scowling," she teased, heading for her brother-in-law with open arms. "I'm just kidding." As she gave him a hug, she looked at Raven and shook her head, silently mouthing over his shoulder *I'm not kidding . . .*

"Stop putting ideas in her head, Quinn. She's already a handful."

Raven let out an unladylike snort and rolled her eyes. "Whatever, Dad . . ." Then to Quinn she said, "You sneak into one cage-fighting after-party and suddenly you're public enemy number one."

Quinn bit her lip to hold back her laugh but Nikko didn't look amused. Turning his full attention to Quinn, he studied her as if he needed to see for himself she was unharmed. She shifted uncomfortably beneath the scrutiny of Nikko's stare and when those steely silver eyes zeroed in on the mark on her neck, she experienced, for a brief moment, what it must be like for Raven to fall under her father's disapproving eye. For chrissake, she was an adult and yet she wanted to go crawl under the table.

"Where's Asher?" His tone was clipped, and Violet must have picked up on the source of his anger because she stepped up to her husband and slipped her arm around his muscular biceps. "Now, Nikko, what goes on between them isn't any of our concern . . ." she quietly cautioned him.

To her sister's credit, she seemed to diffuse a great deal of his temper. But Raven knew that tone, and as Quinn moved back, her niece shot her an amused *You're in trouble* grin.

"The hell it isn't," Nikko growled. "I didn't send my sister-in-law to him so he could take advantage of her." Then to Quinn he snapped again, "Where is Asher?"

All right, now it was her turn to muscle up to the cranky cage fighter. "Nikko, I love you for caring so much. Really, I do, but no one is taking advantage of me. And Asher is meeting with the head of hotel security right now." No sooner did she finish speaking than the door chirped as the lock clicked and in walked the man of the hour.

The moment the door closed behind him, it locked all that tension and testosterone inside the room with them.

"Come on," Violet said, grabbing Raven's and Quinn's hands as she led them toward the bedroom. "Let's give these two some privacy. I've got a package I think you've been anxious to get your hands on."

CHAPTER

33

Nikko waited for the bedroom door to close and not a second longer before laying into Asher. "Now it makes perfect sense."

Asher's hackles rose. "What's that?"

He was fairly certain the only thing keeping the fighter's fist from flying at his face right now was their friendship forged over fourteen years of blood, sweat, and tears. But that bond would only carry either one of them so far, or cut the other so much slack before this shit turned real, and Del Toro was pushing that line, stepping up on him like this. The accusation in his voice abraded Asher's already frayed nerves. He'd had a pretty intense forty-eight hours with, like, zero sleep, and he was in no mood for the shit he knew was about to hit the fan. But Del Toro was too pissed to care. They didn't call him "The Bull" for nothing, and he was seeing red.

"It makes perfect sense why you put up such a fight when I told you I wanted to take Quinn with us. You're fucking her . . . I can't goddamn believe it!"

The ex-marine turned MMA fighter took another step closer but Asher held his ground. He'd go toe-to-toe with the CFA heavyweight champion if need be, because over his dead body was Quinn leaving with them.

"I trusted you to take care of her, and this is how you treat our friendship? By taking advantage of a vulnerable woman in need of your protection?"

All right, that's it. "Fuck you, Del Toro." He shoved the fighter out of his face, fully expecting him to come back swinging. "It's not like that, and if you ever accuse me of doing something like that again, you and I are not friends anymore. I'm not letting Quinn go because I *can't* let her go. I'm in fucking love with her, man . . ."

Nikko's snort of laughter was anything but amused. In fact, it was downright nasty. "Please . . . you're in love with something, all right, but it isn't her shining personality. I don't know who the fuck you think you're trying to kid, but you forget . . . I know her."

Asher's fist flew into Nikko's jaw. When it connected, pain exploded in his hand. It was like hitting a damn brick wall. He used his momentum to shove his friend back because the only advantage he had was surprise, and once Del Toro retaliated, he knew he was going to get his ass handed to him, but he didn't fucking care. He wasn't going to stand here and let Nikko insult Quinn, even if Asher would have been the first to agree with him a week and a half ago.

"You don't fucking know her," he growled. "That woman you met at the wedding isn't the real Quinn. I'll say it one last time, asshole. I'm. In. Love. With. Quinn. I don't care if you believe me or not."

Perhaps it was the gasping trio who appeared in the doorway that gave Nikko pause, or maybe he felt like a dick for not believing Asher the first time, but that retaliatory haymaker Asher was expecting to pile into his gut didn't come. Del Toro did shove him back, though, and with enough force that his ass would have met the floor if he wasn't so good on his feet.

Quinn stared at him, utterly shocked. Violet grinned bigger than the Cheshire cat, and Raven watched them, enthralled, like she couldn't believe someone was dumb enough to face off with her father outside of the cage.

Yep, that was him. Stupid fucker right over here . . .

Leave it to the kid to break the mounting tension in the room. "You're in love with my aunt Quinn? Holy crap!"

"Why does everybody act like that's so damn surprising?" he grouched under his breath.

"Because it is," Nikko said. "And by the look on her face, I'd say she's just as shocked as we are."

"She knows, I told her yesterday," Asher grumbled as he made his way to the minibar, grabbed out a bottle of vodka for himself, and tossed Nikko a Jack Daniel's. The miniature bottle of booze sailed through the room and Nikko snatched it out of the air with speed that proved why he was the top contender in his weight class. The guy was fast, and had a brick jaw, because Asher hadn't pulled his punch and was a hell of a fighter himself.

"It just . . . sounds a lot more meaningful in English," she confessed.

He arched his brow at Quinn and twisted off the mini cap. "Really? I wouldn't know." He tipped the little bottle of Absolut back and didn't put it down until it was empty.

Quinn stepped away from her sister and moved toward him with slow, determined steps, her eyes 100 percent fixed on him, and it lit up his veins like a fucking Christmas tree. He could feel everyone else's eyes on him too, but they faded to a distant awareness in light of Quinn's nearing presence. She stopped in front of him, slipped her arms around his neck, and said loud enough for everyone in the room to hear, "I love you too, Asher Tate." And then she kissed him. Honest to God, it took every bit of strength he possessed to keep it PG-13. He wished they didn't have an audience, because the emotion swelling inside his chest was just as consuming as her kiss.

He knew what she was doing, taking a stand for him—for them. She was letting Nikko know, in no uncertain terms, that they were together, and not to interfere, which was exactly what her overprotective brother-in-law would do. Not that Asher blamed him. He understood Nikko's unreasonable sense of responsibility. Hell, he shouldered more than his share—carrying around that much guilt and blame for people who had trusted you with their lives yet had died would fuck anyone up.

Asher had his own issues. He sure as shit wasn't going to fault Nikko for his—nor would he just step aside and let the guy take his heart and soul away. When Nikko awkwardly cleared his throat, Asher reluctantly released Quinn. He gave her a lopsided grin and said, "You're right, it does pack a stronger punch in English."

Quinn smiled against his lips and gave him one last kiss before stepping back to address her brother-in-law. "I appreciate everything you're doing for me, Nikko, but I want to stay with Asher. Now that I have my files, hopefully I can finish my story and this will all be over soon."

Asher certainly hoped so, but something told him it wasn't going to be that easy. Whoever was posing as Collin Anderson wouldn't stop until Quinn was dead.

———

He wouldn't be climbing any trees for a while, but he wasn't about to let a bullet wound in the leg stop him from finishing this mission. What didn't kill you only made you stronger . . . The persistent throbbing in his thigh might be keeping him grounded, but he was far from being out of the game. And he was pissed. No longer was he concerned with making this look like an accident. If the fallout for Tate's death blew his way, then he'd just deal with it when the time came. There were other places he could point the blame, bigger fish to fry than him. Perhaps when this was over he'd take an extended vacation. Maybe Mexico . . . someplace his services and expertise would be in high demand without dealing with all the bureaucratic bullshit.

His top objective right now was to get Quinn and that evidence before she went public with a story that would ruin not only his life, but the organization he worked for as well. Not that he particularly gave a shit about the company, but it was the media spotlight he wanted to avoid—kinda hard to hold on to anonymity with your face plastered across CNN.

It was becoming increasingly apparent the only way he was getting to Quinn was through Tate. He'd been staring at an empty house for the last few hours, and was starting to get nervous that he'd run off with her, when a truck came down the driveway and parked up by the front door. The driver's door flew open and out stepped the bastard. But where was Quinn?

His pulse ticked in time with the throbbing in his thigh. His breath froze in his lungs as he waited for her to make an appearance. Was she waiting in the car? From where he watched, he couldn't see that half of the cab. Tate headed for the house without looking back, and he moved through the trees to better his view.

Fuck, she wasn't here . . . Lucky for Tate, or he'd put a bullet in him right where he stood. But where was Quinn Summers? Tate would never leave her alone and unprotected. So if he was here, then where in the hell was he hiding her? That was a question he intended to get answered, right before he put an end to this cat-and-mouse bullshit.

He waited for Tate to unlock the front door and step inside before making his way through the woods toward the house. His steps were a little slowed, his gait uneven, but that didn't matter. His trigger finger still worked just fine. Before he pulled his Glock from his waistband, he rolled his balaclava over his face. Stepping out from the cover of the trees, he quickly cut across the yard to the front door. He was taking a chance that Tate hadn't reactivated the security system, but without risk there wasn't any reward.

The sun was starting to drop in the sky. It wouldn't be long before dusk was upon them. Though he preferred the cover of night, he wasn't sure how much time he had to wait. The longer he dallied, the greater risk he ran of losing the element of surprise. And with Tate, he knew he was going to need every advantage he could get.

He mounted the porch steps, cautious to avoid the creaking of loose floorboards, and slowly opened the front door. When the alarm didn't sound, he released a breath he'd been holding and silently slipped inside. A quick survey of the living room and kitchen told him Tate must be upstairs. His suspicion was confirmed when the floorboards squeaked above his head. He crossed the living room and pressed his back against the wall near the staircase. With Glock in hand, he waited for the bastard to come down.

His pulse ticked with anticipation. Finally . . . this would soon be over. A fine sheen of sweat rose behind his neck, trickling between his shoulder blades. The moisture trapped between his skin and flak jacket was a distracting annoyance.

Footsteps grew closer. The hesitancy in the pattern told him Tate realized he wasn't alone. The click of a cocking gun confirmed it. His steps were slow and cautious, but the occasional groan of a weak floorboard in the stairs gave away his position. Silence.

Tension spiked in the room, as tactile as flesh and bone. Excitement warred with a niggling of fear. He knew Tate wasn't a man to underestimate, and his element of surprise was quickly vanishing. He needed to act—now.

Holstering his Glock, because he'd need both hands, he stepped away from the wall and grabbed Tate's arms, forcing them up. The gun went off, discharging over his head. The ear-ringing pop rendered him momentarily deaf. He grabbed Tate's wrist and twisted sharply as he turned, sending him over his shoulder, but not before the bastard drove his knee into his side. He felt his ribs snap beneath the impact; air exploded from his lungs.

Fuck!

Tate landed on his back. He lunged for the gun still held tightly in Tate's hand. With a firm grip on Tate's wrist, he slammed it onto the hardwood floor—one, twice, three times before the gun clattered across the floor. A fist plowed into his jaw. Pain exploded in his head, stars burst behind his eyes. *Motherfucker* . . .

He reached behind his back and pulled out his Glock, cocking the gun while Tate was still beneath him. He knew it was only a matter of time, though. The bastard was calculating and recalculating his options. He could see it in the fury of his eyes that held no fear, only venomous rage. Admirable . . . for a man about to die.

"Where is she?" he demanded, slowly rising to his feet to put some distance between him and the bastard before he could strike again. When Tate didn't answer, he pointed the Glock at his heart and demanded again. "Where the fuck is Quinn?"

Surprise momentarily flared in his eyes, and then nothing—all trace of emotion vanished. He should have known this wasn't going to be easy.

"Is that bitch really worth dying for, Asher? I'm going to find her one way or another."

That steely glare would have sent a shiver of trepidation through him if he hadn't been standing over that fucker with the barrel of his gun pointed at his chest.

"Fuck you . . ."

Not the response he was hoping for, but one he expected nonetheless. "No, fuck you." And with that final parting comment, he pulled the trigger and put two rounds into Tate's chest.

Turning away, he headed for the door and holstered his Glock, frustration robbing him of his postkill high. He should have known the bastard wouldn't talk. But getting him out of the way was more important than getting his answers. Tonight was a game changer, and he was going to have to adjust his strategy accordingly. Finding Quinn now would be near impossible. If he was going to get his hands on her, she was going to have to come to him—and she would, with the proper motivation . . .

CHAPTER

34

The moment Nikko and her sister left, Quinn went to work. The island separating the kitchen and living room area was covered with papers and printed articles. She had her interviews pulled up on the laptop and was going over each one with a meticulous eye, cross-referencing and highlighting comments, making notes, and digging through others.

Asher watched her from the couch, his gaze flickering to the clock on the wall. It was past midnight. Dark circles under her eyes and the fine lines of exhaustion drawn on her beautiful face spurred him into action. If she wasn't going to acknowledge her limits and take care of herself, then he was going to do it for her.

"Quinn, it's after midnight . . ." he told her, giving her the chance to step away from this on her own.

Her violet eyes didn't even dart up to him as she stared at the screen—scowled was more accurate. "I know what time it is, Asher." Her tone was tense—clipped.

"Then you know it's time to give it a rest for tonight." His tone was equally firm. He was about two minutes from tossing her over his shoulder and putting her to bed.

"I can't. Not until I find it . . ."

"Find what?" He rose from the couch and dragged his hand through his hair in frustration.

"The name of the military team that escorted us into Haiti. I can't remember it and I know I have it written somewhere in my notes. I've been searching over an hour and I can't find it."

She was still staring at the screen when he walked over. It wasn't until he closed the lid on the laptop that her gaze snapped up to his, and it wasn't a happy one.

"I was reading that," she snapped.

"And it will still be here in the morning. You've waited this long for your interviews; one more day isn't going to matter. If you aren't going to take care of yourself, then I'm going to do it for you." Despite her protests, he picked her up and cradled her against his chest as he carried her into the bathroom. When he put her down she no longer looked angry, just defeated, and that hit him in the gut like a sucker punch.

Cupping her face in his hands, he met her tired eyes and said, "Don't worry, you'll find it tomorrow. You just need a break and a fresh approach in the morning." He kissed her forehead because he didn't trust his mouth on any other part of her. Quinn didn't need to be seduced; she needed to be taken care of.

He started filling the Jacuzzi and spotted her toiletry bag on the counter near the sink. "Stay here."

He didn't trust her not to leave and head back out to the kitchen. Quinn was a stubborn woman with a single-minded determination that he both loved and hated. He walked over to her bag and unzipped it, looking for the bottle of lavender oil she kept on the rim of the tub in his bathroom. There were a lot of feminine toiletries amongst the oil, but the one that gave him pause was her packet of birth control pills. They hadn't discussed contraception, but he'd be lying if he said he wasn't glad to discover she had that base covered.

When he came back over with the lavender oil and added a few drops to the water, she was wearing the faintest hint of a grateful smile. The earthy aroma rose in the steam, filling the room and his senses with the scent his olfactory system had learned to associate with Quinn, and, just like Pavlov's dog, his body reacted—instantly growing hard for her.

He didn't say anything as he slowly began to undress her. As much as he could, he kept his gaze averted, because this was not about him or how much he wanted her, and he knew the sight of her naked body would undo any and all of his altruistic intentions.

Quinn's needs were more important than his own, and the protective instinct he felt toward her went far beyond just keeping her out of the hands of a killer. He wanted to take care of her, cherish her. Because he knew this woman's love was the rarest, most precious gift he would ever possess. And he didn't deserve it . . . not after all the lives he'd taken, the mistakes he'd made. But yet, for some miraculous reason, she saw beyond that darkness of his past and she'd given herself to him anyway.

She stood almost frozen and beautifully statuesque, wearing nothing but her bra and panties. Her breaths quickened. He could see the flutter of her pulse in the little divot at the base of her throat and rolled his lips between his teeth to keep from kissing her there. He moved behind her, away from the temptation, but this view was no easier to behold.

When his fingers brushed the column of her spine to slip beneath her bra strap, he heard the slight catch of her breath. The sound rolled through him, sending a rush of heat heading south. He hesitated a moment before unfastening the clasp, struggling to get control of the lust burning through his veins. It only seemed to build; the sexual tension humming between them was off the charts.

When his fingers unhooked her clasp, she released a breath that skated over his flesh like a caress. It was sex to his ears, and his own air left his lungs on a tortured groan. He slowly ran his hands up her back, thumbs applying gentle pressure up her spine and fanning out over the knots of tension in her slender shoulders. As he worked his way up, he slipped his fingers beneath the pale pink elastic straps and slid them off as his palms slowly glided down her arms.

When his hands reached hers, he laced their fingers together to keep from reaching up and cupping her breasts. Quinn tipped her head back, resting it against his chest, and closed her eyes as she exhaled a slow, wanton sigh. The only thing left on was a matching pale pink scrap of lace between her legs.

Unable to resist, he looked down over her shoulder and uttered a deep, masculine groan. Her breasts were beautifully full, with a natural gentle slope to dusky-pink pebbled nipples that made his mouth water. She pressed into him, the top of her bottom nestled against the base of his erection.

"Touch me . . ." Her voice was a soft, throaty plea.

She didn't understand he was fighting like hell not to do just that. With his fingers laced between hers, he lifted her arms up behind his neck. Her small, slender fingers untangled from his and slipped into his hair. He slowly dragged the backs of his hands down the insides of her arms, grazing the outer swells of her breasts. Her nipples pebbled tighter, as if begging for his caress.

The temptation was gutting his control. One hand covered her breast as the other skated down the flat plane of her stomach. When his fingers dipped beneath the lace covering and found her silky folds wet with desire, he couldn't resist dipping a finger inside her. She gasped, her blunt nails scoring his scalp as her fingers knotted into his hair. She was so tight; her little glove gripped his offering and greedily refused to let go. His cock jerked against her bottom, wanting so badly to be inside her. She felt so fucking incredible. So wet, so tight . . . he wanted to feel her wrapped around his cock with no barrier between them, just her silky heat squeezing his steel shaft, milking his release.

He'd never been bare before, and he wanted to experience the intimacy of it with Quinn. His lips fell to the soft skin of her throat, his tongue tracing the battering of her pulse, nipping and sucking at the pale flesh. "Quinn . . ." His voice was barely more than a throaty rasp.

The tension in the base of his spine coiled tighter as the pressure in his balls became an ache that skewed the line between pain and pleasure.

Fuck, he could come just touching her . . . Never before in his life did a woman have this kind of effect on him, this overpowering control over him.

"I want you, Quinn. So bad it hurts."

"Then take me . . ." Her plea was so needy, it rocked his very soul.

"I want to feel just you . . . nothing else but you." He wasn't sure if she hesitated to answer out of surprise or uncertainty. Did she understand what he was asking her? "I swear I'm safe. I'd never do anything to hurt you."

She nodded. "I know you wouldn't. It's okay. I'm safe too."

His heart slammed inside his chest, his hands shaking with the urgency to get inside her as he slipped her panties off and made quick work of shucking his shirt and freeing himself from his jeans. When he gripped his shaft to guide himself between her parted thighs, his cock was already weeping with anticipation. He slipped inside her silky folds, felt the stretch of her flesh yielding to his, and he almost came right then and there.

"Oh, fuck, Quinn . . ." he groaned against her throat as he wrapped her hair into his fist and gripped her tighter. His free hand slipped between her legs and found the bead of her sex, trapping the bud against his cock. She gasped and moaned his name as he began to thrust inside her. Her grip around his neck tightened as her back arched against his chest. The pressure building inside his cock was unbearable. He was going to come. So was she. He could feel *everything*—the tightening of her glove, the early tremors building inside her, the rush of wetness bathing his cock . . . It was amazing.

The moment she came, he exploded. The jolt of cum jetting against her core was euphoric. Her broken cry was drowned out by his harsh bark of rapture and he gripped her tightly, unable to do more than hold on for the ride as she milked him with each sweet spasm.

By the time the final shudders left her body, Quinn was boneless in his arms. He adjusted his grip on her and reached over to turn off the water, then helped her step into the oversize whirlpool tub. He finished stepping out of his jeans and climbed into the steaming bath, settling in behind her. She leaned back against his chest, her head resting against his shoulder as he reached over and turned on the jets. Water rushed around them and the contented sigh that escaped her lips resonated deep inside him.

Neither of them spoke as he held her, his arms wrapped around Quinn's slender frame as they basked in their postorgasmic bliss. Sometimes there were just no words—except maybe for the four simple ones he whispered as his lips brushed against her temple.

"I love you, Quinn . . ."

CHAPTER
35

Asher woke to the sound of vibration on the nightstand. Instead of grabbing his cell, his hand instinctively went for his Sig P226. He bolted upright, arm raised, gun pointing at the bedroom door. It took a few seconds for his mind to engage and overrule his instincts. He'd fallen asleep—really asleep—not that half-dose, half-conscious limbo he usually hovered in, and startling awake was disorientating as hell. He couldn't remember the last time he'd actually slept with no nightmares to haunt him, no screams to pull him from sleep's sweet embrace . . . For the first time there was just blissful silence and the feeling of Quinn's naked body curled up against him.

He scowled at the persistent buzzing on the table and set the gun down to snatch up his cell. His gaze fell to the alarm clock and he was surprised to see it was almost ten. Shit . . . he'd lost half the morning already. The phone quieted in his hand and he cast a quick glance at the woman sleeping beside him. His chest tightened, his heart swelling with fullness, as he took a moment to admire her flawless alabaster skin and the halo of pale blonde hair circling the pillow next to his.

God help him, he loved this woman, and the feeling of free-falling that swept over him when he thought of the danger she was in scared the hell out of him. How was he going to keep Quinn safe and find the fucker hunting her? The idea of putting a bullet between that bastard's eyes filled him with a profound sense of satisfaction.

He leaned down and pressed a soft kiss to her bare shoulder and then carefully slipped out of bed. She hadn't been sleeping well and needed all the rest she could get. He grabbed a change of clothes from his bag and was just fastening his jeans when his cell began to buzz again. The caller ID came up Denver Police Department, which was odd. Why wouldn't Jax just call him from his cell? He left the bedroom and pulled the door closed behind him before answering.

"Hey, man . . ."

"You fucking lied to me."

"Good morning to you too. What the fuck are you talking about?"

"He's not after you. It's Quinn he wants."

Asher stopped midway to the couch, tension settling over him like liquid cement. "How do you know that?"

"Oh, I figured it out pretty fucking fast when that bastard jumped me and demanded I tell him where she was. The fucker put two rounds in my chest."

Cold dread infused Asher's veins, turning his blood to ice. "You're all right?" he demanded, panic gripping his chest and squeezing like a steel band. He'd never forgive himself if something happened to Jax. He never should have called him. Never should have involved him in this shit . . .

"I'm fine. Thank God I was wearing a vest. Just a little sore and a whole lot pissed off. You withheld valuable information from me. I'm not just a cop, Asher, I'm your fucking brother."

"I know . . . Fuck, I'm sorry. I should never have pulled you into this."

"No, you should have pulled me into this from the very beginning. I know who she is, Asher. Quinn Summers isn't your girlfriend. She's a goddamn missing person case."

"She's a what?"

"You heard me—a missing person case. The FBI is looking all over for her."

His heart jumped inside his chest. "Jax, the Feds can't know she's here."

"Why the hell not? And it's a little late for that. They already figured it out. Her name flagged with them when I ran her record. Within forty-five minutes, the fucking Feds were ringing my phone off the hook. Her roommate was murdered, Asher. And they thought whoever did it had Quinn. They have two agents flying in tomorrow and they want to talk to her about a report she made with the attorney general's office."

"Fuck." He dragged his hand through his hair and began to pace. "Quinn thinks whoever is trying to kill her was hired by Mark Madison."

"The attorney general?"

"Yeah . . ."

"That doesn't make any sense. Why would the attorney general want to kill Quinn?"

"Because she uncovered a human-trafficking operation in Haiti while doing a human-interest story for the CGRN. She went to the attorney general for help and her roommate wound up dead before she could get home. No one knew she was back in the States except for Mark Madison, and someone's been trying to kill her ever since. I know it's circumstantial, but if she's right, going to the FBI could get her killed."

Jax cursed. "You could have come to me with the truth a hell of a lot sooner and I might have been able to do more to help you. Either way, you're going to have to bring her in or they're going after you for obstructing justice."

"I don't give a fuck, I'm not handing Quinn over to the Feds."

"No one's asking you to. They just want to talk to her."

"What if this is a ploy to flush her out?"

"It could be. But I don't think it is. Quinn could be wrong and it's entirely possible someone else is trying to kill her. They've made their search for Quinn too high-profile for this to be a conspiracy. Too many people know the Feds are looking for her. She can't just disappear. I've got a friend with the bureau I can call. I'll ask him about the agents they have flying in. I think we need to hear what they have to say, Asher. They'll be at my office tomorrow morning at eleven. Bring her in. No one's going to try to touch her here. I promise she'll be safe."

As much as he hated the idea of bringing Quinn in to the FBI, Jax had a point. This cat-and-mouse game had to end. If there was any chance these Feds were legit, then they could be instrumental in helping him catch a killer. "What about the blood sample? Did you find it?"

"It's already with the CBI, but results will take a few days to get back and then they've got to run it through the databank for a match. At this point, the benefit to having the blood sample will be proof we've got our guy."

"A few days? Are you serious? How come *CSI* can do this shit in an hour?"

"Because *CSI* isn't real life. Listen man, I gotta go. I'll see you tomorrow. Don't be late. It's poor form to keep the Feds waiting."

Jax disconnected the call before Asher could respond. It was just as well. He didn't want to hear the thoughts going through Asher's head right now. Not that any of it mattered. Asher had no choice but to be at his brother's office tomorrow at 11:00 a.m. sharp with Quinn in tow.

He dropped into a chair and propped his elbows on his knees, resting his face in his hands. Fuck . . . how in the hell was he going to convince Quinn it was a good idea to walk into that police station when he wasn't so sure of it himself? For all he knew he could be leading her into a trap, and he'd never forgive himself if anything happened to her.

"What's the matter?"

His head snapped up to find Quinn standing in the doorway, wearing nothing but that damn white USMC T-shirt she'd had on the night she came to stay with him. So much had happened since then. So much had changed between them. And he wasn't entirely confident it wasn't about to all fall apart.

"Still not sleeping?" she asked, coming over to him.

No, for once that had not been his problem. He was dealing with another kind of nightmare. Asher leaned back and opened his arms, inviting Quinn to crawl onto his lap. He didn't have to ask twice. Damn, she was adorable . . . with her long, pale blonde hair hanging loose in a sexed-up mess. Her violet eyes were fresh from sleep and especially bright this morning, her lush lips still red and kiss swollen.

In the worst way he wanted to carry her back into that bedroom and pretend the rest of the world didn't exist. But unfortunately, life wouldn't pause for them. There was a killer out there who probably thought he'd just removed the obstacle between himself and Quinn. With Asher figuratively out of the way, his efforts to find her would intensify. She wouldn't be safe until that bastard was dead.

"Quinn, I need to talk to you about something."

She straightened against him and turned to meet his eyes, caution drawing her brows tight. No doubt she was feeding off his own tension. He was not exactly the model of confidence he'd been hoping to display.

"Jax called me. He knows about Manhattan. The FBI has you listed as a missing person and it flagged with the bureau when he ran your record. They've been looking for you since you disappeared."

"They called Vi looking for me, but I didn't know they were calling me a missing person case. Do they know I'm with you?"

The panic hedging in her voice made his chest ache. He nodded. "Two agents are flying into Denver tomorrow and they want to meet with you. Ask you some questions."

She shook her head and scrambled off his lap, looking at him like he'd just betrayed her. Her wide eyes darted around the room as if she was looking for an escape. He could see her mind racing with options; unfortunately she didn't have many more than he did.

"You're bringing me in."

It was an accusation more than a question. She stepped back and stumbled against the chair. His hand shot out to catch her arm before she fell, but she dodged his grasp and somehow managed not to fall. "Quinn, it's not like that."

"It's exactly like that."

"We need help. I can't protect you and catch this guy at the same time. My hands are tied. That bastard shot Jax last night, thinking he was me."

"Oh no! Is he all right?"

"He's okay. He was wearing a vest. My point is the shooter came back, Quinn. And he's not going to quit. He probably thinks I'm dead and this could be the opportunity I need to get an upper hand on him. His guard will be down. But I can't hunt that bastard and watch over you at the same time."

"And you trust the FBI to do that? To keep me safe?"

She looked at him like he had lost his mind, and who knows, maybe he had. All he knew was that they were running out of time and he had to do something—now. "I don't know. But I trust Jax. He has a friend in the bureau and is calling him to discuss your case. I think we need to meet with the Feds and at least hear them out. Jax and I will be there the whole time. We won't let anything happen to you. I promise. You gotta trust me."

She didn't look like she was sure she did, and fuck if that wasn't a knife in the heart. He stood and walked over to her, counting it as a win when she didn't back away. He moved slowly so as not to frighten her. It'd been a long time since he'd seen that look of doubt in her eyes. Reaching up, he cupped her cheek and gently brushed his thumb beneath her plump bottom lip. "Sweetheart, after everything we've been through, do you honestly believe I'd ever let you go? You're mine, Quinn. I would kill for you and die to protect you."

Tears filled her eyes, turning them into large luminous violet pools he wanted to drown in. When she dropped her gaze and blinked, a drop slipped over her lashes and rolled down her cheek to collect against his hand. When she looked back up at him, the doubt was gone, the fear banished by his vow to love and protect her. Her slender fingers wrapped around his wrist and she pressed her lips into his palm.

"Okay . . ." she whispered against his battle-scarred hand. "I trust you."

Those three words released a dam of emotion inside him and he pulled her into his arms. Holding her tight, Asher promised, "We're going to get through this, Quinn. I won't let anyone hurt you."

CHAPTER
36

He waited until it was almost closing time before entering the office. Violet Del Toro's name was on the outer glass door, confirming he was at the right place. He walked inside and was greeted by a receptionist with long blonde hair. It had a natural curl that made her golden locks a little wild and untameable. The woman's smile was bright as she swept her appreciative gaze over him. There was a touch of mischievousness in those hazel eyes that piqued his interest.

"Hi, you're running late. I didn't think you were coming. We're about to close." When he arched his brow in question, she continued to explain. "Dean called and said he was sending you down to schedule an appointment. Tommy Thorson, right? The newest fighter for the Cage Fighting Association? Congratulations on your contract."

She stood and extended her hand over her desk. This was going to be so fucking easy, he almost felt bad about it. Putting a warm smile on his face, he stepped forward and took her hand—small, delicate fingers wrapped around his.

"How did you know?" He glanced at the nameplate on her desk. Penelope Cantrell—she didn't look like a Penelope.

"Are you kidding? I can spot a cage fighter a mile away. You guys don't exactly blend in well."

She thought he was an MMA fighter? "Guilty . . ." He winked, flashing her a flirtatious grin. "I'd like to schedule an appointment with Violet Del Toro."

Her warm smile fell and something dimmed in those bright eyes. "I'm sorry, Dr. Del Toro isn't scheduling any appointments right now. She's away on a family vacation."

Fuck . . . "That's all right, I don't mind waiting. If you could just book me her next available appointment?"

"She'll be out for the next several weeks. Dr. Morrison is handling all the CFA accounts right now. I can schedule you an appointment with him." She sat back down and turned to her computer, her nails clicking away on the keys.

"That'll be fine," he conceded. "Everyone needs a vacation now and then, right? You know where she went?" he asked offhandedly, making casual conversation.

Her gaze briefly darted to him, then back to the monitor. "No, I don't."

She was lying. This bitch knew exactly where Violet was. He shot a quick glance down the hallway. It was empty. So was the waiting room. They were alone. He looked up at the clock. It was after five—past closing time . . .

He slipped his hand into his pocket and fingered the thin wire garrote.

"I know Dean is anxious to get your contract completed. It looks like I can get you in Tuesday morning. Will eight thirty work for you?"

"Let me check my calendar." He pulled out his cell and came around the side of the desk all casual-like. She didn't pay him any mind as she kept looking through the doctor's schedule.

"Or else we could maybe squeeze you in at the end of the day?"

"Umm . . . you know, neither of those times are really good for me. You got anything else?" He moved closer. Her guard was down. This was going to be easy—a piece of fucking cake. And he couldn't wait to taste her frosting . . .

He returned his cell to his pocket and exchanged it for the thin wire. He was stepping behind her when the front door suddenly opened.

Instead of moving forward, he stepped back and casually leaned his hip against her desk.

Her gaze shot up to the guy walking in and her smile fell. Her tawny brows pulled tight in a scowl. He could see her guard going up. It was like watching one of those old medieval gates crash into place. So this fun little kitten had some claws after all. Interesting . . .

He bet she was a fighter. The thought of her struggling beneath him as his hand tightened against her throat, squeezing as she gasped for breath, shot his dick hard as a rock.

"We're closed," she snapped, jerking him out of his reverie.

He held back his chuckle at the serious case of frostbite this woman was throwing at the guy, who dropped into a seat in the waiting room, stretching out into a negligent sprawl.

"I know. That's why I'm here. I'm taking you home."

She snorted something under her breath about not needing a baby-sitter. Well, this was an interesting dynamic they had going on. There was obviously some history between them—some water under their bridge, and with the fireworks going off between them, he'd bet the guy was fucking her, or at least had been at one time. The guy wasn't particularly tall, but he was built—heavily muscled and well defined. If he had to venture a guess, this was one of those MMA fighters Penelope seemed to think he was. Yeah, this was his cue to hit the road. He could feel the guy's eyes on him, watching him with a hell of a lot more interest than he was comfortable with.

"I need to check my training schedule. How about I call you?"

The woman turned her attention back to him and her beaming smile was on—with an extra halogen he suspected wasn't for his benefit, but rather for the guy burning a hole in his back with a death glare. Time to adios.

"Sure," she said. "Here's an appointment card. Our number is at the bottom—just give me a call and I'll get you scheduled."

"Thanks." He took the card and left, careful to keep his back to the guy watching him like a hawk.

As he walked through the doors and into the hot Nevada sun, he squinted into the blinding light and growled a nasty curse. He was too late. Quinn's sister was gone and, no doubt, far from his reach. Coincidence? He thought not . . .

He'd be lying if he said that loss of leverage didn't piss him off. He hated wasting his time, especially when that was the one thing he was running short on. Oh well, today wouldn't be a total bust. As long as he was here, he could hang out a few more hours and at least compensate himself for the trip.

He watched from his rental as the guy escorted Ms. Cantrell to his car—an old orange Charger that was one door decal and a Confederate flag short of becoming the General Lee. The presumed fighter opened the door for her and she said something to him before getting inside that made him smirk and shake his head.

Yeah, this woman definitely had some fire, and he was looking forward to quenching it.

As they left the lot, he hung back before pulling out, putting a few car lengths between him and the Charger. No one would pay any attention to a minivan; they were a dime a dozen. He might as well be driving a chameleon.

———

"I found it."

Asher looked up from the game of solitaire laid out on the opposite end of the table from Quinn. He wasn't used to being cooped up indoors and he was going bat-shit crazy in here. After fourteen years of spending nearly every day outside, the culture shock was making him antsy—or maybe it was his indecision over bringing Quinn in to meet with the Feds tomorrow.

He had some game-changing options here and the last thing he wanted to do was make an already bad situation worse. He'd sounded a hell of a lot more confident about his decision when he'd been selling it to Quinn. Maybe once he heard back from Jax, and his friend with the bureau could vouch for the agents, he'd feel more at ease with the whole idea of her meeting with them. But one thing was for certain—something had to give, and he was running out of options.

He couldn't take Quinn home. As long as that bastard was on the loose it wasn't safe for her there, and he couldn't keep her here indefinitely. What he wanted to be doing was hunting that bastard down, and sitting here twiddling his thumbs was making him edgy as hell.

"What did you find, Quinn?"

The smile on her face was encouraging. It was a hell of a lot better than the fear he'd put there this morning.

"The name of the military team that escorted us into Haiti. I knew I had it somewhere in my notes, but I couldn't remember where. I've been searching for it since yesterday." Her violet eyes kept scanning the computer screen. "Here it is . . . Eagle Ops."

Asher's fingers tightened on the deck of cards in his hand. "Quinn, Eagle Ops isn't US military."

She looked up at him and met his eyes across the table. "It isn't?"

"No, it's a private security company that hires ex-military officers. They tried to recruit me when I left the Special Forces. I had plans to start my own company so I never met with anyone. I know they've been involved with some questionable dealings in the past. Most of these guys are freelancers and they keep who they work for under wraps. They pick and choose their jobs."

"Well, at least now I know why I couldn't find any connection to the military and the CGRN. There isn't one."

"Did any of the men with the security team know you were digging into the disappearance of those kids? Did you talk to any of them?"

"I don't know if they knew or not. When we traveled, they rode in the vehicles ahead of and behind ours so I never really saw them, except for the night they handed those girls over. But I was so far away I couldn't recognize any of them specifically. I only knew it was them by the way they were dressed."

Before he could respond, his cell began to buzz on the table. "I've gotta get this. It's Jax." He snatched the phone up and answered it as he headed across the living room. Restless energy had him pacing again. By the time he checked out of here, he was going to have to replace the damn carpet.

"I got ahold of Wade and told him what was going on. He assured me the two agents meeting with Quinn are reputable men. He said he'd trust them with his life, and actually has on more than one occasion. He backtracked the query and it was placed by Mark Madison the same day Quinn met with him. Every bit of procedure was followed; the paper trail looks clean. If he had something to hide, this isn't the route he'd take to do it. I'm not doubting that something is going on here. I've got bruised ribs to prove it. I just don't think the attorney general is behind it."

"I'm not so sure either, but she's got a pretty compelling timeline."

"I can't explain the dead roommate or how anyone knew she was back in the country. But I know whoever's after her is a professional killer and Quinn's in serious trouble. You've done a great job of keeping her alive thus far, and I understand you've got your reservations about trusting the Feds, but whatever is going on here, whoever's behind this, I think bringing the FBI in is the right move. Let them do their job. Let them figure out this mess and see how far up the chain it goes. This isn't Quinn's conspiracy to solve—or yours. Your job is to protect her, and the best way to do that right now is to get her the help she needs."

"I know, but she doesn't trust easily and I don't want to let her down. If I'm wrong, if you're wrong, and this goes badly, I'll lose her. She'll never trust me again."

Silence answered him. Then, "Fuck, you're really in love with her, aren't you?"

Exhaling a sigh, Asher turned and made another trek across the living room. "Yeah, I'm afraid I am."

"Hell of a bad time to get your emotions involved."

"Your observations are astounding. I wish I would have thought of that before."

Jax laughed. "Glad to hear you're still a smartass. Wade said the agents are going to want all her notes, interviews, and pictures, so bring them along to the meeting."

"I'll let Quinn know."

"See ya tomorrow then."

The call disconnected and Asher exhaled a pent-up sigh. How was Quinn going to feel about handing all her information over to the Feds? Probably not very fucking good.

CHAPTER

37

He watched her through the bedroom window. Did she realize she'd left her curtains open? Not completely, just far enough to give him a teasing glimpse of creamy bare flesh. Did she do it on purpose or was it an innocent oversight? It was mistakes like this that could get a pretty woman like her killed. She stepped out of view and returned a moment later wearing nothing but a black lace bra and matching panties.

Did women really walk around their houses like that? Of course they did in every guy's fantasy, but this was real life, and every action caused a reaction—a reaction that was now happening in his pants. He reached down and adjusted his hard-on. Movement in the shadows a few houses down the street caught his attention. What the fuck was that? He lifted his binoculars and trained them on the brush, watching as the man dressed in black slowly made his way toward Penelope Cantrell's house.

Interesting . . . Did she know she had a stalker? With the way she flirted with him and flittered around her house half-naked, he wasn't surprised she'd attracted some unwanted attention. Perhaps that was the reason for the escort home this afternoon, and the snide remark about not needing a babysitter.

He was crashing some other guy's party . . .

The man heading toward her house right now wasn't a professional. His movements were too rushed and uncoordinated. He was unaware he was being watched; his sole focus was on that bedroom window when it should have been on the guy who had a Glock with an Osprey 40 silencer trained on his head. One twitch of his finger and Penelope's problems would be over—for about sixty seconds, because he was a hell of a lot worse threat to her than this wannabe.

The low growl of an engine had her secret admirer putting on the brakes and slinking back into the shadows. He cut a glance behind him and saw Dukes of Hazzard heading their way. Fuck . . . this guy was a real pain in the ass. He was starting to wonder if this woman was worth all the effort. As much as he wanted to enjoy a little private time with Penelope Cantrell, he wasn't willing to jeopardize his mission.

Bo Duke climbed out of the car and wasted no time banging his fist against the door. He could feel the tension radiating off the guy all the way over here. Testosterone scented the air. "Pen, I know you're in there. Open the goddamn door."

The familiarity with her name confirmed his suspicion that those two had a history. His gaze shot to her bedroom window. She was gone. Her stalker was still there though, hiding behind an evergreen, watching Bo Duke pound on the door. He couldn't tell if it was panic or anger driving the man—or maybe something else, because Penelope opened the front door, wearing a thin black robe that hung down to midthigh, and the guy had her pressed up against the door before he could even get inside.

The guy's body was up against hers, his mouth devouring her the way he wanted to be right now. One of his hands fisted into her hair possessively, and the other slipped inside her robe to capture her breast. She wasn't fighting him off. Instead, her arms slipped up around his neck.

What a whore . . .

The guy didn't care he was giving the neighborhood a show, and just maybe that was the point. Bo Duke was marking his territory. Penelope belonged to him, and the only way anyone was getting to that woman was through him. It was a risky stance, because he wasn't one to back down from a challenge. The same couldn't be said for her stalker, though. The spineless bastard was slipping away, back into the shadows he'd come from.

As he weighed the quandary of sticking his hand into someone else's cookie jar, his cell went off, alerting him to a message.

> Feds moving in. Arriving in Denver in the morning. Will have the woman's location soon. Be ready to move.

Shit. He'd known it was only a matter of time before the Feds found her. By killing Tate, he'd traded one set of problems for another. He was out of time. Once they got her into protective custody, the game was going to change drastically, and he needed to come up with a plan to get Quinn before that happened. This wasn't just about finding her; this was about stopping a witness. If the Feds got their hands on that SD card, this would become all about damage control and survival, because they were all going to be fucked.

> Getting into position now. Let me know.

Well, that answered that. Penelope Cantrell would live another day. Perhaps when this was all over, he'd come back and pay her another visit . . .

As he fired up the minivan and began to pull away, his cell went off again with another text.

> FYI: Tate's not dead.

———

Quinn's hand gripped Asher's so tightly, his fingers were starting to go numb. Each step they mounted to the entrance of the Denver Police

Department ratcheted her tension until she was a veritable ball of anxiety beside him. Fuck, he didn't want to do this—didn't want to put her through this. If he could bear this burden for her, he'd do it in a heartbeat.

If he thought there were someplace he could take her where she would stay safe, they'd be on the next plane. But the bottom line was Asher wasn't a runner. It wasn't in his blood, and he'd learned a long time ago the best way to deal with a threat was head-on. The last thing they needed was to be hunted by a madman and the FBI. There were too many unknowns at this point—too many variables. But one thing was for certain—they'd be better off aligning with the Feds than making them their enemy. Did that mean Asher was going to just hand them his trust? Hell no, but Jax was vouching for them, so he could at least meet with the guys and hear what they had to say.

As they approached the glass double doors, he pulled Quinn to a stop and bent to look her in the eyes. She'd hardly spoken two words on their drive to Denver. Her walls were back up, and reinforced with galvanized steel. Looking at her now, it was almost impossible to believe this was the same woman who'd come apart for him so sweetly, and he couldn't help but feel she was slipping out of his grasp.

Quinn's trust meant everything to him, and he knew what it was costing her to give it to him now, because every fiber of her being told him she did not want to be here. Not that he blamed her. Finding her roommate dead had been a terrifying experience for her, and seeing something like that would leave a hell of a scar. It was no wonder she didn't trust the government or anyone affiliated with it. Hell, look how long it'd taken him to get her to open up and trust him. And now he was putting it all on the line. He swore to God if those agents fucked this up . . .

"Quinn, it's going to be all right."

She met his eyes and nodded, but looked anything but convinced.

"Remember what I said. We're in this together. I won't leave you."

She nodded again.

He wasn't used to this side of Quinn and much preferred the feisty, sassy version of the woman. Hell, he'd even take the shrew right now—anything but this frightened, insecure female. He wished she'd tell him where her head was at. Then again, he wasn't sure he wanted to know. It wouldn't change what they had to do, which was walk through these doors and have a sit-down with federal agents.

He briefly pressed his lips against hers and then opened the door. He was glad to see his brother waiting for them, and even more glad when he passed them through security without disarming them. He had his Sig in his waistband and a Glock strapped to his ankle. Quinn wore the Beretta he'd given her. They got some strange looks from the desk jockeys as they passed by, which told him Jax must not share much about his personal life, because these guys were rubbing their eyes like they were seeing double.

"It's nice to see you again, Quinn," Jax greeted her as he led them down the hall. "I'm sorry it has to be under these circumstances."

"Me too." The smile Quinn gave him lacked her usual luster. "I'd much rather be playing corn hole with your brother and eating your burned burgers."

An unexpected chuckle rumbled in Asher's throat, and Jaxson's top lip twitched in amusement. Now there was his girl . . . putting on a brave face for his brother. She was rallying her moxie before they walked into this meeting. That she didn't feel the need to pretend with him spoke volumes about her trust in him. Only he knew how hard this really was for her.

"They weren't that burnt," Jax retorted, playing along with the attempt to ease the tension they were all feeling right now. "And so would I. Believe me. A cold beer and corn hole sound pretty damn good right about now."

He led them to an office that felt a lot like an interrogation room. A rectangular metal table sat in the middle of the room with a large one-way glass on the opposite wall. There were two men in dark suits already sitting at the table, each holding a foam coffee cup. One agent had close-cropped salt-and-pepper hair. He looked to be pushing fifty, while the other couldn't be any older than Asher's early thirties. A brief flash of surprise registered in their eyes when Asher and Quinn walked in, reminding him how annoying it was to go places with his brother. It didn't last long though, because the moment Quinn stepped out from behind him, both men rose to their feet, all attention fixed solely on her.

"Ms. Summers . . ." The older agent greeted her, holding out his hand. "I'm Special Agent Tim Meadows. It's a pleasure to meet you."

She stepped forward and shook his hand. His partner was next in line. "Special Agent Maxwell Kellen . . ."

Both men made the same introduction to Asher. He shook their hands and took a seat beside Quinn in the two empty chairs across from them; Jax stood in his periphery.

"I appreciate you taking the time to meet with us," the older man began. "We're very sorry about your roommate."

The guy was upfront, direct. Asher respected that. Quinn didn't look so convinced.

"It hasn't been easy."

"I'm sure it hasn't. When we arrived at the apartment—"

"Wait. You were there?" Quinn interrupted. "You saw Emily?"

The agent shook his head. "By the time we got there, the police had already come and gone. As soon as the query came in from the attorney general to investigate your story, we went to your apartment looking for you. We thought you'd been taken. Look, we want to help you, Ms. Summers, but in order to do that, we need you to help us."

Special Agent Meadows was good . . . his voice was calm and mellow, reminding Asher more of a hostage negotiator than an FBI agent. Now his partner sitting beside him? That guy reeked of "federal officer." Asher knew what Meadows was doing—trying to gain her trust and align himself with Quinn. If the guy thought it was going to be that easy, he was in for a rude awakening. Quinn had her quills out.

Leveling the agent with a cold, hard stare, she asked, "What do you want from me?"

That was his Quinn . . . prickly as a porcupine. He was catching a chill just sitting beside her.

The other agent chimed in. Perhaps it was his turn for the "bad cop" routine. "For starters, you could give us the SD card you told the attorney general about."

He didn't have the patience the other agent did—whether because of youth or temperament, Asher couldn't be sure. But diplomacy was not high on this guy's priority list.

"The pictures aren't any good," she told them. "It was too dark . . . they didn't turn out."

She wasn't lying. They'd looked at the photos together yesterday, and although the images taken in the darkness were graphically disturbing, it was impossible to see the men with any amount of clarity or detail.

"You'd be surprised what IT at Langley can do, ma'am." Meadows gave her an encouraging smile. "Would you mind telling us what happened when you were in Haiti? What you saw?"

Quinn cast Asher a questioning glance, silently asking him for his opinion. Should she trust these men with the truth? He really wasn't sure, and only time would fully answer that question. But he trusted Jax, and right now that would just have to be good enough. He nodded his head and took Quinn's hand beneath the table, giving it an encouraging squeeze.

It wasn't any easier for him to hear Quinn's story recounted a second time. By the time she finished describing in horrific detail the events that led her up to this point, including Emily's murder and the attempts made on her own life, there wasn't a man in the room unaffected. Righteous anger resonated off every one of them. Even the stoic, hard-ass Agent Kellen was looking at Quinn with compassion, and maybe even a bit more concern than he ought to.

She concluded her story by adding, "So if you're not trying to kill me, then who is?"

"That's a good question," Agent Kellen said, suddenly the chatty one. "And we'd like to help you try to figure that out. Until we do, we'd like to take you into protective custody."

No. Fucking. Way. "She's already in protective custody," Asher cut in, leveling the agent with a territorial glare. "Mine."

Meadows spoke up. "With all due respect, Mr. Tate, Ms. Summers has been compromised here. Whoever is after her has gone through a significant amount of trouble to silence her. Whether or not we have the SD card, she's still a witness and a pivotal factor in this case. Right now we have no leads to start tracking this assassin down. Eagle Ops is a low-profile organization. They work very hard to stay under any government radar. It isn't going to be easy finding a link in their chain. And once we do, I'm betting they're not going to be too cooperative. With the information Ms. Summers is providing, I'm hopeful something will turn up, but . . ."

He paused a moment, as if weighing the wisdom of his words. The fucking Fed should have thought about them a little harder.

"I think we need to move fast, and the easiest way to do that is to draw the killer out—"

"Wait a minute," Asher cut in, sitting a little straighter in his chair and trying his damndest not to launch himself across this table. "You want to use Quinn as bait? Not a fucking chance!"

"Asher . . ." Jax's hand rested on his shoulder, and it wasn't to comfort him. His brother wanted hands on him so he could hold him back in case Asher decided to plant his fist in Agent Meadows's face. "Rein it in, Ash. Listen to what the man has to say."

"Ms. Summers is the only connection we have to this case right now."

She wasn't the only connection. But Asher wasn't thrilled about admitting it. He'd worked hard to put that part of his life behind him, to sever those connections. The last thing he wanted to do was drudge up the past and open old wounds that were just starting to scab over.

"It's going to take time to put this investigation together, to mobilize a team to start chasing down leads. The longer it takes to shut this trafficking operation down, the more girls are going to go missing. Do you know what the chances are of us recovering them? Less than 2 percent. But if we can draw him to her, if we can catch this son of a bitch, we can shut this operation down."

"I'll do it," Quinn offered.

"The hell you will!" he growled.

"Asher, they're right. I just want this to be over. The thought of more girls disappearing . . ."

Muttering a curse under his breath, he scrubbed his hand over the back of his neck. "I know someone who's worked for EO. He tried to recruit me when I left the military and he did some freelance work for Tate Security. I'll talk to him and see what kind of information I can get—maybe a name of his contact. At the very least it would give you guys a starting point, but you're going to have to get a call through to the District of Columbia Department of Corrections."

"That shouldn't be too difficult. Who's the guy?"

"Rolland Peterson."

Agents Meadows and Kellen exchanged a concerned look. They knew what Peterson was capable of and were clearly hesitant about making contact with him. But there were no other options, and the agents knew that as well as Asher did. Agent Meadows stood and Jax led him to his office to make the call. They weren't gone more than ten minutes before they returned. The agent didn't look happy. Sitting down in the seat across from them, the special agent said, "He won't take the call. Said if you wanted to talk to him you knew where to find him. Otherwise, I believe his exact words were 'fuck off.'"

Shit, of all the people Asher didn't want to see again, this guy was definitely one of his top five. He was less than thrilled about the idea of leaving Quinn behind in order to do it. But if he didn't find these Feds an EO lead, he wouldn't put it past them to pursue this killer by using Quinn to draw the fucker out.

"I'll go talk to him, under one condition. You take Quinn into protective custody and hide her in a safe house. I want full disclosure and direct contact with both of you. And Jaxson stays with her at all times while I'm gone. I won't have Quinn become collateral damage so you two can fast-track this goddamn case."

Meadows and Kellen exchanged looks but neither of them were agreeing to shit at the moment. Maybe they were hesitant about working with an ex-marine Special Forces commander who was now a civilian, but he still had the security clearance to cut through whatever red tape these Feds needed to make this happen. Fuck, he didn't want to do this, but at this point there wasn't much he wouldn't do to help Quinn or end this nightmare for her.

"Listen, these are my terms. You don't agree and I'll have her out of here so damn fast it'll take you months to find her again. I get your concern for those kids and wanting to expedite this investigation, but Quinn's safety is my most important concern and I won't have you treating her like one of your sacrificial lambs—even if it will help you catch a killer. If you want my help, and right now I'm the best lead you've got to the EO, we're going to do this my way."

The senior agent must have seen the truth in his eyes because he gave Asher a curt nod. "Agreed. I assure you, Ms. Summers's safety is our highest priority as well."

CHAPTER

38

The Feds had located her. According to his boss, they were moving Quinn to a safe house. Getting to her wouldn't be easy. It would take an elaborate setup and planning to get past those agents. The collateral damage was going to be extensive—but it was a cost he was willing to pay. He'd have to figure out a way it couldn't be traced back to him when it was all over. Not even EO knew his true identity, nor did he know that of his boss. It was safer that way, for all of them. If one of them got caught, the integrity of the organization remained intact. Only one other man knew his connection to EO, and he was about to become instrumental in helping him pull this mission off.

He didn't know where his boss was getting his information, but it didn't take a genius to figure out it was someone within the FBI. Up until this point, he'd been on his own with intelligence, but now that the Feds were involved, suddenly it was pouring in.

It was surprising the people who could be bought for the right price. He was a prime example of how the government could corrupt and erode a person's humanity until there was nothing left but anger, hatred, and greed. After a while, killing became as natural as breathing—as essential as eating. It was the only time he truly felt anything anymore. The power of taking a life . . . For just a moment, becoming the mighty hand of God . . . There was nothing like it.

He'd paid his dues with this one, worked hard for his kill. Quinn's life had become his the moment she'd stepped off that truck and onto the barren Haitian dirt—though neither of them had known it at the time. Destiny had intertwined their paths too many times for it not to be fate. She belonged to him, not that self-righteous bastard Tate.

He wouldn't fail again . . .

———

It was all happening so fast, Quinn's head was spinning. One minute they were meeting with federal agents and the next she found herself in protective custody, being stashed away in a safe house outside of Denver. The house was a modest two-story design with two bedrooms on the main level. A kitchen and dining room were divided by an island, and the living room housed a large fireplace. A small sitting room and two other bedrooms shared an adjoining bath on the upper level. The home was secluded, tucked away on a small private lake. She heard Asher commenting to Jax when they pulled up that the location would make the house difficult to approach from the back unnoticed. As far as feeling safe went, she wasn't sure it could get any more secure than two armed FBI agents, a homicide detective, and a retired Special Forces recon soldier holed up inside this house with her. Someone would have to be a suicidal fool to try to attack her here.

But her security detail was about to go down by one. So far, she hadn't gotten any time alone to talk with Asher. He was busy with Agents Meadows and Kellen. Jax had agreed to stay with her while he was gone. The thought of him leaving her, even for a day, made Quinn's heart sink with dread.

She kept her fears and protests to herself, though. Quinn knew he didn't want to go, and refused to make this any more difficult for him than it already was. This situation needed to end, and if Asher could get the answers to help discover who was behind it, then what other choice did she have than to let him go?

It was late. Quinn had had a long day, as had everyone else. She stood at the bedroom window, watching the moon glimmer off the lake's surface, and tried not to panic. Her arms wrapped tightly around herself as she hugged Asher's T-shirt close. She was exhausted—to the point of emotional—but was unable to unwind enough to sit down and rest.

Asher's flight was leaving early in the morning. Quinn wanted to go with him, but as of five o'clock tonight, she was officially in protective custody of the FBI—which basically meant she was a prisoner. Her only consolation was in knowing Asher wouldn't be gone long. He planned to return tomorrow night.

It scared her that in such a short time she could become so reliant on Asher. What was going to become of them when this nightmare was over? Asher had yet to speak of a future together, to offer her any sort of a commitment beyond keeping her alive. Not that that wasn't an important one. It was probably hard to think about tomorrow when you were just trying to survive today.

A soft knock sounded on the door before it opened. She didn't have to turn around to know it was him. She could sense his presence; feel the energy in the room shifting in response to his approach. When he came up behind her, his outdoorsy, masculine scent enveloped her as he wrapped his arms around her and squeezed.

Quinn exhaled a deep breath and sank back into his strength. His chin rested on top of her head and they stood there together in silence, looking out to the glistening water below. "It's beautiful here . . ." she commented offhandedly. "Though not as beautiful as your place. It's only been a few days and already I miss it." She was making small talk for fear that if the conversation turned to him leaving, she'd cry. What if the man who shot Jax realized it wasn't Asher, and that he was still alive? She wasn't this assassin's only target. What if he went after Asher now that she was in protective custody? No doubt when Asher started asking questions about Eagle Ops, it was going to raise red flags and the bastard would figure out quickly enough he was still alive.

His lips pressed against her temple and he drew in a slow, deep inhale. "With any luck, we'll get back there soon . . ."

Was this his way of asking her to stay with him? Was he offering her a chance at something with him that went beyond "protect and serve"? His lips grazed her cheek, her jaw, her neck . . . And all concerns about the future retreated to the background of her mind as the here and now demanded its due. Asher's hand slipped under her shirt to capture her breast as his mouth nipped and sucked the sensitive spot beneath her ear.

As much as she wanted him, she wasn't sure she felt comfortable doing this in a house full of FBI agents, not to mention his brother. She was just about to tell him so when he trapped her nipple between his thumb and finger, sending a dart of painful pleasure zinging into her core. There was something off with him tonight—he was restless . . . edgy. She could sense it in the persistent boldness of his touch, feel it in the demanding abrasiveness of his kiss. He seemed to have an excess amount of testosterone and frustration built up inside him and he wanted to work it out on her. The idea of becoming that outlet for him had her instantly wet and aching for him. Suddenly, she found herself rationalizing her reservations.

"I've wanted to do this all day . . ." he whispered against her ear. "The thought of leaving you tomorrow is tearing me up." He held her tighter, kissing his way down her neck. "I tell myself you'll be fine, but I don't want anyone protecting you but me."

There was his rub . . . the annoyance eating away at him. Asher wasn't a man who gave up control, and she could sense what it was costing him to do so now—even if it was only for one day. Neither she nor Asher had a choice in the matter, not if they wanted this to end. All she could do was be here for him and ease his frustration any way she could.

"I'll be fine with your brother," she assured him with more bravado than she felt. Not that she didn't trust Jax or the other agents; they just weren't Asher. Quinn turned in his arms and slowly slid his shirt up, exposing a roadmap of muscles she wouldn't mind exploring with her tongue. She could see this body every day for the rest of her life and never grow tired of it. "You'll be back tomorrow night. And I'll be here waiting . . ."

He let her go long enough to finish pulling off his shirt, and hers, leaving her standing in nothing but a white lace thong. He took a moment to study her in the glow of the moonlight shining in through the window. She stood there, heart pounding in anticipation at the wild possessiveness reflecting in his eyes. She was long past her shyness. It was impossible to retain any bit of modesty after Asher had made love to her. He'd left no part of her untouched, unexplored, or unclaimed. She belonged to him . . . body, mind, and soul.

When his hungry gaze dragged up to lock on hers, she held it as she knelt before him. Something flared in Asher's eyes—it was the look of a man about to lose control, and a thrill of fear and excitement lit up her veins. Before she lost her nerve, Quinn unfastened his jeans, sliding them down his long, muscular legs, and released his cock from Abercrombie & Fitch.

The rapid rise and fall of his chest, the heat blazing in his eyes, sent Quinn's heart beating at a chaotic tempo. She held fast to that beautiful multicolored stare as she parted her lips and slowly dragged her tongue over his crown.

He hissed a breath and growled a vulgar curse that startled her. She'd never done this before and wasn't entirely sure what she was doing. But she'd definitely underestimated the intensity of his reaction. Asher's eyes broke her stare and his lids fluttered closed as his head tipped back, exposing the thick, corded muscles of his neck. It was the most erotic thing she'd ever seen—this powerful, muscular man submitting himself to her . . .

But not entirely. No, there was always that small element of control he had to hold on to. He could never fully let go, and she felt it now as he gathered her hair out of her face and fisted it into his hand. Slowly, he pulled her head forward, guiding himself into her mouth. As he set the pace, she slipped one hand up his thigh and around to grab the hard muscled flesh of his ass, biting her nails in just hard enough to make sure he remembered who was really in charge here.

"Oh fuuuck . . ." he groaned, his cock jerking in response to the warning, and maybe the pain.

She relaxed her throat and took him deeper as her other hand slowly slid to his hip. Her thumb swept over the muscular indent before her fingers rode up the ridges of his stomach—his entire body was like flesh-covered steel. The tactile foreplay sent her senses into overload. The scent of him, the taste of his essence on her tongue . . . The intimately erotic feeling of him filling her mouth had her moaning with pleasure. She was so close to coming and he wasn't even touching her. The ache between her thighs, the building pressure deep in her core, was almost unbearable. She dragged her nails over Asher's pec and the flat disc of his nipple.

He barked a sharp curse as the first embers of his release slicked across her tongue. His hand fisting her hair tightened and he pulled her mouth away. Before she realized what he was doing, Asher yanked her to her feet and ripped away the scrap of lace between her legs. Lifting her up, he backed her against the wall and thrust inside her.

The sudden invasion ripped a cry of pleasure from her throat. Asher's mouth covered hers, swallowing her release as he relentlessly drove them over the edge. She inhaled his low groan as a rush of heat poured into her, sending her spiraling into ecstasy.

After a few breath-catching moments, Asher leaned back just far enough to meet Quinn's eyes. Where a few minutes ago there had been wild, untamed lust, there was now concern. "Are you all right? I didn't hurt you, did I?"

It had been a rough ride. Luckily, she liked him like that. No doubt she'd be feeling him all day tomorrow.

Before she could assure him she'd never been better, Asher murmured a self-recriminating "Fuck, you make me lose control . . ."

He'd yet to put her down, to leave her heat. Quinn slipped her hand beneath his chin and lifted it so his gaze met hers. "Hey, I'm fine . . ." Giving him a teasing smile she said, "Besides, I like it when you lose control."

Exhaling a sigh, he rested his forehead against hers. "Thank God, because I feel like that's all I do around you."

CHAPTER

39

The moment Asher's plane touched down at Reagan National Airport, he turned his cell on and fired off a text message to Quinn.

Just landed. How is everything there?

At his insistence, the Feds had gotten her an untraceable cell because he didn't want to be out of contact with her. It was hard enough leaving her as it was. His flight out wasn't until 5:00 p.m. and he wouldn't touch down in Denver until nine. Barring any delays, the soonest he could get back to Quinn was ten o'clock tonight.

Perhaps it was just being away from her after being her sole protector, but leaving the job to someone else, even if it was two federal agents and his brother, didn't sit well with him. What-ifs ran rampant through his mind. If he didn't find a way to shut this shit down, he was going to make himself crazy. His cell buzzed and his pulse quickened, anxious for her response. Fuck, he had it bad for this woman.

Doing fine here. Uneventful morning. Miss you . . .

Miss you too. Be back tonight. What's going on there?

Agent Kellen is outside doing a property
sweep. Agent Meadows has been on the
phone with Langley a lot this morning. They
think they can salvage the photos. *fingers
crossed* Your brother made me breakfast.
He burned the toast, but don't tell him I told
you. ;)

He knew what Quinn was doing—trying to lighten his mood and
put him at ease. Unfortunately, the only thing that was going to do that
was having her safe and back in his arms again, but he could play along.
She didn't need to know what it was costing him to do this.

Your secret's safe with me. Just keep him
away from the grill.

He couldn't possibly dread this meeting more. The Feds had been
helpful in cutting through the red tape and getting him an appointment
with the bastard he never wanted to set eyes on again.

LOL! Will do. What time is your meeting?

Two.

The plane rolled to a stop and the seat belt light went off. Passengers
stood and began flooding the aisle, grabbing their luggage from the
overhead compartments.

Hope everything goes well.

That would be nice, but he knew it wouldn't.

Thanks. I'll call you later. Stay safe.

I will. You too. I love you. :)

The weight on his shoulders lightened and his heart swelled inside his chest as he read those three words. He couldn't wait until this was over and they could finally focus on their future instead of trying to survive their past.

Love you too.

———

A loud, obnoxious buzz sounded as the metal lock disengaged and the guard opened the door. Asher stepped in the room, gave the guard a head nod as he walked by, and approached the man sitting at the table. His ankles were cuffed to a metal ring anchored in the cement floor. Suited in orange, the prisoner leaned forward in his chair, head down, wrists shackled. He'd yet to acknowledge Asher's presence. Not a good sign—for either one of them. This wasn't going to end well.

Seeing this bastard again dredged up the past like it was yesterday. Gunfire echoed somewhere in the recesses of Asher's mind, the distant shout of his voice ringing in his ears. *Stand down!* The coppery tang of blood mixed with the sulfuric bite of gunpowder stung his nostrils and anger flooded his veins all over again.

The man's head snapped up, eyes locking with Asher. His cold hard stare carried none of the regret Asher had hoped to see.

"Little late to testify, ain't it? The trial ended days ago. I'd say it was nice to see ya, but fuck you."

Asher pulled the empty chair away from the table and sat across from Rolland Peterson. "I didn't come here to talk about the trial."

"Then why the fuck are you here? Because it sure as hell isn't to talk about the weather."

"I'm here because you wouldn't take my call."

"That's because I wanted to give you the chance to apologize to me in person."

"Are you fucking serious?" This guy was out of his goddamn mind if he thought Asher was going to apologize to him. And he had to bite his tongue to keep from telling the bastard exactly that. He had no interest in dancing around the subject anymore. The sooner he got what he came here for, the sooner he could get the hell out of there. "I want to talk about Eagle Ops." Not a flicker of surprise registered on Peterson's face, but the smug satisfaction tugging his top lip sent a chill of unease racing down Asher's spine.

"What about it?"

"You've worked for them in the past. Who's the point of contact?"

"Why do you want to know? You looking for work?"

"Maybe . . ."

He huffed a derisive snort. "Don't fucking lie to me."

"Well, you pretty much single-handedly fucked my career when you started a shoot-out in Nisour, so the way I see it, you owe me."

"I don't owe you shit!" He slammed his fists on the metal table. Asher didn't flinch, but it was much more difficult to hold back the smile threatening to curl his lips. Peterson was a time bomb. Rattle his cage hard enough, and Asher had no doubt he'd get the answers he was looking for.

"I saved your fucking life! And this is how you thank me? You sanctimonious bastard! Every one of you would have been dead if it wasn't for me. "

Peterson really believed that. It wasn't true, but in this man's grandiose world it was. Asher shook his head with the first embers of pity sparking inside him. "Have you taken any jobs with EO working for the Children's Global Resource Network?"

The grin that crossed Peterson's face was nothing but pure evil. "Sorry, I don't talk about my other missions, and I sure as hell ain't discussing them with you. Who are you working for, Tate?"

"No one." It was true.

"Then what the fuck do you give a shit about the CGRN for?"

Holding on to a thread of hope that the man still had a shred of humanity alive somewhere inside his black soul, Asher took a chance and told him the truth. "Kids are disappearing, man—talk to me. Give me a name and I'll see what I can do about getting your sentence reduced. I'll talk to whomever your lawyer wants. I'll testify at your appeal."

"Ha, you say that like you think your word means shit to me now. It's your fault I'm in this goddamn place. If you just would have come when Jayce asked you to—"

Asher slammed his fist on the table and shot to his feet, sending the chair skidding back behind him. "You're in this goddamn place because you pulled the trigger after I gave you a direct order to stand down! Tell me who else is working for EO! Who's their point of contact?" He was done playing games with this asshole.

A smirk curled Peterson's top lip and Asher's fist tightened. It took all his restraint not to reach across the table and choke the life out of him right here and now.

"When are you going to learn you can't save the world, Tate? Haven't you figured that out by now? They're just some kids on a shit-hole piece of land nobody gives a fuck about. One less mouth to feed—"

Asher launched across the table and grabbed the collar of Peterson's orange jumpsuit. "You goddamn piece of shit! You were trafficking kids right under the nose of the CGRN! Who else is doing it?"

"I'm not saying another motherfucking word until you talk to those Feds you're working with and get me an immunity deal."

With a contemptuous shove, he sent Peterson slamming back in his chair. The guard remained where he was, giving Asher the freedom to let this play out—on whose order, he wondered. He straightened and dragged his hand through his hair. How did Peterson know he was working with the FBI? Dammit, getting his answers was going to take too long. Even if the Feds would agree to bargain for a reduced sentence, he doubted Peterson was going to talk—not if it meant implicating himself.

"Why did you insist I come here if you had no intention of helping?"

"Oh, I'm helping. You just arrogantly assumed that person would be you. By the way, I hear she's a sweet piece of ass . . ."

Asher froze. His eyes shot to Peterson's. Icy fingers of dread slipped down his spine. "Who's that?"

"Your girlfriend. How does it feel to know that at this very moment, while you're wasting your time here with me, there's a killer right outside her door? And there's not a goddamn thing you can do about it."

Was this a trap? An orchestrated ploy to get him away from Quinn? Or just another one of this bastard's sick mind games?

"Quinn Summers, isn't it? That's a beautiful name . . . reminds me of sunshine and butterflies."

Fuck! Asher shot to his feet with a snarled curse and bolted for the door. Peterson's laughter was a chilling taunt that would haunt him forever if anything happened to her.

"You're too late . . ." he called in farewell.

God, he prayed Peterson was wrong.

———

"Gin." Quinn laid her cards on the end table between herself and Jaxson, and gave him a triumphant grin. "What'd I stick you with? Is it enough to go out?"

"Beginner's luck," he grumbled, laying his hand down and showing her two queens and a five.

Quinn laughed, grateful for the distraction Jax offered her. He didn't seem like the kind of guy that sat around playing cards. He was much too stoic, too intense to kick back and while away the day playing games. But Quinn had been a nervous wreck ever since Asher had left that morning.

Jax, bless his heart, was doing his best to keep her distracted without making her feel like a prisoner. He'd even offered to play gin with her. When she told him she didn't know how to play, he'd suggested that learning a new game might help take her mind off Asher for a little while.

She didn't point out that sitting across from an identical replica of the man she was hopelessly in love with, and worried sick about, would make that an impossible task. Quinn was desperate for the chance to think about anything other than Asher being halfway across the country, meeting with someone who had ties to an organization that had more than likely sent someone to kill her, and was involved in human trafficking.

Quinn gathered the cards and began shuffling them. "So . . . do you have a girlfriend?"

Jaxson's blank stare gave nothing away. "I said I'd play cards with you, not talk about my love life. Deal the cards, Quinn."

"Come on, Jax. Don't be so broody. You said you'd help distract me from worrying about your brother, so talk to me. You're always so quiet, even at the barbecue. Tell me about yourself."

He watched her a moment, but hell if she could figure out what was going on inside his head. He was harder to read than Asher, and that was saying something. Just when she didn't think he was going to answer her, he said, "I'm not seeing anyone. I was, and it didn't work out. Dating a homicide detective might sound fun and exciting—until you actually do it. Most women can't stand being in second place to a job, and I married mine a long time ago."

Wow, that was more transparency than she was expecting.

"Now deal the cards."

Quinn finished shuffling the deck and started dealing the cards. *One, one . . . two, two . . . three, three . . .* She could feel Jax watching her—studying her. Her brow rose, a silent *What?*

"Are you really in love with my brother?"

"I am. Why do you sound so surprised by that?" *Four, four . . . five, five . . .*

"He isn't an easy man to love. He's got some sharp edges."

She stopped dealing and met his stare. "Don't we all?" What was he getting at? Did he know something about Asher he wasn't telling her? In the time she'd spent with Jax, she'd quickly figured out that no conversation with him was ever just that. He had a cop's mind—suspicious—always thinking, always trying to figure everything out. She suspected that jaded side of him came from the horrific deeds he'd witnessed over his years on the force. It would take the right woman, a special woman, to soften that out of him.

She resumed dealing. *Six, six . . . seven, seven . . .*

Pop! The muffled sound carried upstairs and Quinn froze. Her eyes locked on Jax, who was already reaching for his gun.

CHAPTER
40

I need on the next flight to Denver," Asher demanded, speaking past the cell phone pressed to the side of his face and the ringing in his ear. Why in the fuck wasn't Jax answering? He'd sent Quinn a *Hey, how are you? Just checking in* text, but hadn't gotten a response yet. He didn't want to scare her unnecessarily if, by some chance in hell, Peterson was fucking with him, but his gut told him this was for real. The guy knew too much about Quinn for this to be anything other than a setup.

When his call rolled over to voice mail, he growled a nasty curse that had the woman behind the counter giving him a disapproving scowl. He ended the call without leaving a message so he could talk to the woman about getting on that damn plane, which was about to leave in the next five minutes.

"What is your name?" The woman asked.

He handed her his ID and she typed his info into the computer.

"It says here you're scheduled to leave on a flight to Denver in an hour and a half."

"I know when my flight is. I'm telling you I need to be on *that* plane," he pointed at the one sitting outside his departing terminal.

"It's leaving in five minutes."

"Thank you. That's why I need to be on it."

"They've closed boarding."

"Ma'am, it's an emergency. I really need to get on that plane. Will you please check to see if they have any available seating?"

When she went back to typing on her computer, Asher checked his cell for any missed messages or calls.

Nothing.

Fuck.

Dear God, he prayed he wasn't too late.

"There is one seat available in the—"

"Great! I'll take it."

She shot him an annoyed scowl, but he didn't give a shit. He wasn't trying to make friends. If she didn't like him now, she really wasn't going to like him if he missed that flight.

"I'll have to call the pilot and make sure they'll still let you board."

As she picked up her phone, Asher dialed Jax again. He was torn over contacting either Agent Meadows or Agent Kellen—unsure right now whom he could trust. They could be the leak, or maybe someone else in the bureau. It was impossible to know, but one thing was for sure—if that assassin knew where Quinn was, then someone on the inside was feeding that fucker intel.

This time when the call went to voice mail Asher left a message. "Jax, it's me. The whole trip was a setup to get me away from Quinn. The killer knows where she is. Peterson knew about Quinn, the EO, and the CGRN. Get her out of there. I don't know if Meadows or Kellen are involved. Call me back as soon as you get this."

He disconnected the call and the woman across the counter was staring at him, pale faced and slack jawed with the receiver halfway between her ear and the desk. She'd obviously heard his message and looked like she was about to shit herself.

"Well?" he prompted impatiently when she didn't say anything. "Can you get me on that plane?"

"Y-yes . . ." She came around the desk and handed him his ticket. "Follow me."

The woman led him through the passenger terminal and down the Jetway, his strides eating up the distance as he rushed toward the plane. Fuck it—if Jax and Quinn weren't answering, he needed to call Meadows.

Asher made one last call as he boarded the Boeing 747. "Sir," the stewardess approached him as he headed for his seat. The engines were already running and the plane began to ferry down the runway. "Sir, you're going to have to hang up your call."

He ignored her, praying to God the agent would pick up on the next ring—or the next—or the next. Asher slid into his seat and fastened his belt as the jet began to pick up speed. "Sir . . . we're ready to take off. Please shut off your phone."

The call went into Agent Meadows's voice mail. Fuck! Panic like he'd never felt before gripped his heart. It was paralyzing. The helplessness of being stuck four hours away from Quinn with no idea if she was all right was the most gut-wrenching experience of his life. There was no doubt in his mind that if anything happened to Quinn, it would be a loss he'd never survive.

———

"Did you hear that?" Quinn whispered. Downstairs there was a ping of breaking glass followed by a dull thud.

The shot of adrenaline flooding her veins jumpstarted her heart, which was now banging a rapid staccato against her ribs.

Jax held a finger to his lips, warning her to be silent as he carefully set his cards on the end table and rose. She could hear the soft vibration of his cell ringing in his pocket. He ignored the call and reached behind his back, pulling his gun from his waistband. He waved her over. She crept up behind him, taking care not to make any noise.

The buzzing stopped as he grabbed her wrist and pulled her close, shielding her with his body. As they inched closer to the railing, his cell began vibrating again. She prayed the low hum wouldn't give away their position. She reached into his front pocket and pulled out the phone.

Asher was calling. The temptation to answer was almost too much to resist. It pained her to swipe her thumb across the screen, silencing the call. She'd give anything right now to hear the deep, assured calmness of his voice.

"We need to get you to the panic room," Jax whispered.

Easier said than done. There was a flight of stairs, a living room, and a dining room separating them from the access door in the kitchen. They approached the railing overlooking the living room and Quinn's hammering heart leapt into her throat. It was the only thing blocking the scream threatening to rip free. Special Agent Meadows sat slumped on the couch with a bullet wound in the center of his forehead. The back of his head was missing; blood and white matter ran down the wall behind the couch.

Quinn's stomach lurched. Her hand flew up to cover her mouth. She turned to make a dash for the bathroom but Jax wouldn't let her go. He spun them away from the railing and pulled her into his arms, holding her tight as he pressed them into the small alcove.

"Shhh . . ." he whispered beside her ear.

Quinn swallowed against the bitter rise of bile burning the back of her throat. But when the agent's cell began to ring, her broken sob was all it took to give away their position.

Pop. Pop. Bullets tore through the Sheetrock above their heads, sending white dust raining down on them.

Jax swore, stepped away from the wall, and returned fire. "You've still got my phone?"

"Yes." She clutched the cell so hard, her fingers were going numb.

"Call 911 and tell them Detective Tate is in a shoot-out at the O'Brian safe house. One federal agent is dead, the other is status unknown."

Where was Agent Kellen? Why wasn't he helping them? Quinn ducked down and made the call to 911 as Jax and the man who'd shot Agent Meadows exchanged another round of gunfire. Jax's gun clicked; he growled a curse and dropped his clip before pulling another from his pocket. He slammed it into the grip of his gun, released the slide, and began shooting again. They couldn't stay up here. Jax was going to run out of ammo. She had the gun Asher had given her, but that was only a nine-round clip.

There was another pause in gunfire and Quinn saw a flash of black cut across the living room. The shooter threw the front door open and ran out. It took a whole two seconds for Jax to chase after him.

"Get to the panic room, Quinn." He charged down the stairs and ran out the front door.

Quinn pulled the gun from the holster on her ankle and started down the stairs. Her sweat-slicked hands shook from the adrenaline coursing through her body. *This is not happening*... Her mind told her the lie, attempting self-preservation of her sanity.

Oh, but it was. There was a dead federal agent with his brains blown all over the living room wall to prove it. As Quinn's feet hit the landing, she kept her eyes averted from the couch. When she passed the front door, she stopped. Another wave of dread crashed over her, threatening to pull her under. Out on the front lawn Jax knelt over Agent Kellen. Both his hands were pressed against the side of the agent's neck. He wasn't moving.

Instead of running for the panic room, she raced to the front door. Her knees threatened to buckle as she gripped the jamb. "Oh, God, is he dead?"

Agent Kellen was pale and still. From where she stood, she couldn't tell if he was dead or unconscious. She prayed the latter and banked on that hope because Jax was still trying to save him. Blood seeped out from beneath his hands, oozing between his fingers as he fought to stymie the flow. There was so much blood . . .

"Quinn, get back in the house!" Jax shouted over his shoulder.

She hesitated to leave him, torn between wanting to help and getting to safety. How many more lives would be lost protecting her? But there was nothing she could do for Agent Kellen now. If she didn't get to that safe room, then their sacrifice would be for nothing.

"Goddammit, Quinn!"

Jax's voice spurred her feet into action. Quinn turned and ran back inside, cutting through the living room and into the kitchen. Her fingers had just grazed the doorknob leading to the basement stairs when a sharp pain bit into her scalp. She let out a startled yelp as her head snapped back and she was yanked off-balance. The gun in her hand went off, a wild shot that sent ceiling dust raining down on them. The weapon was ripped from her grasp as she stumbled back, crashing into a wall of muscle.

A shrill cry of terror tore from her throat. The man's hand clamped tightly around her neck, cutting off her scream. Her lungs burned from lack of oxygen and she began to struggle against the merciless grip.

"Let her go!"

The man spun them both around to face the voice. Using her as a shield, he held Quinn pressed tightly against him. One hand still clamped over her throat, the other now holding her gun. The muzzle bit sharply into her right temple.

Oh my God, I'm going to die . . .

"Get back or I'll fucking kill her!"

Jax was blocking their exit—his gun hand steady and absolutely unwavering. Seeing him from this perspective, the man was almost as terrifying as the one who held a gun to her head. Zero emotion reflected on his face, his eyes so identical to his brother's, yet it was like looking into the face of a stranger. This man was tactical and decisive. Impending doom reached into her chest with icy fingers and took hold of her heart.

"You're going to kill her anyway."

Sirens sounded in the distance—growing closer. As she watched Jax take in the scene, assess the desperation of their situation, what felt like agonizing minutes only took about two seconds. And then she saw the muzzle of Jax's gun shift to her.

"I'm sorry, Quinn . . ."

Before his words could fully register, his gun fired. Fire ripped through her shoulder and she flew back into the man that was already falling. When she landed on the ground, her head smacked on the tile floor, ushering her into blessed blackness.

CHAPTER
41

Quinn woke to her heartbeat in her shoulder. The pain was a throbbing presence somewhere distant in the haze of her mind. Her throat was raw and ash dry. She tried to swallow, sending a little moisture that way. She winced and felt a weight shift beside her. Warm hands enveloped one of hers and gently squeezed. She tried to open her eyes but the invisible sandbags wouldn't let her.

Confusion clouded her mind, the pain an annoying presence anchoring her to consciousness when she'd much prefer to escape to oblivion—where there was no pain and no one was trying to kill her.

"Quinn . . ." The deep masculine voice held strained emotion that pulled at her heartstrings. She tried again to open her eyes and this time succeeded, but her vision was blurred. She gave her best effort at a smile when she met that beautiful multicolored stare. Worry lines creased his forehead, tension bracketing his mouth.

"Asher . . ." Her voice was barely more than a hoarse rasp.

"No, it's Jax."

She blinked a few times, trying to focus her eyes through the haze of painkillers. She abandoned her smile and replaced it with a confused frown. "You . . . shot me."

Jax's grip on her hand tightened and he exhaled a deep sigh. "Jesus, I know. Fuck, I'm so sorry, Quinn. I couldn't let him take you. I knew if he did, you'd be dead before we ever found you."

"You shot me to save me . . ." she managed weakly, cracking what she could of a smile. "You know how messed up that sounds, right?"

His chuff of laughter held no humor. "Believe me, I know. You can imagine how it went trying to explain myself to Asher. Telling my brother I shot his girlfriend did not go well. He's off-the-charts pissed at me. I expect him to be barreling in here any moment. If it helps, I shot you because your shoulder was right in front of that fucker's heart. The bullet went through you and into his left ventricle."

"So he's dead?" The idea of having this nightmare over, to know that the man who killed Emily and so many others was dead, almost made it worth the bullet.

Jax nodded. "He is. They're working on IDing him now. Hopefully we'll hear something soon."

"What about Agent Kellen?"

Jax looked away and softly shook his head. Tears filled Quinn's eyes as guilt washed over her in a crushing wave. Two more lives, gone because of her. Her only consolation was that no one else would die trying to protect her. Thanks to Jax, it was finally over.

She squeezed his hand to draw his eyes back to hers. When they met, she saw all the emotion he'd kept bottled up at the safe house churning inside him—grief, guilt, anger, fear . . . Jax wasn't the emotionless, hard-hearted cop she'd mistaken him for. He was struggling with the decision he'd made to pull that trigger, no doubt second-guessing his choice. If he'd stayed with Agent Kellen, kept the pressure on his neck, would he have lived? When she put herself in his place—the impossible decisions he'd been faced with—Quinn's heart ached. The last thing she wanted him doing was feeling bad about the choice he'd made. Most likely he'd saved her life, because Jax was right—the man who held that gun to her head had planned to kill her.

"I forgive you for shooting me." She squeezed his hand tighter. "You saved my life. Thank you." The look he gave her was a little surprised—like he hadn't been expecting her gratitude. "If it helps you feel any better, I'd do the same thing for you."

A smile tipped his mouth. It wasn't much, but she'd take it.

"Thanks. I think that's the nicest thing you've ever said to me."

The door flew open and Asher rushed to her side. He took the vacant spot on the other side of her hip and framed her face with his hands. "Quinn, sweetheart, are you all right?" His deep voice was choked with emotion, making it strained and raspy. Just the sight of him made her lose the battle with her tears and they spilled down her cheeks.

Quinn nodded as relief swept over her. "I'm okay," she told him, trying to sound braver than she felt. "It's over. He's dead."

Asher pressed a chaste kiss to her mouth, holding the contact long enough to draw a deep breath, as if needing the extra moment to compose himself. Jax let go of her hand and stood, giving them their space. Now that Asher was here, her bravado crumbled and Quinn lost it. A culmination of fear turned to relief, and now the regret and grief over the loss of so many lives had her sobbing.

"Shhh . . ." he whispered against her cheek. His nose nuzzled against her temple as he gently gathered her into his arms. She wrapped her good arm around him and held on like he was the lifeline he'd become.

"I'll give you two some privacy." Jax's voice was strained.

"Don't go far. I want to talk to you."

The chill in his voice made Quinn shiver.

"I'll be down at the cafeteria."

The door clicked closed softly. Neither of them spoke for several minutes, both seeming to grapple with emotions too powerful for words. He just held her with his face buried in the side of her neck. When his strong muscular shoulders softly shook, she understood the reason for his silence.

"I'm all right, Asher. I promise. I know you're mad at Jax—"

He lifted his head and met her eyes. Quinn's breath caught in her throat at the raw emotion she saw reflecting at her through the breathtaking prism of color. "Mad? Quinn, I'm furious. My brother nearly took my life from me. I trusted him to protect you, to keep you safe."

"He did. Asher, you weren't there. That man . . . he had a gun to my head. He was going to kill me."

"Jax shot you."

"Jax saved my life. He did what he had to do at the moment. You owe him thanks and, I suspect, an apology. Don't let this drive a wedge further between you two. I can't live with that guilt, Asher. Not on top of everything else."

He seemed to concede after taking a moment to contemplate her words. "When this is all over, I'm taking you someplace far away from here."

When this is all over . . . Wouldn't that be nice? Hearing those words was a sad reminder that just because someone wasn't trying to kill her anymore, it didn't mean this was over. There was a group of men running a human-trafficking trade on the other side of the world, and she'd vowed to do whatever it took to stop them. She was going to have to testify to what she saw that night—to relive that nightmare all over again. But as long as she had Asher's love and support, she had no doubt she would make it through this.

"I'd really love that."

He leaned forward and pressed a kiss against her forehead. "I should go talk to Jax. You need anything before I go? Do you want me to have the nurse come sit with you?"

"No, I'm fine. I'm just going to try to get some more rest. I'll see you when you get back."

Asher rose from the bed, but instead of leaving, he tucked the covers in around her. Cupping the side of her cheek, he whispered, "I love you, Quinn."

She turned her face and kissed the center of his palm. "I love you too, Asher."

He left and quietly closed the door behind him. Quinn hit her PCA button, giving herself another dose of pain medication before closing her eyes to rest. She'd just started to drift off when she heard a soft knock on the door.

———

As Asher walked down the hall, a prickle of unease needled at him. He hated leaving Quinn, especially after what she'd just been through, but the conversation he planned to have with his brother would be best not spoken in front of her. He ignored the feeling of fire ants that had been crawling over his flesh since the moment he stepped off the plane, and followed the signs to the cafeteria.

He'd been a wreck ever since he'd landed and discovered a message from Jax telling him the safe house had been hit. He'd never come so close to losing his fucking mind. When he'd called Jax and gotten the details, nuclear didn't begin to describe the emotions rocketing through him. Now that he'd seen for himself that Quinn was all right, he no longer wanted to murder his brother, but that didn't mean he wanted to star on the next Doublemint commercial with the guy either.

In his heart he knew Quinn was right. He needed to get over this and forgive Jaxson for shooting her. The truth of it was he probably did save her life. And as much as it angered Asher about how it was done, it equally upset him to know that if he'd been in his brother's shoes, he never would have been able to do it. He would have hesitated and Quinn would most likely be dead right now. And quite possibly a murderer would be running free.

That was the one good thing about all this. At least that fucker was dead. Asher still had questions—lots of them, like how that bastard knew the location of the safe house. Or how Peterson knew about

Quinn. Had he been a part of the trafficking before the Nisour Square indictment? All of those were answers he expected would come out in the next few days as the FBI headed up its investigation, because they had two dead agents and the bureau was pissed. Heads were definitely going to roll.

Jax was on the phone when Asher walked into the cafeteria. This late at night, the place was empty. The only food anyone was getting would be out of a vending machine. Not that he could eat. The thought of it made his stomach churn. He quickly checked his own phone for any missed messages. He was waiting for the enhanced pictures to come in from Langley any time. They wanted him to show the photos to Quinn to see if she recognized any of the men.

"Call me as soon as you get the prelim back. I want a name and positive ID on that fucker ASAP."

Jax disconnected the call and glanced up, locking eyes with Asher. It was like looking in a mirror.

"No word, huh?" Asher came over to the table closest to Jax and dropped into the chair.

"Not yet. Soon, though."

"You couldn't have just shot him in the fucking head?"

Jax exhaled a sigh and took the chair across from him. "I couldn't. He had a gun to her temple and I was afraid if I shot him in the head his muscles would contract and he'd pull the trigger. By hitting her first, she buckled and moved out of the line of fire. You think if there were any other way out I wouldn't have taken it?"

Asher knew he would have. He needed to let his brother off the goddamn hook. "You're right, Jax. I shouldn't have lit into you like that on the phone. You saved Quinn's life, and I'm forever in your debt." He reached across the table and offered his brother his hand. Jax looked at him a little surprised, as if he couldn't believe Asher was forgiving him.

"I don't want any thanks." He took Asher's hand and gave it a firm shake. "I just wish it didn't have to happen like that."

Asher's cell buzzed, alerting him to an incoming e-mail. "That should be the photos from Langley." He retrieved his phone and opened the attachment, then began downloading the pictures.

"They got them enhanced, huh?"

"Yeah. Hopefully Quinn will recognize these guys. It'll make their arrest a hell of a lot faster when we know who we're looking for."

"Forward the e-mail to me, will ya? Maybe one of these guys will be our shooter."

Asher forwarded it and opened the first picture. Jax's cell chimed and he downloaded the pics. The images were still a little shadowed, but Asher could see faces now, and they were much closer than the—

"What the fuck?" He zoomed the pic in and out, readjusting the image to get a better look at the man standing off to the side. There had to be some mistake . . . but the fucking camera didn't lie.

"What's the matter? You recognize one of the guys?" Jax asked.

Before he could answer, Jax's cell began to ring. He had it to his ear before the tone could sound a second time. "Tate. What's the word on that ID?"

His brother's conversation drifted to the background as Asher's mind tried to reject what he was seeing. *No fucking way . . .* He'd fought beside this bastard—bled for the motherfucker.

"What the hell do you mean he's not our guy?"

Asher's head snapped up, eyes locking on his brother.

"Hang on." Then to him, Jax said, "Blood type wasn't a match to the sample I got from your place. He's not our shooter."

"Fuck!" Asher jumped up, knocking the chair to the floor as he ran for Quinn's room.

CHAPTER
42

"Come in . . ." Quinn called at the soft knock sounding on the door. It opened slowly and she was surprised to see the man standing there. "Jayce? What are you doing here?"

"I heard about what happened from Asher's father. I stopped by to check on you. Are you all right?" He peeked his head inside and glanced around the room. "Asher here?"

Quinn glanced up at the clock. It was almost 11:30 p.m. Pretty late to be stopping by for a visit, but she also knew that men who served together in the military were close—Semper Fi and all that. He probably wouldn't let something like the time of day stop him from being there to support a friend in need. Maybe it was the morphine fogging her mind and messing with her judgment, but something about this didn't quite feel right.

"He ran to the cafeteria. I expect him back any minute."

"Great. You won't mind if I wait inside then?"

He didn't give her a chance to say either way. Jayce stepped inside and the door closed behind him. He took another step and that was when she noticed his limp. Her heart raced as her mind made the connection. The staccato of her panic displayed on the monitor above her head. The beep, beep, beep of her spiked pulse drew Jayce's gaze to the monitor.

The smile that he gave her held the warmth of a rattlesnake about to strike. "I see you've finally figured it out." He tapped two fingers against his temple. "About fucking time . . . I saw you that night."

"Excuse me?"

"In Haiti. You were there in the bushes, taking pictures of us. I wondered why you didn't recognize me that day you showed up to Asher's. But it makes sense now. Your pictures weren't any good. Do you have any idea how many times you've slipped between my fingers? After a while, you just needed to die on principle alone. Fuck, you're like a goddamn cat with nine lives.

"I managed to snag your laptop and camera at the airport before they loaded your luggage into the cargo hold. Imagine my dismay to find the SD card missing from your camera. It was helpful that you had your name and address on the luggage tag though. I knew right where to find you. Only you weren't there."

Emily . . . Tears pricked her eyes but she held them back, refusing to give this bastard the satisfaction of seeing her cry.

Jayce pulled a gun from the inside of his jacket and pointed it at her. There was no doubt in her mind she was going to die and this was his confession—right before he pulled that trigger.

"Just do it," she told him, losing the battle with her tears. "Before Asher comes back. You can slip away and no one will know it was you." She was desperate for him to leave before Asher returned. There wasn't anything she wouldn't say or do to save his life, and any moment he was going to walk through that door and it would be too late.

"That might have been true at one time, Quinn, but it's too late for that now. Believe it or not, it gives me no pleasure to kill him. But you, on the other hand . . . I'm going to enjoy this—just a little."

The door flew open, slamming into the wall as Asher burst into her room. The feral rage on his face when his eyes locked on Jayce was murderous. In the weeks they'd spent together, Asher had told her several times he was a killer, but it wasn't until this moment, seeing the bloodlust in his eyes, that she truly believed him.

His hand shot behind his back.

"Ah-ah-ah . . . slowly . . ." Jayce warned. "Set the gun on the floor and kick it over here."

Asher's gaze flickered from Jayce to her—and then back to Jayce, who kept the barrel pointed at his chest as Asher withdrew the gun from his waistband and did as instructed.

"I'm glad to see you made it. A little late to the party, but you're here nonetheless. Shut that door and block it with a chair."

When Asher didn't comply right away, Jayce moved his aim, pointing the gun at Quinn's chest. "How long do you think it'll take for her to bleed out? Should we find out? It took Collin five minutes. You think you could save her in time? You couldn't save Anderson."

Asher snarled a nasty curse and grabbed a chair, jamming it beneath the door handle so it couldn't turn.

"There. Now we won't have to deal with interruptions."

"Why are you pointing that gun at her?" Asher growled. "She's no threat to you."

"No, you're right. She's not, but I know you, and you don't give a fuck if you live or die, so it's rather pointless to aim it at you. But you care about her. I knew you were lying to me when you told me you didn't—that you weren't fucking her. Not that I blame you. I've had plans for her myself . . . You should have left to go testify on Peterson's behalf when I called you and asked you to go the first time. You wouldn't have been there when she showed up at your house, and we wouldn't be here right now."

"You know I'm going to fucking kill you, right?" Asher growled. "And when I do, I'm going to make sure you suffer."

It was a promise that made the fine hairs on the nape of Quinn's neck prickle. Did Asher really believe either of them stood a chance in hell of surviving this? They were being held at gunpoint by a madman.

"What happened to you?" Asher asked with a snarl of disgust. Quinn wasn't sure if he was stalling, trying to buy himself some time to figure a way out of this, or if he genuinely wanted to know.

"The same thing that happened to you, so you can drop that self-righteous, sanctimonious bullshit. You forget, I fought beside you. I watched you kill, over and over and over again. Those bureaucratic bastards didn't just steal my humanity—they got yours too. The government wanted to create a monster . . . Well, they sure as hell got one!"

"There was a time I would have agreed with you, but you're wrong. I am *nothing* like you. At least now I know why you wanted me to testify on Peterson's behalf. I couldn't figure out why you spoke at his trial, why you cared so much when you clearly don't give a fuck about anyone else. You lost your partner in your little side operation. And now you're another player short after the hit on the safe house. How many more of you are there? You know the Feds are going to shut EO down, right? It's over. They're already tracing calls made from Quantico in the last twenty-four hours to find the leak. And when they do, I suspect it's going to lead them straight to your boss."

The door handle rattled, catching against the back of the chair. The momentary distraction was all Asher needed, and perhaps was what he was waiting for, to make a move. The second Jayce's eyes flickered to the door, Asher dove for him. Jayce swung his gun toward Asher, but before he could fire off a shot, Asher forced his gun hand up. The weapon discharged into the ceiling with a deafening pop before they both hit the floor. Quinn's ears rang, the high-pitched sound slowly fading to the riotous banging on the door and the dull thuds of fists hitting flesh combined with the occasional pained grunt amidst the chaos. She couldn't see them from where she lay in the bed, but knew this was her only chance to act.

She tore the monitor cables from her chest, and pulled off her blood pressure cuff and the O2 monitor from her finger before disconnecting her IV. A rush of light-headedness hit her when she tried to sit up. She struggled through it, forcing her legs over the opposite side of the bed from Asher and Jayce. The pain in her shoulder made her nauseous, but the adrenaline coursing through her veins gave her the extra strength to get to her feet. Steadying herself against the bed, Quinn came around the end to search for the gun Asher had kicked across the floor. There it was, beneath a chair in the corner . . .

Dizziness made it hard to focus and she feared if she took her eyes off the weapon, she might pass out. It was maybe ten feet away, but with the effort it took to take each step, it might as well have been one hundred. Keeping her left arm tucked tight against her side, her other hand gripped the windowsill to steady her as she forced one foot in front of the other, slowly making her way toward Asher's gun.

———

Air exploded from Jayce's lungs when Asher linebackered him. The momentary distraction was a costly mistake and the misfire of his weapon sent ceiling debris raining down on them. He stumbled to catch his footing but the impact sent him and Asher to the ground. He turned in midair, forcing Asher to absorb the brunt of the impact, and slammed the butt of his gun against his temple. The hit momentarily rocked him and Jayce took the opportunity to finish what he'd started. Quinn had to die.

He shoved up past the side of the bed and pulled the trigger twice in rapid succession, expecting her to be in the bed. The bullets drilled into the empty mattress. He panned his gaze and his weapon a little to the left and found her staggering across the room. As he pulled the trigger, something slammed into his ribs, knocking his aim off. Glass shattered above her head and Quinn let out a frightened scream.

God, he loved that sound. He'd had so many plans for her . . . *Fucking Tate . . .*

Asher went for Jayce's gun arm, grabbing his wrist with both hands and forcing it down. Jayce's free hand locked on Asher's throat and he squeezed. The thunder of Tate's pulse beneath his fingertips was a rush. The blaze of hatred radiating in those eyes, glaring at him as he fought for his life . . . It was more thrilling, more satisfying than he'd ever imagined. His only regret was that Tate wouldn't live to see Quinn's brains splattered all over that white wall.

———

Rage licked through Asher's veins, hot and ravenous as he fought for control of the gun. Jayce's grip tightened, his fingers digging into his neck. The fucker smiled down at him, arrogant and triumphant. Asher knew the moment he let go of Jayce's wrist to pry his hand from his throat, he was going to shoot Quinn.

From his back, he didn't have the strength to control Jayce's arm without using both hands, and the bastard knew it. He couldn't speak to warn Quinn to get down. Fuck, he couldn't breathe!

Asher couldn't stay like this. In this position, he was fighting a losing battle. Jayce was strong and he had too much leverage over him. Strategy warred with his instinct for self-preservation. It was a conscious fucking effort not to let go of Jayce's wrist. Tightening his grip, Asher slammed his knee into Jayce's injured ribs and bucked his hips up as he rolled, using his momentum to put Jayce on his back and reverse their position.

He pinned Jayce's gun hand to the floor, easily controlling it from this angle, and palm-struck Jayce's elbow with his free hand, knocking Jayce's grip from his throat. The bastard wasn't smiling anymore—especially not after Asher drove his fist into Jayce's nose. Bones crunched at the impact. Blood coated Jayce's face, pouring down his throat. He coughed and sputtered, struggling to breathe.

In this, Jayce was right—Asher *was* a killer. And this son of a bitch was about to experience the death Asher had promised him minutes ago. Asher's only regret was that Jayce had just one life to lose. For the suffering he'd caused so many others, he deserved a hundred deaths, but Asher found comfort in knowing he was sending this bastard to hell. His reign of terror in this world was about to come to an end.

But Jayce wasn't going down easy. He was as ruthless a fighter as he was a human being. He bucked his hips and displaced Asher's weight, driving his knee into Asher's side. His ribs cracked with the force of the blow. Jayce reached down, and when he swung his arm up a glint of metal flashed in the air a moment before sharp searing pain slashed across Asher's chest.

Asher dove for Jayce's gun, his fingers curling around the grip as he rolled onto his back and took aim, firing two rounds into the fucker's chest. Jayce Rivers was dead before he hit the ground—an end too merciful for this bastard, but an end all the same.

CHAPTER

43

"Are you just about done?"

The ER doc's brow rose as he glanced up at Asher over his wire-rimmed glasses, then went back to stitching up the knife wound across the left side of his chest—thirty-eight stitches and counting. His brother stood in the corner, arms crossed over his chest, stonily watching him.

"Will you go check on Quinn?" Irritability made his tone sharp. He wanted to be with her himself, but instead he'd been stuck down here getting stitched up.

"You know I can't do that. You turned room 2415 into a crime scene. The only reason you're not under arrest right now is that you're my brother and I told the chief I would stay with you."

"It was self-defense."

"You know that. And I know that. But until it's officially been declared such and the charges have been dropped, you're stuck with me."

"Aw, fuck . . . Sorry," he told the doc when the man gave him the bushy brow again. "It was an accident. The guy shouldn't have come up behind me like that. Will you at least call and see how she is?"

He hadn't gotten a chance to talk to Quinn since the shooting. Jax had busted his way inside seconds after Asher had shot Jayce, and the charge nurse for the floor was right behind him. She'd taken one look at the dead man on the floor and then at Asher's chest and called a rapid response. Within a minute, a swarm of medical staff was trying to force him on the gurney. He hadn't wanted to leave Quinn, and had been quite adamant about not doing so, which had prompted the Code 21 being called, and before he knew it a syringe full of ketamine was being shot into his leg and he was lights out.

He wasn't sure how much time had gone by, but he woke to this doctor stitching up his chest and the disapproving scowl of his brother from the corner of the room.

"She's fine. I checked on her right before you woke up. They're getting her settled into another room, and I'll take you up to her as soon as we're done here. I've already given my statement to the Feds, and when you're up to it, they're going to want to talk to you. Rivers's blood type matches the DNA sample I got from your place. Although it's not conclusive yet, it looks like we've got our shooter. But just in case, I put an officer outside Quinn's room. I should have done it right from the beginning. If I had— "

"If you had, a killer would still be on the loose. I'm just glad we figured it out when we did—before it was too late. All I want to do right now is hold her in my arms and never let her go again."

"I'm sure you do. Just hold tight a little bit longer. I know she's anxious to see you too."

Several minutes later, the doc set down his needle and thread. "That's it. Keep it covered, clean, and dry. Sutures come out in seven to ten days. You can shower after twenty-four hours. The nurse will be by shortly to get you bandaged up."

The doc shoved his chair back and stood as he removed his gloves and tossed them in the trash. As he walked out, he pressed the button on a com device attached to his scrubs and spoke. "Room twenty is ready for a dressing and discharge."

Asher tapped his foot with restless anticipation, anxious to get out of there and back to Quinn. All he could think about was that look of terror on her face. He wanted to take her in his arms and promise her no one would ever harm her again. If he had to spend every day for the rest of his life fulfilling that promise, he'd count it an honor.

"Does Quinn have any idea how much you're in love with her?"

The incredulity in Jax's voice told him he was having trouble believing it himself.

"If she doesn't, she's going to—if I could just get the hell out of here."

As if on cue, the door opened and in walked a nurse. She came in backward, speaking to someone else in the hall about another patient that needed an EKG. As she turned around and got a look at him, her big doe eyes grew impossibly larger. He knew the cut was bad, but didn't expect an ER nurse to be so squeamish.

She set the supplies on the table and rushed over to him. "Jax! What happened to you?"

Before Asher could correct her, the nurse's hands were on him—one cupping the hard angle of his jaw as the other ran from his collarbone down the right side of his chest. She touched him like a woman who was well familiar with his body. And it shocked the shit out of him, rendering him momentarily speechless.

A month ago, this would have been on his list of top five erotic fantasies—cue the porn music—but it did zero for him now. In fact, he was really uncomfortable. The only woman he wanted touching him like this was Quinn.

Jax cleared his throat from the corner of the room. The busty brunette's golden-amber eyes darted up and over his shoulder. She gasped and stumbled back like he'd scalded her.

"Glad to know you still care, Doe."

"Jax?" She looked from him to his brother, and the confusion on her face quickly turned to anger. "You have a twin brother and you didn't tell me?"

Jax shoved away from the wall and came toward her. "Calm down, Doe."

"Don't tell me to calm down. I just felt up your brother! And don't call me that. You lost that right six months ago."

Then she turned her big golden eyes on Asher. It didn't take a rocket scientist to figure out where she got that nickname. "I'm so sorry. I thought you were Jaxson."

"It's fine. It happens all the time, really." He looked at his brother. "Seriously, dude, don't you tell anyone I exist?" But his brother wasn't paying any attention to him.

"I have to go. I'll send someone else in to do your dressing."

"Eve . . ."

Jax stepped forward and reached for her hand, but she pulled it away before he could touch her. And then she was gone—out the door and running down the hall. Asher was going to give his brother a hard time, but the razz died on his lips when he looked at his twin. The guy looked as gutted as Asher felt. Guess he wasn't the only one to get shot by cupid's arrow.

"You should go after her."

"She doesn't want to talk to me."

"Yes, she does. The only other woman that's ever touched me with that kind of emotion is Quinn. She's in love with you, man. Don't be a dick. Go after her."

Jax—the brother who was always cool, rational, and reserved. The guy who thought with his head and never his heart, for the first time in his life, looked completely shredded.

"Hey, I'm no love guru, but I know what it's like to be alone. And I know what it's like when you find that missing part of your heart. Some things are worth swallowing your pride for, brother, and the love of a good woman is one of them. Go."

Jax hesitated another second, then, muttering a self-damning curse, he took off out the door. Asher really hoped his brother could find happiness, because if anyone deserved it, it was Jaxson.

———

"Is there anything else I can get you?" the nurse asked, pulling up the covers around Quinn.

They'd moved her to another wing and posted a guard outside her door. She was still shaken, but refused the nurse's offer of medication to help calm her. She didn't want to be drugged when Asher finally returned. She needed a clear head for what she had to say.

"No, thank you. I'm just going to rest."

Her mind was still trying to process everything that had happened. The shock of discovering Jayce had been trying to kill her since the day she'd fled Haiti left her shell-shocked. She couldn't imagine the betrayal Asher must be feeling right now. To have a brother-in-arms turn on you like that . . . It would be a blow that would no doubt leave a very raw and open wound for a long time to come.

She couldn't help feeling responsible for bringing this nightmare to his doorstep, and she couldn't conceive how he didn't blame her, even just a little bit, for turning his life upside-down. She'd nearly gotten him and his brother killed—more than once. She stopped to consider the death toll and the guilt nearly consumed her. How could Asher possibly want her after this? Now that the threat was over, would he decide she just wasn't worth the trouble and send her packing like he'd threatened to do the day she showed up on his doorstep?

Even now, he was down in the ER getting a knife wound stitched up. At the thought of all that blood, her nauseous stomach flipped and bile rose up her throat. Tears pricked her eyes. She knew she'd reached her limit of what she could endure when all she wanted to do was cry. And that's exactly what she did. She cried for Emily, the first of many to lose their lives because of her. She cried for Aileen and all those other girls whose lives had been stripped away from them—their innocence stolen. She cried for the burden she'd been on Asher and the unfairness of it all . . .

A soft knock sounded on the door and Quinn grabbed a tissue from the table stand, quickly drying her eyes and blowing her nose before answering.

"Come in . . ."

———

The guard opened the door and let Asher inside. He could tell right away she'd been crying. Her bright violet eyes were luminous with unshed tears; the tip of her nose was rosy red. She looked so small lying in that bed. So fragile . . . How long had she been left in here by herself crying? Someone should have gotten him, dammit. After everything she'd been through, she shouldn't be alone. Well, he was here now, and a pack of wild horses couldn't drag him away from her again.

"Are you all right?" Her voice broke and it cut through him like glass.

"Sweetheart, I'm fine," he assured her, coming over to the side of her bed. "It's just a few stitches . . . I'll heal."

"I'm so sorry . . ."

He winced at the pain in her voice, feeling it as deeply as Jayce's blade, only sharper. That bastard had cut through flesh and muscle, but Quinn held the power to carve out his soul. "What do you have to be sorry for? Quinn, none of this was your fault."

"How many times are you going to have to save me?"

Tears slipped down her cheeks as he took her hand in his and he knelt on the floor at the side of her bed. He looked into those beautiful eyes that held the key to his heart and saw his redemption and his demise. She was the only woman in the world that could bring him to his knees. Didn't she get it? He would die for her, kill for her . . .

"As many as it takes. Quinn, I'm so in love with you, it terrifies me. Before you came into my life, I had nothing to live for. Guilt and regret consumed me. I knew the moment I met you that you were going to turn my life upside-down. I just never thought you'd become my salvation."

The smile she gave him was worth any fires of hell he'd have to walk through. He was hers to possess, and the rightness he felt every time she looked at him filled him with such a deep sense of peace, there was no doubt in his mind he wanted to spend the rest of his life with this woman.

"I thought about where I want you to take me when this is all over."

Keeping his eyes on hers, he dipped his head and pressed a kiss to the back of her hand held tightly in his. "Oh yeah? Where is that?"

"Home."

EPILOGUE

12 Months Later

"Do you have any idea how difficult it is to ride a horse in a wedding dress?" Quinn called to her husband, who had been leading them through a narrow trail for the last hour. He pulled Marley around and waited for her and Jack to catch up, giving her a smile that was pure sin and promised he'd make it worth her trouble.

He snagged Jack's reins and guided the stallion a step closer before bending over to whisper near her ear, "Do you have any idea how difficult it is to ride a horse with a hard-on?" His husky voice sent a shiver of anticipation rushing through her.

Quinn laughed at his plight. "You get zero pity. This was your idea, honeymooning in your cabin."

"Are you kidding? It's a fabulous idea. You, me, and nothing but nature for six long days and nights . . ." There it was, that smile again that sent tingles all the way to her garter belt. "After the media circus you've been through, and now that the EO trial is over, I want you all to myself—no lawyers, no reporters . . ."

"No courtrooms . . . It sounds heavenly."

"Oh, sweetheart, I'm going to show you heaven," he promised. "Come on, we're almost there."

With a gallant sweep of his arm, he indicated for her to lead the way. She didn't know where she was going, but there was only one trail, so she stayed the course. She'd never been to his cabin before. He'd spoken of bringing her many times, but this year had been a roller coaster ride of highs and lows. She was encouraged to discover this week that the US government was putting together a Special Ops team to go into Haiti and vet out the traffickers.

Asher had been offered the job of leading the unit, but it would have required reinstatement into the USMC-MARSOC division. After much deliberation, he'd decided to officially retire from any further military service work in favor of helping his father run The Rabbit Hole. But Quinn knew the real reason he stayed—Asher refused to leave her. He told her he'd served his country for fourteen years; now it was his turn to have the life he'd always wanted, the family he'd dreamed of but never thought possible until he met her.

Another team was going in, and they were leaving next week. The soldier heading the operation was an old friend of Asher and Nikko's— Gunnery Sergeant Hunter Gerrard. He was a highly decorated Special Forces officer and more than qualified to find those bastards and shut them down. The second part of their mission was a search and rescue. She prayed they'd find those girls alive and get them back to their families.

It wouldn't be easy, but Quinn knew she needed to put this behind her. She'd done what she could to be the voice for those girls and to see justice served for her friend Emily. She was eager to start her new life with Asher. And that was exactly what this would be—their fresh start, a chance to get away from the distractions of the world and reconnect with each other.

"How much farther?" she asked over her shoulder, more than ready to get out of this saddle and then out of her dress. She was looking forward to Asher's assistance.

"Just through those trees up ahead."

As they entered the clearing, Quinn brought Jack to an abrupt halt. The sight of the small cabin nestled on a flat plane of meadow brought tears to her eyes. White gossamer and LED lights wrapped up the two log posts framing the archway. Large white bows decorated the porch railing, and hanging above the door was a sign reading *Just Married.*

"You like it?" Asher asked, stopping beside her.

"Like it? I absolutely love it! Asher, it's perfect . . ."

"You should see the inside."

"I can't wait!" This was quite possibly the most romantic thing Asher had ever done for her. He wasn't a guy who got hung up on the little details, or so she'd thought. He was good to her—protective, considerate, and passionate, but he was also pragmatic, and not just a little hardheaded. Decorating a cabin in wedding blitz and bling was . . . swoon-worthy romantic.

"Now I know what you and Jaxson were up to when you were gone for so long yesterday." What was an even bigger surprise was that he'd gotten his brother to help him with all this. Now Fisher? That she could see. But Jax? Definitely not the decorating type. But over the last year, she noticed the efforts Asher had made to mend his relationship with his twin brother. And they were growing close—as close as anyone would expect twins to be.

Asher gave her a lopsided grin that was sexy as hell as he led the horses over to the lean-to and hopped down. After removing Marley's bridle and saddle, he opened the gate to let him inside. Turning to Quinn, he wrapped his hands around her waist and plucked her from the saddle. Before her cowboy boots could touch the grass, she was in his arms. His mouth came down on hers like she suspected he'd been wanting to do ever since the pastor said, "You may kiss the bride," but out of respect for the church full of guests, their parents, and the pastor, their union-sealing kiss had been G-rated and chaste.

But there was nothing innocent about this kiss—it was full of wicked promise Quinn felt all the way to her toes. Asher's tongue swept past her lips, taking his first taste of his wife. His throaty groan of approval rolled through her like an electric current, lighting up every one of her nerve endings. He tasted more intoxicating than the Crown Royal his brothers had passed between them at the head table. The whiskey's sinful bite teased her senses as his tongue plundered and possessed, laying claim to what was now in the eyes of the law, and God—his.

A forceful nudge on his shoulder made him take a step forward, knocking Quinn off-balance. Her arms flew up around his neck, steadying herself. Her laughter rang out, echoing off the Rocky Mountains and infusing into the air. She felt the vitality of nature in a way that could only be described as magical.

"I think someone wants us to get a room," she teased as Asher reluctantly let her go and quickly removed Jack's bridle and saddle. He opened the gate one last time, and the large black stallion slipped into the pasture and began grazing next to Marley.

Turning toward Quinn, Asher swept her up into his arms. As he carried her to the cabin and up the steps to the threshold, he dipped his head and whispered huskily, "That was my thought exactly . . ."

ACKNOWLEDGMENTS

First and foremost, I want to thank God for blessing me with the opportunity to pursue my passion. Many thanks to my wonderful editor, Melody Guy, and the amazing staff at Montlake for your dedication and commitment to Asher and Quinn's story. To my agent, Nalini Akolekar, you've literally made my dreams come true overnight. I can never thank my fabulous critique group enough for all your hard work. Sally, Mikayla, Linda, John, and Lyanne, you make my stories shine, and I love you dearly! Last but certainly not least, I want to thank my wonderful family for your patience and continual support, for all the times you've heard "In a minute" or "Just a second" and patiently waited for me, knowing it was going to be at least another hour. I love you with all my heart!

ABOUT THE AUTHOR

Melynda Price is a multipublished author of contemporary and paranormal romance. She enjoys writing stories that make her readers fall in love—over and over again. Her greatest challenge as a writer is making the unbelievable believable, while taking her characters to the limit with tales full of passion and unique twists and turns. Salting stories with undertones of history whenever possible, Price strives to plant her characters so deep into her readers' hearts that they will live on forever. She currently resides in Northern Minnesota with her husband and two children. On snow-filled days, she likes to curl up in front of the fireplace with her Chihuahua and a hot cup of coffee to write.